SETTLING
SCORES

SETTLING SCORES

Sporting Mysteries

edited and introduced by
MARTIN EDWARDS

BRITISH LIBRARY

First published 2020 by
The British Library
96 Euston Road
London NW1 2DB

Cataloguing in Publication Data
A catalogue record for this publication is available from the British Library

ISBN 978 0 7123 5321 2
eISBN 978 0 7123 6750 9

Illustration of the Tennis at Wimbledon by W. Bryce Hamilton in
The Sphere, 12 June 1926 © Illustrated London News Ltd/Mary Evans

Typeset by Tetragon, London
Printed and bound by TJ International, Padstow, Cornwall

CONTENTS

INTRODUCTION

The detective story "is a sporting event", said S. S. Van Dine, as long ago as 1928, when he published his twenty "rules of the game" in the *American Magazine*. The following year, in a famous early anthology of the genre, *Best Detective Stories*, Britain's Ronald Knox expressed a similar view. According to Knox, "the detective story is a game between two players, the author... and the reader", and laid down his own set of rules—just ten this time, the famous "Detective's Decalogue".

The association of sports and games with stories of crime and detection is therefore long-established, and it isn't too fanciful to discern various other types of connection. The most daring criminals, especially murderers who set out to commit the perfect crime, resemble gamblers who bet on the outcome of a race or sporting contest as well as those sportsmen and women who are prepared to take extraordinary risks in pursuit of a coveted prize. It is perhaps no surprise that when E. W. Hornung, Arthur Conan Doyle's brother-in-law, created one of fiction's most legendary rogues, A. J. Raffles, "the amateur cracksman" was also a gifted cricketer.

Sports and games can also provide an appealing background for tales of crime and detection, as many inventive novelists and short story writers have demonstrated over the years. This book gathers short mysteries set in Britain and published from the late nineteenth century to the second half of the twentieth. As with other anthologies in the British Library Crime Classics series, this mysterious medley is designed to be eclectic, in the hope that it will please the most jaded palette. This collection also shines a light on the part played by sport in British life, and the way that sport, as well as wider society, has changed over the years.

How fascinating it is, for instance, to read "The Double Problem", a story about athletics first published almost a century ago, in an age when soccer is an industry worth billions and star players are international celebrities and multi-millionaires. Lord Rockpool suggests in the story that athletics is supplanting football in the public affections: "the exaggeration of professionalism is gradually killing the public interest in Association football... The professionals... have deprived the game of a feature of robustness... which still keeps the Rugby game healthy... the finicking exactness of the professional player has robbed the game of its goal-getting possibilities..." Suffice to say that his crystal ball suffered a serious malfunction.

Rockpool's inaccurate prophecy reminds us that these stories were mostly written in an age which drew a strict dividing line between amateur sportsmen, typically well-bred young men with inherited wealth, and professional players from humble backgrounds whose earnings were so modest that on occasion they were tempted into crime. Time and again, this anthology illustrates the workings and consequences of the class divisions in British society.

The authors featured range from the famous, including Doyle, to such long-forgotten (at least in the context of crime fiction) figures as F. A. M. Webster and David Winser. Webster, author of "The Double Problem", was a prominent athletics coach and writer; there can be little doubt that Lord Rockpool's sentiments reflected Webster's. Winser was an accomplished oarsman before his life was cruelly cut short during the Second World War.

People with first-hand experience of sport at the highest level have often turned to writing crime fiction, usually thrillers rather than cerebral whodunits. The outstanding example is Dick Francis, whose much-lauded books benefited from his expert understanding of the horse racing world as well as from his personal knowledge of the exciting but dangerous life of a high-profile jockey.

The first landmark mystery set against the world of horse racing was Doyle's "Silver Blaze", and the sport has supplied a popular backdrop to crime fiction ever since. Another National Hunt champion jockey, John Francome, followed Dick Francis' lead by publishing his first thriller in 1986. He continued to turn out a book a year for a quarter of a century before giving up, as he has explained, "because I simply couldn't think of any more ways of killing anyone". Francis died in 2010, but by then the Francis "family business" of thriller writing had been joined by his son Felix, who continues to write bestsellers branded as "Dick Francis novels".

Cricket is probably the sport which has produced the most distinguished literature, and although it is (on the surface at least) a much gentler sport than horse racing, it has often featured in crime stories. Dorothy L. Sayers' multi-talented Lord Peter Wimsey was a fine batsman, and *Murder Must Advertise* (1933) includes a memorable cricket scene. Among cricketers who have written crime fiction was Sayers' friend Henry Aubrey-Fletcher, a wealthy baronet who played the game as an amateur for Buckinghamshire. Writing as Henry Wade, he featured a country house cricket match in a key scene in his finest novel, *Lonely Magdalen* (1940), while his familiarity with the country racing set is evident in *A Dying Fall* (1955).

Ted Dexter, a charismatic figure nicknamed "Lord Ted", was one of England's most dashing sportsmen during the 1950s and

1960s. He captained the national cricket team and was also an accomplished golfer. In collaboration with the sports journalist Clifford Makins, he produced *Testkill* (1976), concerning the murder of an Australian cricketer during a Test Match at Lord's.

Dexter and Makins returned to sporting crime three years later with *Deadly Putter*, set in the world of golf. This is another sport which has given rise to a host of crime novels and short stories. Several authors have made a speciality of golfing mysteries. They include the highly collectable Golden Age writer Herbert Adams as well as, in more recent times, authors such as Keith Miles (the real name of the prolific crime novelist who has also achieved success as Edward Marston), Barry Cork, and Malcolm Hamer. In 1997, Thomas W. Taylor produced *The Golf Murders*, an extensive and lavishly illustrated catalogue of books and short stories featuring the sport; he pointed out that golf features in numerous mysteries by Agatha Christie, one of the few female crime writers to show a deep interest in golf. Taylor also listed the different murder methods employed in golfing mysteries, e.g. exploding ball; exploding club head; explosive charge in the cup; exploding golf course (believe it or not); speared with the flag stick; trick club; and sabotaged golf cart.

Among famous footballers to turn to writing thrillers after hanging up their boots, perhaps the most notable is Terry Venables, who played for England and also managed the national team. He and the Scottish novelist Gordon Williams co-wrote three novels under the pen-name P. B. Yuill about the private eye James Hazell which led to a television series starring Nicholas Ball as the Cockney answer to Philip Marlowe.

The former World Number One women's tennis player Martina Navratilova dabbled in thriller writing during the 1990s, again working in collaboration. To this day, the overwhelming majority of sports-related crime fiction is written by male authors, and sports mysteries with female protagonists are uncommon, although this is likely to change as the media belatedly pay more attention to women's sports.

Of course, being a prominent sportsman or woman is not an essential qualification for writing an authentic sports-based crime story. Leonard R. Gribble, a prolific writer with a keen commercial instinct, enjoyed his greatest success with *The Arsenal Stadium Mystery* (1939), a football whodunit in which famous players from Arsenal F.C. became characters in a mystery. The book became a popular film and has recently been republished as a British Library Crime Classic. Gribble returned to the beautiful game with a story featuring the leading English soccer star of his era, *They Kidnapped Stanley Matthews* (1950).

Bernard Newman, one of whose short stories appears in this book, tried a similar approach with a novel about tennis. Victor Gollancz emblazoned the dust jacket of *Centre Court Murder* (1951) with words taken from the book's opening sentence: "Gorgeous Gussie Moran made a mistake when she paraded in lace panties: and a bigger mistake when she told the world about her love affairs". Today this serves as a reminder of some of the more bizarre sexism of the past, not only in fiction, but in real life: Moran was an American tennis star whose revealing dress prompted the All England Club to accuse her of having brought "vulgarity and sin into tennis". After that, even Newman's book about murder at the home of cricket, *Death at Lord's* (1952), was likely to be an anti-climax.

Peter Lovesey is today renowned as one of the world's leading detective novelists, but he began his career as a published author with a book which grew out of his interest in the history of athlet-ics and charted the careers of five great distance runners. This was followed by *Wobble to Death* (1970), a prize-winning novel about a six-day endurance race which introduced the Victorian detective Sergeant Cribb, and *The Detective Wore Silk Drawers* (1971), set in the world of bare-knuckle boxing. Lovesey's body of work includes *Goldengirl* (1977), published under the pen-name Peter Lear and written in anticipation of the Moscow Olympics.

The links between sport and fictional crime were celebrated in Ellery Queen's landmark anthology *Sporting Blood* (1942), although that book also included such activities as poker, chess, and the collecting of coins and butterflies. There has been at least one anthology of horse racing stories, and also a book of chess mys-teries. This collection is, as far as I know, the first major attempt in the UK to gather together short mystery stories, each of which features a different sport and a different author. Putting it together has been a pleasure enhanced by the help and encouragement of classic crime experts Nigel Moss, Jamie Sturgeon, and John Cooper, as well as by information supplied by Philip Harbottle and the support of the team in the Publishing Department at the British Library.

And now it's time to fire the starting pistol...

MARTIN EDWARDS
www.martinedwardsbooks.com

THE LOSS OF SAMMY CROCKETT

Arthur Morrison

Arthur Morrison (1863–1945) was a journalist, author, and nineteenth century EastEnder who was born in Poplar, the son of an engine fitter. He made good use of his knowledge of the East End of London in books such as *Tales of Mean Streets* (1894)—yes, he wrote about the mean streets long before Raymond Chandler—and *A Child of the Jago* (1906). In his youth, he was an enthusiastic cyclist and boxer; in later years, as his literary fame grew, he could afford to indulge in his artistic tastes, and he assembled a valuable collection of Japanese works of art, many of which are now held in the British Museum.

When Sherlock Holmes' apparent demise in the Reichenbach Falls in 1894 created a vacancy for a popular detective, Morrison was commercially astute enough to seize the opportunity. That year saw the first appearance of his series investigator Martin Hewitt, an amiable but shrewd private enquiry agent, and the stories were snapped up by the *Strand Magazine*; Sidney Paget, famous for illustrating the Holmes stories, also supplied illustrations for Hewitt's case-book. The series continued for a decade and the American author and critic Ellery Queen went so far as to describe Hewitt as the only important contemporary of Holmes among private detectives. In the early 1970s, Hewitt was played on television in *The Rivals of Sherlock Holmes* by a well-cast Peter Barkworth. This story, which first appeared in the *Strand* in April 1894, has occasionally been reprinted under an alternative title, "The Loss of Sammy Throckett"; the reasons for the change are themselves a mystery.

IT WAS, OF COURSE, ALWAYS A PART OF MARTIN HEWITT'S business to be thoroughly at home among any and every class of people, and to be able to interest himself intelligently, or to appear to do so, in their various pursuits. In one of the most important cases ever placed in his hands, he could have gone but a short way toward success had he not displayed some knowledge of the more sordid aspects of professional sport, and a great interest in the undertakings of a certain dealer therein. The great case itself had nothing to do with sport, and, indeed, from a narrative point of view, was somewhat uninteresting, but the man who alone held the one piece of information wanted was a keeper, backer, or "gaffer" of professional pedestrians, and it was through the medium of his pecuniary interest in such matters that Hewitt was enabled to strike a bargain with him.

The man was a publican on the outskirts of Padfield, a northern town pretty famous for its sporting tastes, and to Padfield, therefore, Hewitt betook himself, and, arrayed in a way to indicate some inclination of his own toward sport, he began to frequent the bar of the "Hare and Hounds." Kentish, the landlord, was a stout, bull-necked man, of no great communicativeness at first; but after a little acquaintance he opened out wonderfully, became quite a jolly (and rather intelligent) companion, and came out with innumerable anecdotes of his sporting adventures. He could put a very decent dinner on the table, too, at the "Hare and Hounds," and Hewitt's frequent invitation to him to join therein and divide a bottle of the best in the cellar soon put the two on the very best of terms. Good terms with Mr. Kentish was Hewitt's great desire, for the information he wanted was of a sort that could never be extracted by casual questioning, but must be a matter of open communication by the publican, extracted in what way it might be.

"Look here," said Kentish one day, "I'll put you on to a good thing, my boy—a real good thing. Of course, you know all about the Padfield 135 Yards Handicap being run off now?"

"Well, I haven't looked into it much," Hewitt replied. "Ran the first round of heats last Saturday and Monday, didn't they?"

"They did. Well"—Kentish spoke in a stage whisper as he leaned over and rapped the table—"I've got the final winner in this house." He nodded his head, took a puff at his cigar, and added, in his ordinary voice, "Don't say nothing."

"No, of course not. Got something on, of course?"

"Rather—what do *you* think? Got any price I liked. Been saving him up for this. Why, he's got twenty-one yards, and he can do even time all the way! Fact! Why, he could win runnin' back'ards. He won his heat on Monday like—like—like that!" The gaffer snapped his fingers, in default of a better illustration, and went on. "He might ha' took it a little easier, *I* think—it's shortened his price, of course, him jumpin' in by two yards. But you can get decent odds now, if you go about it right. You take my tip—back him for his heat next Saturday, in the second round, and for the final. You'll get a good price for the final, if you pop it down at once. But don't go makin' a song of it, will you, now? I'm givin' you a tip I wouldn't give anybody else."

"Thanks very much—it's awfully good of you. I'll do what you advise. But isn't there a dark horse anywhere else?"

"Not dark to me, my boy, not dark to me. I know every man runnin' like a book. Old Taylor—him over at the Cop—he's got a very good lad—eighteen yards, and a very good lad indeed; and he's a tryer this time, I know. But, bless you, my lad could give him ten, instead o' taking three, and beat him then! When I'm runnin' a real tryer, I'm generally runnin' something very near a winner, you bet; and this time, mind, *this* time, I'm runnin' the certainest winner I *ever* run—and I don't often make a mistake. You back him."

"I shall, if you're as sure as that. But who is he?"

"Oh, Crockett's his name—Sammy Crockett. He's quite a new lad. I've got young Steggles looking after him—sticks to him like wax. Takes his little breathers in my bit o' ground at the back here. I've got a cinder sprint path there, over behind the trees. I don't let him out o' sight much, I can tell you. He's a straight lad, and he knows it'll be worth his while to stick to me; but there's some 'ud poison him, if they thought he'd spoil their books."

Soon afterward the two strolled toward the tap-room. "I expect Sammy'll be there," the landlord said, "with Steggles. I don't hide him too much—they'd think I'd got something extra on, if I did."

In the tap-room sat a lean, wire-drawn-looking youth, with sloping shoulders and a thin face, and by his side was a rather short, thick-set man, who had an odd air, no matter what he did, of proprietorship and surveillance of the lean youth. Several other men sat about, and there was loud laughter, under which the lean youth looked sheepishly angry.

"'Tarn't no good, Sammy lad," someone was saying. "You a makin' after Nancy Webb—she'll ha' nowt to do with 'ee."

"Don' like 'em so thread-papery," added another. "No, Sammy, you aren't the lad for she. I see her—"

"What about Nancy Webb?" asked Kentish, pushing open the door. "Sammy's all right, anyway. You keep fit, my lad, an' go on improving, and some day you'll have as good a house as me. Never mind the lasses. Had his glass o' beer, has he?" This to Raggy Steggles, who, answering in the affirmative, viewed his charge as though he were a post, and the beer a recent coat of paint.

"Has two glasses of mild a day," the landlord said to Hewitt. "Never puts on flesh, so he can stand it. Come out now." He nodded to Steggles, who rose, and marched Sammy Crockett away for exercise.

On the following afternoon (it was Thursday), as Hewitt and Kentish chatted in the landlord's own snuggery, Steggles burst into the room in a great state of agitation and spluttered out: "He—he's bolted; gone away!"

"What?"

"Sammy—gone. Hooked it. *I* can't find him."

The landlord stared blankly at the trainer, who stood with a sweater dangling from his hand, and stared blankly back. "What d'ye mean?" Kentish said, at last. "Don't be a fool. He's in the place somewhere; find him."

But this Steggles defied anybody to do. He had looked already. He had left Crockett at the cinder-path behind the trees, in his running-gear, with the addition of the long overcoat and cap he used in going between the path and the house, to guard against chill. "I was goin' to give him a bust or two with the pistol," the trainer explained, "but when we got over t'other side, 'Raggy,' ses he, 'it's blowin' a bit chilly. I think I'll ha' a sweater—there's one on my box, ain't there?' So in I coomes for the sweater, and it weren't on his box, and when I found it and got back—he weren't there. They'd seen nowt o' him in t' house, and he weren't nowhere."

Hewitt and the landlord, now thoroughly startled, searched everywhere, but to no purpose. "What should he go off the place for?" asked Kentish, in a sweat of apprehension. "'Tain't chilly a bit—it's warm—he didn't want no sweater; never wore one before. It was a piece of kid to be able to clear out. Nice thing, this is. I stand to win two years' takings over him. Here—you'll have to find him."

"Ah—but how?" exclaimed the disconcerted trainer, dancing about distractedly. "I've got all I could scrape on him myself; where can I look?"

Here was Hewitt's opportunity. He took Kentish aside and whispered. What he said startled the landlord considerably. "Yes, I'll tell you all about that," he said, "if that's all you want. It's no good or harm to me, whether I tell or no. But can you find him?"

"That I can't promise, of course. But you know who I am now, and what I'm here for. If you like to give me the information I want, I'll go into the case for you, and, of course, I sha'n't charge any fee. I may have luck, you know, but I can't promise, of course."

The landlord looked in Hewitt's face for a moment. Then he said, "Done! It's a deal."

"Very good," Hewitt replied; "get together the one or two papers you have, and we'll go into my business in the evening. As to Crockett, don't say a word to anybody. I'm afraid it must get out, since they all know about it in the house, but there's no use in making any unnecessary noise. Don't make hedging bets or do anything that will attract notice. Now we'll go over to the back and look at this cinder-path of yours."

Here Steggles, who was still standing near, was struck with an idea. "How about old Taylor, at the Cop, guv'nor, eh?" he said, meaningly. "His lad's good enough to win, with Sammy out, and Taylor is backing him plenty. Think he knows anything o' this?"

"That's likely," Hewitt observed, before Kentish could reply. "Yes. Look here—suppose Steggles goes and keeps his eye on the Cop for an hour or two, in case there's anything to be heard of? Don't show yourself, of course."

Kentish agreed, and the trainer went. When Hewitt and Kentish arrived at the path behind the trees, Hewitt at once began examining the ground. One or two rather large holes in the cinders were made, as the publican explained, by Crockett, in practising getting off his mark. Behind these were several fresh tracks of spiked shoes. The tracks led up to within a couple of yards of the high fence bounding the ground, and there stopped abruptly and entirely. In the fence, a little to the right of where the tracks stopped, there was a stout door. This Hewitt tried, and found ajar.

"That's always kept bolted," Kentish said; "he's gone out that way—he couldn't have gone any other without comin' through the house."

"But he isn't in the habit of making a step three yards long, is he?" Hewitt asked, pointing at the last footmark and then at the door, which was quite that distance away from it. Besides," he added, opening the door, "there's no footprint here nor outside."

The door opened on a lane, with another fence and a thick plantation of trees at the other side. Kentish looked at the footmarks, then at the door, then down the lane, and finally back towards the house. "That's a licker," he said.

"This is a quiet sort of lane," was Hewitt's next remark. "No houses in sight. Where does it lead?"

"That way it goes to the Old Kilns—disused. This way down to a turning off the Padfield and Catton Road."

Hewitt returned to the cinder-path again, and once more examined the footmarks. He traced them back over the grass toward the house. "Certainly," he said, "he hasn't gone back to the house. Here is the double line of tracks, side by side, from the house—Steggles's ordinary boots with iron tips and Crockett's running pumps—thus they came out. Here is Steggles's track in the opposite direction alone, made when he went back for the sweater. Crockett remained—you see various prints in those loose cinders at the end of the path where he moved this way and that, and then two or three paces toward the fence—not directly toward the door, you notice—and there they stop dead, and there are no more, either back or forward. Now, if he had wings, I should be tempted to the opinion that he flew straight away in the air from that spot—unless the earth swallowed him and closed again without leaving a wrinkle on its face."

Kentish stared gloomily at the tracks, and said nothing.

"However," Hewitt resumed, "I think I'll take a little walk now, and think over it. You go into the house and show yourself at the bar. If anybody wants to know how Crockett is, he's pretty well, thank you. By-the-bye, can I get to the Cop—this place of Taylor's—by this back lane?"

"Yes, down to the end leading to the Catton Road, turn to the left, and then first on the right. Anyone'll show you the Cop," and Kentish shut the door behind the detective, who straightway walked—toward the Old Kilns.

In little more than an hour he was back. It was now becoming dusk, and the landlord looked out papers from a box near the side window of his snuggery, for the sake of the extra light. "I've got these papers together for you," he said, as Hewitt entered. "Any news?"

"Nothing very great. Here's a bit of handwriting I want you to recognise, if you can. Get a light."

Kentish lit a lamp, and Hewitt laid upon the table half-a-dozen small pieces of torn paper, evidently fragments of a letter which had been torn up, here reproduced in facsimile.

The landlord turned the scraps over, regarding them dubiously. "These aren't much to recognise, anyhow. *I* don't know the writing. Where did you find 'em?"

"They were lying in the lane at the back, a little way down. Plainly they are pieces of a note addressed to someone called Sammy or something very like it. See the first piece with its 'mmy'? That is clearly from the beginning of the note, because there is no line between it and the smooth, straight edge of the paper above; also, nothing follows on the same line. Someone writes to Crockett—presuming it to be a letter addressed to him, as I do for other reasons—as Sammy. It is a pity that there is no more of the letter to be found than these pieces. I expect the person who tore it up put the rest in his pocket and dropped these by accident."

Kentish, who had been picking up and examining each piece in turn, now dolorously broke out:—

"Oh, it's plain he's sold us—bolted and done us; me as took him out o' the gutter, too. Look here—'throw them over'; that's plain enough—can't mean anything else. Means throw *me* over, and my friends—me, after what I've done for him. Then 'right away'—go right away, I s'pose, as he has done. Then," he was fiddling with the scraps and finally fitted two together, "why, look here, this one with 'lane' on it fits over the one about throwing over, and it says 'poor f' where it's torn; that means 'poor fool,' I s'pose—*me*, or 'fathead,' or something like that. That's nice. Why, I'd twist his neck if I could get hold of him; and I will!"

Hewitt smiled. "Perhaps it's not quite so uncomplimentary after all," he said. "If you can't recognise the writing, never mind. But if he's gone away to sell you, it isn't much use finding him, is it? He won't win if he doesn't want to."

"Why, he wouldn't dare to rope under my very eyes. I'd—I'd—"

"Well, well; perhaps we'll get him to run after all, and as well as he can. One thing is certain—he left this place of his own will. Further, I think he is in Padfield now—he went toward the town I believe. And I don't think he means to sell you."

"Well, he shouldn't. I've made it worth his while to stick to me. I've put a fifty on for him out of my own pocket, and told him so; and if he won, that would bring him a lump more than he'd probably get by going crooked, besides the prize money, and anything I might give him over. But it seems to me he's putting me in the cart altogether."

"That we shall see. Meantime, don't mention anything I've told you to anyone—not even to Steggles. He can't help us, and he might blurt things out inadvertently. Don't say anything about these pieces of paper, which I shall keep myself. By-the-bye, Steggles is indoors, isn't he? Very well, keep him in. Don't let him be seen hunting about this evening. I'll stay here tonight and we'll proceed with Crockett's business in the morning. And now we'll settle *my* business, please."

In the morning Hewitt took his breakfast in the snuggery, carefully listening to any conversation that might take place at the bar. Soon after nine o'clock a fast dog-cart stopped outside, and a red-faced, loud-voiced man swaggered in, greeting Kentish with boisterous cordiality. He had a drink with the landlord, and said: "How's things? Fancy any of 'em for the sprint handicap? Got a lad o' your own in, haven't you?"

"Oh, yes," Kentish replied. "Crockett. Only a young 'un—not got to his proper mark yet, I reckon. I think old Taylor's got No. 1 this time."

"Capital lad," the other replied, with a confidential nod. "Shouldn't wonder at all. Want to do anything yourself over it?"

"No—I don't think so. I'm not on at present. Might have a little flutter on the grounds just for fun; nothing else."

There were a few more casual remarks, and then the red-faced man drove away.

"Who was that?" asked Hewitt, who had watched the visitor through the snuggery window.

"That's Danby—bookmaker. Cute chap; he's been told Crockett's missing, I'll bet anything, and come here to pump me. No good though. As a matter of fact, I've worked Sammy Crockett into his books for about half I'm in for altogether—through third parties, of course."

Hewitt reached for his hat. "I'm going out for half an hour now," he said. "If Steggles wants to go out before I come back, don't let him. Let him go and smooth over all those tracks on the cinder-path, very carefully. And, by-the-bye, could you manage to have your son about the place today, in case I happen to want a little help out of doors?"

"Certainly; I'll get him to stay in. But what do you want the cinders smoothed for?"

Hewitt smiled and patted his host's shoulder. "I'll explain all my little tricks when the job's done," he said, and went out.

On the lane from Padfield to Sedby village stood the "Plough" beerhouse, wherein J. Webb was licensed to sell by retail beer to be consumed on the premises or off, as the thirsty list. Nancy Webb, with a very fine colour, a very curly fringe, and a wide-smiling mouth revealing a fine set of teeth, came to the bar at the summons of a stoutish old gentleman with spectacles, who walked with a stick.

The stoutish old gentleman had a glass of bitter beer and then said, in the peculiarly quiet voice of a very deaf man: "Can you tell me, if you please, the way into the main Catton Road?"

"Down the lane, turn to the right at the cross roads, then first to the left."

The old gentleman waited with his hand to his ear for some few seconds after she had finished speaking, and then resumed, in his whispering voice, "I'm afraid I'm very deaf this morning." He fumbled in his pocket and produced a note-book and pencil. "May I trouble you to write it down? I'm so very deaf at times, that I—thank you."

The girl wrote the direction, and the old gentleman bade her good morning and left. All down the lane he walked slowly with his stick. At the cross roads he turned, put the stick under his arm, thrust the spectacles into his pocket, and strode away in the ordinary guise of Martin Hewitt. He pulled out his note-book, examined Miss Webb's direction very carefully, and then went off another way altogether, toward the "Hare and Hounds."

Kentish lounged moodily in his bar. "Well, my boy," said Hewitt, "has Steggles wiped out the tracks?"

"Not yet—I haven't told him. But he's somewhere about—I'll tell him now."

"No, don't. I don't think we'll have that done, after all. I expect he'll want to go out soon—at any rate, some time during the day. Let him go whenever he likes. I'll sit upstairs a bit in the club-room."

"Very well. But how do you know Steggles will be going out?"

"Well, he's pretty restless after his lost *protégé*, isn't he? I don't suppose he'll be able to remain idle long."

"And about Crockett. Do you give him up?"

"Oh, no. Don't you be impatient. I can't say I'm quite confident yet of laying hold of him—the time is so short, you see—but I think I shall at least have news for you by the evening."

Hewitt sat in the club-room until the afternoon, taking his lunch there. At length he saw, through the front window, Raggy Steggles walking down the road. In an instant Hewitt was downstairs and at the door. The road bent eighty yards away, and as soon as Steggles passed the bend the detective hurried after him.

All the way to Padfield town and more than half through it Hewitt dogged the trainer. In the end Steggles stopped at a corner and gave a note to a small boy who was playing near. The boy ran with the note to a bright, well-kept house at the opposite corner. Martin Hewitt was interested to observe the legend "H. Danby, Contractor," on a board over a gate in the side wall of the garden behind this house. In five minutes a door in the side gate opened, and the head and shoulders of the red-faced man emerged. Steggles immediately hurried across and disappeared through the gate.

This was both interesting and instructive. Hewitt took up a position in the side street and waited. In ten minutes the trainer reappeared and hurried off the way he had come, along the street Hewitt had considerately left clear for him. Then Hewitt strolled toward the smart house and took a good look at it. At one corner of the small piece of forecourt garden, near the railings, a small, baize-covered, glass-fronted notice-board stood on two posts. On its top edge appeared the words "H. Danby. Houses to be Sold or Let." But the only notice pinned to the green baize within was an old and dusty one, inviting tenants for three shops, which were suitable for any business, and which would be fitted to suit tenants. Apply within.

Hewitt pushed open the front gate and rang the doorbell. "There are some shops to let, I see," he said, when a maid appeared. "I should like to see them, if you will let me have the key."

"Master's out, sir. You can't see the shops till Monday."

"Dear me, that's unfortunate. I'm afraid I can't wait till Monday. Didn't Mr. Danby leave any instructions, in case anybody should inquire?"

"Yes, sir—as I've told you. He said anybody who called about 'em must come again on Monday."

"Oh, very well, then; I suppose I must try. One of the shops is in High Street, isn't it?"

"No, sir; they're all in the new part—Granville Road."

"Ah, I'm afraid that will scarcely do. But I'll see. Good day."

Martin Hewitt walked away a couple of streets' lengths before he inquired the way to Granville Road. When at last he found that thoroughfare, in a new and muddy suburb, crowded with brick-heaps and half-finished streets, he took a slow walk along its entire length. It was a melancholy example of baffled enterprise. A row of a dozen or more shops had been built before any population had arrived to demand goods. Would-be tradesmen had taken many of these shops, and failure and disappointment stared from the windows. Some were half covered by shutters, because the scanty stock scarce sufficed to fill the remaining half. Others were shut almost altogether, the inmates only keeping open the door for their own convenience, and, perhaps, keeping down a shutter for the sake of a little light. Others again had not yet fallen so low, but struggled bravely still to maintain a show of business and prosperity, with very little success. Opposite the shops there still remained a dusty, ill-treated hedge and a forlorn-looking field, which an old board offered on building leases. Altogether a most depressing spot.

There was little difficulty in identifying the three shops offered for letting by Mr. H. Danby. They were all together near the middle of the row, and were the only ones that appeared not yet to have been occupied. A dusty "To Let" bill hung in each window, with written directions to inquire of Mr. H. Danby or at No. 7. Now, No. 7 was a melancholy baker's shop, with a stock of three loaves and a plate of stale buns. The disappointed baker assured Hewitt that he usually kept the keys of the shops, but that the landlord, Mr. Danby, had taken them away the day before, to see how the ceilings were standing, and had not returned them. "But if you was thinking of taking a shop here," the poor baker added, with some hesitation, "I—I—if you'll excuse my advising you—I shouldn't recommend it. I've had a sickener of it myself."

Hewitt thanked the baker for his advice, wished him better luck in future, and left. To the "Hare and Hounds" his pace was brisk. "Come," he said, as he met Kentish's inquiring glance, "this has been a very good day, on the whole. I know where our man is now, and I think we can get him, by a little management."

"Where is he?"

"Oh, down in Padfield. As a matter of fact, he's being kept there against his will, we shall find. I see that your friend, Mr. Danby, is a builder as well as a bookmaker."

"Not a regular builder. He speculates in a street of new houses now and again, that's all. But is he in it?"

"He's as deep in it as anybody, I think. Now, don't fly into a passion. There are a few others in it as well, but you'll do harm if you don't keep quiet."

"But go and get the police—come and fetch him, if you know where they're keeping him; why—"

"So we will, if we can't do it without them. But it's quite possible we can, and without all the disturbance and, perhaps, delay that calling in the police would involve. Consider, now, in reference to your own arrangements. Wouldn't it pay you better to get him back quietly, without a soul knowing—perhaps not even Danby knowing—till the heat is run tomorrow?"

"Well, yes, it would, of course."

"Very good, then, so be it. Remember what I have told you about keeping your mouth shut—say nothing to Steggles or anybody. Is there a cab or brougham your son and I can have for the evening?"

"There's an old hiring landau in the stables you can shut up into a cab, if that'll do."

"Excellent. We'll run down to the town in it as soon as it's ready. But, first, a word about Crockett. What sort of a lad is he? Likely to give them trouble, show fight, and make a disturbance?"

"No, I should say not. He's no plucked 'un, certainly—all his manhood's in his legs, I believe. You see, he ain't a big sort o' chap at best, and he'd be pretty easy put upon—at least, I guess so."

"Very good, so much the better, for then he won't have been damaged, and they will probably only have one man to guard him. Now the carriage, please."

Young Kentish was a six-foot sergeant of Grenadiers, home on furlough, and luxuriating in plain clothes. He and Hewitt walked a little way towards the town, allowing the landau to catch them up. They travelled in it to within a hundred yards of the empty shops and then alighted, bidding the driver wait.

"I shall show you three empty shops," Hewitt said, as he and young Kentish walked down Granville Road. "I am pretty sure that Sammy Crockett is in one of them, and I am pretty sure that that is the middle one. Take a look as we go past."

When the shops had been slowly passed, Hewitt resumed: "Now, did you see anything about those shops that told a tale of any sort?"

"No," Sergeant Kentish replied. "I can't say I noticed anything beyond the fact that they were empty—and likely to stay so, I should think."

"We'll stroll back, and look in at the windows, if nobody's watching us," Hewitt said. "You see, it's reasonable to suppose they've put him in the middle one, because that would suit their purpose best. The shops at each side of the three are occupied, and if the prisoner struggled, or shouted, or made an uproar, he might be heard if he were in one of the shops next those inhabited. So that the middle shop is the most likely. Now, see there," he went on, as they stopped before the window of the shop in question, "over at the back there's a staircase not yet partitioned off. It goes down below and up above; on the stairs and on the floor near them there are muddy footmarks. These must have been made today, else they would not be muddy, but dry and dusty, since there hasn't been a shower for a week till today. Move on again. Then you noticed that there were no other such marks in the shop. Consequently the man with the muddy feet did not come in by the front door, but by the back; otherwise he would have made a trail from the door. So we will go round to the back ourselves."

It was now growing dusk. The small pieces of ground behind the shops were bounded by a low fence, containing a door for each house.

"This door is bolted inside, of course," Hewitt said, "but there is no difficulty in climbing. I think we had better wait in the garden till dark. In the meantime, the gaoler, whoever he is, may come out; in which case we shall pounce on him as soon as he opens the door. You have that few yards of cord in your pocket, I think? And my handkerchief, properly rolled, will make a very good gag. Now over."

They climbed the fence and quietly approached the house, placing themselves in the angle of an outhouse out of sight from the windows. There was no sound, and no light appeared. Just above the ground about a foot of window was visible, with a grating over it, apparently lighting a basement. Suddenly Hewitt touched his companion's arm, and pointed toward the window. A faint rustling sound was perceptible, and as nearly as could be discerned in the darkness, some white blind or covering was placed over the glass from the inside. Then came the sound of a striking match, and at the side edge of the window there was a faint streak of light.

"That's the place," Hewitt whispered. "Come, we'll make a push for it. You stand against the wall at one side of the door and I'll stand at the other, and we'll have him as he comes out. Quietly, now, and I'll startle them."

He took a stone from among the rubbish littering the garden and flung it crashing through the window. There was a loud exclamation from within, the blind fell, and somebody rushed to the back door and flung it open. Instantly Kentish let fly a heavy right-hander, and the man went over like a skittle. In a moment Hewitt was upon him and the gag in his mouth.

"Hold him," Hewitt whispered, hurriedly. "I'll see if there are others."

He peered down through the low window. Within, Sammy Crockett, his bare legs dangling from beneath his long overcoat, sat on a packing-box, leaning with his head on his hand and his back towards the window. A guttering candle stood on the mantelpiece, and the newspaper which had been stretched across the window lay in scattered sheets on the floor. No other person besides Sammy was visible.

They led their prisoner indoors. Young Kentish recognised him as a public-house loafer and race-course ruffian well known in the neighbourhood.

"So it's you, is it, Browdie?" he said. "I've caught you one hard clump, and I've half a mind to make it a score more. But you'll get it pretty warm one way or another, before this job's forgotten."

Sammy Crockett was overjoyed at his rescue. He had not been ill-treated, he explained, but had been thoroughly cowed by Browdie, who had from time to time threatened him savagely with an iron bar, by way of persuading him to quietness and sub-mission. He had been fed, and had taken no worse harm than a slight stiffness from his adventure, due to his light under-attire of jersey and knee-shorts.

Sergeant Kentish tied Browdie's elbows firmly together behind, and carried the line round the ankles, bracing all up tight. Then he ran a knot from one wrist to the other over the back of the neck, and left the prisoner, trussed and helpless, on the heap of straw that had been Sammy's bed.

"You won't be very jolly, I expect," Kentish said, "for some time. You can't shout and you can't walk, and I know you can't untie yourself. You'll get a bit hungry, too, perhaps, but that'll give you an appetite. I don't suppose you'll be disturbed till some time tomorrow, unless our friend Danby turns up in the meantime. But you can come along to gaol instead, if you prefer it."

They left him where he lay, and took Sammy to the old landau. Sammy walked in slippers, carrying his spiked shoes, hanging by the lace, in his hand.

"Ah," said Hewitt, "I think I know the name of the young lady who gave you those slippers."

Crockett looked ashamed and indignant. "Yes," he said; "they've done me nicely between 'em. But I'll pay her—I'll—"

"Hush, hush!" Hewitt said; "you mustn't talk unkindly of a lady, you know. Get into this carriage, and we'll take you home. We'll see if I can tell you your adventures without making a mistake. First, you had a note from Miss Webb, telling you that you were mistaken in supposing she had slighted you, and that as a matter of fact she had quite done with somebody else—left him—of whom you were jealous. Isn't that so?"

"Well, yes," young Crockett answered, blushing deeply under the carriage-lamp; "but I don't see how you come to know that."

"Then she went on to ask you to get rid of Steggles on Thursday afternoon for a few minutes, and speak to her in the back lane. Now, your running pumps, with their thin soles, almost like paper, no heels and long spikes, hurt your feet horribly if you walk on hard ground, don't they?"

"Ay, that they do—enough to cripple you. I'd never go on much hard ground with 'em."

"They're not like cricket shoes, I see."

"Not a bit. Cricket shoes you can walk anywhere in."

"Well, she knew this—I think I know who told her—and she promised to bring you a new pair of slippers, and to throw them over the fence for you to come out in."

"I s'pose she's been tellin' you all this?" Crockett said, mournfully. "You couldn't ha' seen the letter—I saw her tear it up and put the bits in her pocket. She asked me for it in the lane, in case Steggles saw it."

"Well, at any rate, you sent Steggles away, and the slippers did come over, and you went into the lane. You walked with her as far as the road at the end, and then you were seized and gagged, and put into a carriage."

"That was Browdie did that," said Crockett, "and another chap I don't know. But—why, this is Padfield High Street!" He looked through the window and regarded the familiar shops with astonishment.

"Of course it is. Where did you think it was?"

"Why, where was that place you found me in?"

"Granville Road, Padfield. I suppose they told you you were in another town?"

"Told me it was Newstead Hatch. They drove for about three or four hours, and kept me down on the floor between the seats so as I couldn't see where we was going."

"Done for two reasons," said Hewitt. "First, to mystify you, and prevent any discovery of the people directing the conspiracy; and, second, to be able to put you indoors at night and unobserved. Well, I think I have told you all you know yourself now as far as the carriage.

"But there is the 'Hare and Hounds' just in front. We'll pull up here and I'll get out and see if the coast is clear. I fancy Mr. Kentish would rather you came in unnoticed."

In a few seconds Hewitt was back, and Crockett was conveyed indoors by a side entrance. Hewitt's instructions to the landlord were few but emphatic. "Don't tell Steggles about it," he said; "make an excuse to get rid of him, and send him out of the house. Take Crockett into some other bedroom, not his own, and let your son look after him. Then come here, and I'll tell you all about it."

Sammy Crockett was undergoing a heavy grooming with white embrocation at the hands of Sergeant Kentish, when the landlord returned to Hewitt. "Does Danby know you've got him?" he asked. "How did you do it?"

"Danby doesn't know yet, and with luck he won't know till he sees Crockett running tomorrow. The man who has sold you is Steggles."

"Steggles?"

"Steggles it is. At the very first, when Steggles rushed in to report Sammy Crockett missing, I suspected him. You didn't, I suppose?"

"No. He's always been considered a straight man, and he looked as startled as anybody."

"Yes, I must say he acted it very well. But there was something suspicious in his story. What did he say? Crockett had remarked a chilliness, and asked for a sweater, which Steggles went to fetch.

Now, just think. You understand these things. Would any trainer who knew his business (as Steggles does) have gone to bring out a sweater for his man to change for his jersey in the open air, at the very time the man was complaining of chilliness? Of course not. He would have taken his man indoors again and let him change there under shelter. Then supposing Steggles had really been surprised at missing Crockett, wouldn't he have looked about, found the gate open, and *told* you it was open, when he first came in? He said nothing of that—we found the gate open for ourselves. So that from the beginning, I had a certain opinion of Steggles."

"What you say seems pretty plain now, although it didn't strike me at the time. But if Steggles was selling us, why couldn't he have drugged the lad? That would have been a deal simpler."

"Because Steggles is a good trainer and has a certain reputation to keep up. It would have done him no good to have had a runner drugged while under his care—certainly it would have cooked his goose with *you*. It was much the safer thing to connive at kidnapping. That put all the active work into other hands, and left him safe, even if the trick failed. Now you remember that we traced the prints of Crockett's spiked shoes to within a couple of yards of the fence, and that there they ceased suddenly?"

"Yes. You said it looked as though he had flown up into the air; and so it did."

"But I was sure that it was by that gate that Crockett had left, and by no other. He couldn't have got through the house without being seen, and there was no other way—let alone the evidence of the unbolted gate. Therefore, as the footprints ceased where they did, and were not repeated anywhere in the lane, I knew that he had taken his spiked shoes off—probably changed them for something else, because a runner anxious as to his chances would never risk walking on bare feet, with a chance of cutting them. Ordinary, broad, smooth-soled slippers would leave no impression on the coarse cinders bordering the track, and nothing short of spiked shoes would leave a mark on the hard path in the lane behind. The spike tracks were leading, not directly toward the door, but in the direction of the fence, when they stopped—somebody had handed, or thrown, the slippers over the fence and he had changed them on the spot. The enemy had calculated upon the spikes leaving a track in the lane that might lead us in our search, and had arranged accordingly.

"So far, so good. I could see no footprints near the gate in the lane. You will remember that I sent Steggles off to watch at the Cop before I went out to the back—merely, of course, to get him out of the way. I went out into the lane, leaving you behind, and walked its whole length, first toward the Old Kilns and then back toward the road. I found nothing to help me except these small pieces of paper—which are here in my pocket-book, by-the-bye. Of course, this 'mmy' might have meant 'Jimmy' or 'Tommy,' as possibly as 'Sammy,' but they were not to be rejected on that account. Certainly Crockett had been decoyed out of your ground, not taken by force, or there would have been marks of a scuffle in the cinders. And as his request for a sweater was probably an excuse—because it was not at all a cold afternoon—he must have previously designed going out—inference, a letter received; and here were pieces of a letter. Now, in the light of what I have said, look at these pieces. First there is the 'mmy'—that I have dealt with. Then, see this 'throw them ov'—clearly a part of 'throw them over'; exactly what had probably been done with the slippers. Then the 'poor f,' coming just on the line before, and seen, by joining up with this other piece, might easily be a reference to 'poor feet.' These coincidences, one on the other, went far to establish the identity of the letter, and to confirm my previous impressions. But then there is something else. Two other pieces evidently mean 'left him,' and 'right away'—send Steggles 'right away,' perhaps; but there is another, containing almost all of the words 'hate his,' with the word 'hate' underlined. Now, who writes 'hate' with the emphasis of underscoring—who but a woman? The writing is large and not very regular; it might easily be that of a half-educated woman. Here was something more—Sammy had been enticed away by a woman.

"Now, I remembered that when we went into the tap-room on Wednesday, some of his companions were chaffing Crockett about a certain Nancy Webb, and the chaff went home, as was plain to see. The woman, then, who could most easily entice Sammy Crockett away was Nancy Webb. I resolved to find who Nancy Webb was and learn more of her.

"Meantime I took a look at the road at the end of the lane. It was damper than the lane, being lower, and overhung by trees. There were many wheel tracks, but only one set that turned in the road and went back the way it came—towards the town—and they were narrow wheels, carriage wheels. Crockett tells me now that they drove him about for a long time before shutting him up—probably the inconvenience of taking him straight to the hiding-place didn't strike them when they first drove off.

"A few inquiries soon set me in the direction of the 'Plough' and Miss Nancy Webb. I had the curiosity to look round the place as I approached, and there, in the garden behind the house, were Steggles and the young lady in earnest confabulation!

"Every conjecture became a certainty. Steggles was the lover of whom Crockett was jealous, and he had employed the girl to bring Sammy out. I watched Steggles home, and gave you a hint to keep him there.

"But the thing that remained was to find Steggles's employer in this business. I was glad to be in when Danby called—he came, of course, to hear if you would blurt out anything, and to learn, if possible, what steps you were taking. He failed. By way of making assurance doubly sure, I took a short walk this morning in the character of a deaf gentleman, and got Miss Webb to write me a direction that comprised three of the words on these scraps of paper—'left,' 'right,' and 'lane'—see, they correspond, the peculiar 'f's,' 't's,' and all.

"Now, I felt perfectly sure that Steggles would go for his pay today. In the first place, I knew that people mixed up with shady transactions in professional pedestrianism are not apt to trust one another far—they know better. Therefore, Steggles wouldn't have had his bribe first. But he would take care to get it before the Saturday heats were run, because once they were over the thing was done, and the principal conspirator might have refused to pay up, and Steggles couldn't have helped himself. Again I hinted he should not go out till I could follow him, and this afternoon when he went, follow him I did. I saw him go into Danby's house by the side way and come away again. Danby it was, then, who had arranged the business; and nobody was more likely, considering his large pecuniary stake against Crockett's winning this race.

"But now, how to find Crockett? I made up my mind he wouldn't be in Danby's own house—that would be a deal too risky, with servants about, and so on. I saw that Danby was a builder, and had three shops to let—it was on a paper before his house. What more likely prison than an empty house? I knocked at Danby's door and asked for the keys of those shops. I couldn't have them. The servant told me Danby was out (a manifest lie, for I had just seen him), and that nobody could see the shops till Monday. But I got out of her the address of the shops, and that was all I wanted at the time.

"Now, why was nobody to see those shops till Monday? The interval was suspicious—just enough to enable Crockett to be sent away again and cast loose after the Saturday racing, supposing him to be kept in one of the empty buildings. I went off at once and looked at the shops, forming my conclusions as to which would be the most likely for Danby's purpose. Here I had another confirmation of my ideas. A poor, half-bankrupt baker in one of the shops had, by the bills, the custody of a set of keys; but *he*, too, told me I couldn't have them; Danby had taken them away—and on Thursday, the very day—with some trivial excuse, and hadn't brought them back. That was all I wanted, or could expect in the way of guidance; the whole thing was plain. The rest you know all about."

"Well, you're certainly as smart as they give you credit for, I must say. But suppose Danby had taken down his 'to let' notice, what would you have done then?"

"We had our course even then. We should have gone to Danby, astounded him by telling him all about his little games, terrorised him with threats of the law, and made him throw up his hand and send Crockett back. But as it is, you see, he doesn't know at this moment—probably won't know till tomorrow afternoon—that the lad is safe and sound here. You will probably use the interval to make him pay for losing the game—by some of the ingenious financial devices you are no doubt familiar with."

"Aye, that I will. He'll give any price against Crockett now, so long as the bet don't come direct from me."

"But about Crockett, now," Hewitt went on. "Won't this confinement be likely to have damaged his speed for a day or two?"

"Ah, perhaps," the landlord replied; "but, bless ye, that won't matter. There's four more in his heat tomorrow. Two I know aren't tryers, and the other two I can hold in at a couple of quid apiece any day. The third round and final won't be till tomorrow week, and he'll be as fit as ever by then. It's as safe as ever it was. How much are you going to have on? I'll lump it on for you safe enough. This is a chance not to be missed—it's picking money up."

"Thank you; I don't think I'll have anything to do with it. This professional pedestrian business doesn't seem a pretty one at all. I don't call myself a moralist, but, if you'll excuse my saying so, the thing is scarcely the game I care to pick up money at in any way."

"Oh! very well, if you think so, I won't persuade ye, though I don't think so much of your smartness as I did, after that. Still, we won't quarrel—you've done me a mighty good turn, that I must say, and I only feel I aren't level without doing something to pay the debt. Come, now, you've got your trade as I've got mine. Let me have the bill, and I'll pay it like a lord, and feel a deal more pleased than if you made a favour of it—not that I'm above a favour, of course. But I'd prefer paying, and that's a fact."

"My dear sir, you have paid," Hewitt said, with a smile. "You paid in advance. It was a bargain, wasn't it, that I should do your business if you would help me in mine? Very well, a bargain's a bargain, and we've both performed our parts. And you mustn't be offended at what I said just now."

"That I won't. But as to that Raggy Steggles, once those heats are over tomorrow, I'll—well—!"

★

It was on the following Sunday week that Martin Hewitt, in his rooms in London, turned over his paper and read, under the head "Padfield Annual 135 Yards Handicap," this announcement: "Final Heat: Crockett, first; Willis, second; Trewby, third; Owen, o; Howell, o. A runaway win by nearly three yards."

THE ADVENTURE OF THE
MISSING THREE-QUARTER

Arthur Conan Doyle

Arthur Ignatius Conan Doyle (1859–1930) is a towering figure in British popular literature, the creator of the most renowned character in the history of fiction. So frustrated was he by the way that his Sherlock Holmes stories overshadowed his other work that he went to the extreme length of killing off his hero, only to be persuaded to bring him back in *The Hound of the Baskervilles* and then reveal in "The Empty House" that Dr. Watson's reports of the detective's death were exaggerated. Doyle was a keen sportsman who played ten first class cricket matches and took the wicket of the legendary W. G. Grace (admittedly Grace was in his fifties at the time). He also enjoyed boxing, which features in books such as *Rodney Stone*, football, golf, ski-ing—and even baseball.

This story was first published in the *Strand* in 1904, and was collected in *The Return of Sherlock Holmes*. As the leading authority on Holmes, Leslie Klinger, has pointed out, it is the only case in the canon which directly involves amateur sport, although Dr. Watson was just as keen a sportsman as Doyle. We learn in "The Sussex Vampire" that Watson played rugby, while his multi-talented friend was an accomplished exponent of fencing, singlestick, and boxing—despite disclaiming here any sporting connections. It is significant that Holmes refers to amateur sport as "the best and soundest thing in England"; there can be little doubt that he was speaking for his creator.

WE WERE FAIRLY ACCUSTOMED TO RECEIVE WEIRD telegrams at Baker Street, but I have a particular recollection of one which reached us on a gloomy February morning some seven or eight years ago and gave Mr. Sherlock Holmes a puzzled quarter of an hour. It was addressed to him, and ran thus:—

"Please await me. Terrible misfortune. Right wing three-quarter missing; indispensable tomorrow.—OVERTON."

"Strand post-mark and dispatched ten-thirty-six," said Holmes, reading it over and over. "Mr. Overton was evidently considerably excited when he sent it, and somewhat incoherent in consequence. Well, well, he will be here, I dare say, by the time I have looked through the *Times*, and then we shall know all about it. Even the most insignificant problem would be welcome in these stagnant days."

Things had indeed been very slow with us, and I had learned to dread such periods of inaction, for I knew by experience that my companion's brain was so abnormally active that it was dangerous to leave it without material upon which to work. For years I had gradually weaned him from that drug mania which had threatened once to check his remarkable career. Now I knew that under ordinary conditions he no longer craved for this artificial stimulus, but I was well aware that the fiend was not dead, but sleeping; and I have known that the sleep was a light one and the waking near when in periods of idleness I have seen the drawn look upon Holmes's ascetic face, and the brooding of his deep-set and inscrutable eyes. Therefore I blessed this Mr. Overton, whoever he might be, since he had come with his enigmatic message to break that dangerous calm which brought more peril to my friend than all the storms of his tempestuous life.

As we had expected, the telegram was soon followed by its sender, and the card of Mr. Cyril Overton, of Trinity College, Cambridge, announced the arrival of an enormous young man, sixteen stone of solid bone and muscle, who spanned the doorway with his broad shoulders and looked from one of us to the other with a comely face which was haggard with anxiety.

"Mr. Sherlock Holmes?"

My companion bowed.

"I've been down to Scotland Yard, Mr. Holmes. I saw Inspector Stanley Hopkins. He advised me to come to you. He said the case, so far as he could see, was more in your line than in that of the regular police."

"Pray sit down and tell me what is the matter."

"It's awful, Mr. Holmes, simply awful! I wonder my hair isn't grey. Godfrey Staunton—you've heard of him, of course? He's simply the hinge that the whole team turns on. I'd rather spare two from the pack and have Godfrey for my three-quarter line. Whether it's passing, or tackling, or dribbling, there's no one to touch him; and then, he's got the head and can hold us all together. What am I to do? That's what I ask you, Mr. Holmes. There's Moorhouse, first reserve, but he is trained as a half, and he always edges right in on to the scrum instead of keeping out on the touch-line. He's a fine place-kick, it's true, but, then, he has no judgement, and he can't sprint for nuts. Why, Morton or Johnson, the Oxford fliers, could romp round him. Stevenson is fast enough, but he couldn't drop from the twenty-five line, and a three-quarter who can't either punt or drop isn't worth a place for pace alone. No, Mr. Holmes, we are done unless you can help me to find Godfrey Staunton."

My friend had listened with amused surprise to this long speech, which was poured forth with extraordinary vigour and earnestness, every point being driven home by the slapping of a brawny hand upon the speaker's knee. When our visitor was silent Holmes stretched out his hand and took down letter "S" of his commonplace book. For once he dug in vain into that mine of varied information.

"There is Arthur H. Staunton, the rising young forger," said he, "and there was Henry Staunton, whom I helped to hang, but Godfrey Staunton is a new name to me."

It was our visitor's turn to look surprised.

"Why, Mr. Holmes, I thought you knew things," said he. "I suppose, then, if you have never heard of Godfrey Staunton you don't know Cyril Overton either?"

Holmes shook his head good-humouredly.

"Great Scot!" cried the athlete. "Why, I was first reserve for England against Wales, and I've skippered the 'Varsity all this year. But that's nothing! I didn't think there was a soul in England who didn't know Godfrey Staunton, the crack three-quarter, Cambridge, Blackheath, and five Internationals. Good Lord! Mr. Holmes, where *have* you lived?"

Holmes laughed at the young giant's naïve astonishment,

"You live in a different world to me, Mr. Overton, a sweeter and healthier one. My ramifications stretch out into many sections of society, but never, I am happy to say, into amateur sport, which is the best and soundest thing in England. However, your unexpected visit this morning shows me that even in that world of fresh air and fair play there may be work for me to do; so now, my good sir, I beg you to sit down and to tell me slowly and quietly exactly what it is that has occurred, and how you desire that I should help you."

Young Overton's face assumed the bothered look of the man who is more accustomed to using his muscles than his wits; but by degrees, with many repetitions and obscurities which I may omit from his narrative, he laid his strange story before us.

"It's this way, Mr. Holmes. As I have said, I am the skipper of the Rugger team of Cambridge 'Varsity, and Godfrey Staunton is my best man. Tomorrow we play Oxford. Yesterday we all came up and we settled at Bentley's private hotel. At ten o'clock I went round and saw that all the fellows had gone to roost, for I believe in strict training and plenty of sleep to keep a team fit. I had a word or two with Godfrey before he turned in. He seemed to me to be pale and bothered. I asked him what was the matter. He said he was all right—just a touch of headache. I bade him good-night and left him. Half an hour later the porter tells me that a rough-looking man with a beard called with a note for Godfrey. He had not gone to bed and the note was taken to his room. Godfrey read it and fell back in a chair as if he had been pole-axed. The porter was so scared that he was going to fetch me, but Godfrey stopped him, had a drink of water, and pulled himself together. Then he went downstairs, said a few words to the man who was waiting in the hall, and the two of them went off together. The last that the porter saw of them, they were almost running down the street in the direction of the Strand. This morning Godfrey's room was empty, his bed had never been slept in, and his things were all just as I had seen them the night before. He had gone off at a moment's notice with this stranger, and no word has come from him since. I don't believe he will ever come back. He was a sportsman, was Godfrey, down to his marrow, and he wouldn't have stopped his training and let in his skipper if it were not for some cause that was too strong for him. No; I feel as if he were gone for good and we should never see him again."

Sherlock Holmes listened with the deepest attention to this singular narrative.

"What did you do?" he asked.

"I wired to Cambridge to learn if anything had been heard of him there. I have had an answer. No one has seen him."

"Could he have got back to Cambridge?"

"Yes, there is a late train—quarter-past eleven."

"But so far as you can ascertain he did not take it?"

"No, he has not been seen."

"What did you do next?"

"I wired to Lord Mount-James."

"Why to Lord Mount-James?"

"Godfrey is an orphan, and Lord Mount-James is his nearest relative—his uncle, I believe."

"Indeed. This throws new light upon the matter. Lord Mount-James is one of the richest men in England."

"So I've heard Godfrey say."

"And your friend was closely related?"

"Yes, he was his heir, and the old boy is nearly eighty—cram full of gout, too. They say he could chalk his billiard-cue with his knuckles. He never allowed Godfrey a shilling in his life, for he is an absolute miser, but it will all come to him right enough."

"Have you heard from Lord Mount-James?"

"No."

"What motive could your friend have in going to Lord Mount-James?"

"Well, something was worrying him the night before, and if it was to do with money it is possible that he would make for his nearest relative who had so much of it, though from all I have heard he would not have much chance of getting it. Godfrey was not fond of the old man. He would not go if he could help it."

"Well, we can soon determine that. If your friend was going to his relative, Lord Mount-James, you have then to explain the visit of this rough-looking fellow at so late an hour, and the agitation that was caused by his coming."

Cyril Overton pressed his hands to his head. "I can make nothing of it," said he.

"Well, well, I have a clear day, and I shall be happy to look into the matter," said Holmes. "I should strongly recommend you to make your preparations for your match without reference to this young gentleman. It must, as you say, have been an overpowering necessity which tore him away in such a fashion, and the same necessity is likely to hold him away. Let us step round together to this hotel, and see if the porter can throw any fresh light upon the matter."

Sherlock Holmes was a past-master in the art of putting a humble witness at his ease, and very soon, in the privacy of Godfrey Staunton's abandoned room, he had extracted all that the porter had to tell. The visitor of the night before was not a gentleman, neither was he a working man. He was simply what the porter described as a "medium-looking chap"; a man of fifty, beard grizzled, pale face, quietly dressed. He seemed himself to be agitated. The porter had observed his hand trembling when he had held out the note. Godfrey Staunton had crammed the note into his pocket. Staunton had not shaken hands with the man in the hall. They had exchanged a few sentences, of which the porter had only distinguished the one word "time." Then they had hurried off in the manner described. It was just half-past ten by the hall clock.

"Let me see," said Holmes, seating himself on Staunton's bed. "You are the day porter, are you not?"

"Yes, sir; I go off duty at eleven."

"The night porter saw nothing, I suppose?"

"No, sir; one theatre party came in late. No one else."

"Were you on duty all day yesterday?"

"Yes, sir."

"Did you take any messages to Mr. Staunton?"

"Yes, sir; one telegram."

"Ah! that's interesting. What o'clock was this?"

"About six."

"Where was Mr. Staunton when he received it?"

"Here in his room."

"Were you present when he opened it?"

"Yes, sir; I waited to see if there was an answer."

"Well, was there?"

"Yes, sir. He wrote an answer."

"Did you take it?"

"No; he took it himself."

"But he wrote it in your presence?"

"Yes, sir. I was standing by the door, and he with his back turned at that table. When he had written it he said, 'All right, porter, I will take this myself.'"

"What did he write it with?"

"A pen, sir."

"Was the telegraphic form one of these on the table?"

"Yes, sir; it was the top one."

Holmes rose. Taking the forms he carried them over to the window and carefully examined that which was uppermost.

"It is a pity he did not write in pencil," said he, throwing them down again with a shrug of disappointment. "As you have no doubt frequently observed, Watson, the impression usually goes through—a fact which has dissolved many a happy marriage. However, I can find no trace here. I rejoice, however, to perceive that he wrote with a broad-pointed quill pen, and I can hardly doubt that we will find some impression upon this blotting-pad. Ah, yes, surely this is the very thing!"

He tore off a strip of the blotting-paper and turned towards us the following hieroglyphic:—

Cyril Overton was much excited. "Hold it to the glass!" he cried.

"That is unnecessary," said Holmes. "The paper is thin, and the reverse will give the message. Here it is." He turned it over and we read:—

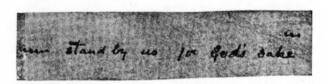

"So that is the tail end of the telegram which Godfrey Staunton dispatched within a few hours of his disappearance. There are at least six words of the message which have escaped us; but what remains—'Stand by us for God's sake!'—proves that this young man saw a formidable danger which approached him, and from which someone else could protect him. '*Us*,' mark you! Another person was involved. Who should it be but the pale-faced, bearded man, who seemed himself in so nervous a state? What, then, is the connection between Godfrey Staunton and the bearded man? And what is the third source from which each of them sought for help against pressing danger? Our inquiry has already narrowed down to that."

"We have only to find to whom that telegram is addressed," I suggested.

"Exactly, my dear Watson. Your reflection, though profound, had already crossed my mind. But I dare say it may have come to your notice that if you walk into a post-office and demand to see the counterfoil of another man's message there may be some disinclination on the part of the officials to oblige you. There is so much red tape in these matters! However, I have no doubt that with a little delicacy and finesse the end may be attained. Meanwhile, I should like in your presence, Mr. Overton, to go through these papers which have been left upon the table."

There were a number of letters, bills, and note-books, which Holmes turned over and examined with quick, nervous fingers and darting, penetrating eyes. "Nothing here," he said, at last. "By the way, I suppose your friend was a healthy young fellow—nothing amiss with him?"

"Sound as a bell."

"Have you ever known him ill?"

"Not a day. He has been laid up with a hack, and once he slipped his knee-cap, but that was nothing."

"Perhaps he was not so strong as you suppose. I should think he may have had some secret trouble. With your assent I will put one or two of these papers in my pocket, in case they should bear upon our future inquiry."

"One moment! one moment!" cried a querulous voice, and we looked up to find a queer little old man, jerking and twitching in the doorway. He was dressed in rusty black, with a very broad brimmed top-hat and a loose white necktie—the whole effect being that of a very rustic parson or of an undertaker's mute. Yet, in spite of his shabby and even absurd appearance, his voice had a sharp crackle, and his manner a quick intensity which commanded attention.

"Who are you, sir, and by what right do you touch this gentleman's papers?" he asked.

"I am a private detective, and I am endeavouring to explain his disappearance."

"Oh, you are, are you? And who instructed you, eh?"

"This gentleman, Mr. Staunton's friend, was referred to me by Scotland Yard."

"Who are you, sir?"

"I am Cyril Overton."

"Then it is you who sent me a telegram. My name is Lord Mount-James. I came round as quickly as the Bayswater 'bus would bring me. So you have instructed a detective?"

"Yes, sir."

"And are you prepared to meet the cost?"

"I have no doubt, sir, that my friend Godfrey, when we find him, will be prepared to do that."

"But if he is never found, eh? Answer me that!"

"In that case no doubt his family—"

"Nothing of the sort, sir!" screamed the little man. "Don't look to me for a penny—not a penny! You understand that, Mr. Detective! I am all the family that this young man has got, and I tell you that I am not responsible. If he has any expectations it is due to the fact that I have never wasted money, and I do not propose to begin to do so now. As to those papers with which you are making so free, I may tell you that in case there should be anything of any value among them you will be held strictly to account for what you do with them."

"Very good, sir," said Sherlock Holmes. "May I ask in the meanwhile whether you have yourself any theory to account for this young man's disappearance?"

"No, sir, I have not. He is big enough and old enough to look after himself, and if he is so foolish as to lose himself I entirely refuse to accept the responsibility of hunting for him."

"I quite understand your position," said Holmes, with a mischievous twinkle in his eyes. "Perhaps you don't quite understand mine. Godfrey Staunton appears to have been a poor man. If he has been kidnapped it could not have been for anything which he himself possesses. The fame of your wealth has gone abroad, Lord Mount-James, and it is entirely possible that a gang of thieves have secured your nephew in order to gain from him some information as to your house, your habits, and your treasure."

The face of our unpleasant little visitor turned as white as his neckcloth.

"Heavens, sir, what an idea! I never thought of such villainy! What inhuman rogues there are in the world! But Godfrey is a fine lad—a staunch lad. Nothing would induce him to give his old uncle away. I'll have the plate moved over to the bank this evening. In the meantime spare no pains, Mr. Detective! I beg you to leave no stone unturned to bring him safely back. As to money, well, so far as a fiver, or even a tenner, goes, you can always look to me."

Even in his chastened frame of mind the noble miser could give us no information which could help us, for he knew little of the private life of his nephew. Our only clue lay in the truncated telegram, and with a copy of this in his hand Holmes set forth to find a second link for his chain. We had shaken off Lord Mount-James, and Overton had gone to consult with the other members of his team over the misfortune which had befallen them.

There was a telegraph-office at a short distance from the hotel. We halted outside it.

"It's worth trying, Watson," said Holmes. "Of course, with a warrant we could demand to see the counterfoils, but we have not reached that stage yet. I don't suppose they remember faces in so busy a place. Let us venture it."

"I am sorry to trouble you," said he, in his blandest manner, to the young woman behind the grating; "there is some small mistake about a telegram I sent yesterday. I have had no answer, and I very much fear that I must have omitted to put my name at the end. Could you tell me if this was so?"

The young woman turned over a sheaf of counterfoils.

"What o'clock was it?" she asked.

"A little after six."

"Whom was it to?"

Holmes put his finger to his lips and glanced at me. "The last words in it were 'for God's sake,'" he whispered, confidentially; "I am very anxious at getting no answer."

The young woman separated one of the forms.

"This is it. There is no name," said she, smoothing it out upon the counter.

"Then that, of course, accounts for my getting no answer," said Holmes. "Dear me, how very stupid of me, to be sure! Good morning, miss, and many thanks for having relieved my mind." He chuckled and rubbed his hands when we found ourselves in the street once more.

"Well?" I asked.

"We progress, my dear Watson, we progress. I had seven different schemes for getting a glimpse of that telegram, but I could hardly hope to succeed the very first time."

"And what have you gained?"

"A starting-point for our investigation." He hailed a cab. "King's Cross Station," said he.

"We have a journey, then?"

"Yes; I think we must run down to Cambridge together. All the indications seem to me to point in that direction."

"Tell me," I asked, as we rattled up Gray's Inn Road, "have you any suspicion yet as to the cause of the disappearance? I don't think that among all our cases I have known one where the motives are more obscure. Surely you don't really imagine that he may be kidnapped in order to give information against his wealthy uncle?"

"I confess, my dear Watson, that that does not appeal to me as a very probable explanation. It struck me, however, as being the one which was most likely to interest that exceedingly unpleasant old person."

"It certainly did that. But what are your alternatives?"

"I could mention several. You must admit that it is curious and suggestive that this incident should occur on the eve of this important match, and should involve the only man whose presence seems essential to the success of the side. It may, of course, be coincidence, but it is interesting. Amateur sport is free from betting, but a good deal of outside betting goes on among the public, and it is possible that it might be worth someone's while to get at a player as the ruffians of the turf get at a race-horse. There is one explanation. A second very obvious one is that this young man really is the heir of a great property, however modest his means may at present be, and it is not impossible that a plot to hold him for ransom might be concocted."

"These theories take no account of the telegram."

"Quite true, Watson. The telegram still remains the only solid thing with which we have to deal, and we must not permit our attention to wander away from it. It is to gain light upon the purpose of this telegram that we are now upon our way to Cambridge. The path of our investigation is at present obscure, but I shall be very much surprised if before evening we have not cleared it up or made a considerable advance along it."

It was already dark when we reached the old University city. Holmes took a cab at the station, and ordered the man to drive to the house of Dr. Leslie Armstrong. A few minutes later we had stopped at a large mansion in the busiest thoroughfare. We were shown in, and after a long wait were at last admitted into the consulting-room, where we found the doctor seated behind his table.

It argues the degree in which I had lost touch with my profession that the name of Leslie Armstrong was unknown to me. Now I am aware that he is not only one of the heads of the medical school of the University, but a thinker of European reputation in more than one branch of science. Yet even without knowing his brilliant record one could not fail to be impressed by a mere glance at the man, the square, massive face, the brooding eyes under the thatched brows, and the granite moulding of the inflexible jaw. A man of deep character, a man with an alert mind, grim, ascetic, self-contained, formidable—so I read Dr. Leslie Armstrong. He held my friend's card in his hand, and he looked up with no very pleased expression upon his dour features.

"I have heard your name, Mr. Sherlock Holmes, and I am aware of your profession, one of which I by no means approve."

"In that, doctor, you will find yourself in agreement with every criminal in the country," said my friend, quietly.

"So far as your efforts are directed towards the suppression of crime, sir, they must have the support of every reasonable member of the community, though I cannot doubt that the official machinery is amply sufficient for the purpose. Where your calling is more open to criticism is when you pry into the secrets of private individuals, when you rake up family matters which are better hidden, and when you incidentally waste the time of men who are more busy than yourself. At the present moment, for example, I should be writing a treatise instead of conversing with you."

"No doubt, doctor; and yet the conversation may prove more important than the treatise. Incidentally I may tell you that we are doing the reverse of what you very justly blame, and that we are endeavouring to prevent anything like public exposure of private matters which must necessarily follow when once the case is fairly in the hands of the official police. You may look upon me simply as an irregular pioneer who goes in front of the regular forces of the country. I have come to ask you about Mr. Godfrey Staunton."

"What about him?"

"You know him, do you not?"

"He is an intimate friend of mine."

"You are aware that he has disappeared?"

"Ah, indeed!" There was no change of expression in the rugged features of the doctor.

"He left his hotel last night. He has not been heard of."

"No doubt he will return."

"Tomorrow is the 'Varsity football match."

"I have no sympathy with these childish games. The young man's fate interests me deeply, since I know him and like him. The football match does not come within my horizon at all."

"I claim your sympathy, then, in my investigation of Mr. Staunton's fate. Do you know where he is?"

"Certainly not."

"You have not seen him since yesterday?"

"No, I have not."

"Was Mr. Staunton a healthy man?"

"Absolutely."

"Did you ever know him ill?"

"Never."

Holmes popped a sheet of paper before the doctor's eyes. "Then perhaps you will explain this receipted bill for thirteen guineas, paid by Mr. Godfrey Staunton last month to Dr. Leslie Armstrong of Cambridge. I picked it out from among the papers upon his desk."

The doctor flushed with anger.

"I do not feel that there is any reason why I should render an explanation to you, Mr. Holmes."

Holmes replaced the bill in his note-book. "If you prefer a public explanation it must come sooner or later," said he. "I have already told you that I can hush up that which others will be bound to publish, and you would really be wiser to take me into your complete confidence."

"I know nothing about it."

"Did you hear from Mr. Staunton in London?"

"Certainly not."

"Dear me, dear me; the post-office again!" Holmes sighed, wearily. "A most urgent telegram was dispatched to you from London by Godfrey Staunton at six-fifteen yesterday evening—a telegram which is undoubtedly associated with his disappearance—and yet you have not had it. It is most culpable. I shall certainly go down to the office here and register a complaint."

Dr. Leslie Armstrong sprang up from behind his desk, and his dark face was crimson with fury.

"I'll trouble you to walk out of my house, sir," said he. "You can tell your employer, Lord Mount-James, that I do not wish to have anything to do either with him or with his agents. No, sir, not another word!" He rang the bell furiously. "John, show these gentlemen out." A pompous butler ushered us severely to the door, and we found ourselves in the street. Holmes burst out laughing.

"Dr. Leslie Armstrong is certainly a man of energy and character," said he. "I have not seen a man who, if he turned his talents that way, was more calculated to fill the gap left by the illustrious Moriarty. And now, my poor Watson, here we are, stranded and friendless in this inhospitable town, which we cannot leave without abandoning our case. This little inn just opposite Armstrong's house is singularly adapted to our needs. If you would engage a front room and purchase the necessaries for the night, I may have time to make a few inquiries."

These few inquiries proved, however, to be a more lengthy proceeding than Holmes had imagined, for he did not return to the inn until nearly nine o'clock. He was pale and dejected, stained with dust, and exhausted with hunger and fatigue. A cold supper was ready upon the table, and when his needs were satisfied and his pipe alight he was ready to take that half comic and wholly philosophic view which was natural to him when his affairs were going awry. The sound of carriage wheels caused him to rise and glance out of the window. A brougham and pair of greys under the glare of a gas-lamp stood before the doctor's door.

"It's been out three hours," said Holmes; "started at half-past six, and here it is back again. That gives a radius of ten or twelve miles, and he does it once, or sometimes twice, a day."

"No unusual thing for a doctor in practice."

"But Armstrong is not really a doctor in practice. He is a lecturer and a consultant, but he does not care for general practice, which distracts him from his literary work. Why, then, does he make these long journeys, which must be exceedingly irksome to him, and who is it that he visits?"

"His coachman—"

"My dear Watson, can you doubt that it was to him that I first applied? I do not know whether it came from his own innate depravity or from the promptings of his master, but he was rude enough to set a dog at me. Neither dog nor man liked the look of my stick, however, and the matter fell through. Relations were strained after that, and further inquiries out of the question. All that I have learned I got from a friendly native in the yard of our own inn. It was he who told me of the doctor's habits and of his daily journey. At that instant, to give point to his words, the carriage came round to the door."

"Could you not follow it?"

"Excellent, Watson! You are scintillating this evening. The idea did cross my mind. There is, as you may have observed, a bicycle shop next to our inn. Into this I rushed, engaged a bicycle, and was able to get started before the carriage was quite out of sight. I rapidly overtook it, and then, keeping at a discreet distance of a hundred yards or so, I followed its lights until we were clear of the town. We had got well out on the country road when a somewhat mortifying incident occurred. The carriage stopped, the doctor alighted, walked swiftly back to where I had also halted, and told me in an excellent sardonic fashion that he feared the road was narrow, and that he hoped his carriage did not impede the passage of my bicycle. Nothing could have been more admirable than his way of putting it. I at once rode past the carriage, and, keeping to the main road, I went on for a few miles, and then halted in a convenient place to see if the carriage passed. There was no sign of it, however, and so it became evident that it had turned down one of several side roads which I had observed. I rode back, but again saw nothing of the carriage, and now, as you perceive, it has returned after me. Of course, I had at the outset no particular reason to connect these journeys with the disappearance of Godfrey Staunton, and was only inclined to investigate them on the general grounds that everything which concerns Dr. Armstrong is at present of interest to us; but, now that I find he keeps so keen a look-out upon anyone who may follow him on these excursions, the affair appears more important, and I shall not be satisfied until I have made the matter clear."

"We can follow him tomorrow."

"Can we? It is not so easy as you seem to think. You are not familiar with Cambridgeshire scenery, are you? It does not lend itself to concealment. All this country that I passed over tonight is as flat and clean as the palm of your hand, and the man we are following is no fool, as he very clearly showed tonight. I have wired to Overton to let us know any fresh London developments at this address, and in the meantime we can only concentrate our attention upon Dr. Armstrong, whose name the obliging young lady at the office allowed me to read upon the counterfoil of Staunton's urgent message. He knows where the young man is—to that I'll swear—and if he knows, then it must be our own fault if we cannot manage to know also. At present it must be admitted that the odd trick is in his possession, and, as you are aware, Watson, it is not my habit to leave the game in that condition."

And yet the next day brought us no nearer to the solution of the mystery. A note was handed in after breakfast, which Holmes passed across to me with a smile.

"Sir," it ran, "I can assure you that you are wasting your time in dogging my movements. I have, as you discovered last night, a window at the back of my brougham, and if you desire a twenty-mile ride which will lead you to the spot from which you started, you have only to follow me. Meanwhile, I can inform you that no spying upon me can in any way help Mr. Godfrey Staunton, and I am convinced that the best service you can do to that gentleman is to return at once to London and to report to your employer that you are unable to trace him. Your time in Cambridge will certainly be wasted.

"Yours faithfully,
"LESLIE ARMSTRONG."

"An outspoken, honest antagonist is the doctor," said Holmes. "Well, well, he excites my curiosity, and I must really know more before I leave him."

"His carriage is at his door now," said I. "There he is stepping into it. I saw him glance up at our window as he did so. Suppose I try my luck upon the bicycle?"

"No, no, my dear Watson! With all respect for your natural acumen I do not think that you are quite a match for the worthy doctor. I think that possibly I can attain our end by some independent explorations of my own. I am afraid that I must leave you to your own devices, as the appearance of *two* inquiring strangers upon a sleepy countryside might excite more gossip than I care for. No doubt you will find some sights to amuse you in this venerable city, and I hope to bring back a more favourable report to you before evening." Once more, however, my friend was destined to be disappointed. He came back at night weary and unsuccessful.

"I have had a blank day, Watson. Having got the doctor's general direction, I spent the day in visiting all the villages upon that side of Cambridge, and comparing notes with publicans and other local news agencies. I have covered some ground: Chesterton, Histon, Waterbeach, and Oakington have each been explored and have each proved disappointing. The daily appearance of a brougham and pair could hardly have been overlooked in such Sleepy Hollows. The doctor has scored once more. Is there a telegram for me?"

"Yes; I opened it. Here it is: 'Ask for Pompey from Jeremy Dixon, Trinity College.' I don't understand it."

"Oh, it is clear enough. It is from our friend Overton, and is in answer to a question from me. I'll just send round a note to Mr. Jeremy Dixon, and then I have no doubt that our luck will turn. By the way, is there any news of the match?"

"Yes, the local evening paper has an excellent account in its last edition. Oxford won by a goal and two tries. The last sentences of the description say: 'The defeat of the Light Blues may be entirely attributed to the unfortunate absence of the crack International, Godfrey Staunton, whose want was felt at every instant of the game. The lack of combination in the three-quarter line and their weakness both in attack and defence more than neutralised the efforts of a heavy and hard-working pack.'"

"Then our friend Overton's forebodings have been justified," said Holmes. "Personally I am in agreement with Dr. Armstrong, and football does not come within my horizon. Early to bed tonight, Watson, for I foresee that tomorrow may be an eventful day."

I was horrified by my first glimpse of Holmes next morning, for he sat by the fire holding his tiny hypodermic syringe. I associated that instrument with the single weakness of his nature, and I feared the worst when I saw it glittering in his hand. He laughed at my expression of dismay, and laid it upon the table.

"No, no, my dear fellow, there is no cause for alarm. It is not upon this occasion the instrument of evil, but it will rather prove to be the key which will unlock our mystery. On this syringe I base all my hopes. I have just returned from a small scouting expedition and everything is favourable. Eat a good breakfast, Watson, for I propose to get upon Dr. Armstrong's trail today, and once on it I will not stop for rest or food until I run him to his burrow."

"In that case," said I, "we had best carry our breakfast with us, for he is making an early start. His carriage is at the door."

"Never mind. Let him go. He will be clever if he can drive where I cannot follow him. When you have finished come downstairs with me, and I will introduce you to a detective who is a very eminent specialist in the work that lies before us."

When we descended I followed Holmes into the stable yard, where he opened the door of a loose-box and led out a squat, lop-eared, white-and-tan dog, something between a beagle and a foxhound.

"Let me introduce you to Pompey," said he. "Pompey is the pride of the local draghounds, no very great flier, as his build will show, but a staunch hound on a scent. Well, Pompey, you may not be fast, but I expect you will be too fast for a couple of middle-aged London gentlemen, so I will take the liberty of fastening this leather leash to your collar. Now, boy, come along, and show what you can do." He led him across to the doctor's door. The dog sniffed round for an instant, and then with a shrill whine of excitement started off down the street, tugging at his leash in his efforts to go faster. In half an hour we were clear of the town and hastening down a country road.

"What have you done, Holmes?" I asked.

"A threadbare and venerable device, but useful upon occasion. I walked into the doctor's yard this morning and shot my syringe full of aniseed over the hind wheel. A draghound will follow aniseed from here to John o' Groats, and our friend Armstrong would have to drive through the Cam before he would shake Pompey off his trail. Oh, the cunning rascal! This is how he gave me the slip the other night."

The dog had suddenly turned out of the main road into a grass-grown lane. Half a mile farther this opened into another broad road, and the trail turned hard to the right in the direction of the town, which we had just quitted. The road took a sweep to the south of the town and continued in the opposite direction to that in which we started.

"This *détour* has been entirely for our benefit, then?" said Holmes. "No wonder that my inquiries among those villages led to nothing. The doctor has certainly played the game for all it is worth, and one would like to know the reason for such elaborate deception. This should be the village of Trumpington to the right of us. And, by Jove! here is the brougham coming round the corner. Quick, Watson, quick, or we are done!"

He sprang through a gate into a field, dragging the reluctant Pompey after him. We had hardly got under the shelter of the hedge when the carriage rattled past. I caught a glimpse of Dr. Armstrong within, his shoulders bowed, his head sunk on his hands, the very image of distress. I could tell by my companion's graver face that he also had seen.

"I fear there is some dark ending to our quest," said he. "It cannot be long before we know it. Come, Pompey! Ah, it is the cottage in the field!"

There could be no doubt that we had reached the end of our journey. Pompey ran about and whined eagerly outside the gate where the marks of the brougham's wheels were still to be seen. A footpath led across to the lonely cottage. Holmes tied the dog to the hedge, and we hastened onwards. My friend knocked at the little rustic door, and knocked again without response. And yet the cottage was not deserted, for a low sound came to our ears—a kind of drone of misery and despair, which was indescribably melancholy. Holmes paused irresolute, and then he glanced back at the road which we had just traversed. A brougham was coming down it, and there could be no mistaking those grey horses.

"By Jove, the doctor is coming back!" cried Holmes. "That settles it. We are bound to see what it means before he comes."

He opened the door and we stepped into the hall. The droning sound swelled louder upon our ears until it became one long, deep wail of distress. It came from upstairs. Holmes darted up and I followed him. He pushed open a half-closed door and we both stood appalled at the sight before us.

A woman, young and beautiful, was lying dead upon the bed. Her calm, pale face, with dim, wide-opened blue eyes, looked upwards from amid a great tangle of golden hair. At the foot of the bed, half sitting, half kneeling, his face buried in the clothes, was a young man, whose frame was racked by his sobs. So absorbed was he by his bitter grief that he never looked up until Holmes's hand was on his shoulder.

"Are you Mr. Godfrey Staunton?"

"Yes, yes; I am—but you are too late. She is dead."

The man was so dazed that he could not be made to understand that we were anything but doctors who had been sent to his assistance. Holmes was endeavouring to utter a few words of consolation, and to explain the alarm which had been caused to his friends by his sudden disappearance, when there was a step upon the stairs, and there was the heavy, stern, questioning face of Dr. Armstrong at the door.

"So, gentlemen," said he, "you have attained your end, and have certainly chosen a particularly delicate moment for your intrusion. I would not brawl in the presence of death, but I can assure you that if I were a younger man your monstrous conduct would not pass with impunity."

"Excuse me, Dr. Armstrong, I think we are a little at cross-purposes," said my friend, with dignity. "If you could step downstairs with us we may each be able to give some light to the other upon this miserable affair."

A minute later the grim doctor and ourselves were in the sitting-room below.

"Well, sir?" said he.

"I wish you to understand, in the first place, that I am not employed by Lord Mount-James, and that my sympathies in this matter are entirely against that nobleman. When a man is lost it is my duty to ascertain his fate, but having done so the matter ends so far as I am concerned; and so long as there is nothing criminal, I am much more anxious to hush up private scandals than to give them publicity. If, as I imagine, there is no breach of the law in this matter, you can absolutely depend upon my discretion and my co-operation in keeping the facts out of the papers."

Dr. Armstrong took a quick step forward and wrung Holmes by the hand.

"You are a good fellow," said he. "I had misjudged you. I thank Heaven that my compunction at leaving poor Staunton all alone in this plight caused me to turn my carriage back, and so to make your acquaintance. Knowing as much as you do, the situation is very easily explained. A year ago Godfrey Staunton lodged in London for a time, and became passionately attached to his landlady's daughter, whom he married. She was as good as she was beautiful, and as intelligent as she was good. No man need be ashamed of such a wife. But Godfrey was the heir to this crabbed old nobleman, and it was quite certain that the news of his marriage would have been the end of his inheritance. I knew the lad well, and I loved him for his many excellent qualities. I did all I could to help him to keep things straight. We did our very best to keep the thing from everyone, for when once such a whisper gets about it is not long before everyone has heard it. Thanks to this lonely cottage and his own discretion, Godfrey has up to now succeeded. Their secret was known to no one save to me and to one excellent servant who has at present gone for assistance to Trumpington. But at last there came a terrible blow in the shape of dangerous illness to his wife. It was consumption of the most virulent kind. The poor boy was half crazed with grief, and yet he had to go to London to play this match, for he could not get out of it without explanations which would expose his secret. I tried to cheer him up by a wire, and he sent me one in reply imploring me to do all I could. This was the telegram which you appear in some inexplicable way to have seen. I did not tell him how urgent the danger was, for I knew that he could do no good here, but I sent the truth to the girl's father, and he very injudiciously communicated it to Godfrey. The result was that he came straight away in a state bordering on frenzy, and has remained in the same state, kneeling at the end of her bed, until this morning death put an end to her sufferings. That is all, Mr. Holmes, and I am sure that I can rely upon your discretion and that of your friend."

Holmes grasped the doctor's hand.

"Come, Watson," said he, and we passed from that house of grief into the pale sunlight of the winter day.

THE DOUBLE PROBLEM

F. A. M. Webster

Frederick Annesley Michael Webster (1886–1949) is remembered today rather for his contribution to the world of athletics than as a writer of detective stories. He won the national javelin championship in 1911 (a feat he repeated twelve years later) and was a member of the Cyclists Section of the Territorial Army prior to the First World War. He became Hon. Secretary of the Amateur Field Events Association, which was formed in 1910, and whose chairman was Arthur Conan Doyle. Might his involvement with Doyle have inspired him to turn to writing? At all events, he began to produce books about athletics, including *The Evolution of the Olympic Games* (and his son Dick later competed in the pole vault in the Berlin Olympics of 1936). A severe knee injury sustained while playing football seems to have kept him away from service on the front line in France during the war, but he joined the King's Africa Rifles and spent some time in East Africa, the setting for several later books. In peacetime he developed a reputation as an outstanding athletics coach and in 1936, he founded the School of Athletics, Games and Physical Education at Loughborough College.

Webster had a separate career as an author of thrillers and detective stories, although his fiction never scaled the heights. In 1933, Dorothy L. Sayers subjected *Gathering Storm* to scathing criticism for "the stale re-hashing of old material", and noted that "he cannot plead inexperience for his crimes, since he has written many mystery tales"; she did at least praise his characterisation of his detective, the unfortunately named Detective Inspector Oaf. This story features his principal investigator, Old Ebbie Entwistle, and was collected in the improbably titled *Old Ebbie: Detective Up to Date* a year after its first appearance in *The Blue Magazine* in April 1922.

I N RECORDING THE CRIMINAL INVESTIGATIONS OF MY FRIEND, Ebenezer Entwistle, the old Pimlico chemist of gentle birth, who, unable to fulfil his early desire of becoming a doctor, had adopted this humbler branch of the science of Æsculapius I find so much that is terrible and horrific, as in the Secret of the Smaller Stain, that it is at times a relief to turn to some lighter phase of his researches.

"We are about to move among important people, my dear Hicks," was the remark with which one evening he greeted my arrival at the little shop which stands at the corner of Tolnody Street.

"Indeed," I answered; "if this is another investigation you will have seriously to consider the question of engaging an assistant, since criminology and not chemistry seems now to occupy the major portion of your time."

As I made this remark, I noticed that he held in his hand a copy of "The Sportsman," a paper it was his habit sometimes to peruse.

"I learn from this newspaper," he said, holding it up, "that a young man who hurls a sixteen pound hammer a matter of between one hundred and seventy and one hundred and eighty feet, is regarded by the sporting public of this country as something of a genius?"

"Yes, indeed," I answered, "especially when a Freshman, in his first year of open competition, breaks British record and bids fair to eclipse the World's Champion, whose performance has stood unchallenged since 1913; for I assume that your remark relates to the Oxonian, J. C. McLaglan, who is attaining fame so rapidly in the world of sport. He seems, also, to have courted a quite unnecessary degree of notoriety by growing a beard. The papers have been full of his pictures."

"I gather, further," said Old Ebbie, following his original train of thought, "that the taste of the British public is gradually changing. Football furnishes an absorbing interest for two-thirds of the year; cricket, which has fallen into disfavour with the uneducated and unintelligent, has small claims to general attention during the summer months, so that the more exciting, but no less scientifically practised sport of athletics proper bids fair to provide the popular spectacle from April to September."

"Yes," I answered, "but it is not a matter of satisfaction to the best class of amateur athlete."

"Indeed, and why is that?" asked Ebbie.

"Because the growing popularity of the pastime has attracted the attention of the bookmakers. For example, there is almost as much betting this year upon the result of the Inter-University Sports at Queen's Club as on the Boat Race."

"Ha!" ejaculated Old Ebbie, and not another word did he speak for upwards of half-an-hour.

"Well," he said at last, "I have here a letter from the Dean of St. Luke's College, Oxford. There has been some trouble about a cheque which he asks me to investigate privately. It appears that some person, posing as an undergraduate and wearing the St. Luke's College colours, purchased certain goods from a local tradesman, for which he paid with a cheque; this, upon presentation at the London bank upon which it was drawn, was returned and marked 'no account'; and neither the name of the drawer nor his handwriting in any way resembles those of any undergraduate of the college in question. Not unnaturally the dean would prefer to have the problem solved privately, and in the meantime he has reimbursed the tradesman out of his own pocket."

"And has the origin of the cheque form been ascertained?" I queried.

"Yes," answered Old Ebbie, "it was torn, with its counterfoil, from Lord Rockpool's private cheque book."

"Hum," I said, "I know young Rockpool slightly, having served on the staff of his father, the Earl of Hartland, for a short time."

I met Ebbie at Paddington pretty early next morning, and together we journeyed down to Oxford, where the courteous old dean entertained us to lunch at his college, refusing to say one word concerning the case until we had eaten.

After lunch he took us to his study and placed the returned cheque, signed "James Vivian," in Old Ebbie's hands. There was absolutely nothing which he could tell us personally about the affair, but I could see that my friend was keenly interested from the manner in which he scrutinised the pink, engraved slip of paper.

"The hand is disguised, and will tell us nothing more than that the cheque was drawn by a well educated man who used a fountain pen," he said; "the name of 'James Vivian' has been assumed by someone who, having written the first letter, hesitated a moment before choosing the nom de plume he would employ. He is either an American or one who has lived in the United States long enough to have become accustomed to American business methods."

"Dear me," exclaimed the dean, "how do you deduce these circumstances?"

"It is simple enough," answered Old Ebbie with a slight smile. "You will observe that the writing is fine and well formed; the broadening of the letters shows that they have been written slowly, which would hardly be the case with an educated man, unless he was giving to those letters an unfamiliar or seldom employed shape. If you will look at the writing you will notice a certain hardness of outline and also a degree of blackness, which proves that no blotting paper has been employed; now a shop-keeper almost invariably offers a customer who writes a cheque the use of a sheet of blotting paper, unless, as in this case, the writing dries at once, as is the way with some fountain pen ink. There is a slight, but none the less significant, thickening at the termination of the final up-stroke of the initial 'J,' where the man paused an instant before inscribing the next letter. On the whole, I should say that he was used to writing the 'J,' but not the 'a' which follows it. Finally, you will observe that in dating the cheque he has placed the number representing the month first, the number representing the day of the month second, and the number representing the year last, as is the American custom."

"It all sounds very simple as you explain it," said the dean, "but I must confess that I had overlooked all those little details which you make to appear so painfully simple and obvious."

"Ah," said Old Ebbie, "d'you remember what Stevenson said? 'There is nothing more disenchanting to man than to be shown the springs and mechanism of any art.'"

"Surely this is a very slight affair with which you occupy your valuable time, my dear Ebbie," I remarked as, having said good-bye to the dean, we strolled down the High to the small jeweller's shop at which the cheque had been given in payment for goods to the extent of some fifty pounds.

"There is nothing macabre about it, certainly," he answered, "but there are some unusual circumstances which raise this case above the category of commonplace crimes. We shall see."

"Well," said Ebbie to the jeweller, whose shop was small and dark, "the dean of St. Luke's has sent us to see you about this bad cheque."

"Yes, sir, I shall be pleased to answer your questions," said the man.

"Have you a list of the things purchased?"

"There was only one purchase, sir; a ring comprising a single large diamond held in a woman's hand."

"But surely that was an extraordinary piece of jewellery for an undergraduate to acquire?"

"So I thought, but the gentleman seemed much taken with it, and quite turned up his nose at a stone of the first water in a simple setting, which I offered, and even recommended, in preference to the other. But he said it was for his own use and he preferred it."

"Hum! Had you ever seen this customer before?"

"No."

"Would you know him again?"

"I'm afraid not; I was just closing the shop and most of the lights were out; moreover, he wore a heavy ulster with the collar turned up and had a scarf of St. Luke's colours wrapped right up round his chin."

"Did you notice anything peculiar about him?"

"Nothing, except his arms, sir, which were abnormally long."

"Come," said Ebbie, "that is at least something to go upon. Had he any accent?"

"Not an accent, sir; but, now that you mention it, I remember that he seemed to choose his words with some care. But a great many young gentlemen do that nowadays in their first term."

"By the way," said Ebbie, as we were leaving the shop, "he wrote the cheque with a fountain pen, didn't he?"

"Why, yes, sir," replied the man in some surprise.

"It is always something to have one's deductions confirmed as one goes along," said Ebbie, when we found ourselves once more upon the pavement. "It would appear that despite a certain degree of education our man is not quite a gentleman."

"Because he chooses his words carefully?" I asked.

"No, but because he buys a ring better suited to the hand of a professional boxer than to that of an Oxford undergraduate."

From the terse manner in which the answer was given I gathered that my companion did not wish to converse, and so I remained silent as we walked to "Green Lawns," a large house standing in its own grounds, at which we had been informed that Lord Rockpool was staying. It was a low, prepossessing building, well sheltered by trees, the front facing the road and the back looking across a stretch of smooth lawn, which ran almost up to the wall, towards St. Cuthbert's College, from which, also, it was screened by a row of trees.

The rooms occupied by Lord Rockpool were immediately over the dining-room and drawing-room, which opened straight on to the lawn by way of French windows, set in three-sided bays, which projected from the main structure, the windows being protected by shutters at night. We ascertained later, that these shutters were always closed at tea-time, that is to say, before it was quite dark, during the winter months. These twin bays were covered with lead, their flat roofs being some ten and a half feet above the ground.

The manservant who answered the door informed us that his lordship was at present attending a committee meeting of the Oxford University Athletic Club, of which he was at that time President, but that he would most certainly be in at six o'clock.

Leaving our names and a message that we had been asked to call upon Lord Rockpool by the dean of St. Luke's, we made our way to the Randolph Hotel, whither our baggage had preceded us, and where we now ordered tea.

At six o'clock precisely we presented ourselves again at "Green Lawns," where the door was answered by the same manservant, who informed us that his lordship was in and would see us. I noticed at the moment that the man was perturbed, if not actually agitated.

I was behind my companion as we entered Rockpool's room, and was amused to observe the slight start of surprise caused by the somewhat bizarre appearance of the old chemist, who was clad, as usual, in square-tailed morning coat, with large flap pockets, Gladstone collar, and crossover bird's-eye cravat. A moment later Rockpool caught sight of me, and came quickly forward.

"How d'you do, Captain Hicks?" he said. "We have not met since you stayed at Hartland more than a year ago."

"The last time I saw you was at Queen's last March, when you won the Mile," I answered; "but upon that occasion I had no opportunity of speaking to you."

To my intense surprise a shadow crossed his face upon my mentioning his victory against Cambridge. And then I noticed that the window was wide open; another surprising circumstance, for the evening was cold, even for early March.

Before anything further could be said, Lord Rockpool turned to Old Ebbie.

"And you," he said, holding out his hand, "are the famous Mr. Ebenezer Entwistle, whose brain is said to be one of the acutest at present employed in criminal research. Well, sir, I am delighted to make you welcome, for you come at a most opportune moment."

"You, my lord, are interested then in this affair of the false cheque which has been uttered?" asked Old Ebbie in his quiet, cultured voice, which seemed always to place him at once upon a friendly footing with those with whom he was brought into contact, no matter what their station in life might be.

"But very indifferently, I fear," answered Rockpool. "The affair is trivial, after all: the tradesman has been paid and the dean can afford the money, so it seems the only loser is the poor devil who allowed himself to be tempted to the commission of such a petty and pitiful felony."

"But how do you suppose the person in question was afforded the opportunity of extracting a cheque from your book?" asked Ebbie.

"Nothing could be easier," answered Rockpool. "I have several banking accounts, and usually carry a book in the pocket of whatever coat I happen to be wearing. Why, it was only the other day that the ground man at the Iffley Road track returned to me a cheque-book which he had found in the breast-pocket of an old blazer I had given him to throw away, and which had been hanging on a peg in the dressing-room for months."

"And was it from that particular book that the cheque-form was purloined?"

"No, but from another, with which I am afraid that I was equally negligent. I shall be more careful in future, since this unsavoury episode has aroused my sense of responsibility and I now realise that my carelessness has in some measure led another man into crime. So strongly have I felt this, indeed, that I asked the dean to allow me to reimburse the silversmith the 'pair of ponies' of which he was defrauded, but Dr. Seaton would not hear of it, a circumstance which has annoyed me greatly."

"I see," said Ebbie; "but have you no idea as to the approximate date upon which this cheque-form was purloined?"

"Not the least in the world, for I had not used the book myself for more than three months; so you see that it is no use for us to discuss that matter any further; and, meantime, I have a much more extraordinary problem to offer you, if you would care to undertake the investigation?"

"I must first hear the nature of the case before I can say whether I will undertake it or not," my friend answered guardedly.

"Very well," said Rockpool, "I will relate the circumstances; but whether you undertake the case or not, what I am about to say must, of course, be treated in the strictest confidence. I ask for this assurance, since the matter affects the University as a whole. If I alone were concerned, I should be perfectly content to rely upon your discretion."

"You may do so in any case, my lord," said Old Ebbie, with equal formality.

For some moments Rockpool sat at the table considering the situation before committing it to speech.

"I wonder," he said at length, "if either of you is sufficiently interested in sport generally to have observed that the exaggeration of professionalism is gradually killing the public interest in Association football, which, for many years, has been a sort of fetish with the masses. The professionals, by eliminating the charge, have deprived the game of a feature of robustness which was, at one time, closely allied to the art of tackling, which still keeps the Rugby game healthy. Furthermore, the finicking exactness of the professional player has robbed the game of its goal-getting possibilities, and, therefore, the public are looking around for some other form of sport upon which to fasten their affections. Athletics, a branch of sport which has hitherto been almost entirely free from professionalism and the betting evil, has, in consequence, come in for a quite unpleasant boom."

"So I have already gathered," interrupted Old Ebbie.

"Not unnaturally," continued Rockpool, "both here and at Cambridge we have been pestered to death by newspaper people and Press photographers, since the daily papers are concentrating upon the approaching Oxford and Cambridge sports in a most unprecedented manner."

"In fact," I interposed, "the sports this year are creating just as much public interest as the Boat Race?"

"Yes," answered Rockpool, "and I am afraid that people are betting equally freely upon both events. And then, of course, that infernal fellow McLaglan growing a beard gave the Press photographers an excellent opportunity of exploiting us."

"But surely it is unusual for a Fresher thus to go against the wishes of his associates?" I said.

"An ordinary Fresher, yes," replied Rockpool, "but McLaglan has come up late and must be nearly thirty years of age. I should think he has been abroad a good deal. He is very independent."

"I see," I answered.

"We had a meeting with the C.U.A.C. Committee a week ago," he continued, "when it was agreed that we should do all in our power to support the Amateur Athletic Association in its endeavour to combat the betting evil, for which reason it was decided that, contrary to previous custom, we should not this year publish the selected teams until the eve of the contest. You must quite understand," he added impressively, "that we do not object to publicity or to providing sport for the genuine sport-loving public, but we do resent being exploited for the benefit of those people who follow sport purely and simply for what they can get out of it."

"Yes, the point is quite clear," answered Ebbie.

"This afternoon," continued Rockpool, "the committee of the O.U.A.C. met to award Blues; a point of contention arose, and it was some considerable time before we finally selected the team which will meet Cambridge at Queen's, at the end of the month. Even so, those who are to have their Blues will not be told yet, but everyone who has been training has been requested to continue work at Iffley Road."

"And what was the particular point of contention?" asked Ebbie.

"As to whether McLaglan should be given his Blue," answered Rockpool.

"What!" I exclaimed, "exclude the British record holder from the team, impossible! Besides, my dear fellow, it seems to me that Oxford and Cambridge are so evenly matched this year that McLaglan's hammer throwing is the one thing which may prevent the sports from resulting in an inconclusive tie."

"That was what the majority of the committee thought," said Rockpool drily, "but McLaglan has not the right outlook in relation to sport. This is not snobbishness," he added, "for a board-school boy would be equally as welcome in the team as an Etonian, if he was a sportsman, which McLaglan is not. He is boastful and a bad loser, and has already done a number of things well calculated to bring University athletics into bad repute."

"Such as growing a beard?" queried Old Ebbie, with a sly smile.

"Yes, that amongst other things."

"Such as?"

"A suspicion of shadiness in money matters."

"But what made him grow a beard?" I interposed.

"Heaven alone knows," replied Rockpool. "But we are getting away from the main issue. I returned here from the committee meeting a few minutes after you had called, and immediately sent Smithers, my man, out to get an evening paper. I placed the list of Blues who will compete against Cambridge upon my desk, and then it suddenly occurred to me that some of those infernal newspaper fellows would be along at any moment, pestering me for information. I ran downstairs to give the parlour-maid instructions to tell them, should they call, that I had nothing to communicate. I found the girl laying my landlady's dinner table.

"As I was giving my instructions in the dining-room, which is immediately beneath this study, I heard a slight thud overhead, and asked the girl what it could be.

"'I'm sure I don't know, sir,' she answered, 'for there is no one else in the house, except you and me and cook, who is down in the basement.'

"I ran upstairs immediately and found the window wide open and the list of Blues vanished from my desk.

"You will observe that this room is approached by a long passage, from which the bathroom and lavatory open; there was no one in either of those rooms, and no one could have got downstairs, for the parlour-maid, seeing my excitement, had followed me to the foot of the staircase. A moment later Smithers returned, and together we searched every inch of the house, while Helen remained on guard at the foot of the stairs."

"One moment," interrupted Ebbie, "did your man know that you had the list!"

"No!"

"Did you look out of the window?"

"Yes, but there was no sign of anyone upon the lead flat of the dining-room window below, nor could I see any means by which anyone could have mounted to my window from beneath."

"And were the blinds drawn in the dining-room when you were speaking to the parlour-maid?"

"Yes, the blinds were down and the shutters closed and fastened."

"Good! and what did you do next?"

"I decided to await your arrival, since the matter was far more in your province than in mine."

"Good again," said Ebbie; "if you have a strong electric torch we will examine first the lead flat and then the garden."

"I can give you something better than a torch, for I have one of those petrol-gas storm lanterns; it gives a tremendous light."

While the lamp was being fetched, Old Ebbie examined the room minutely, but apparently without result. This inspection finished, he slipped off his boots and stepped out on to the lead flat in his stockinged feet.

"There are numerous indentations in the lead," he said, after a momentary inspection, "but it is impossible to say whether they are new."

He got down on to his knees and I peered over the edge of the flat roof, holding the lantern out before him.

"By Jove!" he exclaimed, "the lead guttering has been completely crushed right in the centre of the bay, and yet the break is a single one and not very wide, so that it can hardly have been made by a ladder, and yet it is too broad for the imprint of a rope. Well, well! let us go below and see if the ground has any secrets to reveal."

Outside the dining-room window we found a single deep impression in the ground, circular and about nine inches in circumference; from the imprint upon the frosty grass it appeared as if a stout rope had been dragged back perpendicularly some fifteen feet from the hole. Closer inspection of the circular impression in the turf revealed three slightly deeper holes, breaking the circumference triangularly. A mat having been fetched, Old Ebbie lay down to make a more minute examination by the aid of a magnifying-glass and the concentrated beam of a power-torch, which Smithers procured. Presently he passed the torch to me and took out his knife. From the triangular area enclosed by the three slightly deeper holes he delicately extracted a very thin layer of hard earth, in which were embedded infinitesimally small white flecks; in two places the edge of this dry crust was broken as if it had been pierced.

"I do not think there is anything else to be learned here," said Old Ebbie, standing up and putting the thin layer of earth carefully away in his pocket case. "Have you ever been in the fen country, my lord? No? Ah, well, it is an interesting district. I was brought up there."

Rockpool, Smithers and I regarded Entwistle with frank amazement, for to us it appeared that he was drivelling.

"By the way," he added, as if to change the conversation, "could you tell me when Mr. McLaglan began to grow a beard?"

"Yes," said Rockpool, "it was some weeks before Christmas. I remember, because he came to ask me about the Rhodes scholars coming over from the United States, and I told him he had at least nothing to fear from the American hammer-throwers, who would be up this term."

"Is he a heavy man?"

"Oh yes; he has need of weight, you know, as a hammer-thrower."

"Thank you," said Ebbie, "and now have you such a thing as a tape, I want to measure the height of that lead flat from the ground."

Smithers having procured a tape, the measurement was made and the height found to be exactly ten feet six inches.

"Hum!" said Ebbie, "now how the deuce d'you think that anyone got up there so quickly without the aid of a ladder?"

"I'm sure I don't know," answered Rockpool. "But I'm quite certain it was one of those damned journalists, and that the composition of the team will appear in one of the papers tomorrow morning."

"Ah, well, we shall see," said Ebbie, and with that we walked back to the Randolph Hotel, where we stayed the night.

Rockpool was wrong in his surmise; at least, none of the daily papers published a list of Blues next morning.

At breakfast, Ebbie was quite cheerful.

"You were sports officer to your battalion at one time, weren't you?" he asked.

"Yes," I answered.

"Very well then," he said, "let us walk out to Iffley Road today, where, I understand, that the Blues and the problematical Blues will be training, and you shall explain to me some of the mysteries of athletics, about which, I must confess, that I know but little. I want, moreover, to see this wonderful hammer-thrower. I have been thinking a lot about his performances and have worked out a few most interesting mathematical calculations; the strength and skill which enable him to throw a sixteen pound ball nearly one hundred and eighty feet must be simply phenomenal, as you will see for yourself if you work out in foot-pounds the resistance of the whirling hammer-head to the body while the thrower is turning. It would be interesting to know his weight and measurements."

"As it happens, I can tell you his weight and height," I answered; "he stands just six feet and weighs two hundred and thirty-five pounds; his reach, I believe, is abnormal."

"Well, I should much like to see him," said Ebbie.

This wish, however, was not to be gratified. Rockpool was just leaving the track after a training spin, when we arrived at Iffley Road; as we stood chatting, I asked him if McLaglan had been down that morning.

"No," he replied, "he is most particular about his training, and will only throw at that time each day which most nearly corresponds with the hour at which he will have to compete at Queen's, thus he ensures being at his best at the same hour each day."

"By the way," asked Ebbie, "at what school was McLaglan educated?"

"I do not know," Rockpool replied; "he always appears in the programme as 'Privately and St. Luke's College.'"

That afternoon we returned to Iffley Road, but the hammer-thrower did not put in an appearance. Ebbie was disappointed, but still I could see that he was enchanted with the evolutions of the hurdlers and high jumpers. Also we stood for a long time watching the pole-vaulters at work, and it was with difficulty that I was able to make the old chemist believe that more than one American had beaten thirteen feet in this event.

"Really, that seems quite incredible, but what height can these men accomplish?" he said, as we stood beside the sawdust-filled pit into which the vaulters were landing over the high bar after flinging back their spiked poles.

I turned to an undergraduate standing by to get the information.

"Oh, I don't know," he said; "Washburn Thorne, the Rhodes fellow from Cuthbert's, will do something better than twelve feet, I believe, but we've no one else who can reach ten feet; but neither have the Cantabs, for that matter."

Over tea Old Ebbie remained silent, except for such muttered soliloquies as I had learned to regard as an infallible sign that he was rapidly arriving at his final conclusions, although, for the life of me, I was unable to see how he could have fixed upon one single circumstance in this present case.

The "dottle" fell from his third pipe, as he knocked it against the mantelpiece before rising with assured determination.

"Let us go to see Lord Rockpool," he said, "there is someone to whom I wish him to present me."

Rockpool, as mystified as myself, took us round to St. Cuthbert's, where we found that Washburn Thorne had sported his oak, but since Old Ebbie had said that the matter was urgent, the O.U.A.C. president did not hesitate to hammer upon the door, which was opened presently by a typical American of the best type, a youth whose high cheek bones, aquiline features and sensitive hands attested his nationality. He stood about five feet eight inches, and must, I should say, have weighed all of a hundred and fifty pounds, since his arms and shoulders bulked big through his clothes.

"Sorry to bother you, Thorne," said Rockpool, "but this gentleman, Mr. Ebenezer Entwistle, wants to see you on a matter which is most urgent."

"Sure! Won't you all come right in?" answered the young American, in pleasant, well assured tones. I must admit that I took to him at once.

"Well, what can I do for you, Mr. Entwistle?" he asked, when we were all seated.

Old Ebbie looked around the room until his eyes rested upon a couple of bamboo, tape-bound vaulting poles in one corner.

"I believe that you have reduced pole-vaulting to a fine art, Mr. Thorne," said Ebbie.

"Why yes, sir, I reckon to get over the bar with the least margin of waste each time."

"And you can fall from considerable heights without sustaining the least injury?"

At this question the American fidgeted a little and a strange look came into his eyes.

"Yes," he said, more curtly, "if you land anyhow you tire yourself out long before the competition is over."

"And you use a pole with three spikes set triangularly at the point?"

"See here!" exclaimed Thorne, springing up, "I don't mind answering your question; but what is there back of all this?"

"Nothing; except that Lord Rockpool would be interested to know why you entered his rooms last evening and extracted the list of those athletes who will represent your University against Cambridge at the end of the month."

"Eh?" interrupted Rockpool, "how the deuce could Thorne have entered my rooms?"

"The thud you heard overhead, my lord, when you were in the dining-room was caused by Mr. Thorne alighting on the lead flat which he reached by means of his vaulting-pole. I saw the place where it touched the soft lead guttering; we all saw the small circular indentation in the turf pierced triangularly, and I, being a fen-man, knew that it was made by the point of a spiked vaulting-pole, the imprint of which was left on the grass where it fell, and which you and Hicks mistook for the mark made by a rope. The thin layer of dried earth fell from between the spikes when the pole was planted, but I'll admit the white flecks puzzled me until I saw the sawdust in the pit at Iffley Road today."

"But why do you fasten this affair on to Thorne with such certitude?" asked Rockpool.

"Because the height of the lead-flat from the ground is ten feet six inches, and Mr. Thorne is the only man at either Oxford or Cambridge who can beat ten feet at present."

Washburn Thorne was about to speak, but Old Ebbie held up his hand.

"Lord Rockpool," he said, "was anxious to ascribe the business to some too enterprising journalist; I, personally, suspected that the betting fraternity had bribed someone to obtain early and accurate information for them, but since I have seen Mr. Thorne the matter admits of a different significance, and I think McLaglan, too, may play a part, conscious or otherwise, in this affair.

"You, my lord, have told us that the controversy was some-what hot as to whether he should be given his Blue, and I have wondered if he knew of this and had been anxious to satisfy himself, hence my question concerning his weight. The fact that he weighs nearly two hundred and forty pounds put him out of court as a pole-vaulter, but I still have a feeling that Mr. Thorne knows something about McLaglan and wanted to see the list of Blues on that account.

"It struck me as odd that McLaglan, a man of thirty, should be so foolish as to antagonise his associates by growing a beard, but you will remember that you, my lord, told us he was not quite a gentleman and had been much abroad, and that he did not begin to grow his objectionable beard until he knew the names of the Rhodes scholars expected from America. In other words, I wondered if anyone coming over had knowledge of his previous career which would be detrimental, and if for that reason he was growing a beard.

"Mixed up with all this is a fantastic second, or perhaps I should say first, problem—that of the false cheque.

"The man who wrote that cheque was an American, or had lived in America, as witness the method of dating it; the silversmith says his customer had abnormally long arms, by which, in common with other hammer-throwers, Captain Hicks tells me McLaglan is distinguished; the shop-keeper tells me, moreover, that his customer chose his words carefully, as, I told myself, one might do who wished to conceal his American accent. You must remember, too, that McLaglan had been educated privately, and that nothing is known as to his antecedents. Finally, Lord Rockpool has told us that some suspicion attaches to the man of being not quite straight in money matters. I have no proof of his guilt in the matter of the cheque.

"And now, Mr. Thorne, what have you to say to all this?"

Washburn Thorne, who had been regarding Old Ebbie with ever-growing amazement, laughed nervously.

"I admit entering Lord Rockpool's rooms in the manner you have mentioned," he said, "but not from any evil motive. I was at Cornell before I came to Oxford, and I went with the U.S.A. Olympic team to the last celebration of the Olympic Games.

There was a hammer-thrower aboard the U.S.A. ship who made himself pretty obnoxious, and who, after the Games, turned professional and then disappeared. This was the so-called J. C. McLaglan, and once I spotted him I was determined he should not bring discredit upon Oxford University by representing us against Cambridge; but all the time I did not like to speak in case he should be trying to get a good education for honest ends; but I knew I'd have to tell Rockpool if the Committee had given him his Blue. I only meant to look at the list, but I heard Rockpool running upstairs, and so I grabbed the paper, slipped through the window, and jumped down from the lead flat. I played 'possum in the bushes awhile, and then slipped over the wall back to College."

"Ah!" said Old Ebbie, "then McLaglan's beard didn't deceive you?"

"It did absolutely."

"Then how did you recognise him?"

"In the strangest possible way," answered Thorne, smiling. "On board the boat bearing the U.S.A. Olympic team the hammer-thrower in question used to recite a poem he himself had written all about a man called James Vivian, and here in Oxford I heard McLaglan recite the same puerile verses, and spotted him at once."

"Well, now, that is most extraordinary," exclaimed Old Ebbie with a dry chuckle, "for we have solved the double problem. The false cheque given to the silversmith was signed 'James Vivian'; McLaglan has borrowed the name of his invented hero."

"I think we had better go and call on McLaglan," interposed Lord Rockpool. "As a professional he is, of course, altogether outside the pale, but I wonder what has been his object in this masquerade."

"I fancy he was brought over by a bunch of bookmakers who wanted to make sure of an Oxford victory," said Washburn

Thorne, "but I'm afraid you won't find him. I warned him last night that he must not dare to represent the 'Varsity at Queen's Club or I would show him up, and I believe he quitted Oxford early this morning."

In this assumption the Rhodes scholar was correct, nor did the pseudo-amateur hammer-thrower again put in an appearance at that ancient seat of learning.

FISHERMAN'S LUCK

J. Jefferson Farjeon

Joseph Jefferson Farjeon (1883–1955) came from a literary family; his father, brother, and sister were all capable authors. After a decade working in the editorial department of Amalgamated Press, he established himself as a thriller writer with books such as *The Master Criminal* (1924) and *Number 17* (1926), which was filmed by Alfred Hitchcock. He became a prolific and popular novelist, but his work slipped from sight after his death until *Mystery in White* (1937) was published by the British Library in 2014 and became a runaway bestseller. *Thirteen Guests* (1936) and *The Z Murders* (1932) have also been republished in the Crime Classics series.

Farjeon was a cricket lover, as is evident from *Thirteen Guests*. The website Cricket Country points out that the game forms "a vital cog in the wheel of a complex plot. A scorecard of a match between MCC and Somerset emerges from one of the drawers. And an act of fielding practice has a defining role in the unravelling of the final mystery, and thereby the devious twist in the tale." This story, however, features angling. One of a long series of short tales featuring Detective X. Crook which Farjeon wrote for the magazine market in the mid-1920s, it appeared in *Flynn's Magazine* on 18 July 1925.

The Boar's Head stood on the fringe of a big pine forest, and the proprietor often said that if only there were as many customers in the district as there were trees, he would possess a fortune. He was saying so now to Detective X. Crook, who had turned into the little inn for a drink before completing a journey to the Crofts.

"'Ot day like this, customers oughter be swarmin' in like hinsecks," complained the innkeeper. "But, there! Besides yourself, sir, there's them two yonder, and that's all the warm weather's brought *me!*"

Crook smiled, and took his glass to a seat near the other two inmates of the bar parlour—a squat, beard-fringed man with fishing tackle by his side, and a taller, sandy-haired fellow with light blue eyes.

"No, I've not been there this last day or two," the squat little fisherman was observing. "Found a better pitch."

"Last time I met you," replied the sandy-haired fellow almost with a note of complaint in his voice, "you told me you were going to live and die there. Said you'd never known such a pool for fish."

"So I did. And maybe I will go back some time. But I tried Barsham Pond the day after I saw you, and I struck lucky. Been right among 'em ever since."

"Good size?"

"Not bad."

"Not bad, eh? Now, over at the other pond, there's a sixteen-pounder waiting to be caught. Some one told me it was seen jumping about like a young lamb yesterday. You go and get that fish today—or some one else will."

"No, not today," replied the angler shaking his head. "My bait's laid. Tomorrow, p'r'aps."

He rose, collected his rod and tackle, nodded round the parlour, and departed.

Conversation departed with him. For a couple of minutes there was silence, broken only by the breathing of the innkeeper as he polished his glasses. Then the sandy-haired man rose, tossed a coin on the counter, and walked to the door.

"Are *you* going off to catch that sixteen-pounder?" asked the detective.

The sandy-haired man stopped abruptly.

"Me?" he exclaimed, and laughed. "I've got something better to do. Mug's game!" He opened the door, then suddenly paused to add, "P'r'aps *you* fish?"

"No," answered Detective Crook. "I've also got something better to do."

"Then it's no good my directing you to the pond," returned the other. "Good morning." And he swung out of the inn.

"Sixteen pounds is a pretty good size," commented Crook to the innkeeper.

"Sixteen pounds!" scoffed the innkeeper. "More likely sixteen ounces! Bless me soul, these lakes is magnifying glasses. Big enough fish below 'em—but when they come out, more like peanuts!"

"What particular lake were they talking of?"

"That was Lydd Water. That's it. Lydd Water. That fishing chap uster go there hevery day, but now 'e's gone over to Barsham. Sixteen-pounder! Oh, yes. Very likely!"

It was nearly three o'clock when the detective reached the Crofts, a large turreted house standing in spacious grounds. He was shown at once into a sitting room, where a tall girl rose to greet him. She was a pretty girl, but her cheeks were unnaturally pale this afternoon, and there were dark shadows under her eyes.

"Oh, I'm so glad you've come!" she exclaimed immediately. "I was beginning to wonder. I expected you earlier."

"I came as soon as I could after receiving your wire, Miss Holt," replied the detective gravely. "But I was delayed. What is your trouble?"

She hesitated for a moment, then suddenly took a piece of paper from the bosom of her dress and held it out.

"That will explain, I think," she murmured.

Crook took the small sheet. It bore a few scribbled words, and the detective's eyes recognised at once the agitation in the handwriting. The words themselves explained the agitation.

Life has become too great a burden to me. Others can never understand the agony in a man's own soul, and I will not try to explain the agony in mine. But I am finished. Good-by. Try and forget me, and forgive me. You have done all you could—there is no bitterness against you in my heart. I alone am to blame.

P. H.

The detective read the note through slowly, read it again, and then laid it down, writing upward, on the table. With his eyes still upon the note, he asked:

"Well? And then?"

"It was written two days ago," replied Miss Holt. "My brother has not been seen since. Oh, you can't think of the agony I have been through! My father is very ill, too—dangerously ill—and we haven't been able to keep the news from him."

"Naturally not. The note, I suppose, was addressed to him?"

"No, to me. That is," she corrected herself, "it was left in my room."

"I see," murmured Crook, and reread the note. Then he asked, "Do you know the nature of the trouble that was pressing on your brother's mind?"

"No. I can't think of anything. There was only father's illness."

Crook looked thoughtful. "He may have had some trouble you knew nothing about," he said. "Young men often conceal their difficulties—as long as they can. But, tell me, Miss Holt; he speaks of something you have done for him. What does that refer to?"

She shook her head despairingly. "I have done nothing. I don't know what he means."

"Do you know why he should harbour any bitterness against you?" pursued the detective. Again she shook her head. "Well, a man on the verge of suicide—assuming this to have been his mood when he wrote that note—does not always act rationally. Delusions step in, distortions, and exaggerations of small incidents or feelings. Perhaps your brother had debts?"

"I have wondered about that," responded Miss Holt. "I can't trace any though. Two years ago he got into a fearful tangle, and, when father helped him out, he promised he would never borrow a penny again. Before that, father had been continually getting him out of scrapes."

"And you think he has kept that promise?"

"Until these last two days, I've always thought so. Father increased his allowance, you see, and we have no difficulties of that sort. Then the property is entailed, so Peter's future was assured."

II

Crook considered her words for a moment. "Failing your brother, the property passes to you, of course?"

"No. To a cousin."

"How is that?" asked the detective, raising his eyebrows.

"Though I am called Miss Holt, I am only Mr. Holt's adopted daughter," she explained.

"I see. Now, please forgive me if my next question gives you pain, but I must ask it, frankly. Were you engaged to Peter Holt?"

"Oh, no!" she answered flushing slightly. "Mr. Holt—Peter's father—wanted it, because he said he wished me always to live here, he has been wonderfully good to me. But Peter and I never loved each other in that way. I am engaged to Peter's cousin. No, not the one I mentioned before," she added quickly. "A younger brother."

"I see," responded Crook with an odd expression. "The position is quite clear. Your fiancé is third on the list—"

He stopped speaking suddenly. Miss Holt looked at him, and saw that his eyes were fixed on a photograph on the mantelpiece.

"That is Peter's cousin—Arthur Cleyne," she said.

"Your fiancé?"

"No, the elder cousin. My fiancé's name is Edward—his picture is on the other end of the mantelpiece."

The detective transferred his gaze from one picture to the other, but it was noticeable that his interest in the picture of Edward Cleyne was considerably less than his interest in the picture of Arthur Cleyne.

He was about to put another question when the door suddenly burst open and a maid ran in.

"Oh, miss—please, come quick!" she cried. "Mr. Holt—he's—he's—"

With a cry, Miss Holt jumped up from her chair, and hastened out of the room. Five minutes later the detective learned that old Mr. Holt, owner of the Crofts, was dead.

It was a butler who gave the detective this information and who brought Miss Holt's excuses. Would the detective kindly call back a little later? Miss Holt was not in a condition at the moment to continue the interview, but perhaps, at six—?

"Please assure Miss Holt that I understand," interposed Detective Crook, "and give her my sincere sympathy. I will not call again this evening, but will be here tomorrow at mid-day. Tell her I am proceeding with my investigations—she has given me enough information to go on with—and that, if she wants me, I shall spend the night at the Boar's Head."

The detective did not waste any time. Leaving the Crofts, he returned briskly to the Boar's Head, engaged a room, and then proceeded to the railway station. Half an hour later he was walking into the police station of the neighbouring town of Tarrant.

The local inspector, a genial man, advanced smiling.

"So they've got you on this Holt job, too, eh?" he exclaimed. "Well, the more the better. Bit of a puzzle, isn't it?"

"What's your theory?" asked Crook.

"Suicide," responded the inspector. "That's clear enough. But the puzzle is—where's the body? Vanished. We've not found that yet."

"Nor have you found the motive for the suicide," said Crook.

"Common enough motive, I should say," observed the inspector. "A woman—or debts. Peter Holt used to be a bit of a spendthrift from all accounts."

"But that was a couple of years ago."

"Was it?" The inspector shrugged his shoulders. "I see you've been supplied with dates. Anyway, I happen to have found out that a certain money-lender of this town was seen in the locality of the Crofts four days ago."

"That's interesting," admitted Crook. "Was he seen actually entering or leaving the Crofts?"

"I don't believe so. But there'll be time enough to go into that when we find the body. Meanwhile—well, one can put two and two together."

"But Miss Holt told me Peter Holt had no debts?"

"She couldn't know that, sir!" declared the inspector. "Love affairs and debts are two things we don't brag about."

"Quite true," nodded the detective. "Who is this money-lender you speak of?"

"Hubert Bowersby, 69 High Street, lends sums from ten pounds to ten thousand pounds, and will be delighted to see you any time." The inspector laughed, then grew serious again. "No, there won't be much trouble about the motive, I'm thinking, when the time comes to dig into it. And, anyway, there's the poor chap's letter."

"Ah," murmured Detective Crook and produced it. "You've no doubt, I suppose, as to its genuineness?"

"Well, scarcely!" exclaimed the inspector. "*You're* not suggesting it's a forgery, are you?"

"No, it's not a forgery," answered Crook. "The unfortunate man wrote it."

"And meant to do away with himself afterward?" pursued the inspector.

"Without a doubt Peter Holt contemplated suicide when he wrote that note. Have you a handwriting expert on the premises?"

III

Twenty minutes later Detective Crook left the police station and called upon Mr. Hubert Bowersby, of 69 High Street, Tarrant. Mr. Bowersby was out, frightening a creditor who had borrowed ten pounds from him a few weeks ago and was now unable to pay back fifteen, but the detective waited until the money-lender returned, asked him two questions, and then returned to the station.

Back at the Blue Boar, he ordered a light dinner and found the angler whom he had encountered earlier in the day seated at the next table.

"Good evening," said Crook. "Well, did you have any luck?"

"No," grunted the angler. "Not a single bite!"

"You ought to have taken your friend's advice and gone to Lydd Water."

"Hello! What do *you* know of Lydd Water?" exclaimed the angler in surprise.

"Nothing," answered the detective, "excepting that a sixteen-pound fish is supposed to be waiting for you there. Is your friend an authority on fishing?"

"Don't know," said the angler. "Don't know anything about him. He's dropped in here once or twice and I happened to mention I'd been fishing in Lydd Water. Now he's trying to lure me back to it again."

"Why not take his advice?"

"What! Do you think I'll find that sixteen-pounder?"

"You may find something even bigger."

The angler looked at the detective. Then he broke into a smile.

"Say, I'm a fisherman, not a big game hunter," he laughed.

"There's no hippopotamuses around here! What's it all about, anyway?"

"If you care to stroll to Lydd Water after dinner, you may find out," responded Crook inscrutably. "I'll wander with you, if you like. You can show me the way."

"Right!" cried the angler. "And if we find that sixteen-pounder jumping after evening gnats, I'll bring my tackle along tomorrow and have him out!"

The sun was low upon the horizon when, each with a pipe between his lips, the detective and the angler began their evening walk to the lonely lake in the middle of the woods, where a sixteen-pound fish was reported to be enjoying too much freedom.

The long shadows of the trees pointed with eerie significance toward the water. During the first part of the journey, the angler was talkative, but toward the end he fell into a silence, reflecting his companion's quieter mood and only making one remark on the final stretch of their walk.

"Say, what's your interest in Lydd Water?" he demanded curiously.

"I'll answer that later," replied Crook, "if Lydd Water doesn't answer for me."

An hour afterward, the innkeeper watched them return, and, commenting on their expressions, observed to his wife that if he couldn't enjoy an evening stroll more than that, he'd stay at home with the newspaper, so he would.

The angler went thoughtfully to bed, but Detective Crook's activities for the day were not quite over. He walked again to the station and made use of the station telephone. Then he returned to the Boar's Head and, seated in the parlour, wrote a letter to Miss Holt.

It repeated the message which he had given to the butler, told her that he had made some progress in his investigations, and asked her to arrange a meeting at twelve o'clock on the morrow at which the late Mr. Holt's will should be read.

He emphasised this request, saying that while he realised the difficulties of summoning the meeting at such short notice, it was urgent. "Let all the interested parties you can gather together be present," he wrote. "Some will doubtless be in the neighbourhood, and can be summoned by wire. By complying with this request, you will help me to accomplish the task you have set me, and may also avoid many weeks of worry, uncertainty, and delay."

He delivered the note personally, leaving it at the door of the Crofts. Then he returned to the inn and went to bed.

Next morning, shortly before noon, he was back again at the Crofts, and when he was ushered into the sitting room where on the previous day he had had his interrupted interview with Miss Holt, he found several people already assembled there. This gratified him, and his grave smile, as Miss Holt approached him, reflected his appreciation of the manner in which she had complied with his request.

"I have done my best, you see," said Miss Holt quietly. "Over there is our solicitor, Mr. Barley—he has the will in his hand. That lady by his side is Miss Ellertree, Mr. Holt's sister, and next to her is another sister, Mrs. Grahame."

"And who is that on Mr. Barley's other side?" asked the detective, indicating a sandy-haired young man with light blue eyes. "Is he the cousin who comes into the property?"

Miss Holt nodded. "Yes. Arthur Cleyne. And that's Edward Cleyne—my fiancé—standing by the window."

"Thank you," said Detective Crook. "Then everything is ready—as far as I am concerned."

She threw him a curious look; then, after a moment's hesitation, went across to the solicitor and said a few words to him. The solicitor nodded, cleared his throat and gained immediate attention.

"These proceedings are merely preliminary and informal," began the solicitor. "In fact, it was only at Miss Holt's urgent wish to have the will read today that we are here so closely on the heels of—ah—this very sad event. I would like, if I may, to express my very great sympathy with all present over their sad loss—"

He droned on. The detective's eyes wandered slowly round the room and paused when they met those of Arthur Cleyne. Cleyne nodded almost imperceptibly, in recognition of their previous casual meeting in the inn.

"We come now to the will itself," said the solicitor, unfolding the blue paper before him. "It is of interest to all present, and to a few, also, who are absent. The property itself, of course, being entailed property, passes automatically to—er—that is, it would fall first to Mr. Holt's son, Peter, or, failing him, to Mr. Holt's nephew, Mr. Arthur Cleyne—"

"Or, failing him, Mr. Edward Cleyne," interposed Crook quietly.

The solicitor frowned and, readjusting his glasses, stared at the interrupter.

"That would be so," he observed dryly, "if the contingency arose."

"That was what I meant," replied the detective. "If the contingency arose."

Arthur Cleyne was frowning now, and his brother Edward wore a slightly heightened colour as he glanced across at his fiancé. There was a short pause in the proceedings.

IV

Then the solicitor inquired icily:

"And how, pray, can that contingency arise, since Mr. Arthur Cleyne is with us in this room?"

"Well, the claim is not valid just yet at any rate," responded the detective blandly. "For one thing, we are not even sure that Mr. Peter Holt is dead. And, for my part," he added, "I don't believe he is."

The solicitor drummed with his fingers on the table.

"Is this the time to discuss your personal opinions, sir?" he asked.

"Why, it seems to me a most appropriate time," said the detective. "We are reading the late Mr. Holt's will in the absence of the most important beneficiary."

The solicitor, annoyed and surprised to find his brisk little personality overshadowed by the quieter authority of his opponent, shrugged his shoulders impotently, and Edward Cleyne stepped into the breach.

"What makes you so certain that Peter Holt is still alive?" he demanded.

"I cannot see any possible motive for suicide," replied Crook. "Can you?"

"Frankly, I can't," admitted Edward Cleyne. "I put it down myself to money difficulties."

"So did the local police," nodded Crook. "But I could not accept that view. You see, as Miss Holt herself informed me, Peter Holt had mended his ways. His future was assured, and he no longer troubled money-lenders, or allowed them to trouble him."

"Very well—perhaps that's right," interposed the young man quickly. "But why did the local police believe he had got into money trouble?"

"Aha!" chirped the little solicitor, anxious to be in on any turn. "Tell us that!"

"The local police," responded Crook, "acted upon the assumption that, since Peter Holt had left a note implying suicide, he *must* have got into trouble, and they somewhat hastily concluded that the trouble surrounded a certain money-lender named Hubert Bowersby, of 69 High Street, Tarrant, who was seen in this neighbourhood a few days ago. I anticipated their inquiries myself and interviewed Mr. Bowersby yesterday. He has had no transactions of any kind with Peter Holt."

"But, damn it, there must have been some other reason then!" snapped the solicitor. "There's the poor boy's note! P'r'aps you'll suggest, sir, it was forged?"

"No. He wrote it."

"Ah! For a lark, eh?"

"No. He intended to commit suicide afterward. But—"

A sharp rat-tat on the front door interrupted him, and he paused. In a few moments, an apologetic, anxious-faced butler entered the room with a telegram in his hand.

"For me?" queried Miss Holt, as the butler walked toward her hesitatingly.

"Er—no, miss," he stammered. "It's—it's for—for Mr. Holt."

The discussion, for the moment, was forgotten. A telegram addressed to a dead man was somewhat more interesting. Miss Holt held out her hand.

All eyes were upon her when she tore open the orange envelope and took out the pale pink form. The next moment she gasped, and the form slipped from her hand. Edward Cleyne darted to her side.

"What is it?" he asked anxiously.

He stooped and picked up the form; then he, also, gave a gasp of astonishment.

"Good Heavens! It's from Peter!" he exclaimed. "From *Peter!* Good Lord—then, after all, he's not— Listen!" He read the wire out:

Please forgive me. I couldn't do it when the time came. I am leaving today for Canada.

PETER.

Detective Crook glanced round the room. For a second there was dead silence. Then a sharp voice cut through the silence and, hardly knowing why, two or three of the company shivered at the sound of it.

"I tell you—it's impossible!" cried the voice. *"Impossible!"*

Now all turned their eyes toward Arthur Cleyne, startled by his involuntary utterance. Bright flushes had appeared upon his cheeks. It was the detective who answered him.

"Why impossible?" he inquired quietly, but with a new note of sternness in his voice. "Many a man on the verge of suicide has hung back on the brink. And besides, in this particular instance, Peter Holt's impulse had had plenty of time to cool."

"What do you mean?" demanded Arthur Cleyne.

"I mean that the note he assumably left behind him was written two years ago," said the detective. "I realised that the ink was not recent as soon as Miss Holt showed it to me yesterday, and I have since had this point verified by an expert.

"And two years ago, Mr. Cleyne, Peter Holt *was* in financial difficulties and his father refused to help him." He paused. "On the verge of suicide, Peter drew back. He could not go through with it. His father weakened, also, and matters were patched up.

But, unfortunately, the tragic note was not destroyed. Some one got hold of it."

"Look here, I don't understand this," exclaimed Edward Cleyne, facing the detective. "You suggest that Peter never contemplated suicide when—when he last disappeared. Well, if that's so, why in Heaven's name has he sent this telegram?"

While he flourished the pale pink missive still in his hand, the little solicitor, who did not know where he was and strongly resented it, repeated his formula:

"Aha! Tell us that!"

"I can tell you very simply," answered Crook, "and so can Arthur Cleyne—Peter Holt never sent that telegram—"

"But that's nonsense, sir!" interposed the solicitor, who had been peering at the wire. "It was handed in at Liverpool this morning—"

"By a young assistant of mine who travelled up to Liverpool last night, on my instructions, with the one object of sending that wire. Its purpose has been achieved, I think. Have you anything to say, Arthur Cleyne?"

"I?" cried the man addressed. Anger blazed from his eyes. "I could say a great deal, but, for the sake of peace, I shall refrain from saying it! Who is this man?" he demanded, turning to the others, "and why is he allowed to interfere with our conference? I've had enough of him. I'm going!"

"I am Detective X. Crook," replied the detective grimly, "and I do not think I would go just yet, if I were you. Peter Holt is dead, but not by his own hand. He was murdered at Lydd Water, to which spot the murderer has been trying to entice a local angler in order that some one, not himself, might discover the body of the supposed suicide." His eyes bored into Arthur Cleyne's soul.

"It would be natural, would it not, for the only man who knew that Peter Holt's body lay dead at Lydd Water to be the only man, also, who knew that the Liverpool wire—as you yourself knew, Arthur Cleyne—was impossible?"

There was a tense silence. For a full half minute no one spoke. Then Arthur Cleyne smiled suddenly, and regained his composure.

"I take off my hat to you, Detective Crook," he said. "I killed Peter Holt. I suppose I really have to thank our mutual friend, Mr. Hubert Bowersby, for finally confirming your suspicions."

"When I learned that you owed him over three thousand pounds, I discovered the motive for your action, which Peter Holt lacked," replied the detective dryly, and paused. "Will you step outside with me, Cleyne? We shall find some one waiting for us in the hall."

"With pleasure," nodded Cleyne, "though it will not be necessary for him to officiate. I swallowed my quietus a minute ago." He swayed slightly. "Mug's game. Your way's best, Detective Crook. Congratulations to you on having chosen the wise path in time!"

Crook slipped his arm round the swaying murderer and led him gently from the room.

"Bless my soul!" murmured the solicitor, pink with unaccustomed emotion as he stared at Miss Holt and Edward Cleyne. "Then the—ah—contingency *has* arisen, after all!"

THE FOOTBALL PHOTOGRAPH

H. C. Bailey

The literary career of Henry Christopher Bailey (1878–1961) fell into three distinct phases. In his early twenties, he published his first novel, *My Lady of Orange*, and proceeded to establish himself as an assiduous purveyor of historical and romantic fiction. But his breakthrough as a writer came after the First World War when he created the detective Reggie Fortune, who appeared in a long series of short stories and—eventually—novels which received widespread acclaim. In the early years of the Golden Age of detective fiction, Bailey's fame was at least equal to that of Agatha Christie and Dorothy L. Sayers. He also created a second-string series character, a crafty solicitor who rejoiced in the name Joshua Clunk.

Bailey's storylines were often powerful and compelling, but his mannered prose was very much a product of its time, and his style of writing began to fall out of fashion. By the time the Second World War was over, his reputation was already in decline and it is fair to say that it has never recovered, although his work has retained a small band of devoted admirers. Yet Bailey does not deserve to be forgotten. Quite apart from the historical importance of his detective fiction, the best of his stories are compelling and often memorable for their unflinching exploration of the nature of evil. Sport crops up occasionally in his work, and "The Football Photograph" was included in *Mr. Fortune Explains* (1930).

T HE SHOP OF DURFEY AND KILLIGREW SOLD JEWELLERY TO Queen Anne. Perhaps it was a little dowdy even then. Its low-browed windows are not for the smart or the millionaire, but for people who want value for money. Yet Durfey and Killigrew show some perception of the progress of mankind since Queen Anne's death. The doors and windows of their shop are closed with rolling steel shutters.

It was a Monday morning in August. Mr. Fortune was explaining to Mrs. Fortune without hope that duty would prevent his going to the house in Scotland to which she had promised to take him. In grouse he has no interest till they are dead; in venison, none, dead or alive. He does not care to kill anything or to see it killed except in the way of his profession. A place in which there is nothing to do but take exercise he considers bad for his constitution, and the conversation of country houses weakens his intellect. All this he set forth plaintively to Mrs. Fortune, and she said, "Don't blether, child," and the telephone rang.

Reggie contemplated that instrument with a loving smile. "How wonderful are the works of science, Joan. What a benefi-cent invention." He jumped at it. "Yes, Fortune speaking. What? Durfey and Killigrew? Of course I know 'em. My grandmother bought me studs there. Like warming-pans. Burglary? Yes, I'll come if you want me. Not much in my way, is it? Oh, all right." He turned to Mrs. Fortune. "Well, well. Duty, Joan, 'Duty, stern daughter of the voice of God'; thou dost preserve the stars from wrong—me too, darling."

"Pig," said she. "You are a fraud, Reggie."

"Oh no. No deception. Some poor beggar's been killed." He kissed her hair. He departed.

The roll shutters of Durfey and Killigrew were still down when his taxi came to the shop. A large man met him and took him round the corner. In a narrow side-street the shop has another window and an entrance, and over these also the shutters were drawn. But in the shutter at the entrance was a small steel door, and that stood ajar.

The lights were on inside. Some men were crowded into a corner, talking softly, watching others who moved about the shop. From behind the counter rose the square form of Superintendent Bell. Reggie came to his beckoning finger. It pointed down to the space between the counter and the unrobbed showcase of silver on the wall. A man lay there in what had been a pool of blood. He wore a long coat of olive green with purple cuffs and collar. "It's the porter, sir," said Bell.

Reggie crouched over the body. Its brow was torn and bruised, but the blood came from a wound in the throat. He worked upon both... The clenched hands and the blood on their knuckles interested him... From the man's coat he scraped something sticky and shapeless and put it in a specimen box. He opened the dead mouth.

Then he stood up and gazed round the shop. "Well, well," he murmured. "Too many people."

"That's the manager and the assistants, sir." Bell nodded at the group in the corner. "Waiting to check what's been taken. And we'll have to check them off, too."

"Oh yes. Yes. But there must be an office or something. Shut 'em up there." So the staff of Durfey and Killigrew's was removed while Reggie contemplated the dead man with large and dreamy eyes.

Bell came back briskly. "Well, sir, what about it?"

"Has he been moved?" said Reggie.

"They say this is where they found him."

"Yes. It could be," Reggie murmured. He wandered away, bent and poring over the floor. He dropped on hands and knees. His finger-tips moved upon the linoleum. He stooped close, he cut some small pieces out of it. "Yes, blood, I think. I'll verify it. But I should say this is where he was knocked on the head." Reggie sat on his heels and looked up at Superintendent Bell with plaintive wonder.

"What was he doing here at all?"

"Ah. If we knew that we'd know something. He didn't live here. Nobody lives here. He wasn't the watchman. They don't have one. He doesn't lock up. There's always two of 'em do that together, manager and one of the assistants. He was just the porter. He pulled down the shutters and made 'em fast one o'clock Saturday and went off home. That's the routine. Then the other chaps went out through the side-door there. Come and have a look, sir. See? The shutter comes down over the entrance and is fastened to the floor with those bolts inside. That little door in it lets 'em out and when they're outside they lock that up. Well, they went off like that on Saturday and the manager swears there was nobody left in the shop. When he came this morning, the door was still locked all right, but as soon as he got inside he saw the place had been robbed. Then he found the porter lying dead behind the counter." Bell put his head on one side and looked at his Mr. Fortune with a paternal smile. "Now, sir, the place was still locked up safe, but the porter had got inside and been killed and somebody had gone off with a bag full of jewellery. Do you see how it was done?"

"Not wholly. No."

Bell chuckled. "Ah. It beats Mr. Fortune! Then I'm going to get some of my own back for once. Look here, sir." He bent to the bolts which should have held the shutter to the floor.

"Oh, that," Reggie murmured. "I saw that when I came in. Some fellow's cut through the bolts. From outside. There's a mark or two on the base of the shutter. What was the tool? I don't do much burglary myself."

"Thank Heaven there's something you don't know," Bell growled. "Yes, it was a queer tool. A cold chisel uncommon long and thin—they slid it under the shutter and hammered it through the bolts. And that's pretty queer, too. These fellows knew just what they needed to make a short cut into this funny old shop; they got their tool made and they had the almighty cheek to stand in the street and hammer at the door."

"Yes, quite bold. But I suppose it wouldn't take long."

"Matter of minutes, sir. Still, hammering at a jeweller's door in the open street! It is so blooming impudent. Once they cut the bolts, of course they had a soft job. Ran the shutter up a little, came underneath and—"

"And brought the porter in to kill him. Yes. All very clear, Bell."

"I don't know what the porter was doing, sir. That beats me."

"I wouldn't say that," Reggie murmured. "I think I know what he was doing, Bell. But why did he come inside? And why did they kill him? Not according to plan. Some error. I should look into the porter." He gazed at Bell dreamily. "By the way, what are you looking into?"

"Everything, as you might say. We haven't got a line yet. No finger-prints. Glove job. Professionals, of course. We'll have to put some work in. It's a kind of insult to the police, breaking in in this barefaced way. When I told Mr. Lomas he said it was the most infernal impudence of his wretched career."

"Yes. Yes. It is cheek." Reggie nodded. "I feel that. I don't like being ignored myself. I'll go and sympathise. When you've looked up the porter's record you might come along."

The Hon. Sidney Lomas at his desk was surprised by the touch of a gentle hand.

"Alas, my poor brother!" Reggie sighed.

"Ha, Reginald! Bell said he would get you on to it. Good man!"

"I am. But unrecognised. Treated as negligible. Same like you, Lomas. I resent this."

"Deuced impudent, isn't it? Burgle a West End jeweller's from the street with a hammer. Damme, it's defying the whole police force."

"Yes. Not respectful. I think there were precautions, you know. Still, not nice of 'em. But they've behaved shocking to me. Killing a poor wretch crude and casual in the course of the job as if they could get away with a murder as easy as nothing. My only aunt! I exist, I suppose; I am still extant."

"My dear fellow," Lomas chuckled, "highly extant."

"Yes. Yes, I think so. I resent being ignored by an elementary person with a cold chisel."

"By all means. And what are you going to do about it, Reginald?"

"Well, I was going to provide some work for our active intelligent police force. There are one or two little points left lying about by our nasty friend with the cold chisel. Hallo, here's Bell, nice and quick."

"Got the outlines, sir. Pretty well all the jewellery in the place is gone, except some things in the safe. That's not been touched.

The silver and gold plate seems all there. You might say they cleared out the light stuff. The manager puts it at ten thousand pounds provisional."

"And very nice, too." Lomas smiled. "All anywhere by now. Looks easy, doesn't it, Bell? Mr. Fortune says he has some work for you."

"I thought he had," Bell said gloomily. "I can see plenty of work myself. But nothing that leads anywhere. What's your line, sir?"

"It's the porter, you know," Reggie murmured.

"The manager says he'd answer for him absolutely. Been employed a dozen years. Always straight."

"Poor beggar," Reggie sighed. "And how does the manager think he came to be inside, Bell?"

"The idea is, he saw something wrong at the side-door and came inside to see what was up and the burglars killed him."

Lomas nodded. "Reasonable enough. We've had cases like it before. What's the matter, Reginald?"

"Well, you haven't, you know. Not cases like this. Think again, Lomas. At one o'clock Saturday the porter went off duty. The first thing he ought to do is to get out of his highly coloured livery. By the way, where is his home? What about his people? Nobody's reported him missing and he's been dead since Saturday."

"Has he, though?" said Lomas quickly.

"Oh yes. Yes. Forty hours or more. His blood's been drying quite a long time."

"Nobody reported him missing because he lived alone," said Bell. "Rooms in workmen's dwellings, Clerkenwell. No family."

Reggie sighed. "We don't have much luck. Well, well. He didn't go home and change on Saturday. He hung about. The burglars couldn't begin to work till everybody was well away from the shop. Nevertheless, when they did begin the porter was handy in his livery all complete. What about it, Lomas?"

"You mean he was an accomplice."

"Yes. That is indicated. If he wasn't—why did he go in? Suppose he saw the fellows at work—the natural thing is to challenge 'em and make a row. Suppose he came along when they'd gone inside—they wouldn't have left the shutter up, and while it's down nothing shows. He must have been an accomplice or he wouldn't have gone in. And that explains the remarkable cheek of hammering at the door in the street. Nobody would interfere with them while Durfey and Killigrew's own porter stood by. They'd pass for lawful workmen mending the shutters."

"You've got it, sir," Bell cried. "That's neat."

"Yes. I am neat," Reggie sighed. "So were they. Up to a point. Then the thing got away with 'em." ·

"Yes, sir. That often happens in crime," Bell said solemnly.

"Or where would we be?" Reggie smiled.

"When you two have finished chirping at each other!" Lomas cut in. "It isn't so dam' clear, Reginald. Take it your way. The porter was an accomplice. He stood by to guarantee them while they forced the shutter. Good. That explains their confounded cheek very nicely. But it don't explain in the least why he went in after 'em. Or why they killed him."

"No. I noticed that," Reggie murmured. "I don't know everything, Lomas; I don't know why he went in. Not according to plan, I think. Some error. And the thing got away with 'em."

"You might take it he went in to see how much they got," Bell suggested. "So he shouldn't be done out of his fair share of the swag. And there was a row about it and they did him in. We've had cases like that, sir."

"Yes, it could be," Reggie murmured.

"Yes, I dare say you're right, Bell." Lomas settled deeper in his chair. "That'll do for a theory. Quite nice. But it's only a theory. It doesn't give you anything to work on."

"I never thought it did," Bell said gloomily. "One of those cases where you've got a lot of donkey work. It was a professional job and well planned out beforehand. We'll have to go through all the burglars on the list. I don't mind owning, there's nothing in it that's any fellow's particular style. It's too simple."

"Simplicity is the mark of ability," Reggie mumbled.

"I dare say. You are often obscure, Reginald." Lomas yawned and lit a cigarette. "Same old game, what? Same dull old game. Sorry, Bell. You're in for it."

Reggie reached for a cigar. "Thank you so much. Yes." He lay back and blew smoke rings. "'Do the work that's nearest. Though it's dull at whiles,'" he murmured. "The nearest, Lomas old thing. I don't like burglars. I want a murderer."

"Quite. Very proper taste. Happy to oblige. Name and address, please?"

"I don't know his name. Or his address. He's a shortish man, agile, of considerable strength; he has dark red hair which is rather long and oiled, and he has lost a triangular piece from one of the two middle teeth in his upper jaw. At this moment he has a bruised cut on his face. And he uses chewing-gum."

"Good gad!" said Lomas. "Were you there?"

"Do you mean there was only one man in it, sir?" Bell cried.

"Oh no. No. He had a companion. I don't know much about him. He was heavier and I should think older. But the little man did the killing. The porter came in, and they were all three together in the middle of the shop, and there was a quarrel. The small man got his face punched—the porter's knuckles are broken and there was some red hair in the blood. The porter also hit the little man in the mouth and broke his tooth, and the beggar spat out blood and chewing-gum and the bit of tooth, and it all stuck on the porter. Then the little man got some long weapon and hit him on the head. He fell stunned. They hid him behind the counter, and to make sure jabbed him in the throat with a sharp long tool. No doubt it was that long chisel they had made for the job."

"Thank you. Very brilliant, Reginald. And now all we have to do is to find a little man with red hair and a broken tooth. That's going to be quite easy."

"It is wonderful what you get, sir," Bell said reverently.

"Quite," Lomas chuckled. "Makes me feel like the man in the play when they show him Peter Pan's shadow. 'It's nobody I know.'"

"No. You're not suspected at present," Reggie murmured. "Any other helpful suggestions? I want to get on."

"Quite. Very right and proper. Where to?"

"I was thinking of the porter's humble home."

"Man there, sir," said Bell.

"Good. May I go and help him?"

Lomas chuckled. "By all means. If there's anything else you want to do, don't mind us. We like it. Forgive our existence, Reginald."

"My dear chap! Oh, my dear chap!" Reggie stood up and contemplated him benignly. "It's beautiful."

"Thanks so much. Sometimes something seems to say that you feel the Department superfluous."

"Oh no. No. Who ran to lift me when I fell and kissed the place to make it well? My Lomas! I like to feel something safe and solid in the background. Come on, Bell."

The workmen's dwelling in Clerkenwell where the porter lived stood in a by-way, a drab, respectable mass. Children swarmed in the courtyard. The clean staircase was full of the steam of washing-day. "Not the sort of place for a crook, sir," Bell muttered.

"He wasn't," said Reggie.

The porter's rooms were at the top. A detective opened the door to them. "No fresh news of him, sir. The woman below comes in and cleans up for him twice a week. She was here Saturday morning and saw him go off, and the bed's not been slept in since. Down at the office they say he's lived here a matter of ten years. Reckoned a very steady man. He was well liked in the dwellings." He looked round the room. "Decent place in a plain way."

The porter had taken some pride in it. The room smelt fresh and clean, its scanty furniture was in good order—he had curtains up, and a picture or two; a fair show of china and pots and pans; a home-made shelf bore a collection of objects of art.

Reggie looked at them with some care. Reggie stared at the wall. "Well, well," he murmured, and went into the bedroom. That had no decorations but a coloured print of the King. Its furniture was a bed and a chest of drawers. Reggie opened one after the other. The first was empty. The others contained a few clothes. He came back to the other room where the detective was conferring with Bell. "Have you found anything?"

"No, sir, nothing. He doesn't seem to have had any papers at all. There's nowhere for 'em to be."

Bell shook his head. "Somebody's been here before us, Mr. Fortune."

"Yes. That is indicated. I was wondering what they came for. Ask the woman who did the rooms to come up."

She came, a large woman wiping red arms on her apron, breathing hard. "There's something you can tell us, I think," said Reggie amiably. "Has anything gone from this poor chap's rooms?"

She snorted. "Wodsher mean gawn? I ain't took nuffink. Ain't never been in the place since Sat'dy. Tike my dyin' oaf I ain't."

"Of course you haven't. We want to know if anybody else has. And there's only you who can tell us what was in his rooms before he was killed."

"Can I? Dunno so much. I ain't no Nosey Parker. I never poked into 'is fings." She fixed Reggie with a choleric eye. "'E didn't 'ave no golden jools lyin' abaht. 'E kep' 'is bit o' money in the top drawer."

"Just show us, will you?" Reggie murmured.

She waddled into the bedroom. She opened the drawer. "Lummy, it's gawn," she wheezed. "Bit of a tin box it was, guv'nor, so big. I swear it was vere last week."

"Did you ever see it open, mother?" said Bell.

"Yus, I seen it. 'E 'ad 'is money in it and some bits o' pipers."

"They got away with his papers, then. Thank you, mother, that's all." He led the way back to the sitting-room.

"One moment," Reggie murmured. "One moment. Has anything else been taken?"

"Ardsher mean?" she wheezed. "Ain't nuffink else to tike only 'is bits o' sticks." But Reggie was looking round the room, and she stared about her with puzzled eyes. She moved to the shelf of odds and ends and moved one or two. "Yus, 'is pretties are all 'ere."

"What about the pictures?" said Reggie.

"Gorblime!" she gasped. "One of 'is picshers is gone. 'Ere. 'E 'ad one 'angin' up 'ere. Yer can see w'ere ve nile wos, guv'nor."

"Yes, I did see," Reggie smiled.

"Nah, w'at'd anyone want to tike that for?"

"I wonder. What was it?"

"Jest a blinkin' set o' footballers."

"A football team. Was he in it?"

"Not 'im, no. Don't know none of 'em. Don't know w'at 'e 'ad it for."

"Any name to it?"

"I don't know. Yus. Some nime. Couldn't tell yer. But w'at the 'ell does anyone want to pinch a blinkin' photo of footballers for?"

"Quite so. Yes," Reggie murmured. "Don't you worry. Thanks very much." And with professional exhortations not to talk about it Bell got rid of her.

Then he stared heavily at Reggie. "And what's going to happen next, if you please? I begin the day with a murder and a ten-thousand-pound burglary and come on to a stolen football photo."

"Yes. Yes. Very careful mind at work," Reggie smiled. "Quite a pleasure to deal with him."

"Deal with him! He's dealing with us all right. But we don't get near him. He breaks up every clue before we find it."

"I wouldn't say that. No. I wouldn't say that. Dangerous move destroying clues, Bell. He had to, of course. He couldn't let us see that photo. But he's told us he was in it."

"What, you mean the chap that did the murder was one of this football team? That's only a guess, sir."

"Quite. Others possible. But the best guess is that my little red-haired friend was in the photograph."

"Well, suppose he was. That don't help me, sir. How many football teams get photographed every year? You set me to look for a red-haired man with a broken tooth; now you've got it he plays football. I dare say. But it leaves me a nice long job."

"Yes. Yes," Reggie agreed cheerfully. "Better look for a short cut. Somebody at the shop ought to know where the porter had his drop of beer. You might find out what football team was his fancy. Good-bye."

The interesting thing about this case, he has been heard to say, is that it provides some justification for the existence of an expensive police force. He will explain that he always thought he would want to have the Department in his theory up to the neck or they would not have gone through with it. In fact, he took the case as a game of chess (Lomas says a game of poker), which is not his habit. He was for once without emotions. And Bell and his men worked like beavers, and Reggie saw his wife off to Scotland and played with biochemistry and his marionette theatre.

After some days Lomas rang him up. "Is that you, Reginald? Good. Come round, will you. Bell thinks he's on to something."

Reggie went round. Bell was conferring with Lomas more solemnly than ever. "Well, well. And are we yet alive and see each other's face? How do you do, Bell?"

"I've had a heavy week, sir. Now, take it from the beginning. We've found a clerk who was working after hours in an office by Durfey and Killigrew's that Saturday afternoon. When he went home he noticed some men hammering at the shop door. Thought it was a bit queer, so he had a look at 'em. Didn't look much because he saw Durfey's porter standing by and supposed it must be all right. But he noticed there were two of 'em, and one was a little chap with red hair. Well, then, we've got on to a chap who's caretaker at a block of offices round the corner. He knew the porter. He came along between three and four o'clock. There was nobody at Durfey's door then, but he saw the porter hanging about in a doorway opposite. Bit surprised to see him in uniform so late on a Saturday. He called out something about it and he thought the porter was a bit short with him."

"Yes. He would be," Reggie murmured. "Poor devil. So that's how he got murdered."

"All fits what you said," Bell nodded. "The porter was there in his uniform so that nobody should meddle with 'em while they were breaking in. If anything was said about it afterwards I suppose he'd have sworn it wasn't him, it was somebody in a sham uniform. That's been done before. But this chap came by who knew him and could swear he was outside while the burglary was being done. He got the wind up and went in to warn his pals. Most likely he wanted 'em to clear off without the swag to save his face. Then there was a row and they did him in. I dare say it all happened like that."

"'Some error and the thing got away with them,'" Lomas chuckled. "Your game, Reginald. You told us so and you told us right."

"No butter, thank you," Reggie murmured. "What's the matter with our Superintendent? Your manly brow is depressed, Bell. You make me uncomfortable."

"I'm not easy in my mind about it, Mr. Fortune. I don't like a case to look so neat when I'm only half-way through it. Pretty often I've found, if we've got a theory all fixed up half-way, in the end it turns out we made a big bloomer. You know that, too. You're fond of having us on that way."

"Oh, Bell! Oh, my Bell! How can you? I never did. I only look beyond a theory when it don't take in all the evidence."

"You're satisfied, Reginald?" Lomas nodded. "So am I. This is good enough to go on with, Bell."

"I don't say it isn't, sir." Bell frowned. "But Mr. Fortune talks about taking in all the evidence. That's the trouble. I don't know if we have." He turned to Reggie. "Mr. Lomas thinks I've got a bee in my bonnet. But I put it to you, the chances are these two chaps that were seen had someone else in the job with 'em. A big jewel robbery has to be worked out very careful, to study the place and fix up the plans and to get rid of the stuff afterwards."

"Of course there was somebody behind 'em," said Lomas impatiently. "Some fence in a large way of business. There always is. How often do we get these rascals? Once in a score of cases. We'll stick to the red-haired footballer, please."

"Yes, I think so," Reggie murmured.

But Bell was stubborn. "I'm not talking about a fence, sir. What if there was another man actually in the job, Mr. Fortune? It's like this. Yesterday we had notice a man who lived in Barkham Mansions, Marble Arch, was missing."

"Quite a gentlemanly address."

"Yes, sir. He was quite the gentleman, they say. But he was last seen that Saturday afternoon. When our men had a look over his flat they found some queer things. Harvey Stroud was the name he used, and we don't know it, and we can't recognise his description. But he was in touch with a diamond merchant in Amsterdam that does some very shady business, and he kept an outfit that'd come in useful for burglary. He's vanished absolutely. Him and his car. Ever since that Saturday."

"Yes. Very interesting. What was he like?"

"Dark chap, going bald. Smiled a lot, showed his teeth. Several gold ones. Tall and thin. Very spry. Any age."

Reggie shook his head. "I don't think so, Bell. The other man in the shop had large flat feet. And the gentlemanly Mr. Harvey

Stroud don't sound like a chap to hammer at a street door. He may have gone off with the swag. I'd like my red-haired little friend first, thank you."

"Quite, just my view." Lomas rubbed his hands. "We'll get on with him, Bell."

"Oh! Are you getting warm?" said Reggie.

"I hope so. Bell's put in very sound work. But he's never happy unless he has a certainty."

"I like to be sure, it's a fact," Bell grumbled.

Reggie looked at him with half-shut eyes. "Which do you mean? Sure a man ought to be hanged, or sure you can get him hanged? Well, what have you got, Bell?"

"It's going like this, sir. We've got a man who saw a motor-bike with side-car left in Broadlands Rents that afternoon. You know the place. Light vans and such get parked there ordinary weekdays, nothing much on Saturdays. So he noticed it. And he saw two fellows go off with it. Each of 'em was carrying a workman's tool-basket. He thought they looked like builders' men. But the one that rode the bike was a little chap with red hair. Do you notice, Mr. Fortune, these chaps that saw 'em can't tell us anything about the other?"

"Yes. Rather a pity. Yes. But I don't infer that he was the tall and spry and gentlemanly Harvey Stroud. I should say he was somebody who looked the ordinary British workman. Well, any further trace of our red-haired friend?"

"He goes off on the motor-bike and we lose him. But there's the football clue, sir." He stopped. "You know this is all your case really. Everything we've got is what you made for us."

"Oh no. No. Not my case. Not in my way at all," said Reggie quickly. "It's a job for the whole department."

"Quite, quite," Lomas agreed. "Building things up."

Bell glanced at him. "Yes, sir," he said respectfully. "Well, this is what we've built up, Mr. Fortune. The porter used to have his dinner at a little eating-house round the corner. And they say there he talked a lot of football, and his pet club was London City. They got into the Final of the Cup, last year, you know. Well, their outside left is a little red-haired man, Percy Clark. Been with 'em a long time. Regular popular favourite they tell me."

"The football burglar. Quite a new type," Lomas chuckled.

"And is Mr. Clark known to the police?" Reggie asked.

"Not at all, sir. He's in the regular team, though he isn't a professional. And you can take it First League football players don't do much crime. They train too hard."

"Mr. Clark plays as an amateur. Yes. And how does he get his living?"

"He's got a business of his own, sir; motor and cycle depot; specialises in motor-bikes."

"Well, well!" Reggie murmured, and Lomas laughed. "It does all fit, doesn't it, Bell?"

"You mean he could ha' made that queer long chisel they used in his own workshop. Yes, I thought of that. But it is quite a respectable business, old standing; his father had it before him."

"Yes. Yes." Reggie smiled. "What are his teeth like?"

Bell breathed hard. "Ah. I reckon that's up to you, sir. I've had some fellows look at him, but all they can say is he has a scar on his face, healing. Playing football, he might get that easy."

"Do they play football in August?"

"Oh yes, sir. Practice games. League season begins before summer's over. What I was thinking—his team has a practice game this evening—if you'd come up and have a look at him."

"If you like. Anything I can do," said Reggie meekly. "What about it, Lomas?"

"Safety-first idea, isn't it?" Lomas shrugged, "I should have said we have enough of a case to bring the fellow here and ask him a few questions. But there's no harm in looking him over beforehand. I take it the thing turns on his tooth. If he's lost the piece you found, then we've got him cold. If he hasn't, then we shall have to work up something more."

"I don't know about working up," Bell grumbled. "We shall want something more. I thought of taking the chap who saw the burglars at work up to the ground to see if he could identify Clark."

"Oh no. No. I wouldn't do that," Reggie said hastily. "It's not fair, Bell. The red-haired man he saw was in ordinary clothes. Mr. Clark may look very different stripped for football. Try him in a regular identification parade."

"Very good, sir," Bell frowned. "You don't mind my saying so, but you're uncommon careful to have us do everything in the regulation routine way for you in this case."

"It's that kind of case, you know." Reggie was plaintive.

"Quite," Lomas approved. "Quite. You're perfectly right, my dear fellow."

The huge amphitheatre of the London City ground was sparsely populated for that practice match. Two men who strolled in just before the kick-off had no difficulty in finding places against the rails. The players ran on to the field and lined up. The red head of Percy Clark glistened in the sun.

"Yes. Quite oily," Reggie murmured. "And the right red, thank you." He smiled. "Cut over the eye nearly gone. Sturdy little wretch, isn't he?"

"He could have struck that blow?" Bell said under his breath.

"Oh lord, yes! Just the man. Short and powerful. I told you he would be. Quick on his feet, isn't he?" Clark was making rings round the opposing half. "That also. Oh, damn!" Clark had come into contact with the back. They had some badinage.

"I didn't see," Bell muttered. "What is it? Tooth there, sir?"

"No, it isn't. The whole tooth's gone. He's had it out, confound him. And that is that." He turned away.

"What do you want to do now, sir?" Bell said when they reached the street.

"Carry on, carry on. You'll have to ask Mr. Clark to come to Scotland Yard, and if he won't come—take him."

"I'll tell Mr. Lomas, sir."

"Oh yes. Yes. Let's be correct," Reggie smiled.

And everything was done in order as he desired. That night two grave men called on Percy Clark in the neat little house beside his garage. They asked him to come and give Superintendent Bell a little information. He laughed. He wanted to know what about. They said the Superintendent would tell him. He replied that he had no time to go running round to police stations. They said he would have to make it. He went with them.

"Cut it short, will you, old friend?" He greeted Bell jauntily. "I'm a busy man."

"All right," said Bell. "You just tell me what you were doing the afternoon of Saturday the 20th."

"I don't think!" Clark winked. "Want to pinch me for something, do you? Nothing doing, old bean. There's been too much in the papers about what a chap gets by talking to the police."

"You can't account for your time that afternoon?"

"Not 'arf," said Clark. "I'm saying nothing, mate."

"If you're innocent, you're a fool," Bell frowned.

"You've got nothing against me. I know that. Not being a fool, old friend, I'm not going to help you fake up a charge. Got that? Now, what about it?"

"You'll be detained as a suspected person," said Bell.

"What of?" said Clark.

"You'll hear when the time comes."

In the morning, Bell put him up for identification by the man who had seen the burglars at work and the man who saw two workmen go off in a side-car. Both of these witnesses picked him out, both declared that they had seen a little man with red hair like his. Neither would say he was the man. His house and his garage were searched and such a tool as the long chisel which had been used in the burglary was found: more than one queer tool of no lawful use.

Then Bell charged him with burglary and murder, and he grinned and asked to see his solicitor.

Reggie was called out of his laboratory to the telephone. "Well, Reginald, Mr. Percy Clark is going to be put through it," said the voice of Lomas. "In the police court tomorrow. Happy now?"

"Not happy, no. Tranquil. I thought you'd have to."

"Quite. You're satisfied? Good. So am I. Come round, will you? The Public Prosecutor wants to talk."

Reggie came into a room which seemed to be occupied by a large man in front of the fireplace, who lectured.

"Oh, my aunt!" Reggie moaned. "Lomas—oh, you are there. I couldn't see you for the noise. Hallo, Bell! You look disgruntled." He turned at last to Mr. Montagu Finchampstead, the Public Prosecutor. "What's the matter with you, Finch?"

"He's explaining that he doesn't think much of the case," said Lomas.

"Fancy that," Reggie murmured. "Haven't we been correct, Lomas? How would Finch have done it?"

"The question is not how I should have done it, but whether the evidence you have will obtain a conviction. And—"

"Is it?" said Lomas. "I should say if the police have good evidence a man was guilty of murder he ought to go for trial."

"Good evidence, yes," Finchampstead fumed. "There's practically nothing but Fortune's story."

"My what?" Reggie was hurt. "I don't tell stories, Finch."

"We have some other striking facts," said Lomas. "A man very like this chap was on the scene of the murder. He has the motorbike equipment and the burglarious tools which the murderer required. He's a footballer, and a football photo was stolen from the murdered man's room after the crime."

"A lot of detail," Finchampstead snorted.

"Of course it's detail," said Lomas. "Every case is made up of detail: and when each scrap fits, the cumulative force is strong."

"Juries don't bother about cumulative force," Finchampstead announced. "We come down to this. The only clear evidence you've got is Fortune's statement about the hair and the piece of tooth. And in my opinion it's not satisfactory."

"Thank you for all these kind words," Reggie murmured. "Why isn't it satisfactory? The murderer left hair on the dead man's fist which is just the colour of Percy Clark's. He left a bit of a front tooth, and Percy has lost all that tooth."

"Just so. All of it," said Finchampstead. "Which means that the bit you found is not evidence against him at all. A man can't have something broken off a tooth he hasn't got."

"How true, Finch! How brilliant!" Reggie looked at him reverently. "But don't you see, dear, that raises the little questions, when did he have that tooth taken out, and why did he have that tooth taken out? For he had his front teeth all present and correct quite recently. I've found a smiling photograph."

"That's right, sir," Bell nodded. "In the football papers. And I've found customers of his who want to swear he hasn't lost a front tooth at all."

"Satisfied now?" Lomas smiled.

Finchampstead scowled at him. "No, I am not satisfied. I am bound to say the evidence is inadequate."

"Now, what exactly do you mean, Finch?" Reggie murmured. "That you don't think Percy was the murderer or that you don't think you can make a jury say he was?"

Finchampstead hesitated. "I don't mind owning it's a queer case," he said reluctantly. "You show a strong probability that he is guilty. But I have to make a proof, Fortune."

Lomas laughed. "Just so. You admit it's a case for trial."

"I agree we must go through with it." Finchampstead rose. "Don't forget, we have no idea what his defence is going to be."

"No. Not a notion," Reggie murmured. "That'll make it very interesting."

The conference broke up. But Bell took Reggie aside. "Mr. Fortune, do you believe this man's guilty?" he said.

"Oh yes. Absolutely. Not a doubt. Why?"

Bell drew a long breath. "Well, I'm glad. I did think you were keeping out of it: leaving it all to us."

"Yes. That is so." He looked at Bell with half-shut eyes. "You notice things," he murmured. "I wanted you fellows to work up the case yourselves. It makes you all nice and keen. I couldn't force a prosecution. But Lomas can. And he has."

The arrest of a First League player for murder was a fortune to newspapers in the depths of the silly season. The great heart of the people was taught to yearn over Percy Clark. Pages of stories, pages of pictures, set forth his deeds on the football field, his beauty and his charm. He became a popular hero persecuted by the police.

The prosecution went on its slow prosaic way. Before the magistrate an old solicitor of renown in criminal cases appeared for Mr. Clark, played lightly with the evidence against him and announced that he would reserve his defence. Mr. Clark was committed for trial.

When the case came on, a crowd fought to get into the court, a crowd remained outside. The driest, hardest little Judge on the bench took the case. "Looks in form," Lomas smiled. "He'll hang the fellow if he can."

"He will keep the jury to the evidence," said Finchampstead with dignity, glancing at the fleshy advocate who was leading for the defence.

But Mr. Justice Blackshaw had no chance for his noted snubs. Sir Edward Pollexfen did not use the melodramatic style which has made him the idol of the criminal classes. He took the case as quietly as the neat counsel for the prosecution. The dangerous evidence of Reggie did not excite him, his cross-examination treated Mr. Fortune with careless respect. "Your evidence is that the murderer had red hair and lost a portion of a tooth in his struggle with the dead man. Very good. I suggest that many men have red hair, Mr. Fortune."

"Yes. Not so many this shade of red."

"Still, a good many. You produce one hair and a piece of a front tooth. You don't suggest that piece is missing from any of the prisoner's teeth."

"Not from any that he has now. He has had the tooth in the position from which this piece came removed."

"If he had lost that tooth before the murder, this piece cannot be his?"

"If he had," said Reggie, and was told that was all.

Lomas looked at Finchampstead. "Taking it easy, what?"

"Much too easy," Finchampstead frowned.

Reggie came from the witness-box to sit beside them. "Well, well. I should say we're going to hear some good hard swearing, Finch."

"I should say they have a good answer. I was afraid of that, Fortune."

"Yes, yes. I know you were," Reggie murmured.

The defence continued to take it easy. The men who had seen a red-haired little fellow at the time and place of the murder were let go with the admission that they could not swear to Percy Clark. The woman telling of the stolen football photograph was only required to admit she did not know who was in it. The customers of Clark who swore he had had all his teeth till the eve of the murder were contemptuously challenged. Bell's own evidence of strange tools in Clark's workshop was dismissed with a few technical questions to confuse the jury.

Pollexfen arose to open the defence with expansive confidence. The jury must be amazed at the weakness of the case which they had been brought to hear. In all his long experience he had never known a criminal charge supported by such scanty, flimsy evidence. It would be apparent to them that no rational man could find the prisoner guilty. But his client was not content to be acquitted for lack of evidence against him. He claimed the right to prove his innocence. And he would show that he could have had no part in the crime.

"That means we're going to have an alibi," said Lomas.

But they began with the tooth. Some of the other players in Clark's football team swore that he had an accident in practice the week before the murder and stood out of training.

"Yes, I dare say they're telling the truth," Reggie murmured. "He'd want time off to make his little arrangements."

They testified that Clark had a kick in the face, complained that it had loosened his teeth, told them the front one had gone so shaky he had to pull it out.

"Thus avoiding any dentist's evidence," Reggie murmured.

The prosecuting counsel, going gingerly, brought out that they had no knowledge how the tooth was lost except what Clark had told them.

And then came a man who said he lived at Gilsfield. It is a little place fifty miles out of London, away from main lines and main roads.

Reggie lay back and gazed at him with mild and dreamy eyes.

The man said he was a retired grocer, and he looked it. He had a habit of going out for a stroll and getting a cup of tea at a wayside inn, the "Billhook." He knew Mr. Clark by seeing him there pretty often. He was at the "Billhook" on the Saturday of the murder. He saw Mr. Clark there. Under cross-examination he was sure of the date, but vague about the time. It was tea-time: might have been four or five. "Or six or seven?" counsel suggested. But he was sure it was before the bar opened. The Court laughed.

"Pretty vague," said Lomas.

"Yes. Yes. Mr. Clark will want them to do better than that," Reggie murmured, and contemplated the sharp, impudent face in the dock.

The landlord of the "Billhook" came next, an oldish, fattish man, sweating freely. He also knew Mr. Clark. Mr. Clark often came to the "Billhook" when he was out on his motor-bike. He came that Saturday. Came for a bit o' lunch. Stayed on till it was getting dark. Had a bit o' game with the darts in the afternoon. He knew the date, he'd got it scored up. Mr. Clark lost half a dollar to him and hadn't paid yet. Again the Court laughed. And cross-examination made nothing of the landlord. He was anxious to oblige, in the manner of a publican, he wheezed and he sweated, but he stuck to his story.

"So that's that," Reggie murmured, watching him out of the box. "Now, what's little Blackshaw going to do about it?"

Pollexfen's speech for the defence took that for granted. He boomed assurance. The charge had collapsed; it was atoms, dust. The prisoner was proved innocent before God and man.

And for the first time the little Judge had his chance to snap. Some lovers of football were applauding. He scarified them.

The reply for the prosecution was in a minor key, ironic about alibis, sarcastic upon dentistry by hearsay, bitter in emphasis on the anxiety of someone to destroy the evidence that the murdered man had a footballing friend.

Mr. Justice Blackshaw took snuff. The summing up came in his driest style. The jury would not be misled by counsel's complaints that a grave charge had been made without proof. They would observe that facts had been given in evidence which were in substance unchallenged and which pointed to the prisoner's guilt. They would also observe that evidence had been given to weaken the strongest part of the case and other evidence which would disprove it all. He made it plain that he did not think much of the explanation of the tooth. He treated the alibi with more respect. If they believed the witnesses for the defence, the foundation of the charge, that Clark had been at the shop at the time of the burglary, was destroyed. They must consider that evidence carefully and the evidence as a whole.

"Fair little beggar, isn't he?" Reggie smiled. "He knows Clark did it all right."

"He knows what your evidence is worth," Finchampstead growled. "That's a direction to acquit."

"I know. I know," Reggie murmured. He gazed pensively at the man in the dock. The gap where the tooth had been showed in a queer, sneering grin.

The jury did not consider long. They came back with a verdict of not guilty, and at the words a cheer rose from the back of the crowded court, rose louder, to the impotent rage of the little Judge, as it was swelled by a boom of cheering from the crowd outside.

"I told you so, Lomas," Finchampstead growled. "You've made a nice thing of it. This is what comes of relying on Fortune's theories."

"No, it isn't. It comes of doing one's job," said Lomas. "Well, let's get away before they tear us limb from limb. Where is Fortune?" But Mr. Fortune had gone.

On the next day a young man on a motor-bicycle stopped at the "Billhook" for lunch. His clothes were loud, his speech Cockney. He confided in the landlord that he was having his fortnight off: mooching round the country on the old jigger: rather thought of putting up somewhere for a bit. The landlord, who looked like the morning after a wet night, said the "Billhook" had no beds. "Sorry. You got some good beer. 'Ave one with me." The landlord had one and another. "Prime stuff. I'll be coming this way again, dad"—the young man winked. "Cheerio!" He rode off and found a bed in Gilsfield. He was Mr. Fortune's chauffeur, Sam, a young man of versatility.

The country round the "Billhook" is lonely, a picturesque and barren region of sandhills which grew heath by nature and have been made to grow larch and pine. Here and there the ponds, which such country is apt to produce, give variety to the vegetation. About this time a botanist, complete with vasculum, was noticed working over the heath. The solitary woodmen and gamekeepers found him affable. He was Mr. Fortune.

Sam continued to mooch round and he often recurred to the bar of the "Billhook," and the men who used it agreed that he was a lad.

From them his bicycle took him often to the hotel in the county town where Mr. Fortune unostentatiously resided.

They had been rusticating thus for something more than a week, and Sam was sitting in the "Billhook" at lunch when he heard the telephone ring. "Yes," the landlord's wheezy voice answered; "yes, this is the 'Billhook.' I'm the landlord. What?" His voice made throaty noises. "Don't know what you mean. Who's that speaking? Who is it?" There was a silence. Then a rattling of the telephone. "I say, miss, who was that rang me up?" And again silence.

Sam finished his lunch and went into the bar. The landlord was gulping down a glass of brandy; his hand shook and his face was a mottled yellow. Sam grinned. "And I'll 'ave a spot o' sloe gin myself, guv'nor." He was served without a word and his money was taken. The landlord watched him go out, shut the door and went back to the telephone.

In the evening Sam related these events to Mr. Fortune. "It gave 'im a rare turn, sir. Pity you can't over'ear what's coming from the other end of the telephone."

"Don't worry," Reggie murmured. "And then?"

"Well, then 'e went back to the telephone and rung up someone and 'ad a long talk. 'E saw me off the premises first careful, so I don't know who that was. But I 'ung about down the road an' presently 'e came out and 'e went walking round by that old pond under the wood. Sort o' mooning about. Didn't do anything. Just starin' like. And then 'e came back lookin' that queer."

Over Reggie's face came a slow benign smile. "No. No. He couldn't do anything," he murmured. "Now we'll do a little more telephoning. Good-bye, Sam. I'm afraid you'll have a night out. I want the 'Billhook' watched tonight."

"All right, sir. I'd love to do the blighter in. The beastly swipes I've drunk in his place! But what do you mean, more telephoning? That message 'e 'ad—"

"Oh yes. Yes. That was me. Good-bye."

As soon as it grew dark Sam went into hiding behind a clump of gorse in the road above the "Billhook." He saw the regular drinkers of that respectable inn arrive and cheerily depart. At the legal hour the "Billhook" closed its door and the light behind the red blind of its bar went out. Two lights upstairs announced that the landlord and his maid-of-all-work had gone to bed. Then those lights also vanished, and the inn was a vague mass in the dark.

The night was silent but for the whirr of bats and an owl hooting. After a while Sam made out the beat of a motor engine

far away, a bicycle engine efficiently silenced. It came nearer at
a great pace, rushed past him, stopped at the inn, and without a
knock or a word the door opened and the man and the bicycle
were inside.

For a moment Sam thought he heard a car purring down the
road, then lost the sound. But soon other faint sounds came.
A man was nearly treading on him, a hand felt for him, a torch
flashed into his face. "All right, son," a voice whispered. "I'm Bell."
The bulk of the Superintendent lay down at Sam's side. "You've
got a good nerve. Anything doing?"

"Not 'alf," Sam muttered. "Chap and his motor-bike gone into
the pub. Couldn't see him."

"Don't you worry."

"But what's up, sir?"

"Search me. No more talk now."

They lay there some while longer. Then a light came out of the
inn, a stable lantern in a man's hand. He was the landlord. With
him walked a smaller man, who carried a spade on his shoulder.
They turned off the road. "'Ere," Sam gripped at Bell, "goin'
down by the pond. That's where the old 'un went this afternoon.
What's the game?"

"Shut up," Bell muttered. He let the two go well ahead before
he stood up. Four other men rose out of the ground behind him.
They moved on towards the pond silently. The lantern light was
glimmering over the water: there was a squelching, splashing
sound. The landlord stood in the pond a little way from the bank,
digging, and the other man held the lantern. Something came
away with a gurgling and sucking, which took two hands to lift,
was taken out of the water and the landlord hurried away with
it, leaving his companion to bring lantern and spade.

As they came, Bell turned his torch on them, and other torches flashed out. They were held in the glare while his men closed. "We're police officers," said Bell, with a heavy grip on the landlord's arm. "Now, what have you got for us?"

"Oh, police, are you?" It was the other man who answered. "Going to make another bloomer, then?"

"I know you, Clark," Bell said.

"You bloomin' well do, Mr. bloomin' Superintendent. An' you know you can't do anything more against me. I've been found not guilty, I have, and you can't touch me. I know my rights and I ain't going to stand for any rough stuff. Come off it."

"And this is your alibi," Bell said mildly. "Well, what's he giving us now?" He took from the landlord's shaking arms a big metal box. "Thanks. Bring 'em back to the pub."

"Now, what do you think you're doing?" Clark cried. "You've got no right to pinch me again. You can't touch me. I tell you—" One of the detectives, hustling him along, advised him to stow the gab. "You wait till I get to my lawyer, you bloomin' stiff. I'll have the hide off you for this. I'll have you turned out of the force."

"Want to talk now, Clark?" said Bell. "Let it out. You hadn't much to say last time."

"I want to know what the bally charge is?" Clark growled.

Bell laughed. "Well, what is it?" He held up the box. "Seems heavy."

They came into the bar of the "Billhook" and the lamps were lit. Bell looked at his prisoners. The landlord's fat face sagged pallid. Clark scowled. "Going to give me the key?" Bell tapped the box.

"I dunno nothing about it," the landlord whined. "I—I was jus' keeping it for—"

"Don't you say anything, George," Clark said quickly. "He'll only twist it against you."

"Yes, who were you keeping it for, George?" Bell smiled. There was no answer. "All right. I dare say we can tell you. Put 'em in there." He opened the door of the bar parlour.

"Here, now, wait a bit. What's the charge?" Clark protested.

"Detained on suspicion," Bell said.

"Oh yes, I don't think. You had that before."

"And now I've got some more," Bell said, and the two were taken away. "Well, Forbes, what about it?"

One of his men was already opening the box. It was full of a bundle in leather cloth. Out of that came jewellery. Forbes spread out a printed list and began to examine things. "This is Durfey and Killigrew's stuff all right, sir."

"Good work," said Bell, and went to the telephone. "That Mr. Fortune? Bell speaking. We've got 'em, sir. With the stuff. They had it buried in this pond here. What, sir? You don't mean—?" He brushed his hand over his face. "Very good, sir. I'll keep 'em here." He hung up the receiver. He sat down heavily and lit a pipe. It took many matches…

Until dawn they waited in the inn, a long watch broken by the complaints of Clark. With the light came a car. Mr. Fortune and Lomas and the Chief Constable of the County. "Hallo, Bell." Reggie was brisk. "Nobody else in the place?"

"There's a woman servant upstairs, Sam says. I haven't got her up, sir. She seems to have slept through it."

"Yes. Been trained not to hear too much. Well, one of your men had better take her off. We shall want her statement. Don't let her see these fellows. I—"

A lorry groaned past the door.

"Well, let's get on, what?" He turned away. "When I want these two beauties I'll whistle."

Through the window of the bar parlour the sharp red face of Mr. Clark could be seen peering after the lorry. It carried some country policemen in uniform. As near the pond as it could get, it stopped. The policemen clambered down and hauled out a cumbrous apparatus of iron and rope.

The Chief Constable strode up to the pond. "It's not so big, Mr. Fortune. We'll soon make sure one way or the other."

"Yes, yes." Reggie walked round the bank and measured distances with his eye. "We're going to make quite sure. They couldn't throw him further than this. Begin from here and work towards that end."

The drags were put in and the constabulary hauled and the black water grew turbid and yellow. The ropes strained. "Got something," the Chief Constable grunted. "Go steady, lads." Out of the depths of the pond into the shallows came a shapeless mass of cloth. Policemen splashed in and lifted on to the bank something that had been a man.

Lomas turned away. The Chief Constable pulled out a flask and drank and passed it to his men. Reggie knelt down by the body... When he stood up again he dabbled his hands in the pond. "Could you blow a whistle, Lomas?" he murmured.

The Chief Constable did that. "Is it the chap you were looking for?"

"Oh yes. Gold teeth, as per invoice. The late Harvey Stroud."

"Was he drowned?" said Lomas.

"No, not drowned. Skull fractured. Injury to bones of the face. Hit and jabbed by hard, heavy weapon. Same like the porter. Ah, here come the operators." Under the propulsion of Bell's men,

Mr. Clark and the landlord reluctantly approached. "Come along," Reggie called. "Just want you to recognise the deceased."

The landlord caught sight of that shapeless face and gave a gasping cry and swayed round, hanging on the arms that held him.

"Yes. Your error," Reggie said. He contemplated the little red face of Percy Clark. Its look of impudence was fixed, but his jaws worked fast. "Still chewing gum, Mr. Clark?"

Then Clark swore at him…

That afternoon the Public Prosecutor was asked to come and see the Chief of the Criminal Investigation Department. He found Mr. Fortune with Lomas. "My dear old Finch," Reggie beamed. "Journeys end in lovers meetin'. And now we live happily ever after. You've been so useful. How wonderful that is! But how gratifyin'! Another nice case for you now."

"Good heavens!" Finchampstead exploded. "Another case of yours? I should have thought that last exhibition was sufficiently ignominious. What is this, now?"

"Percy Clark, dear. Yet once more, oh ye laurels, and once more."

"Are you mad? You can't charge the man again."

"Not the same murder. No. This is another one. And thus we will establish your shaken reputation, Finch."

"My reputation!" Finchampstead gobbled.

"Yes, old thing. Yes, it was too bad." Reggie soothed him. "But necessary, you know. All for your country's good. We had to prosecute the beggar. We had to make him show his hand. And you did it beautifully, Finch."

"What does this mean, Lomas?" Finchampstead groaned.

"He's quite right," Lomas chuckled. "He generally is, confound him. Don't you see, the prosecution drove Clark into a corner. His only chance was to set up that alibi. And the alibi gave him away."

"It was perjured evidence? I dare say. If you hadn't been so hasty—"

"Not hasty. No. Forcin' the game," Reggie smiled. "When he put that fat landlord into the box, he put the rope round his neck. We had it sworn that he was a pal of the landlord's, and that he'd been at the 'Billhook' on the evening of the burglary. So I went down with my chauffeur to look into the landlord. And we found another fellow came to the 'Billhook' that night. A tall, dark fellow who came in a car, went into a back room with the landlord and Mr. Clark, and was never seen to go away. His car was there days after. Well, you know, there was a man reported missing from that Saturday who had interests in burglary—Mr. Harvey Stroud. Bell was always worrying about him. Bell thought he might be the man who put up the job. It looked as if he was. We knew the murder of the porter wasn't according to plan. If Mr. Stroud came quietly down to the 'Billhook' to collect the swag and found he'd been mixed up in a murder, he wouldn't be pleased. There might well have been a row. Another little affair not according to plan. So I rang up the landlord and said, 'What's become of Harvey Stroud?' Only that and nothing more. Just to see the reaction. He reacted very nicely. He gargled. Then my man saw him go out and wander round the adjacent pond, just looking at things. And then he went back and telephoned to Mr. Clark. Soon as the evening shades prevailed, Clark buzzed down to the 'Billhook.' In the night they went out and dug the swag out of the pond. And Bell got 'em with the goods all present and correct."

"We can convict them the burglary, then?" said Finchampstead.

"Oh yes. Yes. And the murder of Stroud. We dragged the pond this morning. Harvey Stroud was there with his head bashed in and his pockets full of stones. And now your fat friend the landlord is coughing up confessions."

"I always knew that rascal Clark was guilty," Finchampstead announced. "This is very satisfactory, Fortune."

"Yes, I think so," Mr. Fortune murmured. "One of my neater cases. Pure art. No vulgar emotion."

THE RED GOLF BALL

Gerald Verner

John Robert Stuart Pringle (1897–1980) wrote breezy crime thrillers in the Edgar Wallace mould. His first story, using the pseudonym Donald Stuart, was "The Clue of the Second Tooth", written in 1927, the first of forty-four stories contributed to the Sexton Blake Library. In 1933 Pringle began writing for publishers Wright & Brown as Gerald Verner, which became his principal pen-name, although he was so prolific that, in order to avoid saturating the market, he started to write under the pseudonyms of Nigel Vane and Derwent Steele as well as Donald Stuart. His detective Trevor Lowe featured in fourteen full-length novels, and several short stories; his debut, *Phantom Hollow* (1933), was dedicated to Mrs. Edgar Wallace.

Sport features in several of Verner's tales, including *The Silver Horseshoe* (1938) and *The Tipster* (1949). In *The Jockey* (1937), a man calling himself "The Jockey" sends a letter to a crooked book-maker, demanding thousands of pounds. This proves to be the first salvo in a campaign against those he claims have besmirched the good name of horse racing, but have escaped conviction because of a lack of evidence. When murder follows, the Jockey becomes the prime suspect. This story, originally titled and published in 1939 as "The Fatal 13th", as by Donald Stuart, was revised to become "The Red Golf Ball", a Trevor Lowe story written by Gerald Verner.

THAT FAMOUS DRAMATIST, MR. TREVOR LOWE, FOUND Glen Hill Golf Course a very pleasant place that afternoon. A heavy programme of work leading up to the opening of his latest West End production had kept him busy night and day for several weeks, and the relaxation was welcome.

He had not been playing too well, probably because of his lack of practice, and at the thirteenth hole he essayed a rather difficult putt in some trepidation. The little white ball, however, behaved beautifully, rolled gently across the smooth green, paused for the fraction of a second at the lip of the hole, and dropped neatly in. Lowe gave a sigh of relief and his opponent Colonel Grayling uttered a grunt.

"Never thought you'd bring that off," he said. "That makes you three up."

The dramatist retrieved his ball and smiled.

"I'm getting back some of my old form," he remarked. "You won't find it such a walkover as you thought, old man."

The colonel stabbed the flag viciously back into its socket, picked up his clubs, and started for the next tee.

"Don't count your chickens," he growled over his shoulder, his red face a shade redder with annoyance. "There's nothing in it so far. Five more holes to go yet."

Lowe lighted a cigarette without replying and strolled after him. Obviously Grayling was a little disgruntled at the prospect of what he had imagined an easy victory being snatched from his grasp at the last minute. He watched the colonel as he carefully teed his ball, addressed it, and with a determined expression, drove off. The drive was a terrible fiasco. The ball, badly sliced, flew to the right at an acute angle, struck a hillock at the side of the fairway, and vanished into a thick clump of trees twenty yards away.

Grayling glared after it in speechless rage.

"Hard luck, old man," said Lowe sympathetically, and the colonel found his voice.

The air quivered with a concentrated selection from a vocabulary acquired during thirty-five years in the Indian Army, and the dramatist listened admiringly. Lack of breath eventually brought the astonishing flow to an end, and without waiting to see his companion's shot Grayling snatched up his bag of clubs and set off angrily in search of his errant ball.

Lowe watched him until his stout figure disappeared in the shadow of the trees, and then set about preparing for his own drive.

But that drive was never made. The club was swinging up over his shoulder when Grayling shouted his name.

Uttering a mild imprecation—mild at least in comparison with the colonel's previous outburst—the dramatist stopped in the midst of his swing and looked towards the sound of his opponent's voice. Grayling was standing on the edge of the clump of trees beckoning frantically, with every sign of acute agitation.

"What is it?" called Lowe impatiently, not unreasonably annoyed at having his stroke interrupted.

"Come here, will you?" shouted Grayling. "I—it's something pretty serious, I'm afraid."

There was a quiver in his voice, and wondering what could be the cause of it Lowe hurried over to him.

"What's happened?" he demanded when he reached him, for Grayling's ruddy colour had left, and he was as nearly pale as many years' tan would permit.

For answer the colonel grabbed his arm and led him in among the trees.

"Look there!" he grunted hoarsely, and pointed with a stubby finger that was not quite steady.

Lowe looked and caught his breath. By the tangle of bushes a man lay face upwards, his eyes staring fixedly at the gently moving branches above him, and he was dead! The sprawling limbs, the unnatural position, the pallor of the face were eloquent testimony.

"Rather horrible, isn't it?" breathed Grayling at his elbow. "Gave me quite a turn, coming on him like that..."

"Who is he—do you know?" asked Lowe, and the question was prompted by something in the colonel's tone.

Grayling nodded.

"Yes," he said. "It's a fellow called Stanwood—a member of the club. What do you think it was—a groggy heart?"

"I think we ought to get hold of a doctor as soon as possible," answered the dramatist gravely.

"I'll go back to the clubhouse and phone Faversham," volunteered Grayling, and was turning away when Lowe stopped him.

"You'd better notify the police as well," he said.

"The police!" The colonel's voice was startled and he came to a sudden halt. "Why? Good heavens, you aren't suggesting..."

"Look at that mark behind his left ear," broke in the dramatist quietly. "That doesn't look like a heart attack to me."

Grayling came slowly back and bending forward, peered down at the dead man. His head was twisted sideways on his right shoulder, and just behind the lobe of his ear was a contused lump—a purple bruise showed clearly against the white skin. The colonel looked up at Lowe with an expression on his face in which doubt and horror were curiously mixed.

"I say," he whispered huskily, "you don't think—that possibly—that it could have been my ball…"

He stopped abruptly, but the dramatist knew what he meant.

"I shouldn't think so," he answered. "By the time it reached here most of its force must have been spent. Besides, it would be near the body. You didn't find it, did you?"

Grayling shook his head, and there was relief in his eyes.

"Didn't have time to look," he said.

"We may as well make certain what happened to your ball," remarked Lowe. "The question almost certainly will be raised."

He began to look about him, but it was Grayling who found the ball. It was lying a few inches away from the trunk of a tree nowhere near the body.

"Don't touch it," warned the dramatist. "Leave it where it is. Its position proves that it could have had nothing to do with Stanwood's death."

"Well, that's something to be thankful for," grunted the colonel. "For the moment I thought it hit the poor beggar. I'll get off to the clubhouse."

He hurried away and Lowe went back to wait beside the body. Stanwood had been a middle-aged man of medium height and inclined to stoutness. The dark hair on his square-shaped head was liberally flecked with grey, but his face was smooth and unlined. The dramatist guessed his age at forty-five and learned later that he was a year behind in his reckoning. The well cut suit of grey flannel, the thin platinum chain that crossed the waistcoat, suggested he was fairly well off. The question was why had he come by his death? Had he fallen and struck his head against the root of a tree or some similar object or had that mark behind his ear been caused in a more sinister way? In other words, was this accident or murder?

Trevor Lowe made a search of the ground in the immediate vicinity of the body and particularly of the head. The grass was thick and rank, and there was nothing in the shape of a root or a brick-bat which could have caused the ugly bruise. It looked as though accident could be ruled out. A splash of colour near Stanwood's feet attracted his attention, and looking closer, he saw a little red object lying half-concealed by the dead man's trousers. Stooping, he picked it up and looked at it with a puzzled frown. It was a nearly new golf ball which had been painted a vivid pillar-box scarlet. He was turning it over in his fingers, wondering at its unusual colour, when he saw that two initials had been scrawled on it in indelible pencil. J. C.

His forehead wrinkled. There was only one member of the club that those letters could stand for—Jack Claymore. Lowe knew him quite well—a pleasant, good-looking, young fellow who lived in the neighbourhood. Rather hasty tempered, but popular for all that.

Was the ball his and if so what was it doing there? Probably it had nothing to do with Stanwood's death, and yet it was curious. Why red? He put it back exactly where he had found it. Just as well not to move anything until after the police had been.

He was smoking a thoughtful pipe when Grayling came back accompanied by Milton, the club secretary.

"I've rung up Faversham and the police," panted the colonel, breathless from his exertions. "They're coming at once."

"This is a terrible business, Mr. Lowe," put in the thin-faced secretary agitatedly. "How do you think poor Stanwood came by his death?"

"I think he was murdered," said the dramatist quietly and then, before either of his listeners could put into words the questions he saw on their faces: "Tell me, Milton, who is the person who uses red golf balls in this club?"

"Red golf balls?" Milton's thin lips repeated the words and he frowned. "Oh, you must mean Claymore. He uses 'em in the winter, after it's been snowing. Quite a number of people do, they show up better. Why?"

Lowe explained.

"Yes, that would belong to Claymore," said Milton, his frown deepening. "He initials all his balls like that."

"But dammit!" grunted Grayling, "it's not winter yet. Why the devil has he been playing with a red ball in the autumn?"

"When was he playing last?" asked Lowe.

"This morning," answered the secretary. "With—Stanwood."

"With Stanwood, eh?" said the dramatist. "Did they come back to the clubhouse together?"

Milton shook his head and his lean face was troubled.

"No," he answered reluctantly. "Claymore came back alone."

There was a short silence, broken by Grayling.

"It's all nonsense," he growled. "Why should Claymore…"

"Nobody said he did," interrupted Lowe shortly. "I wonder how long it will be before the doctor and the police arrive?"

They came in about twenty minutes. Dr. Faversham's round, jovial face was unusually grave as he came up to them. He was accompanied by a thick set man whom Milton introduced as

Inspector Bream, and a constable. The inspector took particulars of the discovery of the body from Lowe and Grayling while the doctor made his brief examination.

"I know Mr. Claymore," he said when he was told about the red golf ball. "Lives at the White House. I shall have to see him. It looks as if he was the last person to see Stanwood alive."

Dr. Faversham's report was what Lowe had expected. Stanwood had died as the result of a heavy blow behind the left ear and death had been almost instantaneous. In the circumstances an accident sounded impossible. So far as the actual time at which death had taken place, the doctor was vague.

"I can't be certain within half an hour or so," he said. "But I should say he's been dead for at least two hours. There'll have to be a post-mortem and an inquest, of course."

The inspector agreed and proceeded with his investigations. A search of the dead man's pockets revealed a wallet containing fifteen pounds in notes, a gold watch, a handful of loose silver, and a bunch of keys. The motive for the murder was evidently not robbery.

"Had Mr. Stanwood any relatives, sir?" asked Bream, and Milton, to whom the question had been addressed, shook his head.

"I couldn't tell you," he answered. "I know very little about him. He only came to live in the district two months ago…"

"He took Fernlow cottage," put in Dr. Faversham. "You know the place—at the corner of Sparrow Lane."

The inspector nodded and made a note in his book. He asked several more questions—heard with raised eyebrows that Claymore had been playing with Stanwood that morning, and closed his book.

"Well, I think that's all for the moment, gentlemen," he said, putting the note-book in his pocket. "I've got your names and addresses and you'll be notified about the inquest. I'll have a word now with Mr. Claymore, I think. You stay here, Turner, until they come with the stretcher."

The constable saluted and the little group made their way to the clubhouse. The course was deserted. The majority of the members were away on holiday, and it was too early in the afternoon for any of the others to have put in an appearance. As they came in sight of the pavilion Lowe saw the slim figure of a girl standing on the veranda, looking towards them.

She was a very pretty girl, dressed in a smartly cut suit of tweeds.

"Mr. Milton," she called, when they were in earshot. "Have you seen anything of Mr. Claymore?"

"Not since before lunch, Miss Morgan," answered the secretary. She frowned.

"He was supposed to meet me here at two," she said. "I've been waiting nearly a quarter of an hour."

"He said he was going home when I last saw him," said Milton ascending the steps. "Rather a dreadful thing has happened, Mr. Stanwood has been murdered!"

Helen Morgan's big eyes widened.

"Murdered—Mr. Stanwood?" she whispered. "How… How awful! Where?"

"Near the thirteenth hole," said the secretary, as she paused. "As a matter of fact the inspector here wants to have a word with Mr. Claymore."

"With Jack?"

Lowe was certain that he saw alarm take the place of horrified surprise in her eyes.

"Why? What can he know about it?"

"Mr. Claymore was playing with Mr. Stanwood this morning, miss," said Bream, answering for himself. "And it's more than likely that he was the last person to see him alive."

"Here he comes now," growled Grayling, jerking his head towards the winding road that connected the clubhouse with the main thoroughfare. "That's his car."

Trevor Lowe watched the little two-seater come swiftly along the track and pull up with a jerk. A hatless, fair-haired man in an open shirt and flannels sprang out, and a moment later joined them on the veranda.

"Hello, Lowe," he greeted the dramatist with a grin. "You're a stranger. Haven't seen you for ages… Sorry I'm late, Helen. I was just setting off when I found one of the tyres completely flat and three inches of glass bottle through the cover…" he broke off and looked quickly from one to the other. "I say, what are you all looking so jolly serious about?"

"It's Mr. Stanwood, Jack…" began the girl, and his face changed. His brows drew together and his mouth set.

"Has that brute been making trouble?" he demanded angrily. "If he has, I'll give him the hiding I promised this morning!"

"Did you quarrel with Mr. Stanwood this morning, sir?" asked the inspector quickly.

"Yes, I did!" snapped Claymore. "I told him a few home truths and threatened that the next time he interfered in my affairs I'd break his neck!"

"Jack!" Helen Morgan's face was white. "You don't know what you're saying…"

"Where did this quarrel take place, sir?" broke in Bream hastily.

"At the thirteenth hole," answered the young man. "We hadn't finished the round, but I left him there. What's the idea of these questions? Has Stanwood been complaining?"

The inspector shook his head.

"No, sir," he said. "Mr. Stanwood is dead."

The quietly spoken words had a startling effect on Claymore. His jaw dropped and he stared at Bream incredulously.

"How did it happen?" he asked huskily.

"He was murdered near the thirteenth hole," answered the inspector.

"Good God!" muttered Claymore, and Bream took the red golf ball from his pocket.

"This was found next to the body," he went on, holding it out. "It's one of yours, I think?"

Claymore looked at the ball in amazement.

"Yes, it's one of mine," he admitted. "But, I don't understand— I only use one of these occasionally, when it has been snowing…"

"You weren't using it this morning?" inquired the inspector.

The other shook his head.

"No, I was playing with an ordinary ball," he replied.

"Then you can't account for this having been found near the body?"

"No."

The inspector dropped the ball back in his pocket.

"I should like to hear, sir," he said, "exactly what did happen this morning between you and Mr. Stanwood?"

Claymore moistened his lips.

"There's not much to tell," he replied, and neither was there. He had dropped into the clubhouse at ten-thirty and found Stanwood having a drink at the bar. There had been nobody else there, and Stanwood had suggested a game. Claymore, although he didn't like the man, had agreed. They got on fairly well until the thirteenth hole, when Stanwood had become offensive. There had been, to use Claymore's own expression, "A hell of a row," and he had left Stanwood, gone back to the clubhouse to leave his bag, and then gone home. Regarding the actual cause of the trouble he was stubbornly silent.

"That's my business," he said shortly when the inspector tried to press the matter, and Bream did not pursue the subject.

"You didn't see what happened to Mr. Stanwood after you'd left him, sir?" he asked.

"The last I saw of him," answered Claymore, "he was practising putting on the green."

"Thank you, sir," said the inspector. "I've no doubt your evidence will be required at the inquest. I'll just go along and have a look at Mr. Stanwood's cottage and then make arrangements with the coroner."

The Inquest was held on the Wednesday morning—two days after the discovery of the crime. Colonel Grayling had suggested that Lowe should stay with him until after the proceedings, and the dramatist, who was intensely interested, had accepted the invitation without much persuasion.

The little school-room was crowded when the coroner opened the inquiry. He was a fussy, bald-headed little man with a dry, nervous cough, and fully aware of the importance of his position.

Milton was the first witness called, and he gave evidence of identification. Dr. Faversham followed him and stated briefly the cause of death, and then Lowe and Grayling gave an account of their discovery of the body. When they had finished Inspector Bream took the stand. He described the circumstances in which he had been called in and gave an outline of his investigations.

Stanwood had, apparently, been something of a mystery. Very little was known about him prior to his coming to live in the neighbourhood, and not very much since. No relations could be traced, nor, with the exception of the few acquaintances he had made in the district, did he appear to have any friends. His balance at the local bank was not excessive but adequate. He had opened an account on his arrival with a cash payment of a thousand pounds, and had since paid in, also in cash, a further five hundred. Of this, nearly nine hundred remained. The inspector had made every effort to discover something of his previous history before he had taken up his residence in Fernlow cottage, but so far without result.

There was a murmur of interest among the audience, sternly suppressed by the coroner, when Bream related his interview with Claymore. The red golf ball was produced, and when the inspector explained where it had been found and to whom it belonged, Lowe saw the jury glance significantly at each other.

Jack Claymore was called, and repeated what he had already told the inspector on the afternoon of the murder. Once again he refused to give any reason for his quarrel with the dead man. He identified the red golf ball as his property, but said he could not account for its presence near the body. The ball that he had been playing with that morning had been an ordinary white one. He explained that he only used the red balls when it had been snowing. He had three of them which he kept with the ordinary ones in his locker at the clubhouse. When he had gone with Inspector Bream to examine this locker he admitted that there were only two of the red balls there, but he was unable to account for this.

He could only affirm that he had not used a red ball for over ten months. To a suggestion that he might have taken a red ball in mistake for a white one, since all the balls were mixed up together, he replied that it was totally impossible. Asked if he had noticed whether there were three red balls in the locker on the morning he had played with the deceased he said he thought there were, but he could not be sure. The locker had a lock, and he kept the key on a bunch with several others. There was no sign that the lock had been tampered with, and so far as he knew the key had not left his possession.

He agreed with the coroner that it seemed as though he had taken the red ball himself, but was quite sure that he had not. Asked if he was engaged to Miss Helen Morgan he looked surprised, and replied that he was, and after some hesitation admitted that Stanwood had, for several weeks past, pestered the girl with his attention, and that he had naturally resented it. He refused, however, to say this was why he had quarrelled with the dead man on the morning of his death. To the coroner's final question as to whether there had been anybody else in sight, either while he had been playing with the deceased or after he had left him, he answered that he had seen no one.

This concluded the evidence, and the coroner prepared to address the jury.

Trevor Lowe had become more and more uneasy during the examination of Jack Claymore, and the coroner's speech did nothing to alleviate his anxiety. He was scrupulously fair, but with every word that fell from his lips the case against Claymore grew blacker.

The dramatist was not surprised when, without leaving the box, the jury returned a verdict of wilful murder against Claymore, and Inspector Bream put him formally under arrest.

Trevor Lowe went back to lunch with Grayling troubled and dissatisfied. In spite of the result of the inquest he was not at all sure that Claymore was guilty. Granting opportunity, and possibly motive—though he thought this was a little weak—no reasonable explanation had been offered for the presence of the red golf ball. It was inconceivable to suppose that Claymore had made a mistake and played with it during his game with Stanwood. And, if he hadn't, how had it got where it had been found? The more he thought of it the more convinced he became that in the correct answer to that question lay the real solution of how Stanwood had met his death. He was silent and preoccupied during lunch, and every effort on Grayling's part to make conversation was met with a grunt or monosyllabic reply.

"Look here," the colonel broke out irritably at last, "what the devil's the matter with you?"

"It's all wrong," muttered Lowe, shaking his head.

"What is?" demanded his host.

"This Claymore business."

"Oh, you think so?" grunted Grayling.

"I'm sure of it," declared Lowe.

"And I suppose, as usual, you want to put it right," said the colonel. "Well, I'm hanged if I can see how you're going to set about it."

Lowe smiled wryly.

"Neither can I," he confessed. "But you must admit that it doesn't make sense. If Claymore wanted to kill Stanwood, why—unless he was crazy—did he do it in such a way that he was bound to be suspected?"

"Probably did it in a fit of temper," Grayling replied. "I don't see there's anything in that."

"And also in that same fit of temper, I suppose he put that red golf ball beside his body," said the dramatist, "in case the evidence against him wasn't sufficient?"

"I'll admit it is peculiar…" began the colonel.

"It's more than peculiar," broke in Lowe impatiently. "It's inexplicable. How…" He stopped suddenly and stared at Grayling. "If only it hadn't been red," he muttered, "there might be an explanation for its presence."

"You mean," put in Grayling, "that if it had been an ordinary ball it might have been the one Claymore was playing with?"

"No," answered the detective to his surprise, and his tone was a little abrupt, "I mean if it had been an ordinary ball it might have been planted by the real murderer to clinch the case against Claymore."

He got up abruptly and began to pace the room.

"But Claymore kept his golf balls locked up in the clubhouse locker," protested the colonel. "Nobody could have…"

"The lock is a simple one," interrupted Lowe. "It wouldn't be difficult to find a key to fit it. That's not the snag. The snag is why was a red golf ball taken when there were lots of white ones to choose from?"

"Aren't you rather taking it for granted that your idea's the right one?" growled Grayling.

"No!" retorted Lowe. "I'm trying to base a theory on the supposition that I'm right."

He lighted a cigarette and inhaled deeply.

"I'm going to get to the bottom of this business, Grayling," he went on. "You've lived in this neighbourhood for years. Tell me everything you know about Stanwood and the people who may have, even remotely, come in contact with him."

The colonel sighed resignedly. He usually slept during the afternoon, but he relinquished a habit of years with a good grace—and it must be admitted that he was interested. By tea-time Trevor Lowe knew as much about the people of the district as Grayling himself, and that was great deal for the colonel was notoriously inquisitive. After tea the dramatist announced his intention of going to London.

"I'll be back sometime tomorrow, I expect," he said, and took his departure, leaving Grayling's curiosity concerning this sudden decision unappeased.

He did not come back on the following day, and it was not until the Friday morning that the colonel heard anything more from him. A telegram arrived which caused him much thought.

"Returning seven-thirty tonight," it ran. "Invite following people to dinner. Got to the bottom of it."

Grayling looked at the four names and went to interview his housekeeper.

Trevor Lowe arrived a little before seven-thirty. He had driven down from town and was in the best of spirits.

"Give me a glass of sherry and don't ask questions," he said, when the colonel demanded to know what it was all about. "You'll know everything in good time. Are all those people coming?"

"Yes," growled Grayling. "And you'll have to make peace with my housekeeper. She thinks I've gone mad!"

By the time Lowe had washed the first of the guests had arrived in the person of Inspector Bream, and the dramatist found him sipping sherry in the colonel's small drawing room. The other three came almost together. Helen Morgan looked a little pale, but otherwise there was no sign of the trouble she was experiencing.

"I understand that it is at your request, Mr. Lowe, that Grayling has invited us here this evening," said Dr. Faversham, as he shook hands.

Lowe nodded, and Milton looked at him curiously.

"Is it permissible to ask why?" he inquired with a smile.

"You will see if you wait," replied the dramatist, and at that moment dinner was announced. Throughout the meal Lowe kept up a string of anecdote and light conversation, and it was not until coffee had been served that he consented to appease the rising curiosity of the people round the table.

"I know you are all wondering why I asked Grayling to invite you here this evening," he began. "Well, the explanation is a simple one. I wanted to tell you the true story of Stanwood's murder."

Helen Morgan gave a little gasp, and Lowe looked round at the expectant faces.

"I may as well begin by saying that I never believed that Jack Claymore had anything to do with the crime," he went on. "There was one thing, in my opinion, that definitely pointed to this belief, and that was the finding of the red golf ball beside the body. I could not account for its presence, except by one supposition: that it had been put there by the real murderer to throw suspicion on Claymore. But there was an obstacle in the way of this theory. If this was what had been done, why had the red golf ball been chosen when a white one would have been so much more convincing?

"For a long time I puzzled over the solution to this, and then, considering all the circumstances, I hit on what I believed was the only plausible one. I will come to it later, I was determined to get to the truth of the matter, and it struck me that a great deal might be learned if more was known of Stanwood's past. I went up to London and had an interview with Detective Inspector Shadgold of Scotland Yard. On my suggestion he sent through to Inspector Bream and asked for a set of the dead man's finger-prints. When the special messenger brought them back we quickly learned whom Stanwood had been and why there was so much mystery surrounding his past.

"His real name had been Felton and he had served a sentence of seven years for blackmail. The date he had been released and the date when he first appeared in this neighbourhood corresponded almost exactly."

He took a sip of coffee and continued:

"This information was most helpful, for it suggested a possible motive for Stanwood's murder. A man who has blackmailed once will do so again. I remembered the thousand pounds in cash, with which he had opened his banking account, and the further five hundred, also in cash, paid in recently. Had he been blackmailing somebody in this district, and was this somebody responsible for his death? It seemed likely, and the next question was who?

"It occurred to me that Stanwood must have had some good reason for coming to live in a small village like Glen Hill, and that probably this reason was because, on coming out of prison, he had marked down a profitable victim to provide him with an income.

"Colonel Grayling, at my request, had given me short histories of the principal people in the neighbourhood. With the assistance of Inspector Shadgold I checked up on these, and discovered there was one person whose past contained an episode that might have been profitable to a blackmailer—if he held proof of what had only been a rumour. I came back to Glen Hill this morning and saw Inspector Bream."

Grayling grunted and Lowe smiled.

"I laid before him everything I had discovered, and offered my theory for the presence of the red golf ball.

"He was interested, and arranged that I should have an interview with Claymore. After a great deal of trouble I persuaded Claymore to tell me the reason for his quarrel with Stanwood, and it confirmed the fact that the man was a habitual blackmailer.

"He had fallen in love with Miss Morgan," Lowe glanced apologetically at the girl, "and having discovered a youthful escapade of Claymore's—I'm not going to say what it was, it has nothing to do with the murder—he threatened to make it public unless Claymore broke off his engagement and gave Stanwood a free hand. Claymore refused to give this as a reason for his quarrel thinking it would only tell against him."

"But who killed Stanwood?" asked Milton impatiently, as the dramatist paused.

"I'm coming to that now," said Lowe quietly. "The person who killed Stanwood is the person whom Stanwood had it in his power to hang, and the person from whom he had obtained one thousand five hundred pounds—the person who, in the concealment of that clump of trees, was a witness between the quarrel of Claymore and Stanwood, and decided to take advantage of it and rid himself of that menace to his safety—the person who struck Stanwood a heavy blow behind the ear with his walking stick, and to make doubly sure that suspicion should fall on Claymore, went to the clubhouse, unlocked Claymore's locker with one of his own keys—the lock is so simple that almost any key will open it—and taking the red golf ball went back and put it beside the body. And that was the great mistake. If he had taken a white ball instead of a red one…"

"Why didn't he?" demanded Grayling.

"He thought he had taken a white ball."

"But—I don't understand…" Helen Morgan's voice was puzzled.

"He couldn't tell the difference," emphasised the dramatist. "White and red looked the same to him. He was colour blind!"

There was a gasp from Grayling.

"Begad!" he breathed. "Then it was…"

"Dr. Faversham," snapped Trevor Lowe, and the jovial-faced doctor, grey-white, sprang to his feet. "He had a practice in the Midlands—where Stanwood came from—and one of his patients died, after leaving him all her money. There were rumours but no proof… Stop him!"

Faversham's hand had gone to his mouth.

Bream sprang forward, but he was too late! Stanwood's murderer was dead before his sagging body reached the floor.

THE BOAT RACE MURDER

David Winser

David Michael de Reuda Winser was born in Plymouth in 1915. His mother died in childbirth, while his father, a submarine commander, was at sea, so he was raised by his grandparents. He was educated at Winchester College, where he showed skill as a marksman as well as becoming a capable oarsman. He earned a scholarship to Corpus Christi College, Oxford, and rowed in the Blue boat in 1935 and the following two years. Quite apart from his sporting prowess, he was a fine poet, and in 1936 his poem "Rain" won the prestigious Newdigate Prize; an earlier winner had been Oscar Wilde, while many years later the prize would go to P. M. Hubbard, who was to become a notable writer of crime and thriller fiction.

Winser studied medicine at Yale University before returning to England to become a doctor. He published five novels, as well as this short story, which benefits from his first-hand experience of rowing in the Boat Race, and was included in Ellery Queen's anthology *Sporting Blood* in 1942. During the war he served as a medical officer, and was awarded the Military Cross. In the Battle of Walcheren in the Netherlands in 1944, he was killed by a mortar bomb while tending to a wounded colleague. He was only twenty-nine years old.

FOR THE THREE WEEKS BEFORE THE BOAT RACE THE OXFORD crew generally lives at Ranelagh. This costs quite a penny, though it is conveniently close to the boat houses, but the question of money doesn't much worry the rowing authorities. The reason for this is that rowing, like every other Oxford sport, is more or less entirely supported by the gate receipts of the Rugger club. So there we lived, in Edwardian comfort, and played croquet on the immaculate croquet lawns in the special croquet goloshes they give you and admired the birds and the ruins. They also fed us remarkably well considering we were in training.

All kinds of things occurred. There was one peacock, an amorous bird, which had a crush on the president, who rowed two. It used to come and display its tail in front of him and wait for him to submit. He never did, though.

But at Ranelagh, in spite of the way they'd sometimes put our names in the papers, we led a completely reporterless life, if that's the word I want. We didn't like the sort of stories that got told about rowing, such as the one which held that the crew that won after Barnes all died in the next five years (they're actually mostly alive still). So what with the O.U.B.C. and Ranelagh, and the fact that all the rowing reporters were friends of ours and of rowing, you didn't hear much. But, now, I think this story needs telling. In fact I more or less have to tell it.

★

You must try and picture a fizz night at Ranelagh. Someone, the coach or some other old Blue, has suddenly produced a dozen bottles of champagne and the coach has said that the crew's been going so well that it damn well deserves the filthy stuff. Actually, as he and everyone else knows, the main purpose of fizz is to stop the crew getting stale. But the tradition's always the same: it's supposed to be a reward for hard work. On this particular night the coach and an old Blue between them had produced *two* dozen bottles, because the second crew, the *Isis*, was coming over to dinner from Richmond.

Perhaps you can imagine the rest already. Solly Johnstone leaning back in his chair and laughing so hard at his own jokes that everyone else is laughing. Once I saw the president try to stop him making jokes because it was hurting him terribly to go on laughing so hard, but Solly didn't stop. And then, after dinner, two crews milling about in the big games room, the president taking cine-camera pictures with an enormous searchlight affair, the *Isis* crew taking on the varsity at billiards and ping-pong, Ronnie playing the piano and someone singing, the gramophone playing "The Donkey Serenade," Solly still making his incredible jokes, and somewhere over in the corner Melvin Green talking about rowing to Dr. Jeffreys, who coached the crew for the first part of training. The noise, and the general tohu-bohu, as Solly said, were both considerable.

I was watching this with a benevolent and yet slightly mildewed eye, because I had a feeling that I didn't deserve to be quite as cheerful as the rest of them. I was the cox, and furthermore I had had some very bad news. And again, when people like Jon Peters and Harry Whitteredge were slightly out of control, their fourteen stone made walking dangerous for coxes.

No one who saw them that night would have credited them with the dignity, the dignity which only their genius stopped short of ponderousness, with which they sent that boat along in the race. They looked about as dignified as a bull on skates. But I happened to know that they were going to get as bad a shock as I had, nearly as bad a shock as Jim Matthews. Jim Matthews was the stroke, and he was going to find himself out of the crew.

Now this may not sound especially serious. Jim Matthews never had the reputation of Brocklebank, or Lawrie, or Sutcliffe, or Bryan Hodgson. You didn't read in the papers that he was going to pull off the race all by himself. And in a way he wasn't. But I heard a conversation once between Jon and Harry, who were wonderful oarsmen in their day, and it was rather significant.

"That fellow Matthews," Jon said, or words to this effect, "doesn't look much, and he doesn't do much, and doesn't talk much. Also I don't like him particularly. But I'm damned if there's anyone else who gives me time to come forward."

"The trouble with us, Jon," Harry said, "is that we need such a hell of a lot of time."

"Yes, but Jim gives it to us. If we have Jim we'll win this race."

"Don't you think we will anyway?"

"Not without Jim."

"I know. Nor do I."

I don't suppose it matters much to you who wins the Boat Race. But, for the purposes of this story, to get the record straight, you have to realise that ten or eleven men think of practically nothing else, for twelve whole weeks of training, than getting

into the crew and seeing Oxford win. It becomes an obsession, a
continual idea at the back of one's mind. Jon had a baby car, and
once, when the crew was travelling by car from Oxford to Henley,
Jon and Harry took an omen. If they could pass and *touch with
their hands* every other O.U.B.C. car, Oxford would win the Boat
Race. So, at considerable risk to their lives (and Oxford wouldn't
have won without them), they touched every car. It was that sort
of thing every day. And now the coaches were going to drop Jim
Matthews, and those two wouldn't have time to come forward.
When that happened all their dignity and poise over the stretcher
went with the wind and they became more of a hindrance than
a help, charging backwards and forwards in the boat. So, not for
you or Oxford perhaps, but for those men who rowed in the crew,
Jim's going was a real tragedy. Everyone knew that once they'd put
in Davis, the dark-haired short-built *Isis* stroke, they'd leave him
there. And Davis, who had plenty of guts and rowed as hard as he
could, was hopelessly short in the water. There'd be hell to pay.

As for Jim, I knew a bit how he felt. I'd been in and out of the
crew myself, because the *Isis* cox was at least as good as I was and
knew the river even better. I wouldn't have been a bit surprised at
anything Jim had done. But, as soon as the coaches told him, he'd
frozen up completely. He hadn't said anything to them, which was
stupid of him. They hadn't wanted to make the change; his own
carelessness, which we knew was designed to save himself for one
of those terrific races he'd row, looked sloppy. The coaches were
worried, and the rowing correspondents started saying Oxford
was stale. Hence the fizz, and hence Davis.

And all Jim said, in front of the coaches, he said to me. "Come
on, Peter," he said. "I'm going to scare the Alacrity bird."

So Jon and I took him back to Ranelagh in my small M.G. and dropped him near the Alacrity bird's usual haunt; the bird was a crane which flew when you chased it. Then I let Jon drive the car into its garage. He wasn't allowed his car or his pipe during the last six weeks of training, and he needed a few luxuries like that. He joined me again before I reached the main house and we walked in together.

"Your petrol's low," he said. He didn't know about Jim yet but he sounded depressed, as if he knew something of the sort was afoot.

"There's enough for tomorrow, isn't there?"

"Provided the gauge is right, you've got half a gallon."

"That's all right then. Don't worry about the outing, Jon. Fizz night tonight."

Somewhere outside in the garden poor Jim Matthews was walking. I think the Alacrity bird was only an excuse because he wanted to be by himself. I was sorry for Jim. He'd have one more outing, with Davis rowing two, and then he'd go.

Next day, as might be expected after a fizz night, everything went wrong. To begin with I left it too late to get down to the river in time, thinking I'd take my car. I was the only one of the crew allowed to go into shops, because the others were thought to be especially susceptible to flu at that stage of training, so I used to take my car with me and go out shopping after the outing. But that morning I found there wasn't any petrol after all, so I had to run all the way across the polo grounds. They were just getting the boat out when I came, with a little boy doing my work. I pushed him aside without saying thanks, and behaved in a thoroughly bad manner. And then Davis, who was pardonably nervous, paddled on hard when I told him to touch her gently and the boat just missed drifting on to a buoy. Jim Matthews, like everyone else, sat there doing nothing, while I swore. The only incident of interest was that Jon and Harry swore back, being apparently by now aware that Davis was coming up to stroke. Davis rowed too fast. They got tired, and the coaches would accuse them of bucketing, and the boat would start stopping. I didn't blame them for swearing. I swore too.

The coach picked up his megaphone. "Ready, cox?" he asked. He didn't ask it out of kindness.

I said Yes.

"Paddle on down to the Eyot," he said. "Jim, make them work it up a bit once or twice."

Now the Eyot is a good fifteen minutes' paddle from the boat houses, and Jim, I suppose because it was his last time at stroke, took them along really hard. When he worked it up he worked it right up, nearly to forty, and he kept it there for a full minute. Then, not so long afterwards, he did it again. And to end up with he put in a terrific burst of rowing. All the time he was steady, swinging them easily along. I could see the great green holes in the water Jon and Harry made. The boat travelled. I wondered whether the coaches were going to change their mind. No one will know that now, not even Jim. I'd noticed Davis' blade wasn't coming through very well at the end of the paddle, but I hadn't thought anything else about it. When we'd easied he leant forward over his oar and stayed there, but again this wasn't very unusual; it had been about as hard work as a paddle like that can be. After a rest I gave the order to come half forward, because we were going to do a rowing start. But Davis didn't move.

"Half forward, two!" I said, still angrily.

Then apparently bow leant forward and touched him, because his body slumped forward, slid over the gunnel, and went into the water. I don't know when he died, but he was dead when the launch reached him. Luckily Dr. Jeffreys was on the spot, waiting to see what difference the change would make. Well, he'd seen.

If I'd ever doubted whether the coaches deserved their positions, and during training you doubt most things, I was all wrong. They took the launch on up to the London University boat house, where no one ever went during the mornings, got Solly's car round there, put Davis' body in it, brought it to Ranelagh without either the crew or the press or the secretary of Ranelagh seeing, and before lunch they'd got the whole crew together, and Dr. Joe Jeffreys was talking to them. One of the chief duties of the coaches was to keep the crew feeling happy.

"Well," said Joe, "you all saw what happened. Poor young Davis died of heart failure. I know how you feel, and you know how I feel. But there's one thing you ought to understand clearly. The reason he died was that his heart was dicky before he started. I never tested it, but I know it was, because your heart doesn't fail at the end of a paddle unless it *is* dicky. And I know all your hearts are damn sound, because I *did* test them. Just to make sure I'm going to test them again today."

And he did, and he was quite right; there was nothing wrong with any of the toughs.

But in the middle, when Jon had just gone out and Solly, Joe and I were alone in the room, Joe suddenly stopped.

"I *did* test Davis' heart," he said.

*

Well, Solly made a rather typical crack about the value of tests, but apparently this was a pretty sound test. Anyway we went and rang up the police.

"That kid was murdered," said Joe. I suppose Solly thought he was just humouring him. Another of the duties of coaches is to keep the other coaches feeling happy. Those last weeks of training are the devil all round.

It was rather typical of the way the Boat Race gets a grip on people that the crew went out that afternoon. Solly insisted he was only doing it to allay any suspicion about Davis in the minds of the press. But anyway the boat went out, and, with Jim stroking beautifully, they rowed the best two minutes they'd ever done, clearing their wash by yards at thirty-six. When Jim was there, that was as good a crew as any.

The police were around when we got back, but that didn't bother us much. You see, we all knew each other pretty well; you don't have murderers rowing with you. Murderers are professionals, probably, as they've worked with their hands. Anyway, you don't.

Well, they found out what had killed Davis. We'll call it diphenyl tyrosine; Jim and I knew what its real name was because we happened to be medical students. Joe Jeffreys knew it too, of course. The odd thing about it is that it's a component of quite a common patent medicine. That's all right, because it only quickens up your heart for a day or so; but when you start with a quickened heart and then row hard in a Boat Race crew your heart gets very quick indeed, so quick that it doesn't really function adequately. It starts to jump about a bit, and then it starts to fibrillate, to quiver all over in rather a useless way. Then, if it's the ventricle fibrillating, you die. Davis had plenty of guts; he went on just as long as his heart did. He had the guts of a good stroke, but he wasn't Jim Matthews. I was sorry for Davis, but, for the crew's sake, I was glad Jim was safe. The funny thing was that whoever killed Davis must have known that he'd got guts.

Now they started in on a long investigation of the crew's movements during the day before. It had to be the day before because they'd got a very interesting bit of evidence. A man had come into a chemist's in Putney and he'd asked for this patent medicine, as no doubt men did every day. He'd worn a mackintosh and an old hat.

But underneath the mackintosh the chemist had noticed he was wearing those queer white blanket trousers the crews wear out of the boat.

The policeman who was doing the detective work then had two very frustrating conversations which he described to us with fair relish.

He'd asked the chemist if the purchaser in the white trousers had been a big man. The chemist said, Yes.

"Bigger than me?"

"Well, maybe."

"Sure he wasn't fairly small?"

The chemist considered. "Well," he said, "you might call him small."

"Could you draw a line against the wall showing just his height?"

The chemist stepped forward confidently, stopped, tried to think, and then said:—

"No. Not exactly, somehow."

"What colour was his hair then?"

"Oh," said the chemist, "if I noticed the colour of all my customers' hair I'd be in a pretty state." He became a little irritable. "All I know is," he said, "he had white trousers on."

The other conversation was the sequel to the discovery that Jon and I brought my car back when the rest of the crew came in. They wanted to find if anyone went *out* of Ranelagh in a car like mine.

The detective people went to the porters at the two gates. "Did you see a small black sports car go out of the grounds?" they asked. "After 5.30."

Those were the days when Hornets and M.G.'s were as common as sneezing. One porter said he'd seen four, colour unnoticed; the other had seen seven, three of them black or dark-brown.

"Well," said the fellows, "did you see any coming back again?"

"Those seven," said the porter, who wasn't colour-blind, "was going both ways." He wasn't shaken from this peculiar belief. In short they didn't get any change out of porters or chemists. Someone in the crew *did* buy this patent medicine and someone *could* have gone out in my car. They never found the bottle, of course. There were hundreds of ways to get rid of it—you might put it down the lavatory and pull the plug, for instance. It was one of those small bottles. You'll be guessing its name in a minute but, luckily, you'll guess wrong.

Then, also in front of me, someone realised that if the chemist had been at all an efficient man he'd have made the fellow in the mackintosh sign for the medicine, simply because, technically, it was poison if you had a whole bottleful. So one of them went off to find out if the chemist was as efficient as all that, and the other started to find out where we'd all been.

Now the curious thing about all this investigation was that it had taken a very short time. It was still only the day after the murder. As soon as they knew it was murder they'd started thinking about heart drugs, the sort you might mix up in someone's milk as they went to bed, or drop in a glass of fizz; so they thought of diphenyl tyrosine and, sure enough, there it was when they did an autopsy on Davis. No one knew when he'd taken it; but they'd decided it must have been in his fizz. Personally the mechanism of this seems pretty difficult to me, but that's what they said. I suppose they'd had experience of that sort of thing. Anyway he'd certainly not have been looking out for it; very few people expect to be poisoned in the middle of a fizz night. They seemed so certain about it all, quite rightly as it turned out, that we didn't like to doubt their word. So we were all terribly efficient when it came to describing our movements.

They only wanted to know about the time between 5.30, when we all came back from the outing, and six. The chemist said the purchaser in the white trousers had come in at about 5.45, and the reason he knew was that it was a quarter of an hour before he closed at six, and the fact that no other customers had come in afterwards had made him think he'd been a sap not to close quarter of an hour earlier. This looked pretty good evidence to me, and the detective fellows liked it a lot.

Most of the crew had been together from 5.30 till six, all in the big games room. Jon, Jim and I hadn't been there at first. We knew where Jim was, outside with the Alacrity bird. The three of us got back from the outing a little later than the rest of them because of that talk with the coaches, and Jim had come into the house again at ten to six. We were sure of that, or very nearly sure, because by six o'clock, when the news came on, he'd played a complete game of ping-pong with Ronnie. That left quarter of an hour of Jim unaccounted for.

Jon said he'd been in his room all the time till six, when he came down for the news.

I said I hadn't been in the games room at all. First of all I'd done the crossword and then I'd been signing autographs for the crew.

"How do you mean 'for the crew'?" one of them asked.

I told him that the rest of them could never be bothered to sign autograph books. All the coxes after Peter Bryan's time had had to forge the signatures of everyone else; it was one of their duties. So long as you had two or three different nibs and patience you could make a very good job of it indeed.

"Oh," they said, laughing. "That's dangerous."

I said not so dangerous as they thought.

Well, one of the detectives walked to the chemist's and back. It took twenty-five minutes, walking hard. That meant that Jon or I could have gone on our feet or by car, while Jim could only have gone by car. On his way there he met the detective who'd been to see if anyone signed. Someone had, all right, but it was probably not his name. *A. G. Gallimage*, someone had written.

They went to work on this clue, rather ingeniously. The detective said he wanted a genuine autograph, and went round to each member of the crew with some sentimental story about his daughter being ill in bed and only needing a genuine autograph to recover. It's wonderful what rowing men will swallow. Jim was the only one who made a fuss. He was playing ping-pong again and he said, as rudely as usual:—

"The cox can forge mine."

The detective said he knew that. His daughter wanted a real one. After that Jim signed, a bit grudgingly; and went on playing.

He signed in a writing very like Gallimage's.

This more or less meant Jim or me. I forgot to say that they'd checked up on Jon and found that a maid had seen him in his room between 5.40 and 5.50. She didn't say so, but I expect he went up there for a smoke. He thought it improved *his* rowing but nobody else's. So Jim and I were left, and the signature did very well for either of us. It was typical of the effect of the Boat Race atmosphere that the detectives came and asked Solly if they could arrest both of us. I know they did because I was in the room at the time.

"Would you mind if we arrested Matthews and your cox?" they asked.

"Yes, old chap," said Solly. "We can get another cox, but we haven't any more strokes. Leave them both if you can."

The detective looked serious. "Evidence is bad," he said.

Solly leant back in his chair. "Trot it out," he said. "The cox and I will spoil it. The cox does the crossword in half an hour every morning."

"Twenty-five minutes with Jon," I said. "That was two days ago."

Then I shut up.

The detective trotted out the evidence. At the end I pointed out a flaw. It wasn't half as hard as the *Times* crossword, let alone Torquemada.

"But if Jim went," I said, "he must have used the car."

"Yes."

"But there wasn't any petrol in the car."

"Sure?"

"Quite sure. You see Jon and I both saw the gauge reading half a gallon. Only next morning it still read half a gallon and there wasn't any petrol in her. It foxed me completely."

"It certainly did," said Solly.

"You realise what you're saying?" asked the detective.

"No," I said.

"If Jim Matthews didn't take your car, then someone walked to the shop. That means you walked, because Jim didn't have time."

"He could have run," I said.

"Ah," said the detective. "That's where you're wrong. *He wasn't out of breath.*"

I suppose I looked pretty shaken by this bit of information, because Solly patted me on the back in a very kindly way. "That's all right," he said. "It'll turn out not to have been either of you. Glad you remembered about the petrol."

I was a good deal comforted by this. "Well," I said, "that fellow who coxes the *Isis* is a damn fine cox, and I've got one Blue already. I know we'll win. But I wish they had wireless sets in prison."

"We'll try and let you know all about it," said the detective. This seemed to me a pretty decent way to speak to a murderer.

That isn't all, and it won't be all either. Oxford won, of course, with one of Jim's beautifully timed spurts. He couldn't have made it without Harry and Jon and they couldn't have made it if he hadn't been there, swinging them along so steadily and easily that you'd have thought they were paddling. That is, until you saw how the boat moved.

Furthermore those detectives forgot one thing. Perhaps you saw what it was. Of course my petrol gauge is a bit odd; they can easily test it and show *that it sticks on the half-gallon mark*.

I'm sorry for Jim. I wish it hadn't happened. To be honest, I don't see any other way we could have won; but even Jim, who was a casual ambitious fellow, didn't mean to pay that price for it. He thought Davis would feel ill and give up in the middle of the paddle. But Davis went on rowing till his heart stopped.

THE SWIMMING GALA

Gladys Mitchell

Gladys Mitchell's enduring popularity as a detective writer is evidenced by a comprehensive tribute website, *The Stone House*, www.gladysmitchell.com, established by Jason Half and containing interesting articles as well as valuable bibliographic material. In an essay about the appeal of detective fiction, Mitchell argued that: "Modern literature is full of plays and films that end nowhere; novels and short stories that leave the playgoer or the reader suspended in mid-air, forced either to impotent irritation or else to having to invent their own outcome. Detective stories, by their very nature, cannot cheat in this way. Their writers must tidy up the loose ends; must supply a logical solution to the problem they have posed; must also, to hold the reader's attention, combine the primitive lust and energy of the hunter with the cold logic of the scholarly mind."

Mitchell (1901–83) was a school teacher by profession who had a lifelong love of sports, notably athletics and swimming; she taught games and coached pupils in hurdling. Her interest in athletics led to her becoming a member of the British Olympics Association and is from time to time reflected in her fiction, notably in the third case of her series detective Mrs. Bradley, *The Longer Bodies* (1930) and *Adders on the Heath* (1963). This little story originally appeared in the *Evening Standard* on 25 July 1952, and was more recently collected in *Sleuth's Academy*, edited by Nicholas Fuller.

W HEN IT ALL CAME OUT AT THE TRIAL THERE WAS NO
doubt the murder had been planned.

Mind you, it turned out that tongues had begun to wag as
soon as young Smith and his sister had been appointed as deputy
superintendents at our Public Baths, especially as old Ford, the
Baths Superintendent, had had no say in the appointments. The
girl was to take over the ticket office—adults ninepence, children
under fifteen fourpence—and the young chap acted as instructor,
mopper-up, and assistant chucker-out of louts.

Both were good swimmers, especially the lad, and he made no
bones about telling the Baths Committee that he was only going
to stay until he had mastered the job. He wanted a Baths of his
own. This was none too satisfactory from our point of view, but
you've got to take what you can get in these days, especially as the
pay isn't any too good, and the brother and sister seemed a well-
spoken young couple and the lad's qualifications were first class.

The couple had been appointed in April, and in the following
September the Swimming Club held its annual gala. The men
and women members held their club practices on different days
of the week, but joined forces for the gala and finished up with a
mixed team race—two men and two girls on each side. This was
the high spot of the evening.

Well, the first I knew of anything being wrong was when my
chauffeur came into the Mayor's Parlour and held out an envelope.

"Found on the floor of the interior compartment of the mayoral car, Mr. Mayor, sir, when I was cleaning her for tonight's do."

Tonight's do happened to be a parent-teacher gathering at the local grammar school, and I was not looking forward to it much. There is something about those BA and MA hoods and gowns that makes me feel I left school at the age of twelve unable to read and write. Besides, the chairman of the parents happened to be the man who thought he ought to have been mayor that year.

Putting aside these thoughts, I opened the envelope.

"You ought to keep your eyes and ears open," the letter read, "but I suppose you can't swim. Don't you know what's going on under your silly old beak? I suppose you take your something bath at home, if any."

It was unsigned, of course. I'm not proud. I showed it to the chauffeur. After all, we had gone to the same primary school.

"What do you make of it?" I asked. To my surprise he looked rather uncomfortable.

"There's been rumours, Mr. Mayor, sir."

"What about? Me?"

"No, about the public baths, sir. Bit of a scandal, it seems."

"There's always some rumour about the public baths, and had been ever since we allowed mixed bathing."

"That's not it this time, Mr. Mayor, sir. This isn't general, it's particular."

"Well, get on with it. What do you know?" The mayor's chauffeur, hanging about for hours and hours during every municipal function is the repository of most of the gossip that's going, as well I knew. "Come on, Henry, let's have it."

"Well, Ted, as man to man I don't exactly know anything, but I can tell you what's going about. There's a sort of fussation about young Bob Smith at the baths."

"But why? The attendance has bucked up no end since he came, and he's taken over the coaching for the swimming club and made a good job of it, so I hear. Doesn't he behave himself with the ladies?"

"It's with one particular lady, Ted—his sister. It's said she's not his sister and she isn't his wife, neither."

"Oh, good heavens. Even if the fellow's a Mormon it doesn't make any difference to his job. It's the usual old pussies making the usual mischief."

"Some councillors didn't ought to have wives," said Henry. "But, all the same, you know, Ted, there's no smoke without fire."

"Now what do you mean by that?"

"I heard it put about as the chairman of the Baths Committee would like to get rid of poor old Ford and give the job to Smith and his sister so as to keep them here."

Well, the Splash Night came, and Henry drove me and the mayoress to the baths. There was the usual bouquet for her and the usual interval speech for me so that the swimmers could get a breather while I was making it, and then came the high spots—the diving competition and the mixed team race.

It was during the latter, when every eye was fixed on the swimmers and you couldn't hear a thing except the din, that a shot was fired and the chairman of the Baths Committee fell dead into the water.

Perhaps I ought to explain the geography of our swimming bath. You enter the building by turnstile and then there are two ways in. Either you charge in at the first doors and find a dressing box—that's the procedure if you've come for a swim—or else you walk along a corridor behind the men's side of the bath and come to the slipper baths, where you get the soap and water caper if you haven't a bathroom at home.

You also come to some swing doors which open on to the deep end of the swimming bath almost opposite the diving boards.

Through this door the murderer had come, and had picked off the victim, who was standing on the opposite side of the bath helping to judge the team race. A child of ten couldn't have missed.

The only clue, if you can call it that, was the Baths Superintendent's overcoat, hat and gloves which the police found, together with the revolver, chucked down in the passage outside, which at that time must have been empty, for everyone was watching the race.

There were no prints on the gun, of course, because of the gloves, and the whole thing turned on a question of motive. Two people only were involved, it seemed, and their motives were completely dissimilar. It appeared for a time as though the only person who could have given a casting vote was the man lying dead in the parish mortuary, to which he had been taken after young Smith had dived in and fished him out of the water.

What it came to was this: either old Ford, the baths superintendent, had shot to save his job, or young Smith had fired to try to keep himself out of prison, for the couple turned out not only to be married but to be bigamously married. But nobody seemed to know whether the dead councillor had known this.

However, the police arrested Smith on the bigamy charge and then went on investigating the murder. I went into a huddle with them, with the Baths Committee and with the full Council, but nobody seemed able to help.

The chief trouble was that nobody had been able to give a description of the murderer owing to the interest that was taken in the team race, and the overcoat and hat were not in themselves enough to incriminate Ford, as his house adjoined the Baths and had been left unlocked as it always was unless he went into the town.

To cut the cackle, young Smith was hanged. The police were able to prove that nobody left the Baths directly after the shot was fired, and that nobody except the officials had used the corridor which was reserved on gala nights for them and for some of the swimmers who were using the slipper baths as dressing-rooms, and these swimmers and officials were all on the Bath level at the time.

Smith had put on the overcoat over bathing trunks, done the deed, flung off coat, hat and gloves and tossed down the revolver.

Then all he had to do was to dash to the rescue of the body just to emphasise the way he was dressed or undressed, if you prefer it. When the police charged him he confessed, and admitted that the dead councillor had known of the bigamous marriage and was threatening to expose him.

Who worked it all out and presented his conclusions to the police? I did.

THE CASE OF THE MAN
IN THE SQUARED CIRCLE

Ernest Dudley

When Ernest Dudley died at the ripe old age of 97, he was described in Marcelle Bernstein's obituary in the *Guardian* as "an actor, a novelist with three books filmed, a radio and television scriptwriter and presenter, a journalist, a screenwriter, playwright, jazz critic, dancer, songwriter, artist and one of the world's oldest marathon runners". Dudley claimed that marathon running helped him to combat depression and he was still running around Regent's Park in the year before his death. Dudley (1908–2006) was born Vivian Ernest Coltman Allen in Wolverhampton and gravitated towards journalism once a career in acting failed to bring him stardom. His interest in boxing, evident in this story, led him to cover the sport for the *People*. In the late 1940s he started to write crime fiction, and he became a founder member of the Crime Writers' Association in 1953.

His most popular character was Doctor Morelle, who first appeared in the radio show *Monday Night at Eight*. Morelle was, according to Bernstein, "conceived in a Bristol cellar during an air raid… [and] based on film actor and director Erich von Stroheim, whom Ernest had met briefly in Paris in the 1930s. With his secretary Miss Frayle—a part written specially for [Dudley's wife] Jane—Dr. Morelle featured in novels, short stories, a film—*The Case of the Missing Heiress* (1949), a play and three radio serials". This story is taken from *Meet Doctor Morelle Again* (1944), the second collection of chapters from the doctor's case-book.

DESPITE HER TIMOROUS AND SENSITIVE TEMPERAMENT, Miss Frayle, on the whole, enjoyed working for Doctor Morelle. At least her duties had the advantage of constant change and variety, and they took her into strange and fascinating places. Through the Doctor she had met many interesting people. At the same time there was a great deal of routine matter to which she had to attend, and she could evince very little interest in these mundane tasks. It afforded her infinitesimal solace that sociology and psychological research was, to the Doctor, more interesting than the most thrilling encounters with murderers, malcontents, blackmailers, and poison-pen writers—that sordid gentry of avarice-ridden social misfits who flit like murky shadows across the life of anyone engaged in crime detection.

She realised full well that the mysteries of the subconscious, to Doctor Morelle, were more breath-takingly exciting than the most complex real-life "who-done-it." That the most glamorous and colourful crook interested him less than the retrogressive stages of dementia praecox. By bitter experience she knew that when the Doctor was engaged in such theoretical research, his preoccupation with the subject would enable him to work untiringly until the small hours of the morning, completely unmindful of the fact that she did not share such interest to that extent. Such things were beyond her mental powers, and when she made foolish mistakes in her note-taking, he would become loquaciously condemnatory of her limited intelligence.

It was with a heart-felt groan, therefore, that Miss Frayle greeted Doctor Morelle's announcement one morning that they would be devoting the next two weeks to intensive research activities.

She tried to hide her boredom by assuming what she hoped was a "poker-face." This did not, however, escape his lynx-like observation.

"Your features possess the fixity of expression of the manic depressive," he snapped. "Am I to assume you do not relish the prospect of our research work?"

"Oh, I dare say it'll be a nice change," she said absently, and resigned herself to days of searching for references in thick, verbose volumes; and the inscribing of the Doctor's endless notes. Actually she need have had no fears of *ennui*, because the research work was fated to be, for Miss Frayle, the most interesting sequence of duties she had ever undertaken.

"I am writing a thesis," the Doctor continued, pacing the study with long raking strides, "and the title is: 'Hedonism and the Masses'."[*]

Miss Frayle looked up brightly. "Hedonism? Let me see, Doctor—isn't that the pursuit of pleasure?"

"Correct, Miss Frayle." He gave a half-derisive smile. "A subject, I presume, well within your limited sphere! This is not a task which I personally relish, however. Nevertheless, the scientist must, for the sake of humanity, forget his own squeamishness. I regret deeply that our research work will take us into numerous sordid places—"

"What places, for instance?"

[*] Subsequently read to the New World Association, London, and reported in *The Times*, but not yet published.

"To the kinema, no doubt—" He gave the word its abstruse Greek pronunciation. "To the theatre, and even to the subterranean establishments where moronic people congregate nocturnally."

"You mean night clubs?" and it was all she could do to prevent herself clapping her hands in excitement. "Now I'll be able to wear my evening frock."

Surprisingly he inclined his head in agreement.

"Throughout these researches it will indubitably assist me if you display your normal reactions towards these various entertainments," he said weightily. "Since you, my *dear* Miss Frayle, are typical of the more cretinous section of the public, your reactions will, I imagine, be representative of the masses. For once, therefore, I shall strive *not* to curb your indiscriminate enthusiasms."

"It's going to be thrilling," she enthused. "It'll take me out of myself."

Her observation prompted him to write one word on his notepad: *"Escapism."*

The Doctor's coldly analytical and often sweepingly denunciatory criticisms of entertainments which are meant to be accepted only superficially afforded considerable amusement to Miss Frayle in the next few days. She had accompanied him to a mammoth Hollywood film, packed with drama, romance, song, and technicolour. On their return the Doctor had dictated:

"The kinema is patently the refuge of the physically lonely and the spiritually lost. The relaxation which the masses apparently attain by sitting in a darkened interior would indicate that they are seeking subconsciously to return to the pre-natal state."

After he had accompanied Miss Frayle to the first night of a society comedy, he dictated:

"The appeal of the theatre would appear to be purely exhibitionistic—both on the part of the players, who cavort and display themselves in a hysterically inspired manner—and on the part of the audience who draw attention to themselves by arriving tardily for the performance, and who preen themselves in a vulgar finery during the intermissions when the illuminations are increased apparently with the sole object that the patrons may exhibit themselves with greater abandon in the confidence that they can be observed."

Of night clubs and people who sleep during the day and play at night, he observed sententiously:

"Garish establishments exist where neurotic persons may set the wheels of evolution turning backwards. These people perform licentious gyrations to cacophonies which have primeval rhythm. Such people, no doubt, through childhood traumas, have cause to fear the world of daylight. Psychologically they are retrograding to the Dark Age."

Indeed, when the *maître* of an expensive night club had obsequiously bowed Doctor Morelle and Miss Frayle to a table on the edge of the narrow dance floor, Miss Frayle could scarcely believe she was not dreaming. While the Doctor toyed distastefully with a shrivelled Lobster Neuborg, she observed him closely. With rude directness he was watching one group of merry-makers after another, as though he was seeking to read their thoughts. Some solitary and peroxided females quite reasonably imagined his interest to be other than academic—and Miss Frayle shuddered as she saw girls ogling him shamelessly. A dance-hostess had even sidled up to their table quite brazenly and, at his request, the creature had actually joined them—though she had quickly left when she realised the Doctor was more interested in her subconscious maladjustments than her physical charms!

Next day, however, it was with regret that Miss Frayle heard the Doctor state that the research was almost concluded.

"To complete my thesis," he announced, flicking the ash off his Le Sphinx, "it only remains for us to visit a display of fisticuffs."

"Oh, a boxing match!" she translated.

"Precisely, my dear Miss Frayle." A thin smile quirked his lips. "I relish this task more than the others. Pugilism can be a manly art for the participants, though the appeal for the onlookers must, for the most part, be grossly sadistic or, in your language, Miss Frayle, the delight in the infliction of pain."

She reached for the telephone. "Would you like me to book ringside seats for some match?" she asked helpfully.

"That will not be necessary." He pulled an envelope from his wallet. "Fortuitously, an acquaintance of mine, Mr. William Royston, who is a coach at the Fencing Club which I attend, has procured me the means of admission to an arena by the name of Ringland. Mr. Royston appeared anxious for me to attend this display, since his young son is one of the leading participants."

As they set out to Ringland on the following Saturday night, Miss Frayle took a note-book and pencil, so that she could write down any notes which the Doctor would suggest as he observed different details. On the other evenings of the week (the Doctor had discovered) the great barn of a place was given over to popular dances, concerts, political meetings and so forth; Saturdays were the only days devoted to the science and noble art of professional pugilism.

Such apparently was the lure of the roped arena, so strong a hold did our modern gladiators have upon the hearts and pockets of the public, that on "fight night" all roads seemed to lead to the large, unhandsome building where programmes always promised action and thrills, and prices were cheap.

On Saturday night Ringland was sure to be jammed. Packed to suffocation with noisy, enthusiastic "fans," and a good time was had by all, with the possible exception—or so the Doctor deduced—of those performers in the ring unfortunate enough to catch a heavy beating from their opponents.

Though even they might be seen again in the same ring upon some subsequent occasion, gamely taking another mauling, or this time, perhaps, handing one out to the other fellow.

Of the thousands who packed the hall, Doctor Morelle was the only one who wasn't tensed eagerly for the fights. Through lowered eyelids he peered across the smoke-filled auditorium with less interest than if he were observing bacteria through a microscope. Occasionally he bent to one side or the other to eavesdrop on the conversation of others. This was purely in the interests of scientific research. The Doctor listened, analytically, to two evident sports fans who were talking enthusiastically on his right.

"Nothink like a nice clean scrap, there ain't," one of the men was saying. "Mind you, it's *boxin'* I wants to see. None o' these sluggin' heavyweights what moves around each other like a couple of elephants and ties theirselves up in clinches all the time."

The man next to him nodded heavily.

"I agree," he said. "Give me the quick and clever ones. Boys with science and skill."

"Like this one 'ere," the first man gestured with his pipe towards the ring, where in the corner nearest them two seconds were ministering to a young boxer.

One of the white-sweatered men was grizzle-haired, but this seemed to be the only evidence that he was past middle age, for he was slim and as active looking as the youngster he was attending and to whom he bore a strong resemblance.

"That person is William Royston," Doctor Morelle informed Miss Frayle. "The younger man will be his son. Rather an exceptionally finely developed youth, do you not agree?"

"He looks awfully strong," she nodded. She saw the young man smiling across to some friends. "He's good-looking, too. I hope he doesn't get hurt."

The Doctor again switched his attention from Miss Frayle's verbal commonplaces to his neighbours' more colourful comments.

"Yes, he's a smart kid, all right," one of them said. "A case of like father like son—though, of course, he's a long way off what the old man was in his prime."

"Only just twenty the boy is, y'know," the other was saying. "His dad's bringin' him along slow and easy-like. Got great 'opes in 'im, 'is dad 'as."

"He certainly has the makings of a champ," observed the other. "And he couldn't be in better hands."

"No more 'e couldn't, and that's a fact." The first man agreed. He glanced sharply at Doctor Morelle, and whispered loud enough for him to hear, "'Ere, I say oo's this nosey geezer 'oo keeps staring at us? Is 'e a friend o' yourn?"

The second man glanced at Doctor Morelle:

"Strewth, no bloomin' fear!"

Quickly the Doctor diverted his gaze across the ropes to the man in the sweater who was busily engaged in massaging the boy's legs.

The Doctor knew that it was the elder man's dream that one day his youngster would hold the middleweight title as he himself had once held it. Royston had often spoken about the boy to patrons of the Fencing Club. Carefully he had nursed the boy along, mindful of the disaster which overtakes many a promising young boxer through being matched with men for whom they are too inexperienced and raw.

Bill Royston wisely kept his boy back, picking each opponent for him with a shrewd eye as to his value as a "trial horse."

Thus for tonight's fight, Sonny Royston was matched against one "Iron" Kelly, a battle-scarred veteran possessed of little real boxing skill, but wily and cunning through the bitter experience of scores of fights, and full of all the cruder tricks of his trade.

Against such an antagonist, a young boxer, provided he knew enough to keep out of the way of the other's destructive but erratic punches, could learn much in ring generalship and ringcraft, and at the same time stand a good chance of scoring enough points to gain him the verdict.

The seconds were out and the boxers were limbering up in their corners. The referee gave them instructions; they touched gloves and the fight was on. It was uneventful enough for the first few rounds, though the fourth round was lively, and ended to roars of applause from the spectators whom young Royston had delighted with his skill and speed. "Iron" Kelly, on the other hand, having earned a number of cautions from the referee for holding and shady tactics generally, had received the crowd's heartily expressed disapprobation.

Sonny Royston had clearly shown he was a true chip off the old block by his cleverness and boxing ability. His attractive style, together with his fair hair and smiling blue eyes, as compared with the rushing, reckless methods of his heavy-featured opponent, had caught the imagination of the crowd.

He had been scoring repeatedly with a beautifully timed left and was ahead on points. Provided he continued to evade the other's vicious, but ill-aimed blows—and his foot-work had so far kept him out of danger—the fight was his.

Doctor Morelle again eavesdropped. He heard his neighbour saying:

"His style's very reminiscent of his father's. I remember when I saw the old chap fight the foreign chap—what's his name?—"

The man went off into a reminiscence of one of Bill Royston's famous fights.

Suddenly Doctor Morelle's attention was diverted by a man who rose from his seat by the ringside and with a smile at his blonde companion, made his way towards the exit.

"A singularly cretinous type—both the man and the woman companion," the Doctor diagnosed. "Typical of the unhealthy section of the parasitic community who watch sport and never participate."

He noted with distaste that the man was short and wasp-waisted, that his wide shoulders in his too slickly cut suit gave him a deformed appearance. Hatchet-faced and of a greyish pallor, the man pulled on a pearl-grey trilby, slanting it over one eye.

As the man swaggered past, Doctor Morelle noticed that two pink ticket counterfoils were stuck incongruously in the hat band. Although the weather was warm and the atmosphere in the Ringland was stifling, the man, strangely enough, was wearing gloves which were buttoned round his wrists.

The man next to Doctor Morelle said in awed tones: "That's Joe Girotti—one of the Girotti boys. A proper race-course crook!"

All this was singularly interesting to the Doctor. Already in his index-like mind he was formulating the meticulously worded notes which he would dictate to Miss Frayle on their return that evening.

He felt a tap on his shoulder and he looked up to see Detective-Inspector Hood of Scotland Yard smiling down at him in his homely way.

"So this is where the great Doctor seeks his recreation," the Inspector grinned widely. "I've heard about cabinet ministers bricklaying, and poets planting potatoes, and I guess you too—"

"My presence here is solely in the interest of sociological research," Doctor Morelle interjected with a cold smile.

The other winked at Miss Frayle. "That's what the vicar said when he was caught talking to a coupla girls in Piccadilly!" He shook the Doctor's hand warmly. "It's nice to see you again." He foraged in his pocket for his pipe, and drew out a slab of candy which he presented gallantly to Miss Frayle.

"Last time we met was at Telbury Halt, if you remember," he reminisced. "I was chasing a gang of house-breakers, and you and the Doctor were of invaluable assistance."

Doctor Morelle lit a Le Sphinx. "It was I who elucidated the mystery for you, was it not?" he remarked innocently, and he added with a smile: "Am I to assume that since you are wearing your cylindrical head-gear, sartorially known as a *bowler*, that you are here on official business?"

"I'm just keeping my eyes on the boys," the Inspector replied, sucking noisily at his acrid-smelling briar. "You get all sorts at a prize fight."

"Would you be particularly maintaining a watch upon one Mr. Joseph Girotti?"

"Well, I was," Hood admitted with a smile. "Seems I can't keep anything from you, Doctor! Girotti's a pick-pocket among other things. He's fly enough to wear gloves as an alibi whenever he spies any of the police. Nasty bit of work he is!"

He raised his bowler affably. "Hope to see you again; must get back to my seat before the next round starts. Enjoy yourselves!"

At that moment the bell rang for the fifth round. With a nod as his father gave him a last-minute word of counsel, young Royston came out of his corner to meet a devastating onslaught from "Iron" Kelly.

Leastways, the attack was intended to be devastating, but Sonny slipped away from the whirl of fists like a shadow, poking his left hand into the other's face with irritating frequency as he did so. Kelly paused for a moment, baffled, then with a ferocious scowl, he charged in again.

This time he slipped and fell upon one knee. With a cheery grin Royston moved forward and helped him to his feet, stepping back to give the man time to steady himself.

The sporting action brought a roar of approval from the fans. Kelly, however, seemed strongly to resent the friendly gesture, for he immediately rushed forward and swung a mighty right which caught the youngster well below the belt. There was a howl of rage from the crowd. "Foul! Dirty! Kick him out, ref!"

The referee seemed to have been unsighted, however, and the fight continued, Kelly doing his utmost to barge in close to the shaken youngster and administer a knock-out.

Crowding him hard against the ropes, he threw in punches from every angle and it looked as if only a miracle could save his victim from sinking beneath the storm. Pandemonium broke out in the hall. Doctor Morelle half stood in his seat so that he could watch with better advantage this astonishing display of mass hysteria—unique even in the case-book of Kraft-Ebbing.

Miss Frayle clung on to his arm, terrified free fights might break out among the spectators and she might lose the new hat she had bought for the occasion. Meanwhile the two dramatic white figures battled beneath the blazing arc lamps. Doctor Morelle observed poor Bill Royston, his face grey with anxiety, crying out to his son to fall into a clinch, and hang on. A section of the crowd found themselves echoing the trainer's frantic appeal, with electric suddenness—which the Doctor could only account for as a phenomenon of mass telepathy.

"Clinch, Sonny!" came the cries. "Clinch!"

But Sonny appeared unable to follow the advice that was now being offered to him from all sides. He lay across the ropes, his protective left shoulder dropped to expose his vulnerable jaw and his adversary drew back his right glove to administer the *coup de grace*.

A mammoth groan came from a hundred throats—and then with a sudden tautening of Sonny Royston's lithe body, the boy's left arm straightened out to smash with terrific force against the other's jaw which *he* had left exposed in his anxiety to deliver the finishing blow.

Kelly stood swaying for a second, his eyes glazing over, then dropped flat on his face.

The voice of the referee, as he began to count, was swamped by the thunder of applause and the ear-piercing whistles of delight which filled the building. The counting-out was, however, a pure formality; "Iron" Kelly never looked like moving inside ten minutes, let alone ten seconds.

Miss Frayle found herself joining wildly in the cheering. She caught the Doctor's mocking gaze, and blushed slightly.

"It would appear that you are quite appreciative of the pugilistic science," he observed calmly.

"I got carried away, Doctor," she smiled. "I'm glad the good-looking young man won. He deserved to."

"Indeed, yes. He certainly displayed more science than his adversary."

"I bet his father's proud of him."

"And justifiably so." The Doctor rose, and pushed through a throng of people. So magnetic and compelling was his personality, that they made room for him immediately.

"Wait for me, Doctor!" called Miss Frayle, fearing she would lose him in the crush.

"Hurry then!"

She caught up with him, and breathlessly tried to keep pace.

"Where are we going to?" she panted.

"To the dressing-room. Courtesy behoves us to congratulate the victor, and his worthy parent."

"Aren't we going to see the rest of the fights?" she queried eagerly. She had never believed that she would enjoy a boxing match so much.

"We may later."

They pushed down a corridor to a door, on which was chalked the name "Sonny Royston," and Doctor Morelle rapped sharply. He turned to Miss Frayle:

"It would be advisable for you to remain outside for the moment," he told her shortly.

He pushed inside the door, and was immediately greeted by Bill Royston.

"Evening, Doctor Morelle," the trainer smiled genially. "Glad you could get along. My lad wants to meet you. He's got into his clothes already. It's a girl he's rushing off to meet."

Doctor Morelle shook hands with the modest young boxer. He

then summoned Miss Frayle and presented her to Sonny Royston. Her eyes were limpid with admiration behind her spectacles.

"He's courting, is Sonny," Bill Royston went on proudly. "Not that that's a bad thing for a boxer when it's the right girl." His genial smile faded for a moment. "But it's a rum business. He has to court on the sly—"

"Rather restrictive, I should imagine," the Doctor observed.

"You're right! You see, his young lady's Kitty Burgess—only daughter of Hal Burgess, the man who promotes the boxing here. I suppose Hal has seen so many boxers become punch-drunk or lose their money he doesn't want his daughter run-ning round with one. Her dad won't allow 'em to meet now he knows they're in love with each other. Won't let her even watch the boy fight."

"That's right, Doctor Morelle," Sonny put in over his shoulder as he carefully knotted his tie in a cracked mirror. "He told me Kitty wasn't for a struggling fighter. Yesterday, that was, when I asked him if we could get engaged. Showed me the door and said I wasn't to see her again."

The young boxer laughed amiably.

"Silly old chump! 'Course it's made no difference to Kitty and me—only now we have to meet on the sly, which we don't like really, and she's not allowed to come and watch me fight. She's waiting for me now in the café across the road."

"Good for her!" Miss Frayle said feelingly, and Sonny grinned widely at her. Then he said to his father: "Wonder if her dad saw me win tonight? Might make him change his mind."

"Try him and see," said the elder man with a grim quirk on his lips.

His son nodded. "Perhaps not," he said.

"Better wait till you're champ," somebody laughed. There was a number of other happily smiling people in Royston's dressing-room, "then he'll give you his daughter—if you'll agree to fight exclusively at Ringland for him!"

There was general amusement at this remark, for Hal Burgess was noted for his shrewd business acumen and his ability to strike a hard bargain. After receiving further hearty slaps on the back and renewed congratulations on his praiseworthy victory, the young boxer hurried off to keep his clandestine appointment.

The dressing-room emptied quickly when he had gone, nearly everybody returning to the auditorium, for there was still some boxing to be seen, until only Doctor Morelle, Miss Frayle, and Bill Royston remained.

Miss Frayle was on tenterhooks to get back to the bouts.

"It's a bit of a worry about Kitty and Sonny," Bill Royston was saying to Doctor Morelle.

"It does seem somewhat unsatisfactory."

"It is." Bill Royston scratched his grizzle-head in puzzlement. "You see, I was pleased about him becoming genuinely attached to the girl, who's a nice kid, and him looking forward to marrying her. After all, the boy's only human and it was much better for him to be really serious over someone like Kitty, than to be chasing after raggle-taggle no-goods."

"Perhaps it'll all come right in the end, Mr. Royston," Miss Frayle put in banally.

"I hope so," he said feelingly. "If it all fizzles out, as it might with Burgess forbidding her to see him, I'll be worried Sonny *may* start running a bit wild." He scratched his head again despairingly—"I wish his mother was here sometimes to give me a hand," he said.

Bill Royston's wife had died several years previously.

Doctor Morelle turned to Miss Frayle with a bland smile. "No doubt Miss Frayle would be able to give you sterling advice," he murmured. "She suffers from repressed maternal instincts."

Royston looked at her hopefully.

"What do you make of it, miss?" he asked.

She thought for a moment. "Speaking as a woman," she began, "I don't think Kitty Burgess is going to stop being in love with your son, Mr. Royston, just because her father tells her to. Why, it'll make her love him all the more. I'm sure of that. Girls of today know their own minds. Sooner or later, Mr. Burgess will have to give in."

"I hope so—and without any ill-feeling," Royston said sincerely.

The Doctor lit a Le Sphinx casually. He was not to know that at that moment Hal Burgess lay dead in his office not far away. He might possibly have known nothing about it except when the promoter's death had become news had he not chanced to meet a sturdy, thick-set individual wearing a bowler hat going up to the offices that lay over the main entrance hall. This was a little while later when, deciding not to stay to see the last bout of the evening, he left Royston and was on his way out with Miss Frayle.

"Doctor Morelle!" the man in the bowler hat hailed. "I've been looking for you everywhere. Thought you'd left. I'd appreciate your help."

The Doctor recognised again Detective-Inspector Hood of Scotland Yard.

"Another little mystery you wish me to elucidate?" he queried.

"Something like that," the other nodded grimly. "Someone's stuck a knife into someone else." He blew a dark cloud of smoke from his strong-smelling briar. "Don't ask me why, Doctor—I don't know yet."

"Is—is it murder?" Miss Frayle stammered.

"I shouldn't be surprised. Suicides don't habitually stab themselves in the back—unless, of course, they happen to be contortionists, or something."

Doctor Morelle dropped his cigarette and trod on it.

"Has the identity of the deceased been established?"

"Yes—it's Hal Burgess, the manager of this place."

Miss Frayle started. She gulped: "Hal Burgess—Kitty Burgess's father! Goodness, but this is terrible!"

The Scotland Yard man gave a grim smile. "Murder usually is," he remarked, and began to climb up the stairs, calling over his shoulder, "the body's up here, Doctor."

They entered an office near the head of the stairway to find a number of police officials already present. Miss Frayle remained in the doorway, too nervous to enter. The Doctor stared down at the shape which lay near the desk and was covered by a sheet.

His narrowed eyes shifted to where, on the desk, beside what was apparently the dead man's grey trilby, a knife was prominently placed upon a handkerchief. He observed the handkerchief was stained red. He removed his gaze from the unpleasant sight, and was eyeing the hat when he heard Hood say:

"Any idea how long ago death took place, Doctor?"

"Approximately half an hour ago. The right lung is punctured, the implement which killed him was evidently used with considerable force."

Meanwhile Hood was surveying the knife on the desk with narrowed eyes. Beneath the glare of a powerful electric bulb, his ruddy features were grim and set. He examined the knife closely.

"Finger-prints seem clear enough," he observed. "Seems as though it's a straightforward case. Probably shan't have to take up your time after all."

From what the Doctor was able to ascertain, it appeared that one of the boxing stewards calling at the office to check some point about the running of the programme had found the promoter dead, and had immediately searched for Detective-Inspector Hood, whom he had previously seen in the auditorium, so conspicuous was this amiable Scotland Yard man.

Inquiries had elicited that no suspicious person had been noticed in the vicinity of the office. But as the attention of everybody was engaged inside the hall, it would have been possible for someone to have come from almost any part of the building and make their way upstairs without attracting attention; or they could as easily have slipped in from the street. The motive for the crime was not robbery; the dead man's well-lined notecase was untouched.

Sounds that the last fight of the evening was over and the noise of the crowd leaving the building reached the office.

Doctor Morelle picked up his walking-stick and beckoned to Miss Frayle.

"As the interception of the murderer would appear to be a foregone conclusion, Inspector, owing to the finger-prints, I take it you will not require my assistance?"

"That's right. Sorry to have bothered you," Hood declared. "Good night, Doctor—good night, Miss."

Outside the office door, Miss Frayle said:

"I've never known you to walk out on a case before, Doctor. Did you really believe that it's almost solved?" she asked quickly.

He tapped his walking-stick on the concrete floor.

"On the contrary, my dear Miss Frayle," he said enigmatically. "I am quite confident that Detective-Inspector Hood will *not* be able to intercept the real perpetrator of the crime."

"Then why don't you do something?"

"I intend so to do," he replied evasively, and then snapped, "as soon as you refrain from your banal interrogations!"

He hurried down the stairs, and stood surveying the people who streamed out of the more expensive seats. He was about to turn towards the exit when he perceived the individual whom he had been informed was Joe Girotti.

His blonde, flashily-dressed companion on his arm, he was swaggering through the crowd. He put on his hat with a dashing gesture, but instead of it slanting over his eyes it seemed to perch on the back of his black, shining head, and the girl looking up at it laughed as with a quick movement he removed it.

Doctor Morelle unexpectedly wheeled round and pulled Miss Frayle towards a telephone booth near the entrance.

"Kindly telephone the Fencing Club," he directed, "and ascertain the address of Mr. William Royston without delay."

A question formed on her lips, but she stifled it when she saw the saturnine set of his feature in the half-light. Ten minutes later they were proceeding in a taxi to the Royston home. There seemed to be a long interval after Doctor Morelle had rung the bell before the door was opened to him by the elder Royston, whose face relaxed with obvious relief when he recognised his visitors.

"Thank heaven it's you, Doctor," he exclaimed. "You are the one person who can help us. For a moment I thought it was the police."

"So you, too, have a latent guilt complex," the Doctor smiled mirthlessly.

Sonny Royston came into the room at that moment. He looked the picture of utter dejection.

"Shall I tell the Doctor, Dad?"

"Yes, go on, Sonny. He'll be able to tell us the best thing we can do."

The young boxer hesitated, then he blurted out: "It's Kitty's father. He's dead—murdered!"

"Of that I am cognisant," the Doctor nodded. "That is the reason I journeyed here. That reason and this—" He handed Sonny a button. "This belongs to you, I presume? I retrieved it from the late Mr. Burgess's office."

Sonny Royston turned to his father helplessly. "You see, Dad," he cried, "the police are going to think it was I who did it!"

"All right, son, take it easy," said his father. Doctor Morelle stared at the boy piercingly, as though he was trying to make up his mind. Young Royston choked and then, his father's grip on his shoulder, proceeded more calmly. "Remember tonight in the dressing-room, Doctor, I joked about asking old Burgess if he'd seen me win my fight and wouldn't he change his mind about Kitty and me? Well, after I'd left you I suddenly thought perhaps after all it wouldn't be such a bad time to speak to him again about our engagement. So I decided to go up to his office before joining Kitty over at the café. There was no reply when I knocked, so I went in. He was on the floor and there was a knife in his back. Without thinking, I knelt down and pulled it out—" He shuddered. "It was horrible, and then some of the blood got on my hand and I wiped it off with my handkerchief. Suddenly I lost my head and rushed out.

"When I reached the street I realised I'd left my finger-prints on the knife. I remembered people knew he and I had quarrelled.

I panicked absolutely and came home—I forgot all about poor Kitty—when I got here I burnt the handkerchief and then I waited for Dad." He glanced at his father. "You know I didn't do it, don't you?" he choked. "You know that what I've told you is true?"

"'Course I believe you," said the elder man. He looked across at Doctor Morelle, his face drawn and harassed.

The Doctor walked across to the boy's side with a purposeful air.

"I must say I am constrained to believe you, young man—" he began.

"I believe you, too," Miss Frayle burst in feelingly.

"It hardly seems consistent," the Doctor continued, ignoring his assistant, "that after you displayed such sportsmanship in the ring you would transfix anyone in the back."

"All the same," said Bill Royston after a moment, "the fact that we all believe him doesn't mean to say that police will, does it? What ought we to do about it?"

"Surely *you've* got a clue, Doctor," Miss Frayle insisted frenziedly, realising that Sonny Royston's freedom—and probably his life—depended on the Doctor elucidating this mystery.

"Regrettably, I fear I have no constructive suggestion to make at this juncture." He stretched out a hand to reach his hat which he had placed on the table. Then, strangely, he turned it round in his hand, gazing at it with a sardonic smile. Suddenly he wheeled round. "May I be permitted to amend my former statement? On the contrary, I *can* elucidate the crime, and in a few minutes put the police on to the true perpetrator."

"Doctor, you're wonderful!"

It was Miss Frayle who said it, but the others in the room evidently thought the same, judging from the relief that came over their anxious faces.

"Now, young man, if you will kindly direct me to the tele-phone."

A short while later found the Doctor on the telephone to Scotland Yard, speaking to Detective-Inspector Hood. The latter was working late on the checking up of the finger-prints found on the knife which had slain Burgess.

"What is it, Doctor?" Hood asked quickly. "Found the murderer?"

"Your powers of deduction amaze me, because your assump-tion is quite correct. If you will kindly assimilate the information I am about to give you…"

The Detective-Inspector acted upon Doctor Morelle's informa-tion forthwith, with the result that some time after midnight Joe Girotti opened the front door of his expensive flat to find himself face to face with Inspector Hood and a couple more formidable-looking officers.

At Scotland Yard he admitted to murdering Burgess—the promoter had refused to pay for his "protection" (another name for blackmail which Girotti extorted from his victims under the threat of being beaten up by the "boys").

Burgess had shown him the door, and the gang-leader, in a burst of rage, had waited until his back was turned and then attacked him with his knife.

The following day, Hood called at the house in Harley Street to thank Doctor Morelle for his assistance, and also to learn how he had so unerringly deduced the identity of the murderer.

"I observed what was to be the vital clue before the murder was actually committed," the Doctor explained laconically. "But, shall I say I observed it only subconsciously? You see, the real object of my presence at the prize-fight was to gather impressions which would form a sociological subject. Not being cognisant of the fact that a murder was to be perpetrated, I was not searching for details. Briefly, I must have noticed two admission tickets fixed in the band of Girotti's head-gear. The observation immediately passed into my subconscious, and then, in Burgess's office I perceived a hat on the table, very like Girotti's. Two tickets were also adhering to that hat.

"Later in the auditorium I perceived Girotti again, and I noticed then the head-gear he now possessed did not appear to fit him properly—and he preferred not to wear it. Later, when interrogating Royston and his son, it occurred to me it was Burgess's hat Girotti had taken in error, leaving his own in the office. No doubt this happened in Girotti's haste to depart."

"I see," said Detective-Inspector Hood, through a cloud of acrid tobacco smoke. "But what was it suddenly brought these clues from your subconscious to your conscious mind, so to speak?"

Doctor Morelle chuckled sardonically. "That occurred when I happened to reach for my head-gear which was reposing on the Roystons' table. I observed that I, too, had inadvertently fixed the boxing arena admission tickets to my own hat, and had omitted to remove them." He lit a Le Sphinx. "And so you have a perfect example of how the subconscious can be brought into use in the elucidation of crime."

"It sounds like Greek to me."

Doctor Morelle walked towards the door. "Now, Detective-Inspector, if you will bear with us, I wish to dictate to Miss Frayle my final notes on a thesis, entitled *Hedonism and the Masses*."

The Scotland Yard man grinned. "Work! Work! Work!" he said. "Don't you ever think of anything else, Doctor? Don't you ever think of—well, *pleasure*?"

I, SAID THE SPARROW

Leo Bruce

Leo Bruce was the pen-name under which Rupert Croft-Cooke (1903–79) wrote detective stories. Croft-Cooke was an extraordinarily industrious author, who produced a book of poetry, *Songs of a Sussex Tramp*, at the age of nineteen and continued to write compulsively for the rest of his life. Barry Pike, a crime fiction critic who has edited a comprehensive collection of Bruce's short mysteries, *Murder in Miniature*, calculates that in all he published 126 books, including thirty-one as Bruce and no fewer than twenty-seven volumes of autobiography. He had, to say the least, a full life which combined wide-ranging achievements with the misery of a prison sentence for homosexual offences and a period of self-imposed exile in Tangier.

His eclectic interests included psychology, wine, gypsies, the circus—and darts, on which he published a book in 1936. In the same year he created Sergeant Beef, who made his debut in the superbly entertaining locked room mystery *Case for Three Detectives*. One of the unlikeliest yet most appealing Great Detectives of the Golden Age, Beef loved his beer and was, almost inevitably, a keen darts player. This story, however, deals with toxophily, and appeared in the *Evening Standard* in the 1950s prior to its inclusion in *Murder in Miniature*.

"A RE YOU A TOXOPHILITE?" ASKED YOUNG THACKERAY.
"No, Church of England," said Sergeant Beef quickly as he bisected a large pickled onion.

The CID man sighed.

"I mean, are you any good with a bow and arrow?"

"You trying to be funny?" asked Sergeant Beef. "It's not that long since I retired from the Force."

Thackeray, who had once served as a constable under Beef, knew him well enough to show no impatience. "I ask because I'm investigating this murder out at Tryfford. You must have read about it. Man shot dead with an arrow."

"Let's hear the details," said Sergeant Beef, unable to keep the eager gleam from his eyes.

Thackeray had got what he wanted.

"Certainly, Ledwick Jayne was the president of the Robin Hood Club of Toxophilites which used to meet at his house once a year for their championship competition. A rich man, Jayne, a widower with one son. This son is a keen-looking type, ex-Army captain, alert and athletic, one of the best archers in the club—if you still call them archers.

"Jayne himself was over 60, a gangling loose-jointed old man. He had a stroke some years ago and it left him not exactly paralysed but stumbling and jerky, with an impediment in his speech and a more or less permanently dropping lower jaw.

"He no longer joined in the archery but never lost his interest in the pastime and made this annual competition a sort of house-party at his great Victorian country house.

"On the night after the finals in which his son Dennis had won the Robin Hood Cup, Ledwick Jayne was standing out on the balcony of his bedroom at ten o'clock before turning in.

"He had said good-night to brother Raymond, with whom he had drunk a last whisky-and-soda in his study and had gone up to bed.

"His son, who was several hundred yards away down at the lake, says that he saw him there in the distance, illuminated by his bedroom light behind him. Dennis, the son, thought nothing of it, for his father was a creature of habit.

"All the younger members of the party had gone down to the lake according to a plan made at dinner. It was a very warm night and they decided that it would be fun to go there and perhaps take a boat out. It was near the field in which the competition had been held, and the little pavilion where they kept their bows and arrows was beside it.

"Ledwick's brother tells the rest of the story. He, Raymond Jayne (an accountant who specialises in income-tax claims), had a last whisky after Ledwick had departed. He had to ring for more soda and chatted with Parkins, the manservant, while he drank it.

"Then he went upstairs. His room was next to his brother's, and the window was open. Suddenly he heard the sound of a fall with breaking wood and ran into Ledwick's room to find him lying over a smashed deck-chair on his veranda.

"It was not very light out there, and only when he had hauled his brother's body into the room did he see the arrow. It had gone straight through the roof of Ledwick's mouth to his brain. The older man was stone dead."

"Let's hear the rest of the facts," said Beef.

"There aren't many.

"A bow, one of those which had been used by the competitors that day, was found among the bushes across the lawn. The angle of the arrow's entry would be just right if it had been shot from there.

"The suspects are necessarily those of the practised toxophilites who were out there in the grounds at the time of the murder."

"Or those of them who had any motive," put in Beef.

"Well, they all had, more or less, except perhaps a Mr. Newnes Drury. You see, they were relatives. The Toxophilite Club was largely a family affair and Ledwick used to ask all those related to him to stay in the house. The rest put up at the village inn a mile or two away and were all in the bar at the time.

"Down by the lake were Raymond's two sons. Keith and Alec, and a girl friend of Keith's called Nancy Maynard. There was also Ledwick's daughter, Grace.

"I say they are all suspects because Ledwick was a very rich man, and his will, which I have examined divides up his fortune in the way you would expect—large shares to his son and daughter, then slightly smaller equal shares to his brother and nephews.

"Any one of them would receive enough money to start him or her in whatever career chosen, and Raymond's share would make the rest of his life comfortable.

"The man without any apparent motive, this Newnes Drury, may possibly have had some understanding with Ledwick's daughter, but I can find no evidence of it. So there you are. Six people all under 30, all out in the grounds when Ledwick was shot, mostly having a motive, and all expert archers."

"Finger-prints?" asked Beef.

"Gloves are worn by archers, I believe. They were by this one, anyway. The arrow hadn't a print. The bow had been used that afternoon by Dennis and Keith, and there were good prints of each of them. Nothing else."

"No footprints?"

"Rubbed out."

"What was the distance from the point where the murderer was believed to be and to Ledwick's position?"

"About 20 yards."

"Was it, though?" said Beef, for the first time showing animation. "Twenty yards? That's interesting."

There was a long silence. Then Thackeray picked up his notes.

"I can tell you what each of the young people claims to have been doing at the time. Of course, they've only got one another as witnesses. Keith and his girl friend had taken the punt and pushed out on the lake…"

"Never mind all that," said Beef brusquely. "Have you got someone down at Tryfford now?"

"Yes. Coles is there."

"Can you phone him?"

"I daresay. What do you want to know?"

Beef sat back in his chair.

"There's several things. I ought really to go down myself. I'm getting old and lazy. Still, you tell your chap to get the manservant to the telephone and I'll do the talking."

Beef thoughtfully poured out a glass of beer while Thackeray did as he was asked.

"We're pretty sure that Parkins never went out that night," he said, with his hand over the receiver. "No other servants lived in the house."

Beef nodded, and when at last the manservant was at the other end asked his questions with great deliberation.

"You remember that night. Did you put the whisky and soda out for Mr. Jayne and Mr. Raymond? You did? Well, how much whisky was there and how much soda?"

Thackeray, leaning close, could hear the man's metallic-sounding reply.

"The siphon was nearly full. The whisky decanter about a third full."

"And when Mr. Raymond rang? Did you notice?"

"Yes. I took particular notice because I was surprised. The siphon was empty. About half the whisky had gone."

"They liked it drowned, did they?"

"No. That struck me as queer at the time. They both liked only a spot of soda."

"Then, when you finally took the tray away?"

"That night, it was. After Mr. Raymond had gone up. The decanter was empty and the new siphon about an inch down."

"You stopped there chatting to Mr. Raymond?"

"I couldn't help it. He kept questioning me about my family and that. I wanted to get back to my fire."

"Thank you, Parkins. You've been most helpful. Are you a toxophilite, by the way?"

"No, sir. I shouldn't know what to do with a bow and arrows."

★

"Nor should I," laughed Beef and replaced the receiver.

"Well?" Thackeray sounded impatient.

"Clever," said Beef. "Dead clever. You'll have to work hard to get the evidence together if you mean to hang him. I can tell you the murderer. At least, I'm pretty sure of it. But you'll have to get the proof."

"Go on," said Thackeray.

"Why did Raymond ring for Parkins?" Beef asked. "And insist on keeping him talking for ten minutes or more? There had been a full siphon of soda. It couldn't all have been used. Why did he squirt it away so that he had an excuse for getting Parkins up to the study if he didn't want to create an alibi for himself?"

"He knew when Ledwick would be shot, then?"

"He knew when Ledwick would die. Let me ask you another question. Do you think that any man with a bow and arrow, *any* man, mind you, could shoot another through his open mouth at 20 yards' range in half darkness?

"If you do you've never played darts. You may be able to get a bull once in three darts, but change your length of throw by two feet and you won't get on the board.

"These archers practised on targets, not on deer in Sherwood Forest. There was not one of them who could even have hit a man's head at an unmeasured range. I saw that at once. Ledwick was not shot from the garden. He was poisoned by his very clever brother.

"All Raymond had to do when he had administered his poison in the whisky was to let Ledwick go to bed and keep Parkins in a closed room far away from the bell. He knew that he would not be disturbed for he had heard the young people's plans and was aware that Parkins was the only resident servant.

"So when he had kept Parkins long enough he went up and found his brother neatly stretched out dead. He had his arrow ready and thrust it through the roof of the mouth to the brain so that he could 'find' his brother shot from the shrubbery.

"He had already emptied away the rest of the whisky which contained the poison and washed out the decanter with soda-water. He broke the deck-chair with a couple of kicks—a nice touch that.

"His alibi was cast-iron. His brother, standing on his balcony with six skilled archers in the grounds, is shot through his notoriously wide open mouth.

"Who's going to suspect poison? The cause of death could never be doubted for a moment, he thought, a cause with which he could have no connection. But you go and get a post-mortem and see if I'm not right. There's something very convincing about a bow and arrow but really, when you come to think of it…"

"Exactly," said Thackeray, "when you come to think of it."

FOUR TO ONE—BAR ONE

Henry Wade

Golden Age detective novelists frequently wrote about country houses and the landed gentry, but few of them had first-hand experience of the life of the aristocracy. Major Sir Henry Lancelot Aubrey-Fletcher, 6th Baronet, CVO, DSO (1887–1969) was a distinguished exception to the general rule. A decorated soldier, he served as High Sheriff of Buckinghamshire and later as Lord Lieutenant of that county. In the 1920s, he played cricket for the county as an all-rounder, and enjoyed considerable success. An enthusiastic sportsman, his love of horse racing is evident in several of his stories. All his crime fiction appeared under the pen-name Henry Wade.

The range of Wade's work in the genre was impressive. He began with a pleasing courtroom novel, *The Verdict of You All* (1926) and his output included inverted mysteries (in which we follow the criminal's activities before seeing whether they lead to his downfall), police procedurals, and classic detection. He showed an admirable determination not to follow a formula, and his deep understanding of police work—not merely investigative procedures but the nature of "office politics" within a police station and the pressures that can lead to corruption—ensured that his mysteries had a touch of authenticity lacking in the work of inferior talents. This story comes from an early collection, *Policeman's Lot* (1933), which includes several cases for Wade's principal detective character, Inspector Poole. But "Four to One—Bar One" is a stand-alone story and although it features horse racing (in particular, betting on races) its bleak tone and focus on violent criminality are quite unusual for Wade and for the period.

T HE BOOKMAKERS IN THE HALF-CROWN RING AT TATTENHAM Park were preparing for the real business of the day. In a quarter of an hour the runners for the big May Handicap would be out, and of the two horses which would almost certainly start favourite it was well known to the fraternity that one had little more than popular sentiment to justify its position in the market. It should be a good race for the Book.

All that concerned the bookmakers now was to get as large a share as possible of the business that was going—and on this warm, cheerful day it should be plentiful; each professional had confidence in his own skill in obtaining that share and in keeping a quick enough ear and eye on the run of the market to keep just on the right side of the quoted odds. Each professional, that is, except old Sam Trapps. Sam was getting old and his nerve was leaving him; that meant that either business or money left him too, and he knew that the time was near at hand when he would have to give up the game, or lose the hard-earned savings of a lifetime's strenuous and fairly honest endeavour.

Already the early silver punters, having caught, or failed to catch, a glimpse of their favourites in the too exclusive paddock, were beginning to move up and down the line of bookmakers, hoping to catch a favourable early price. A small man in a bowler hat and pince-nez approached Josh Blare, at the top of the line.

"Er—what is the favourite?" he asked nervously.

"Any 'orse you like to name, guv'nor. I'll lay yer five to four against any 'orse on yer programme for the race. Duggie 'imself couldn't say fairer than that."

But the pigeon was not quite as blue as all that. He knew that this generous offer contained a catch somewhere, and he took his 2s. off to the Tote. Josh Blare cursed under his breath.

"Five ter four the Field," he yelled, taking up the general cry. "'Three ter one bar one." "'Ere, I lay five ter four *Maiden's Pride*. Five ter four *Maiden's Pride*. Three to one *Jacko*. Five to one bar two."

There was a general rush of "business" all down the line, backers distributing themselves among their favourite bookies, or moving up and down the line in hopes of snatching a longer price. Most of the money, undoubtedly, was going on the two favourites, as it usually did in the big, popular races, but a certain amount was finding its way on to the longer-priced starters. In particular, a horse named *Buzz* was being quietly backed in different places at 100 to 7 and 100 to 8. Business was beginning to be brisk.

Brisk to everyone except Sam Trapps. Old Sam, with his rather bleary eyes and gloomy look, did not impress backers with a feeling of confidence. His old-fashioned suit was too loud for these days, and none too clean; the word "welsher" crept into the minds of the timorous, whilst the knowing hands turned away with a sneer. Business was not coming to old Sam.

Suddenly the old man was seized with an inspiration. He knew that nothing would bring the punters to him now—nothing but a gamble. He was finished anyhow, but he might have a last run for his money, just to show that there was life in the old dog yet.

Although the odds on the longer-priced horses had varied considerably (*Buzz* was down to eights now), and although the bookmakers were kept constantly in touch with the price movements in the bigger rings by their tic-tac men, the two favourites had not budged. "Five to four *Maiden's Pride*" and "Three to one *Jacko*" was still the cry, all the way down the line.

Now suddenly, above the general uproar, there burst a clear bell-like voice:

"Six to four *Maiden's Pride;* seven to two, *Jacko;* five to one bar two!"

"Who's that—stretchin' the odds?" snarled Josh Blare to his clerk. "Sam Trapps? The old fool's balmy. 'Ere, five ter four *Maiden's Pride;* three to one *Jacko*. Five ter four the Field."

But old Sam's wonderful voice, his last remaining asset, had pierced to the brains of the backers. There was a quick movement towards the quoter of more generous odds, and in a minute Sam and his clerk were as busy as ever they had been in their lives.

"Twelve bob to eight *Maiden's Pride*, No. 458. Three-ten to a pound *Jacko*, No. 459. Three pound to two *Maiden's Pride*, No. 460."

The clerk's hand flew; money poured into Sam's bag.

The ring could not ignore it; at the critical moment, when all the (comparatively) big money was going on, here was a price-stretcher jumping in and pinching all the business. There was nothing else for it.

"Six to four *Maiden's Pride*. Seven to two *Jacko*. Six to one *Buzz*," ran down the line.

The crowd in front of Sam Trapps wavered, but Sam did not hesitate.

"Two to one *Maiden's Pride*. Four to one *Jacko*," he cried. Then to his clerk again: "Ten bob to five *Maiden's Pride*, No. 471; eight poun' to two *Jacko*, No. 472. Two bob to one *Maiden's Pride*,

No. 473. Twen'y bob to ten *Maiden's Pride*, No. 474. No, sir, book's closed on *Buzz*. Four poun' to two *Maiden's Pride*, No. 475."

The ring wavered, started to follow suit, and the next moment the bugle blared from the top of the Grand Stand.

"They're off!"

A few more hurried bets were made, but for the most part "bookies" and backers alike were intent upon getting a view of the race. Along the far side of the course the view was interrupted by trees and by the marquees which lined the back of the free enclosures. As the horses swung round the bend, however, it could be seen that *Maiden's Pride* was leading by a couple of lengths; a glance at her ears, however, was enough to tell the tale. A few optimistic bookmakers tried the old trick:

"*Maiden's Pride* wins!" they cried. "Even money *Maiden's Pride*. I take six to four *Maiden's Pride*."

A few mugs rushed into the trap, but there was no money in it.

Jacko, moving nicely, lay third, whilst *Buzz*, away out on the far side of the course, level with the bunch, was going well within herself.

There was a little rush of last-minute bets, mostly among the "bookies" themselves, covering. There was a roar of shouting round and opposite the winning post, and in a second the news flashed down the course; *Buzz* had won; neither of the favourites was placed. It was a great race for the Book, except perhaps in the half-crown ring, where a great many last-minute bets had been accepted on *Buzz* in order to make up for the loss of business on the favourites. To one man in that ring, however, the race had brought a small fortune; Sam Trapps' inspiration had won him more money, probably, than he had won on any single day in the whole course of his career.

As soon as the "Pay, Pay" was over—not a long job—the bulk of the occupants of the half-crown ring, including the bookmakers, went off to get a drink. At the end of the line, however, Josh Blare, having despatched his clerk for what he wanted, remained in scowling contemplation of his book. It was not a bad book, but it might have been so much better. Presently he shut it with a snap and, with a quick look round, jerked his head at a short, thick-set man who, with two weedy-looking youths, was lounging near the entrance ring. The thick-set man strolled forward, the youths following, but at a snarling word from the former these hangers-on dropped back to their former position. As he approached, Blare made off towards the entrance; the two men's paths crossed and a whisper passed between them.

A minute later Sam Trapps, busily engaged in making up his book, heard a husky voice say in his ear:

"Nice race you've 'ad, guv'nor. What'll it be worth?"

Sam glanced up quickly and blanched at sight of the face in front of him. Thin-nosed, thick-lipped, with small pig-eyes that crossed one another in a perpetual leer, it was as cruel a face as the imagination of man could produce. Sam knew it well; he knew the short, thick-set body and the long arms that accompanied it. He shuddered. The stand on each side of him was empty, each occupant having gone off for refreshment. The man with the squint approached closer.

"Fifty, it's worth," he said huskily.

Sam wavered; his nerve was leaving him again. It was rank blackmail, but he knew, only too well, what he was up against.

With a quick movement the man whisked back his coat-flap and quickly, deliberately, exposed two inches of wicked cold steel.

"Remember Bert Larkin," he hissed. "Ten crisps, quick now."

With trembling fingers, Sam counted out the money and thrust it into the hand of his tormentor, who quickly disappeared in the returning crowd. Sam wiped his brow, while his clerk eyed him with horrified amazement.

There was little business on the next race, the crowd not having recovered from the excitement of the big event, but in the last race but one the Book had a really bad turn, a heavily-backed favourite romping home in a common canter. Word passed up the line, however, that John Hallows, a newcomer from the north, had done well, having closed his book early on the favourite and laid off most of what he had accepted.

Blare, now in a thoroughly bad temper, did a thing that he had rarely done in his life before. Thinking he had a greenhorn to deal with, he repeated his trick. With a jerk of the head he summoned Jake, who lounged forward and lit a cigarette within earshot; a minute later John Hallows found himself accosted by the same cross-eyed villain that had fleeced poor Sam.

"That'll be worth twenty, guv'nor," muttered Jake.

"Get out of here!" exclaimed Hallows sharply.

"Remember Bert Larkin."

"Joe, fetch that policeman!"

It was not necessary for Joe, the clerk, to move; Jake had disappeared into the crowd. An easy victory, but John Hallows knew that he had made a dangerous enemy.

Hallows, as has been said, was a north-countryman. He did not speak in dialect, only a slight broadening of vowels and an occasional "Eh, laad" when he was excited, betraying his origin. He was a man of about thirty-five, short but sturdy, with an intense vitality and a sense of independence, almost of superiority, which amounted to something very near conceit. When the last race was over he packed up his traps, then moved down a place or two to speak to Sam Trapps.

"Excuse me, mate," he said, "can I offer you a lift back to town in my bit of a car? You've had a good day, and I think I saw you have a visit from a chap that came to me; maybe there'll be others after you. You can trust me."

Trapps looked at him carefully.

"I think I can," he said. "Thank you kindly; I'd like to come with you."

They threaded their way through the crowd to a huge cheap car park and presently were packing themselves and their paraphernalia into a grimy but serviceable-looking Morris saloon.

"Bought her second-hand," explained Hallows.

If he had said fifth-hand he would have been nearer the mark; still, the car got from one place to another, and that was about all that Hallows asked of it. On the way to London the two bookmakers—one at the beginning, the other at the end, of what they called "the great game"—compared notes on their experiences, and particularly upon the ever-growing activities of the dangerous "race-gangs" that had become much more daring and dangerous since the War. Hallows explained that it was partly because of their activities—robbery and blackmail, freely supported by violence—that he did all the race-meetings within seventy miles of London by car; he was able to avoid the crowds going to and from the railway stations, and—worse still—the "packed" railway carriages. Sam Trapps warned his young friend in particular of Beauty Jake, the man who had tried his hand on them both that afternoon; Jake, he knew, had a little gang of "knifemen"—youths trained in the pleasant art of handling or throwing a weapon far more deadly and less risky to use than a revolver. Sam believed that Jake worked for a boss, but he did not know who he was. Thanking Sam for his warning, Hallows explained that he had been in the Tanks in the War, had been taught to use a pistol, and meant to take care of himself.

By the time the car reached Sam's house in Battersea, the two men were close friends, and Sam parted from his benefactor with many protestations of goodwill and warnings to "take care of hisself." Waving farewell, John Hallows and his clerk, Joe, drove on to the former's home in Bermondsey.

Joe was an older man, who had accompanied Hallows from Lancashire. He was devoted, body and soul, to his boss, and was prepared to do anything that was asked of him. One of the cash bookmaker's difficulties is that, returning late in the evening, very often laden with money, he has no chance of banking his winnings till the following morning. Hallows had met this by installing in his lodging (he was a single man) a heavy safe with a modern lock that would defy anything less than a skilled cracksman with an acetylene outfit. In spite of this, the cautious north-countryman would not leave the safe unguarded, and the arrangement was that Joe should remain on guard while the boss slipped out and got his dinner. After that, Hallows would take charge and Joe was free to go home.

On the present evening Hallows, after "safing" his money, garaged his car and slipped into his accustomed restaurant. He had had very little lunch and he did not hurry over his dinner, but by half-past eight he had finished and, feeling well pleased with himself and his day's work, lit a pipe and started to stroll home. It was still broad daylight, but the shortest way to his lodgings led through some dark and gloomy alleys. He was half-way down one of these when a movement in a passageway caught his eye; instinct caused him to swerve, but he was too late and he fell heavily to the ground with a knife quivering in his back and blood pouring from his mouth.

Fortunately a woman in the house opposite saw what happened, sent her nipper for the doctor, and herself did what she could with a towel to stop the bleeding from the wound itself, in which she wisely left the knife. The doctor came quickly, followed by police and an ambulance, and in ten minutes John Hallows was in hospital, but it was a desperately near thing. For three weeks he lay at death's door; the point of the knife had missed his heart by half an inch and the hæmorrhage from the lung wound was so severe that only his strong constitution and freedom from alcohol and nicotine saved him—that, and the untiring devotion of poor Joe, who had spent a horrible evening waiting for his boss to return, before buttonholing a policeman and eventually tracing "the old man" to hospital. Deserting his wife and children, Joe refused to quit the boss's safe at night-time until Hallows was sufficiently recovered to be able to give him instructions as to how to bank the money.

While still in hospital the bookmaker did some pretty hard thinking. It was evident that he had been the victim of one of the race gangs of which he and Sam Trapps had talked on their way up in the car, and it was fairly certain that as soon as he recovered, the gang would be on to him again. He was faced with a life of perpetual blackmail or perpetual danger—and neither of these alternatives pleased him. He knew he could expect little help from the police, and he decided to take matters into his own hands.

Hallows was out of hospital in five weeks, but it was not till the end of July that he made his reappearance in the silver ring at Fleetwick. He received a welcome from his fellows that was warm, hearty, or effusive, according to their natures; none warmer than old Sam Trapps; none more effusive than Josh Blare's, who declared that nothing in life had given him greater pleasure than the news of Hallows' return from "the valley of the shadow." Sam, who had been to see him in hospital and knew all about it, had kept him a pitch next to himself and swore he wasn't going to let him out of his sight. One sharp-eyed neighbour on the other side observed that Hallows had got a new clerk, and received the information that Joe had got tired of the south and gone home, his substitute having been picked up at a Labour Exchange where he was applying for a post as "secretary and accountant."

The day's racing was uneventful, but John Hallows quickly began to feel the strain of standing about after his long convalescence. Feeling definitely faint, he slipped off to the refreshment room for an unaccustomed brandy and soda, which quickly revived him. As he emerged from the bar, he ran full tilt into no less a person than Beauty Jake, looking, if possible, more sinister than ever. To Hallows' amazement, Jake greeted him effusively, and before he knew what had happened, the bookmaker found himself buttonholed and jockeyed into a quiet corner. Here Jake quickly changed his tone:

"Y've had yer warning," he muttered hoarsely. "Yer know now what yer gits if yer don't pass when y're told. Y'll come that twenty now, quick, and any other time y're asked. See?"

With the utmost difficulty Hallows kept his hands off the man. For one thing he knew that in his weakened state he was no match for the broad shoulders and strong arms of the bully. But he had a better reason than that.

"Hold hard, lad," he said slowly. "You must give me time to think this out. It means a life of blackmail if I give in."

"It means death if yer don't," was the succinct reply.

"What if I tell the police?"

"Where's yer proof? Besides, y'd be dead before yer got in the witness box."

"Well," repeated Hallows doggedly, "you must give me time to make up my mind, anyhow. I'll let you know next week at Dover."

"Beauty," who knew that his boss would rather have a live "passer" than a dead "stick," grunted some form of assent and sidled away. As a matter of fact, there had been no intention to kill Hallows after the Tattenham Park meeting; a knife in the arm to warn him was the idea; but John's swerve had brought the thrown knife on to a more dangerous line.

Hallows returned to his stand, but did not tell Sam what had happened. He had his own reasons for keeping quiet.

Three nights later Hallows was sitting in his lodging smoking a final pipe before turning in, when he heard a tap at his door.

"Come in," he said sharply.

A face consisting of little more than a gigantic grin, appeared round the door—the face of the man who had "got tired of the south and gone home," but bereft of its accustomed moustache and adorned with a pair of wire-rimmed spectacles that rendered it completely unrecognisable.

"Joe!" exclaimed Hallows. "Come in, you old scoundrel."

Joe slipped into the room and sank into an empty chair while Hallows opened a bottle of Bass and pushed it across to him.

"Well, laad?"

"Well, ah've got 'em, boss."

"You have?"

"Ay. Got 'em Toosday, matter o' faact. But ah wanted to mak' sure—and ah have. Saame lot, saame plaace every time."

"How many?"

"Foer. That Josh Blare, t' bookie, is boss."

"My God!"

"'Im and Beauty Jake, and two knife-boys."

"What about Blare's clerk?"

"Not in it. Dead innocent. Thaat's where Blare has t' braains. Clerk knows nowt, would swear his boss knew nowt. It's they foer only."

"And where do they meet?"

"Private bar at the 'Daainty Cheese,' Wigg Street, off Tower Bridge Road. Not twenty minutes from here. Thaat's how they were so quick on to you, yon night—they'd seen you before— where you lodged and fed. Private bar's right away from public bar, down a passage—real private it is—separate entrance."

A slow smile spread over Hallows' still pale face.

"Good," he said. "We'll reconnoitre. Finish your drink, laad, and lead on."

On the following night Hallows sat as usual in the tap-room of the "Broody Hen," drinking his customary modest pint of bitter and discussing the problems of the hour—mostly to do with horse-flesh—with the other patrons of Mr. Chippon's licensed house. Presently he got up and, without saying good-night, slipped quietly out of the room; only the landlord, Dick Chippon, seemed to notice his departure.

Out in the street Hallows found his car waiting, with Joe at the wheel. Without a word, the latter slipped in the gear-lever and the car jerked into motion. A few minutes later they had turned into a quiet street off the Tower Bridge Road and the car pulled up.

"Just give me time to get there, Joe; then come quietly up. Keep the engine running."

Joe nodded without comment, and Hallows, getting out of the car, started down the street away from the crowded thorough-fare. Presently he turned to the right into an even more deserted street; in fact at this hour of the evening—half-past nine—there was not a soul about. Without hesitation Hallows made his way to the entrance to a small public-house—the "Dainty Cheese"—and turned into the passage which led to the private bar. He was wearing rubber-soled shoes and his footsteps made no sound.

Away to his left he could hear loud voices coming from the tap-room, but it was not there that his interest lay. Almost at once the passage turned sharp to the right and led, according to a dingy notice, to the "Private Bar." With one ear cocked behind him Hallows approached the closed door, from behind which he could just catch the murmur of voices. Looking about him, he quietly moved a small table nearer to the door, listened again, and then turned the handle and slipped into the room.

There were four occupants of the private bar, two middle-aged men, one fat and one short and square, and two lanky, vicious-looking youths. They were seated on the far side of a long table, facing the door, with glasses in front of them, their heads together in earnest conversation. At the sound of the opening and closing of the door they looked up, and the next instant, in response to a sharp command, flung their hands over their heads.

"Stand oop!" In the excitement of the moment Hallows was dropping into dialect.

The four men obeyed, staring nervously at the solid, deter-mined-looking figure with its back to the door and a heavy revolver with a clumsy-looking muzzle-attachment in its right hand. As Hallows faced his enemies he had Blare on his right, next to him, Beauty Jake, and then the two "knife-boys."

"Ah've coome to show you two can plaay at this game," said Hallows quietly. "Which of you young swine knifed me?"

The youth on the extreme left jerked his head at his companion.

"Ben," he said, in a husky voice.

"Get across next to Blare, Ben," said Hallows. "Go on, move!"

It was a fatal mistake, though its intention was obvious enough. As Ben passed in front of Jake, the latter's right hand dropped to his side and the next instant a revolver cracked. Hallows felt the wind of the bullet past his ear. Instantly he pulled the trigger and in response to the little cough of his gun Josh Blare collapsed slowly to the floor. As he fired, Hallows sprang to one side and Jake's second bullet ripped down his forearm, searing the flesh like a red-hot iron. Jake was holding the unfortunate Ben in front of him as a shield, whilst the other youth, petrified with terror, still held his arms above his head.

The crack of Jake's second shot was instantly followed by another cough from Hallows' gun, and Ben in his turn collapsed. His falling body threw Jake off his balance for a second, and in that time Hallows had opened the door and slipped out of the room. Flinging the door to behind him, Hallows tipped over the small table. A large man, running from the bar, blocked his way, but Hallows lowered his head and, catching him full in the stomach, sent him flying just as the door of the private bar was jerked open and a pursuing figure crashed over the small table full length to the floor. Hallows dashed out into the street and leapt into the car, which Joe threw into instant and violent motion. A knife crashed against the window, but only splintered the safety glass and fell back harmlessly into the road. Looking back, Hallows saw Jake brandishing his pistol, but evidently thinking better of attracting notice by open-air firing. Ben's companion was retrieving his use-less weapon from the roadway.

Round the corner, Hallows ordered Joe to pull up. Joe looked his inquiries.

"I'm going to finish this job," said Hallows, whose arm was hurting him villainously.

"You're never going back, boss?" exclaimed Joe in consternation.

"I am. No good leaving it half done. They'll never expect me."

"But t' cops?"

"If there are any coming I shall see them; but I don't believe there are. I know this neighbourhood; they're pretty scarce unless they're sent for."

Slipping off his raincoat, Hallows exchanged his hard hat for Joe's disreputable cap.

"Wait here and keep her running."

"Ah'm cooming t' door."

"Wait here!"

Joe, miserable but obedient, sank back into the driver's seat, whilst Hallows slouched slowly off down Wigg Street back to the "Dainty Cheese." He was right; there was no policeman in sight. A small group of loafers, principally consisting of children, stood on the opposite side of the street facing the public-house, but they did not seem greatly excited. Probably no news had reached them; only some boy had seen a brandished pistol and a knife thrown at a retreating car.

Hallows strolled into the side entrance. He had half expected to find it crowded with the occupants of the public bar, but evidently those worthies knew enough of their neighbourhood and business to keep clear of gun-play—if they had even heard Jake's two shots.

Through the half-open door of the private bar Hallows could see the landlord and Jake stooping over a body on the floor. The other youth, if he was still there, was out of sight. Once more Hallows slipped silently down the passage and, entering the room, closed the door behind him. The knife-boy, he saw, was seated at the end of the table, his head buried in his arms.

"Out of the way, landlord," said Hallows, softly. The two men looked up; the landlord flung himself to one side and Jake's hand flew to his pocket, but Hallows' bullet, fired at point-blank range, crashed into his brain and he dropped, a lifeless heap, to the floor. The knife-boy tried to hide under the table, but Hallows' bullet dropped him to his knees and another stretched him beside his companions.

Hallows turned to the landlord.

"Better keep your mouth shut about what you know," he said grimly; then, after a glance at each of the four men on the floor, turned on his heel and left the room. Outside all was as it had been when he left it, the two coughing grunts of his silenced "gun" had conveyed nothing to the group of idlers in the street, even if they had been heard. Hallows lounged out of the side door and strolled down Wigg Street in the direction of Joe and the car. It was the most difficult walk he had ever done in his life; instinct urged him to run, but he knew that his one hope lay in lounging. Nobody was paying any attention to him.

Meantime the landlord of the "Dainty Cheese" was doing some quick thinking. It was a question of what enemies he least wanted to make. Blare's gang he knew—one of the most dangerous of the smaller groups in the game, but it was done, finished, wiped out. On the other hand, if he gave information against the killer—whom he did not know, but who was almost certainly a member of a rival gang—he stood in deadly peril of extermination himself, before he could get into the witness box. So far he got and then, realising that he must not be found doing nothing, with four dead bodies in his private bar, he hurried to the telephone in his small office.

"Tower Bridge Police Station, quick, miss. That the police? Hakett, landlord o' the 'Dainty Cheese,' Wigg Street, speakin'. There's bin a fight in my private bar—four chaps dead. Come at once, fer Gawd's sake."

He hung up the receiver and turned to the difficult task of concocting a tale of convincing ignorance. In five minutes, Inspector Toller, a sergeant, and four uniformed constables were in the house and the crowd outside had grown like magic.

Inspector Toller gazed down upon the unpleasant sight on the floor of the private bar.

"What on earth's been happening here?" he asked.

"Don't know, I'm sure, guv'nor," declared Hakett. "Must 'ave 'ad a quarrel and done each other in."

Toller eyed him sharply.

"Know who they are?"

"Oh, yes, guv'nor, reg'lar customers. That's Josh Blare, the bookie; 'im with the 'ead blown in's Beauty Jake. The red-'aired lad's Ben and t'other's Sloppy Alf. Pals they was come 'ere reg'lar. Can't understand it."

"One of these race gangs, for a monkey," said the inspector to his lieutenant. Then, turning to the landlord: "Now then, Hakett, who shot 'em up?"

"S'welp me, guv'nor, I know nothin' about it. Not till I 'ear the shots; then I rushed in 'ere an' sees these blokes lying bleeding in all directions—all as dead as mutton. Then I rings you up."

"But you must have seen something of the other fellows getting away."

"I tell yer, guv'nor, I didn't see a soul, I believe they did each other in."

"And not a gun to be seen anywhere," said Toller contemptuously. "Race, take one of these constables and question that crowd outside. Somebody must have heard and seen something. Phillips, help me search these fellows for guns, but don't disturb the lie of the bodies before the doc. comes."

DEATH AT THE WICKET

Bernard Newman

Bernard Charles Newman (1897–1968) was a great-nephew of George Eliot, but an author of a very different kind. Like Gerald Verner, he was one of those highly professional mass-producers of commercial fiction who was usually ignored by the critics, but who enjoyed considerable popular success during his lifetime before fading into literary oblivion after his death. He is undoubtedly one of very few writers who met both Adolf Hitler and President Roosevelt, and his books often touched on political themes, especially during the Second World War. *Secret Weapon* (1942) introduced Winston Churchill as a character, while the books he published under the name Don Betteridge included *The Mussolini Murder Plot* (1936). He wrote numerous espionage novels, most notably *Spy* (1936), which is said to have been banned in Germany but used as a textbook in Russia.

Fact and fiction tended to blur in Newman's life as well as in his stories, and although it has been claimed that he worked as a spy in both world wars, Newman denied that this was true; whether his denial was accurate, of course, is a matter for conjecture. Certainly, his sporting activities would have afforded some cover for espionage. He was passionate about cycling and a member of the Cyclists' Touring Club; it is said that he cycled through every country in Europe. His cycling adventures were chronicled in twenty books, while his very first, *Round about Andorra*, sprang from his enthusiasm for walking as well as travel. Three different sports provided him with the background for novels: *Cup Final Murder* (1950), *Centre Court Murder* (1951), and *Death at Lord's* (1952). This is another cricket story, and it was included in the very first Crime Writers' Association anthology, *Butcher's Dozen* (1956), which was edited by Josephine Bell, and two contributors to this book, Michael Gilbert and Julian Symons.

T HERE WAS CERTAINLY PLENTY OF EVIDENCE.

Country house cricket is in danger of becoming extinct, so I had gladly accepted Noxon's invitation. Not that I am a star performer. A country house cricket eleven usually consists of three or four good players, a couple of promising youngsters, three or four people who were once cricketers, and a couple who never were and never would be. I came into the third category, but young Faulkner was emphatically in the first. He was a fast bowler of class, and only the accident of birth in a Minor County had kept him from the public eye. He had played plenty of games for the M.C.C., and had done well; though at Lord's they whispered stories of his queer temper.

Papa Pontivy, once a famous French spy catcher, went down to Malmeston with me. He was not in the least interested in cricket, and within an hour had shocked the company by calling the umpire a referee, and by a comment that Faulkner must be a good bowler, since he hit the bat every time.

This was during a practice game. Over tea, Noxon talked over his strategy for the first match. Faulkner would be his shock bowler: there was a slow left-hander for the other end. After that, he had as changes a selection of has-beens and would-bes.

I am not quite certain how the words "body line" came into the conversation. The phrase was always more dramatic than accurate, but since the unfortunate controversy in Australia it has been dropped—the phrase only, not the method of attack. Many bowlers, when they talk of "leg theory" and "pad play", are really discussing Larwood's method.

Pontivy pricked up his ears when "body line" was mentioned, and a dozen people tried to explain it to him, quite unsuccessfully.

"You may see a bit of it on Wednesday, M. Pontivy," said young Faulkner—rather grimly, I thought. "We're playing Malmeston—and Torris will be there."

I knew that there was bad blood between him and Torris. I confess that I never liked Torris myself. He assiduously cultivated a local reputation as a cricketer, and actually he knew the rules—and dodges—of the game backwards. As captain of the Malmeston Cricket Club he was successful, but very unpopular with his opponents; not because of his success, but because he was no sportsman—he never took a risk, and would insist always on his pound of flesh. There was a famous occasion years ago when Malmeston were facing a score of 260, and had nine men out for 85—and then Torris claimed bad light, and got it.

He used to make a lot of runs, but was not a pretty bat. I never saw a man use his pads more, not even in professional cricket before the new rule. He never played an innings without at least three l.b.w. appeals. He survived all but the last, and unkind rumour said quite a lot about umpires. A country house party is not unlike a school in its atmosphere, and schoolboys' opinions on visiting umpires are notorious. The Malmeston regular umpire was one of Torris's own servants—half the team depended on him for a livelihood, for that matter. It was noted, so exasperated bowlers declared, that Torris was never l.b.w. unless the opponents' umpire had to give the decision, and Torris was always careful when facing his end.

There had been a scene between Faulkner and Torris the previous season, I remembered: Faulkner could stand punishment, but

Torris's pad play made him wild. He promptly packed his leg-field, and served up some real body-line stuff! It wasn't dangerous, for Faulkner was accurate, but it got Torris rattled. And at last he appealed to the umpire!

Unfortunately for him, the umpire wasn't his own man, but a retired Indian officer, Colonel Coffin.

"What?" barked Coffin. "Appeal disallowed! This is cricket, sir, not a test match!"

Old Coffin's unconsciously-coined epigram became almost a classic, and unkind people used to whisper "This is cricket, not a test match!" when they wanted to get Torris wild. Strangely enough, Faulkner himself got unexpectedly ratty when the incident was mentioned. Although he had scored, he hated Torris the more.

But although we all agreed with Faulkner, we tried to calm him down.

"I don't care what you say," Faulkner almost shouted, "but if he tries that pad-stuff, then I give him leg-theory."

"Oh, cut it out, old chap," Taunton protested—another Grade I player. "It'll kill cricket."

"Never heard of in my time," old Knight put in—a grand old tryer, still good for five or six on a perfect wicket. "In my day we used to play the game."

"Play the game!" Faulkner howled. "But Torris…"

"Torris doesn't know how to play the game—never did." This from Bingham, the local doctor. I didn't like him: a good cricketer, but utterly selfish—played for himself first and his side second. When he wasn't batting, he always wanted to bowl. He fancied himself as a fast bowler, but was very erratic—not in the same class as Faulkner. "Nevertheless, I should go steady on the body-line and bumper business, Faulkner. Torris isn't so young as he was, you know—can't get out of the way."

"He's quick enough to stick his pads in front," Faulkner retorted. And he went off into a long defence of body-line—all the old arguments dragged out again, till we were sick of it. I have only mentioned the discussion at length because it was such vital evidence against Faulkner.

Bingham continued to advise caution. I doubted if he were thinking of Torris's welfare! He wasn't Torris's doctor: on the contrary, he disliked him as freely as anybody. Only last winter, so old Knight told me, there had been ugly rumours about Torris and Bingham's wife. Evidently the potential scandal had blown over, for there had been no divorce.

We were to play Malmeston the following Wednesday. Noxon, our host, had fixed up the match in spite of the universal dislike of Torris, for Malmeston were a good side, and had a fine pitch in the middle of a glorious old village green. Noxon had fixed up a full week's cricket for his house party, which was to be assisted by one or two local residents like Bingham. I was quite pleased with my own moderate performances, but Pontivy would have been bored to exasperation but for the lucky accident that the Chief Constable of the county was among the guests. The two men talked shop very contentedly throughout the games.

The house party arrived a few minutes late at Malmeston, but Bingham was already there to represent us: I noticed Torris out in the middle of the green, inspecting the wicket. He won the toss and decided to bat.

I would have witnessed the affair at Malmeston in any case, but chance gave me a front seat for the drama. Early in Malmeston's innings our wicket-keeper knocked up his right thumb rather badly, and had to take off the gloves. Noxon, our skipper, handed them to me.

"Slip the pads on, will you, Newman?" he said.

"But, damn it, Noxon," I protested, "I haven't kept wicket for twenty years!"

"No, but you used to. Stop 'em—that'll do. We don't expect fancy work."

Faulkner was bowling well, getting real pace out of the hard pitch. But I could see that Torris was getting on his nerves. So well positioned behind the stumps, I could now appreciate the irritation of Torris's pad play. Twice Faulkner broke through his guard, and once appealed confidently for l.b.w. But Torris's man was at the other end. I saw Faulkner bite his lip, and guessed what was coming.

I wondered if Noxon would interfere, but Faulkner was his star player, and he himself no more than a keen rabbit. Faulkner set his field deliberately—five men on the leg side. I was a bit anxious— for myself: body-line bowling is no picnic for the wicket-keeper. Torris looked round at the new field in some anxiety—pad-players aren't too fond of being hit.

He certainly got what was coming for him. Faulkner's second ball caught him a nasty blow just below the heart. Play was held up for a minute, and I saw Dr. Bingham look meaningly at Faulkner. But Faulkner was past looks, and had no mercy. Torris stopped the fifth ball of the over on the point of his knee, and almost jumped clear of the ground at its sudden sting—a fast ball on the knee can be *very* painful. He swung his leg to ease it, and took his stance for the final ball.

It was never played. Just as Faulkner began his long run, I noticed that Torris shuddered; a few seconds later—just as Faulkner delivered the ball—the bat fell from Torris's hands. The ball crashed into the undefended wicket; I saw Torris staggering forward, clutching at his chest; a moment later he sank helplessly to the ground.

I ran to his side, and fumbled with my clumsy gloves as he writhed on the crease, his hands pressed towards his heart. But now Dr. Bingham, from mid-off, was kneeling beside Torris. He called out to Knight to bring his bag from his car, and then forced a few drops of red liquid down Torris's throat. At this stage I noticed that Pontivy was on the field, bending over Torris.

"I fear that he is dead," the old man said quietly to the doctor.

"I'm afraid so," Bingham agreed.

The match was of course abandoned at once. I was more than concerned. Sergeant Wilkins, the local policeman, was in the Malmeston team, and I saw him talking to the Chief Constable.

I pulled Noxon on one side. The old chap was naturally tremendously upset. We knew that Torris's death was an accident—Faulkner had never meant to kill him. But that is merely the difference between manslaughter and murder. I did wonder, in fact, if a charge of murder might not be preferred. Manslaughter depends upon involuntary and unplanned conditions, accidents through negligence, and the like. But Faulkner, days before, had planned to bowl body-line at Torris; the fact that the bowling overreached his anticipations was no defence. Noxon thought that manslaughter was quite bad enough! He paralleled the case of a boxer who kills an opponent by a blow which might be classed as unfair. We were unhappy enough, in either case; the idea of giving evidence against Faulkner was not very comfortable!

There was a long wait for an ambulance to take away the body. I heard the Chief Constable ask Bingham to undertake the autopsy, as the usual police surgeon was on annual summer leave. Then he went up to Faulkner.

"I'm sorry, Faulkner," he said, "but from what I hear I shall have to ask you to come along. I'm afraid you'll have to face a charge of manslaughter—no, don't talk now: you're not charged yet. We'll get hold of your solicitor at once. I suggest that Noxon comes with you to arrange for bail."

Faulkner, pale and subdued, acquiesced in silence, and the little party drove off. Half an hour later the ambulance arrived, and Bingham went with the body. It was indicative of the atmosphere of unrest that even Bingham, accustomed to death, had not taken off Torris's pads—these outsize pads which had been the direct cause of the tragedy! I noticed this: so did Pontivy.

"Get those pads off!" he whispered. It was his tone of voice which gave me the first hint of untoward events.

I got into the ambulance and took off Torris's pads and batting gloves, dropping them in a corner of our dressing-room.

"Let the others go!" said Pontivy, softly.

Already players were drifting away. Sergeant Wilkins had taken the names and addresses of those on the field, and had warned me—as the nearest spectator—that I would be needed at the inquest.

"It is not going to be the inquest which the worthy sergeant expects," said Pontivy.

"Look here, Papa, what are you getting at?" I asked.

"You know as much as I do—you saw the man die."

"But…"

"How did he die?"

"He got a blow over the heart."

"Yes, but that did not kill him. He died after a blow on the knee."

"Maybe delayed action," I suggested.

"I repeat, you saw the man die, and should know better. The man was poisoned!"

"What?"

"Once I caught a German spy," said Papa Pontivy. "He knew that he could not escape, and that I had no mercy. So he swallowed a little phial of poison, and died. I do not forget it, or what he looked like. This man, I say, died the same way."

"But he didn't swallow anything!"

"No. But there are other methods of poisoning a man."

"Just a minute, Papa. Bingham saw him die, too, and he's a doctor."

"A country doctor, in a respectable district. I wonder if he has ever seen a man die of poison?"

"Well, he'll find out!"

"Yes. And in the meantime the murderer will have perfected his alibi."

"But—no one was near Torris!"

"His pads were near him. Always look at the obvious, my dear Newman, and don't bother about this circuitous moves of the detective story. The man died after a blow on the knee—that is a *fact*. The doctor will presumably examine the knee. We will examine the pads. His left knee, was it not?"

Pontivy examined the pad with minute care, while I ensured that he was undisturbed. Five minutes later he called over to me.

"Look! These pads are stiffened with cane. A splinter of cane has been bent back—my guess is that it has been impregnated with poison. A devilish scheme! And it worked!"

"So the murderer is someone who knew that Torris was likely to be hit on the pads!"

"Yes—though that appears to be common knowledge—do not touch that splinter!" he cried.

"I wasn't going to! But the bang over the heart…"

"An accident—quite fortuitous."

"Well, what are you going to do? Wait for the result of the autopsy?"

"No. I am quite certain what that will be. But if the murderer is clever, he *must* return to remove this splinter. We will wait, too—and watch."

The pavilion was the usual village hut, with two dressing-rooms under a common roof. I noticed that the rafters supported an accumulation of old nets and other impedimenta. We climbed up to a good vantage point.

Two of the home team came in to collect their kit. Then a long silence. Half an hour must have passed. Then I felt a light tap from Pontivy.

A man had entered the home dressing-room. We could not see him, but heard him turning over the cricket gear. Of course, he would expect to find Torris's pads there. Now he came into our room, and I saw a look of relief on his face as he saw Torris's large-sized pads on the floor.

"I told you that I knew what the result of the autopsy would be," Pontivy whispered, very faintly. "Heart failure—*not* poison!"

Dr. Bingham! I saw him pick up the left pad, and press with a tiny pair of scissors at the inside of the knee-cap. Bingham? Of course; I ought to have suspected him earlier. Swiftly my mind ran the gamut of detection. Motive? The scandal about Torris and his wife. Opportunity? The knowledge that Faulkner would bowl body-line. The early arrival at the ground, while Torris was out on the pitch. The opportunity as a doctor to procure poisons, and the knowledge to use them.

Of course, it *must* be Bingham. Was the absence of the police surgeon fortuitous? No, the crime had been fitted to the period.

Yes, and his character fitted the crime, too—that selfish nature would see another man suffer in his place. Only if another were condemned would his own security be complete.

"Life is a collection of trifles, Dr. Bingham," said Pontivy from the rafters. "If only you could have removed the pads yourself, at the mortuary…"

I saw terror in Bingham's eyes. As I dropped to the ground beside him, I thought that he was preparing to fight. Then he accepted the inevitable, and jabbed his hand sharply against the protruding splinter of Torris's pads.

THE WIMBLEDON MYSTERY

Julian Symons

Julian Symons (1912–1994) was an eminent crime writer and critic of the genre as well as being a biographer, poet, editor, and social and military historian. His early detective novels were relatively orthodox, but he soon became dissatisfied with the conventions of the classic form and began in the early 1950s to develop the British psychological crime novel. He admired the books of Patricia Highsmith, and although his fiction never quite matched the brilliance of her very finest work, he received the Gold Dagger for *The Colour of Murder* (1957) and an Edgar from the Mystery Writers of America for *The Progress of a Crime* (1960). In 1990 he received the CWA Diamond Dagger in recognition of his outstanding career in the genre. He wrote an influential history of the genre, *Bloody Murder* (aka *Mortal Consequences*; three editions) and took particular pride in serving as President of the Detection Club from 1976–85.

Symons was not himself a sportsman, but he enjoyed watching football, tennis, and in particular cricket. Sport occasionally featured in his prolific output of short stories, many of which were written in the 1950s and originally published in the *Evening Standard*. Examples include "Test Match Murder" and "The Grand National Case", as well as this story, known both as "The Wimbledon Mystery" and "Centre Court Mystery". It was included in *Murder! Murder!* (1961), a collection of Quarles's cases; the detective appeared in many short stories but never in a novel.

YOUNG JIMMY CLAYTON, HIS RED HAIR BRILLIANT IN THE sunshine, a small brown zipper bag in his hand, jumped out of a car and pushed his way through a crowd of autograph seekers into the entrance hall of the All England Lawn Tennis Club.

There a tall, thin, tense-looking man hurried up to him. This was Bobo Williams, coach to a generation of British tennis players, among whom Jimmy Clayton was one of the few bright stars.

"Where have you been, Jimmy? We've been searching all over for you. Do you know Parker's two sets up on Van Damm, and you're on after them."

Jimmy flashed him a beaming smile. "And here I am."

"Really, this is no way to prepare—but I won't say anything more now. After you've beaten Gladkov, young man, you and I are going to have a talk."

"Oh, after I've beaten Gladkov," Jimmy said mockingly. "If I don't get changed I shan't get on court with Gladkov. Come on."

He led the way past the two R.A.F. boys on guard at the door of the men's dressing room. "Mr. Clayton," one of them said, "can I have your—?"

"Later, maybe. At the moment my hand's quivering like a leaf in autumn."

The chief men's dressing room at Wimbledon is big—it has to accommodate some ninety players during the championship—and is split down the centre by a row of lockers. At one end of the room are showers and bathrooms, at the other end the cubicles where physiotherapists practise their magical arts of revival. A big television set shows the course of play for those who prefer chatting in the dressing room to watching the reality in the players' stand on the centre court.

Several players were grouped round this set now, and they greeted Clayton cheerfully, and even warmly. For there was something very special about the match Jimmy Clayton was playing this afternoon. He was meeting the first player from the Soviet Union ever to have a chance of winning the men's singles at Wimbledon.

This was Sergei Gladkov, who had quickly become known as the Bear, partly for national reasons and partly because of a deep growl which he uttered on court when things were going wrong. Not that much had gone wrong for Gladkov. Unknown and unseeded, he had reached the last eight without losing a set.

"Better get ready for the Bear, Jimmy," said his doubles partner, Joe Richards. "He's waiting for you now."

"Just waiting to eat you up," somebody else said.

Jimmy had opened his locker, and was quickly changing. Joe Richards patted him on the shoulder. "He won't eat you up, eh, Jimmy? You'll be a pretty tough meal."

Jimmy Clayton merely grinned. Bobo Williams hovered round nervously while he changed. "Now you will remember the tactics we agreed on. His defence is like a wall, you cannot hit past him. Slow up the game, induce him to make mistakes. Don't take things lightly."

"Look, Bobo, I appreciate all you've done for me as a player. But I want to win this championship more than I've ever wanted to do anything. I shan't take it lightly. Satisfied?"

"I suppose so," the other said, and sighed. "After the match we shall plan your tactics against Parker in the semifinal."

The dressing-room attendant called out, "Parker two sets up and leading four-one in the third, Mr. Clayton."

"All right. I'm off." Jimmy Clayton went out of the dressing room and up the steps which, during the tournament, may be used only by those playing on the centre court. He pushed open a door and entered the anteroom where Gladkov was already sitting, reading a book. The Russian nodded to him, unsmilingly.

Five minutes later the doors from the centre court opened, and the American champion, Harry Parker, who obstinately refused to turn professional, and the big Dutchman van Damm came through them.

"Well played, Harry," Jimmy Clayton said. He added, with his grin, "I hope you have the chance to do the same to me."

"Good luck, Jimmy," Parker said. Then he had gone through the door toward the dressing room, and Jimmy Clayton stepped out onto the centre court.

He felt nervous. But once there, once he had bowed to the Duchess of Kent in the Royal box and got the feel of the place, the feel of the crowd rising in massed tiers away from him, once he had absorbed the sensation of being a focal point of attention for thousands of people sitting round this arena, the women radiant in summer dresses, the men using handkerchiefs to protect themselves from the burning sun, Jimmy Clayton was nervous no longer.

He picked up the balls and crashed in his first service, forgetful of everything except that there was a job to be done.

And it was a real job. Gladkov was a player in the pattern of the great Frenchman, René Lacoste. His defence seemed impregnable, his position play was so perfect that he seemed hardly ever to be out of place. Brought up to the net he volleyed, not very powerfully, but with great deftness and cunning. Only overhead did he seem fallible, and Jimmy had agreed with Bobo Williams to feed this apparent weakness with lobs, and to slow up his own natural game in the hope of upsetting Gladkov.

He tried this in the first set, and lost it six-two. Gladkov put away everything lobbed up to him, not so much by power as by intelligent angling of the ball. In the long rallies played at little more than half pace it was not he but Jimmy who made the mistakes.

The crowd, eager to applaud their own player, were slowly silenced. Jimmy could see Bobo Williams biting his nails. In the players' stand there was some shaking of heads. Everybody liked young Jimmy Clayton, but few had supposed that he really stood much chance against the Russian machine.

As they towelled themselves at the end of the set Gladkov smiled at him. The smile was harmless enough, no doubt, even perhaps a friendly smile, but it annoyed Jimmy Clayton by its apparent assumption of superiority.

"I don't care what we agreed," he thought. "I'm going out for my strokes."

He went all out. He stopped lobbing, stepped up the pace of his game, forced his way to the net. He played for the sidelines, determined to make this Russian move.

And he succeeded. He had his luck, in the way of balls that dropped inches in when they might have been inches out. But he succeeded, playing better than he had ever played in his life.

By the end of the second set, which Jimmy won six-three, Gladkov was growling with anger.

In the third set the Russian made a great effort, and even speeded up his own game, pulling up from three-five to five-all.

But when Jimmy took the next two games, Gladkov began to show signs of fallible humanity. In the fourth set he made mistakes, and Jimmy took it six-two to the applause of an almost hysterical crowd that was cheering every point he won.

Back in the dressing room again, he found himself the centre of a cheering, laughing crowd of players. Bobo Williams had tears in his eyes. "Jimmy, you were great, you were great."

"I'm just off to have a shower."

"Yes, have a shower. Then we shall talk. About when you play Parker on Wednesday, the day after tomorrow. Today you were inspired, but—"

"We'll talk," Jimmy agreed. He waved his hand, and disappeared into the bathrooms.

Bobo Williams found himself involved in the crowd of players talking about the match, and about Jimmy's brilliance. It was nearly half an hour before he became aware that Jimmy had not reappeared. He tapped on the door of the bathroom Jimmy had used, then turned the handle.

It was unlocked, and empty.

Bobo went into the physiotherapists' cubicles. Jimmy was not there.

"Typical," Bobo said aloud. "Just typical. Skipped off to enjoy himself before we could have our talk."

To make sure, he spoke to the R.A.F. boys on duty at the main exit. They looked at him blankly. "Mr. Clayton's not come out of here, sir," one of them said. "I've been waiting to get his autograph."

There is another exit, at the other end of the dressing room, also watched by R.A.F. men. Bobo went to it, and was assured that Jimmy Clayton had not come out in the past half hour.

"Couldn't miss him, not with that flaming red hair. Besides, look at the crowd out there waiting to see him."

Bobo was puzzled. "I say, have any of you seen Jimmy come out of the bathroom?" he asked the assembled players. None of them had. "That's a funny thing," Bobo said hesitantly. "He seems to have disappeared."

At first nobody took Jimmy's disappearance very seriously. Bobo Williams was well known to be an old fusspot, and Jimmy could hardly be blamed for getting away from him for an hour or two. In any case, it was generally recognised that Jimmy was a pretty wild and unpredictable character.

So, although Bobo was running around like a scalded cat saying that this was a mystery, nobody paid much attention until Rita Foldes came round to the entrance hall, and met the anxious Bobo.

"Miss Foldes," he said, "have you seen Jimmy? He seems to have disappeared."

"Disappeared?" Rita Foldes was a tall dark girl with beautiful eyes which were suddenly wide with alarm.

"If he'd come out he would have come round to see you," Bobo said. Rita Foldes had become engaged to Jimmy three months back.

"Perhaps not." She spoke perfect English, with no more than a slight accent. "I told Jimmy I might not be able to come. In fact, I got here in the middle of the second set. If you will excuse me I will telephone Jimmy's mother. Perhaps he has gone home."

When she had left them, Bobo Williams said in a voice that was almost a wail, "But he *can't* have gone home. He didn't leave the dressing room."

Joe Richards came up to him. "Why are you looking so solemn? And where's Jimmy?"

"He isn't in the dressing room. And he never left it."

Joe Richards burst out laughing. "Ah, that's one of Jimmy's jokes. You know how he loves a joke."

Rita Foldes came back to them. "Jimmy's not at home. Mrs. Clayton hasn't heard from him since the match."

"Look here," Richards said, "let's make sure Jimmy isn't playing some trick on us. We'll talk to those boys on the doors and have a look in the dressing room. Then we'll come back to you, Miss Foldes."

They talked to the boys on both doors, who repeated with vigour their statements that red-haired, volatile Jimmy Clayton had not come out of the two doors. They searched the dressing room in vain. They looked in Jimmy's locker which contained nothing at all, not even his tennis clothes.

Jimmy Clayton had disappeared.

Later that evening Bobo Williams telephoned Mrs. Clayton. And Mrs. Clayton telephoned detective Francis Quarles.

Francis Quarles was at home when the telephone call came. He was eating dinner, which consisted of an *entrecôte* steak with green salad, accompanied by a glass of claret. While he ate he read a newspaper story headed "Jimmy Lionheart beats the Russian Bear.".

He finished the steak and followed it with Stilton cheese and black coffee. Then he discovered from *Who's Who* that Evelyn Arabella Clayton was the widow of George Morley Clayton of Clayton's Breweries, who had died in 1947, and that James Morley Clayton was their only surviving son. Clearly there was money in the family. Quarles took a taxi to Mrs. Clayton's house in Eaton Square.

Mrs. Clayton was a square-faced practical-looking woman in

her fifties. She received Quarles in a large, badly lit drawing room, furnished in no particular sort of taste. His attention was caught by a full-length portrait that hung over the fireplace, a portrait that showed a young man wearing Army uniform leaning negligently against a bookcase.

There was nothing particularly notable about the picture, but Quarles' attention was caught by the mocking smile on the young man's face, and the fact that he had bright red hair.

He was brought back to the present by Mrs. Clayton, who spoke in a voice as decisive as her appearance.

"Mr. Quarles. It seems that my son James has disappeared. At least, Mr. Williams here believes so. I am by no means convinced that this is not some prank on his part. He is what you might call a rather wild young man. But Mr. Williams is convinced that he is right. He had better tell you his story. Then, if it proves that James has really disappeared I should like you to find him."

Quarles, amused rather than annoyed by this would-be imperial arrogance, listened to Williams' story. At the end of it he said, "But that's impossible."

"Precisely, Mr. Quarles. How do you explain it?" There was sharpness in Mrs. Clayton's voice.

"I don't. I have no data for doing so. I merely say that it is impossible. Your son is engaged to be married, I believe."

"He considers himself so. I have told him that I do not approve."

"Why not?"

"When I die, Mr. Quarles, my son will be rich. I have ambitions for him. Miss Foldes is a perfectly pleasant girl, but her family lives here in exile. As far as I can see, they are never likely to return to their country. It does not appear to me a suitable match."

"Isn't that a rather out-of-date attitude?"

She was unperturbed. "I may be a rather out-of-date person, Mr. Quarles. James is always telling me so. I also object to Miss Foldes' previous engagement—"

"Come on, Aunt Evelyn, don't be so stuffy."

From the shadows of the room, where he had been only dimly visible, came a young man wearing a dark grey suit and a flowered waistcoat.

"She's going to tell you that Rita was engaged to me, but that's all over and done with. My name's Dobson, by the way—Ronny Dobson. And Mrs. Clayton isn't my aunt, though I've known her so long she seems like one. I've known the Clayton family for ages, and so has Rita."

"Thank you, Mr. Dobson... Do you know any reason why your son should want to disappear, Mrs. Clayton? Was he worried about anything?"

"No. In fact, he seemed rather more cheerful than usual, and he was always cheerful."

"Is that he?" Quarles made a gesture at the painting over the fireplace.

"No," said Mrs. Clayton flatly.

Ronny Dobson rocked with laughter. "Really, Aunt Evelyn, it's no use trying to hide the skeleton in the cupboard. That's Ralph, Jimmy's older brother. Jimmy adored him, still does. Ralph became a regular soldier, went over to Korea. He was captured, submitted to brainwashing, and—well, he played ball with the Chinese. British prisoners who came back told how he ran lecture classes and even took part in interrogations, sitting by the side of the Chinese and North Korean officers. They didn't like it, the other prisoners. Some of them were quite savage about what they were going to do to him."

"Ralph's dead," Mrs. Clayton said harshly. "He was killed in one of our bombing raids. He can have nothing to do with this."

"Is he dead?" Ronny Dobson asked softly. "Jimmy never believed Ralph was dead. Or, for that matter, believed he was a traitor. You know that."

Quarles had the curious feeling that there was some other, uncomfortable presence in the dimly lit room. He looked again at the figure in khaki, who stared back with his mocking smile. "When did your son die, Mrs. Clayton?"

"At the end of the war he was not returned with other prisoners. The Chinese authorities said he had been killed in a bombing raid. Ralph was not a bad boy, Mr. Quarles. He was reckless, that is all."

"And Jimmy admired him?"

"Yes. Ralph was three years older and James copied him in everything, even in his enjoyment of ridiculous practical jokes." In Mrs. Clayton's hard face there was some tenderness, as she spoke of her older son.

"This may be a practical joke." Quarles looked at his watch. "It is now half-past nine. Jimmy has, after all, been missing for only five hours. He may be back in the morning."

"He *must* be back," Bobo Williams said. "Tomorrow he has to play in the men's doubles, and on Wednesday there is his semifinal against Parker."

"Do you think we should telephone the police?" Mrs. Clayton asked.

"Yes," Quarles said without hesitation. "In fact, I will telephone them myself. And I think we should go down to Wimbledon tonight to look at this dressing room from which a man can so simply disappear. I happen to know Colonel Macaulay, the secretary of the All England Club. I'll telephone him too."

"I say, can I drive you down?" Ronny Dobson asked. "A real-life investigation sounds like simply terrific fun."

"Do, by all means, although you'll probably find it extremely dull."

They reached Wimbledon quickly in Ronny Dobson's Jaguar. At night the place was oddly ghostlike. The deserted courts and pavilion, stripped of crowd and players, seemed somehow purposeless.

Colonel Macaulay met them at the gate. He was pleasant but sceptical. "I'm very willing to help, Quarles, but I can't help feeling that this is all a fuss about nothing. I should imagine young Jimmy has gone off somewhere for a little quiet celebration. Unwise perhaps, but very understandable."

"I tell you he never left the dressing room," Bobo Williams said, almost crying. "I believe he is somewhere in there now—dead."

"Nonsense, man," Colonel Macaulay said.

Three-quarters of an hour later they had searched the dressing room thoroughly, without finding any body. In the bathroom used by Jimmy Clayton, Quarles had, however, discovered something of interest.

There was a window in this bathroom and on the inside paintwork of the sill Quarles saw four longitudinal scratches, freshly made. He also found on the floor just under the window several fair silky hairs which he examined carefully, and put into an envelope.

"Those aren't Jimmy's," Bobo Williams said immediately. "His is red."

Quarles smiled slightly. "I realised that." He opened the window and peered outside. "What is out here, Colonel Macaulay?"

"This particular window leads to a side passage, which isn't much used."

"Ha. And the other bathroom windows, do they lead in a similar way—?"

"No," Colonel Macaulay said promptly. "Most of the others have no windows, or small ones. This is the only room of its kind."

Quarles seemed in an excellent temper. "You all see the significance of that, naturally?"

They looked at him blankly.

"Those scratches," Ronny Dobson said. "They look as if they might have been made by studs in shoes. Yet that window isn't big enough for anyone to climb out of."

Quarles beamed at him benevolently. "You are quite right, young man. A curious contradiction, is it not? One further question, Colonel Macaulay. You have R.A.F. boys on guard at the doors. How do they recognise those who have a right to come in?"

"By their badges. Absolutely the only people allowed in this dressing room are the competitors, who have a blue cardboard badge, and the club members like Bobo here who wear a mauve and green badge. Our organisation is only human, of course, but we do keep a very careful check on everybody who comes in."

"Do you check equally carefully those who go out?"

Colonel Macaulay was momentarily disconcerted. "Why, no, I don't suppose we do. I really don't know. But anybody as distinctive-looking as Jimmy Clayton would certainly be noticed— in fact, I believe a lot of people were hanging around, waiting for him to come out."

Quarles nodded, looking like a very large and self-satisfied cat. "Well, gentlemen, I don't think there's much doubt about what happened. Jimmy Clayton—"

But they were not destined to hear at this time Quarles' ideas about what had happened to Jimmy Clayton. In the stillness outside came the sound of a car stopping. A voice called, "Hello there. Is anybody about?"

They went outside to see two figures standing by a police car. One of them stepped forward, a grizzled man, square and chunky. "Colonel Macaulay? We were told we should find you here. My name's Leeds, Inspector Leeds, C.I.D. Evening, Quarles."

"Good evening." Quarles was staring at the man with Leeds, who still stood by the car. He went on staring as Inspector Leeds said that they would like to have a look round, and Colonel Macaulay told him that Mr. Quarles didn't seem to take the affair very seriously.

"Ah, Mr. Quarles has ideas of his own," the Inspector said, like a man talking about his favourite nephew. "Very ingenious they are, too, sometimes—and very eccentric."

"I think I must have been wrong," Quarles said. He addressed the man by the car directly. "What in the world are you doing here?"

"This is my colleague Mervyn Briffitt," Inspector Leeds said. "He is interested in the matter from another aspect."

Mervyn Briffitt was a small rosy man with fair curling hair which he wore rather longer than is fashionable, and a long, drooping, silky moustache. Quarles drew him aside as the others went on again to the dressing room. "Why are you here? What has a disappearing tennis player to do with one of the most important representatives of our counterespionage system?"

Briffitt smiled and stroked his silky moustache. He had a pleasant but slightly affected voice. "You flatter me, Quarles. In itself, Clayton's disappearance doesn't interest me at all."

"Then why are you here?"

"Jimmy Clayton is engaged to a girl named Rita Foldes. Did you know that?"

"Yes. Her family is in exile from—" And he named the particular Communist-ruled central European state from which the Foldeses had escaped.

"And her father, Doctor Foldes, used to be Minister of State before the Communists took over and he got out. Did you know that?"

"No. Why should I? What's it got to do with Jimmy Clayton?"

"Nothing perhaps." Briffitt stroked his moustache again. "But Doctor Foldes disappeared yesterday evening—walked out of his flat and vanished. Today Jimmy Clayton, who's engaged to marry his daughter, disappears too. Rather a coincidence, don't you think?"

Mervyn Briffitt said very little as they looked round the dressing room and bathroom yet again, but in some indefinable way the little rosy-faced man with the fair moustache took charge of proceedings.

When they had finished, Inspector Leeds said, "I can handle the routine aspects of this, but I think it's really your pigeon."

"I think so too. I'd like you all to keep quiet about it. And I'd like it kept out of the papers."

"But Jimmy's playing in the doubles tomorrow," Bobo Williams protested. "If he's not here he'll have to scratch."

"My dear Mr. Williams," Briffitt said in his slightly affected voice. "I can assure you that I have more important things to worry about than whether this young man plays in a tennis match. Now, the night is young. I think it might be useful to have a little talk. Are you free, Quarles?"

Quarles looked at his watch. The time was half-past eleven, and he had been up playing poker until four o'clock in the morning. "Of course."

"Good. You are Mr. Dobson, aren't you?" Ronny Dobson started slightly, pulled at his flowered waistcoat, and admitted it. "Can you come along too? I've got a little flat just off Piccadilly and my man will make us a cup of coffee."

A little more than half an hour later the three of them were in the living room of Briffitt's flat, drinking hot black coffee. It was the room of a man of taste, although the taste was slightly unusual. One wall of this room held Victorian conversation pieces, pictures of a kind that are just coming back into fashion; another held drawings and paintings, equally perverse, by Beardsley and Leonore Fini. Miro shared a third wall with some Japanese prints. With the coffee they drank cognac.

"I have asked you to come here, Quarles, because within its limitations I respect your intelligence," Briffitt said.

"I am grateful for the compliment." Quarles had sunk into a big armchair and his eyes were almost closed.

"Besides, this is certainly not a case for ordinary police methods. There are possible diplomatic reactions. No doubt you came to a certain conclusion from what you saw in the dressing room."

"I did," Quarles said doubtfully. "The position of this particular bathroom, the scratches, the hairs, the zipper bag—you know about the zipper bag?" Briffitt nodded. "They all seemed to lead to one conclusion. But I don't understand Doctor Foldes' disappearance, or any of the rest of it, so perhaps my ideas are wrong. Frankly, I don't even understand why Mr. Dobson is here."

"Perhaps I can help," Briffitt said with a faint smile. "Doctor Foldes is one of the most distinguished of his country's exiles. He is chairman of the Committee for National Liberation—that is the exiles' organisation through which they hope one day to regain power. Hungary, Czechoslovakia, Rumania—all these countries have their little groups of fanatical anti-Communist exiles. They talk and talk, scheme and plot, send emissaries home to make contacts and form cells—the usual kind of thing. It is part of my job to keep an eye on them."

"Where does Mr. Dobson come in?"

"Mr. Dobson?" Briffitt looked down at his coffee. "He is also a member of the Committee for National Liberation. He came to this country eight years ago, and his name then was Dombos."

Ronny Dobson laughed. "I speak English pretty well, don't I? I used to come over every year when I was a boy. My family was friendly with the Claytons and I often stayed with them. You are surprised, Mr. Quarles? But it sometimes pays to look a little foolish, and also to appear more English than the English."

Briffitt took a packet of black cigarettes out of his pocket, put one in a holder and lit it. "Recent happenings have caused splits in several of these committees. With the new line, the end of the cult of personality, the release of a good many prisoners, great pressure is being put onto some of the more distinguished exiles to go back. Foldes was one of them. He was visited last week—quite unofficially, of course—by somebody from his country's legation. Probably he was offered a place in the government if he went back. My information is that he had not finally made up his mind."

"Where does your information come from?"

Briffitt waved a hand. "Dobson here is a dedicated anti-Communist. He works with us from time to time, although I don't publicly acknowledge acquaintance with him. Now, yesterday evening Foldes walked out of his flat. He has not been heard of since then."

"You think he has gone back?"

"That is a possibility. There are certain things against it. His daughter Rita says that he would not have gone without telling her. He took no papers, packed no bag. But still, perhaps he has gone. Or perhaps he has been kidnapped by government agents over here. Or perhaps he has been killed by them. I should very much like to know which."

"And where does Jimmy Clayton come in?"

"Ah ha." Briffitt leaned back in his chair, pleased with his own subtlety. "Jimmy is engaged to Foldes' daughter. Jimmy has a brother named Ralph, who is presumed to be dead. Jimmy disappears. Don't those facts suggest anything to you, Quarles?"

With his eyes closed, Quarles murmured, "Not very much."

"I am disappointed. Your mind is less flexible than I had hoped. It suggests to me that Ralph Clayton is still alive, that he is the go-between employed to persuade Foldes to return and that somehow he has employed Jimmy as his tool. Now, the fact that Jimmy Clayton has disappeared suggests further that Ralph Clayton has run into some trouble. That means Foldes is probably still in England. If he is," Briffitt deliberately stubbed out his cigarette and put away the holder, "we're going to find him."

Quarles said nothing. Ronny Dobson began to walk up and down the room. "It fits, you know, it fits. I'm pretty friendly with Jimmy even though he did take my girl away from me. Best man won, and all that. This morning he was very excited, told me he had some wonderful news, but couldn't give me any details."

"You don't think it was about tennis?" Briffitt asked.

"I doubt it. He knew I wouldn't be much interested in that. I'm sure it was something more personal."

"I gathered from Mrs. Clayton that Ralph's death was well established," Quarles said.

Briffitt waved a hand. "Not finally. His body was supposed to have been seen, and the Chinese said he'd been killed in a bombing raid. But isn't that exactly what they would have said if they intended to use him as an agent?"

"Perhaps. I'm afraid you're too subtle for me." Briffitt looked sharply at him, but Quarles showed no sign of having spoken ironically. "We shall all feel a little foolish if Jimmy Clayton turns up in the morning, safe and sound. If he doesn't, I'm prepared to concede that there may be something in your theory. Good night."

In the morning Jimmy Clayton had not returned, and his mother had no news of him. Quarles arrived at his office just after half-past nine and his secretary, pert Molly Player, said disapprovingly, "You're late. Somebody here to see you. Her name's Rita Foldes. Upset, but she's a smasher."

"Thank you for all that information. Ask Miss Foldes to come in."

Looking at her across his big desk, Quarles on the whole agreed with his secretary. Rita Foldes' eyes had shadows round them, but they were still remarkable eyes, dark and lustrous. Her brows were thick, her cheekbones high, and she had that darkly brooding look, rather like that of a bad English tragic actress, which in real life seems to belong exclusively to central and eastern Europeans.

She was the sort of woman, Quarles reflected, capable of immense self-sacrifice, passionate love—and passionate hatred.

She spoke now, abruptly. "Mr. Quarles, I talked to Ronny this morning and he told me you were going to try to find Jimmy. There is something I have to tell you."

She stared at him with painful intensity. The one flaw in her beauty, he thought, was that she might develop a moustache in later life.

"It is something he said I was not to tell anybody."

"My dear Miss Foldes," he said a little impatiently, "please make up your mind whether you are going to tell me this secret. If you are not going to tell me you are wasting my time, as well as your own."

She looked at him reproachfully. "Jimmy's brother Ralph is still alive. Jimmy heard from him yesterday. Is that important?"

"Very important. Tell me the details."

"Jimmy came in to see me yesterday morning. He was excited—oh, so excited. He said to me—I must try to remember the exact words—he said, 'I have had a telephone call from Ralph, Rita. He is still alive. I am going to meet him.'"

"You are sure of those words?"

"I am quite sure, yes. Then he said that I must not tell anybody. He said, 'Ralph says I am not to tell anyone at all, but that can't mean you, Rita. But you promise to say nothing.' I promised." Her voice faltered.

"I am sure he will forgive you. Now, Miss Foldes, you knew Ralph Clayton. What did you think of him?"

She spoke hesitantly. "It is difficult. I have known them a long time—we used to come here for holidays when we were children. Then I did not think anything of Jimmy—he was just the younger brother, you understand."

"But Ralph?"

"Ralph was very charming. He was attractive to women, you know. He was a good talker, played games well, made you feel that you were important to him. And yet—I do not know how to put this so that you understand it—there was always something strange in him, something detached."

"You were not surprised to learn that he had gone over to the Communists?"

"I was shocked, yes. But surprised?" The shrug of her shoulders indicated resignation. "It is the world we live in. Then I came here with my father in 1948, and for a long time I did not meet Jimmy again. I was engaged to Ronny Dobson. But when I met Jimmy again—I knew there could be nobody else."

Quarles leaned forward, large hands stretched palm downward on the desk. "Now, Miss Foldes, I want you to answer this question, although you may think it a strange one. Suppose Jimmy had the choice of meeting you after a long period of absence, meeting his brother after a long period of absence, or playing in the semifinal at Wimbledon—which would he do?"

A smile twitched at the corner of her mouth. "You are joking. It is your English sense of humour."

"Not at all. I was never more serious."

"Then I must be serious too." She thought a moment, finger on chin. "It is ridiculous, of course. I shall never understand the English. But I think he would have played the tennis match."

Quarles sighed, whether from suppressed interest, fatigue, or boredom it would have been hard to say. From the outer office a noise could be heard, a scuffle, a chair overturning, Molly Player's voice raised in protest. Then the door between Quarles' office and his secretary's room opened.

A young man stood there, looking at them, head slightly down like a bull about to charge. He was dark-featured and strikingly handsome, and his resemblance to Rita Foldes was obvious. A revolver gleamed bluely in his hand. His voice was strongly accented. "What has she been telling you?"

"My dear young man, you must put that revolver down."

"You have been telling him secrets, fool?" the young man said angrily.

"*Put that down,*" Quarles said.

The young man raised the gun slowly, and pointed it at Quarles. His lips were drawn up over his teeth in a sneering smile. What happened next was almost too quick for Rita's eye to see. At one moment a heavy brass paperweight lay on Quarles' desk; the next moment it had flown across the room and knocked the gun out of the young man's hand.

Quarles moved across the room with an agility surprising in so big a man and picked up gun and paperweight, while the young man cried out with pain and anger.

"This," Rita Foldes said calmly, "is my young brother Charles. He is, like my father, a member of our National Liberation Committee. He speaks loudly but performs little. You owe Mr. Quarles an apology, Charles."

"I am sorry," Charles Foldes said. He added sulkily, "It was not loaded."

Quarles polished the brass paperweight on his sleeve and returned it to the desk. "Sit down. What secrets were you afraid your sister might tell?"

"It is about their ridiculous committee," she said. "Playing at being conspirators."

"It is very well to talk about playing." Charles Foldes almost shouted the words. "For Andreas and Paul there was no play."

"What happened to Andreas and Paul?" Quarles asked.

"They were sent back home as agents, picked up as soon as they arrived. We have a spy in our organisation, betraying our best men."

Quarles said softly, "And you think your father might have been this spy? That with his work done he might have gone back. Is that what worries you?"

The young man did not answer. There was silence in the room for a moment, then the telephone rang. Quarles picked it up to hear the clipped, yet slightly languid tones of Mervyn Briffitt.

"Look here, we've found a taxi-man who took Foldes down to the dock area on the night he disappeared. Says Foldes met someone there. Would you care to come along to my office while I talk to him?"

Quarles said that he would, and told Briffitt that two members of the family were with him.

"Bring them along by all means."

As they went out of the building, Quarles told them the news. "It looks as though your father may have gone back."

Rita Foldes shook her head in an insistent gesture of denial. And at that moment she slipped on the last step and fell heavily to the ground.

When Quarles and her brother helped her up, her face was twisted with pain. With their help she hobbled to a taxi. "Have you sprained it?" Quarles asked.

"It is nothing, it will be better soon. But I will not believe that my father went back of his own free will. I will never believe it, never, *never*."

This morning Mervyn Briffitt looked rosier and more cherubic than usual. He greeted Rita Foldes and her brother warmly. "Glad you could come along. It really does look as though we're on the track of something. Now, here's our taxi driver, Bill Savory. Just repeat that story you were telling me, Bill."

The taxi driver was a gnarled, hard-bitten little Cockney who showed some sign of regret that he had ever become mixed up in this affair. "I ought to get back on the beat, guv. I'm losing fares, see."

"That's all right, my man," Briffitt said in a lordly manner. "I'll see you're not the loser by it."

The taxi driver sighed, rested his hands on his knees, and gabbled away in a singsong voice. "I'm coasting along that Sunday evening just off Holland Road, see, in Belsiter Gardens, and this old gentleman comes out of a house."

"Number forty-four?" Rita Foldes said.

The taxi driver regarded her with a look of patient pity. "I couldn't say, miss, wasn't looking at the numbers."

"But you recognise this photograph?" With a conjuror's quickness Briffitt produced a photograph. Quarles, looking over his shoulder, saw the face of Doctor Foldes, vaguely familiar from newspaper photographs—the face of a European liberal, shrewd, tolerant, patient, a little sad, the hands clasped together in a gesture expressing resignation, the pince-nez adding an almost comic scholarly touch.

"That's the old gentleman, no doubt about it." Briffitt returned the photograph to his pocket. "Asked me to take him down to the East India Docks—near the Royal Victoria it was. So I did. Took him down there, dropped him off, got paid. Then this other chap comes out of the darkness to meet him. And my fare says, 'You are here, then. You are in time.' And that's the lot."

"Now I have already shown you these, but I will show them to you again," Briffitt said. He did another conjuring act, producing a photograph of Jimmy Clayton, then one of his brother Ralph.

"I couldn't say," the driver said wearily. "I told you before, I just couldn't say. Can I go now, guv?"

"One or two more questions. Just repeat, if you will, how the other man was dressed."

"Wore a raincoat with the collar turned up a bit, and a trilby hat. Wasn't short—medium to tall I should say. But it was dark, I tell you, and I wasn't looking all that hard."

"Just one more question, Mr. Savory," Quarles said. "Those words your fare spoke—in what tone were they uttered?"

"I don't get you."

"Did he sound as though he were pleased to see the other man, as though he knew him well, as though he didn't know him at all, as though he might be afraid of the other man? What was your impression?"

The taxi driver thought, then spoke slowly and deliberately. "I should say it was someone he knew, not much doubt of that. But pleased to see him, no. It was like—you might say it was like a school-teacher talking to a boy just before giving him a dose of the stick. Can I go now, guv? I got to get back on the job."

When Bill Savory had gone, Briffitt looked at them with some satisfaction. His office was a neat small room high up in a building off Grosvenor Gardens. On the walls were, not the criminal mementos one might have expected, but more modern paintings—this time the young English realists, Middleditch and Jack Smith, and their Italian contemporaries.

Stroking his fair moustache, Briffitt said, "We've traced your father to the docks. I wonder if you'd like to say anything about that."

Brother and sister said nothing.

Quarles asked, "Was there any boat in the dock that night which had come from Foldes' country, or was sailing to it?"

Briffitt shook his head, his eyes bright and merry. "None that had any direct connection at all. Yes, Jane my dear, what is it?"

The dark, pretty girl who had put her head inside the door said, "Will your guests have tea or coffee, Mervyn?"

"Tea, my dear, I'm sure. The Earl Grey, so refreshing, with a slice of lemon." When the door had closed he said, "Lady Jane Milberry—Lord Milberry's daughter, of course. Such a charming girl, and so discreet."

Quarles observed him with an ironical eye.

Rita suddenly spoke. "I shall never believe that my father could have been in any way a traitor. I shall never believe that he could have been fool enough to go back."

"Have you any idea at all why he went down to the docks?"

She shook her head. "None, except that I believe it was some kind of trap. And I do not see what this can have had to do with Jimmy."

"Shut up, Rita." Her brother's dark face was brooding, sulky. The slang sounded odd in his heavily accented voice. "Mr. Quarles, about this I have to think. It is serious."

"You mean you know something?"

Charles Foldes ran his hand through his hair, ruffling it. "No. But I think—I think I must go home now. Excuse me, please." He got up and left them.

A couple of minutes later Lady Jane came in. She poured tea, added lemon, and said to Briffitt, "Here's the lunch edition of the evenings. And a note that's just come by hand."

Briffitt opened the papers, gave a furious exclamation, and passed one over to Quarles. The detective read:

WHERE IS JIMMY CLAYTON?

BRITISH STAR DISAPPEARS

AFTER VICTORY

The story briefly reported the fact of Clayton's disappearance, and told of an unsuccessful attempt to get information from his home. Then came the vital paragraphs.

"Bobo Williams, famous British coach, who laid down the brilliant strategy by which Clayton beat the Russian ace Gladkov, admitted today that he was worried. 'My lips are sealed,' he said. 'I have been ordered to say nothing. But I have not seen Jimmy since the match, and am very anxious about him.

"'He is due to play in the men's doubles today, and in his singles semifinal against Harry Parker tomorrow. The affair is in the hands of private detective Francis Quarles, but so far he seems to have done nothing.'

"Mr. Quarles was not in his office when I telephoned. His secretary refused to confirm or deny that he knew anything about Jimmy Clayton's disappearance."

"I never thought it would be possible to keep it quiet," Quarles said. He was stopped by another exclamation from Briffitt. The little rosy-faced man, now almost purple with indignation, handed him the note Lady Jane had brought in. Quarles read:

"To Messrs. Mervyn Briffitt and Francis Quarles—in conference:
    "You might as well give up the search for Foldes. You'll never find him, he's out of your reach. I will try to get Jimmy back in time for his match—if you don't stick your noses in too far.
                                                    "RALPH CLAYTON."

Briffitt fairly pounded the bell on his desk. Lady Jane appeared, looking somewhat disapproving. "When did this note come?"

"A minute or two ago. I waited until the tea was ready before I brought it in."

"And who brought it?"

A certain aristocratic detachment, perhaps indicating resentment that she was being talked to like a mere secretary, became evident in her manner. "I really couldn't say. One of the boys brought it up. I'll make inquiries if you like."

"I do like. And make them quickly."

The stare which Lady Jane gave him was Medusan in its malignancy. But she was back in less than five minutes, to say that the note had been delivered by a small boy who was eating an ice cream cone.

"The usual thing," Quarles observed. "If you trace him you'll find he was given it by a bigger boy who got it from a man outside a post office, or something like that. Not much hope of tracing the note, either. Typewritten on a fairly new machine, or at least one that has no glaring faults of alignment. Flimsy paper. You can put people onto it, but it's long odds against them turning up anything in time for it to be useful."

Briffitt agreed. "You realise what this means. You were followed here from your office—perhaps Miss Foldes and her brother were followed before then. You noticed nothing?"

"No. But I wasn't looking for anyone. It would be interesting to know whether our man was following Miss Foldes and her brother—they came to me at different times—or whether he was trailing me."

Briffitt was stroking his silky moustache. "He knew you were coming to see me, and he knows my Christian name. Still, it's not surprising that Ralph Clayton should know these things."

"You've not remarked the most interesting thing about this note."

"What's that?"

"The fact that it should have been written at all."

Back in his office Quarles patted Molly Player on the shoulder. "You held the fort well against the newspaper onslaught. Thank you."

She smiled sweetly. "Thank *you*. I was helped by the fact that you forgot to tell me anything about the case. But when Miss Foldes called this morning I remembered that she was the girl who got engaged to Jimmy Clayton a few months ago, and I put one and one together."

"Do you know why I didn't tell you about it?" She shook her head. "Because I knew it would give you so much pleasure to work it out for yourself. Now bring me the Blake-Oster file, will you, and order me a sandwich and a glass of milk."

For the next two hours Quarles worked on the Blake-Oster file, collating reports from three different agents about the activities of a drug syndicate which operated in England through a firm of coffee merchants, half a dozen manicurists in top-class hairdressing establishments, and a travelling circus. This ability to switch himself from one case to another at a moment's notice was one of his more considerable accomplishments.

He had just begun to write his report on the drug syndicate when Molly Player buzzed him on the office telephone. "Mr. Williams ringing from Wimbledon. Do you want to speak to him?"

"Yes, put him on." There was a click, and Quarles heard Bobo Williams' thin, protesting voice.

"Mr. Quarles, they've done it. You're too late."

"What do you mean?"

"They've scratched Jimmy from the men's doubles. His name was called, and he wasn't here. Oh, Mr. Quarles, what are we going to do? Is there any news at all?"

"No positive news." He added dryly, "Except of course the news that you gave to the papers."

An anguished bleat came to him down the telephone. "But, Mr. Quarles, I really didn't say anything—"

"You just told anyone who didn't know that I was working on the case," Quarles said pleasantly. "Now, Mr. Williams, I want you to answer a question. You know Jimmy Clayton is devoted to his brother, Ralph?"

"But Ralph Clayton is dead."

"Let us suppose for a moment that he is alive," Quarles said patiently. Williams gasped. "This is the question. Suppose Jimmy had to choose between helping Ralph and playing in the men's singles semifinal, which do you think he would do?"

Bobo Williams was in many ways a foolish man, but his voice now had an impressive earnestness. "Mr. Quarles, I don't believe anything—anything at all—would keep Jimmy away from Wimbledon tomorrow if it was humanly possible for him to get there."

When Quarles put down the telephone his face was grave. He cupped chin in hands for a moment, thinking, then asked Molly Player to ring Mrs. Clayton.

Jimmy's mother was a woman who concealed her emotions as much as possible, but the anxiety in her voice came through the carefully controlled tones that he remembered.

"Yes, Mr. Quarles. Is there any news?"

"Nothing definite, I'm afraid." He then put to her the question that he had put to Bobo Williams, and received an almost equally emphatic reply. "James was mad about tennis. He would let nothing come between him and playing at Wimbledon."

"Not even the chance of helping Ralph?"

There was a pause. "Are you trying to tell me that Ralph is still alive, Mr. Quarles?"

"I don't know. That is something I'm trying to find out."

She said slowly, "Do you know, I almost hope he isn't. But as for your question—I don't think anything but force would stop Jimmy from playing at Wimbledon."

When Quarles had put down the receiver, he said to Molly Player, "Who's our best contact at the War Office?"

"Colonel Pennefether, I should think. He was awfully grateful when you got his wife out of that scrape with the blackmailer, if you remember."

"Get him, will you?"

Five minutes later he was talking to Colonel Pennefether, and explaining what he wanted.

"Ralph Clayton," Pennefether said thoughtfully. "I remember the name, naturally. Give me an hour, and I'll see what I can dig up."

He rang back in less than that time, apologetic. "Sorry, old boy, but there's not much hard information. Clayton's name stinks, no doubt about that. He wasn't a double agent, working for us, if that was in your mind. Just one of the weaker brethren, who hadn't got what it takes. As for his death, there's nothing to contradict that Chinese story that he was killed in one of our bombing raids. Equally, nothing that absolutely confirms it. You could call it ninety per cent certain, I should think."

Quarles thanked him. He had hardly put down the receiver when Molly said, "There's Mr. Foldes on the line. He seems very excited."

Charles Foldes came on, the words bubbling out in his imperfect English. "Mr. Quarles, I had to go home because of something—I was suspecting something. And I have discovered it. I know now how to tell you about my father, why he went to the docks. It was—"

There was a sudden crack that seemed almost to split Quarles' eardrum.

Then a cry.

Then silence.

Francis Quarles shouted to Molly Player, "Ring Mervyn Briffitt and tell him to go to the Foldes flat at once. Something's happened to Charles Foldes. You'll find the number in the black book on my desk."

He ran down the stairs and got a taxi to Belsiter Gardens. He arrived at just the time that Ronny Dobson's Jaguar drew up outside the house. That elegant young man got out, looking a little ruffled.

"I say, I had a call from old Charles a few minutes ago, asking me to come round here urgently. He sounded awfully excited. English really gone quite haywire. Do you suppose?"

"He rang me too, then he was cut off. Come on."

Belsiter Gardens was a street of tall early Victorian terrace houses in decay, the sort of houses that seem the natural homes of unsuccessful artists and exiled political plotters. The names on the doorbells said Marshall, Charambides, O'Brien, Ekberg, Foldes. They rang Foldes' bell first, and then all the others. At last a sluttishly pretty young woman came down, wearing a dressing gown.

"I'm very sorry," Quarles said. "We wanted to see Mr. Foldes, and he doesn't answer his bell."

"Must be out, then. Waking me up! You can't go in there."

"Who are you?" Quarles turned on her a formidable heavy-lidded glare. She returned it defiantly.

"Moira O'Brien. I'm a nightclub singer. Who are *you?*"

"My name is Francis Quarles. I am a private detective and I have reason to believe that something has happened to Charles Foldes. This is Mr. Dobson, a friend of the family. Have you seen or heard anything unusual in the past half hour?"

"Not a thing. I was asleep, I tell you." She yawned. "Suppose it's none of my business if you do go in."

"This is their flat," Ronny Dobson said impatiently. He stepped forward, but Quarles was in front of him.

The door opened at a push. It led into a passage, with doors opening off it. Ronny Dobson named them as they passed. "Charles' bedroom, Rita's, the old man's room, living room, and kitchen off on the right."

They looked into the bedrooms as they passed. They were simply furnished in that anonymous manner characteristic of the homes of exiles who have no emotional stake in the country which harbours them. When Quarles opened the living-room door he stopped. Behind him Ronny Dobson sucked in his breath sharply.

Charles Foldes lay face downward on the carpet, with a neat hole in the back of his head. He had bled very little, but he was quite obviously dead. The telephone was also on the carpet, with the receiver off the hook. In front of Foldes there was an old-fashioned desk, open, with a number of papers on it. More papers were scattered on the floor.

Quarles spoke, more to himself than to Dobson. "He was looking in the desk for papers. On the telephone he told me that he had discovered something—no more than that. While he was talking somebody came in, someone who knew the importance of what Foldes was saying. He shot Foldes through the back of the head, searched the desk, found what he wanted and left. Don't touch," he said sharply to Dobson, who was kneeling by the body.

The young man looked up, his face stricken with grief. "I shall never forgive myself for the fact that I wasn't here on the spot. I had to go out of town first thing this morning, didn't get back until an hour ago. I haven't had a chance to speak to Rita or Charles. If I'd been around so that Charles could phone me earlier, this might never have happened. Is there any news of the old man?"

"He was seen in the dock area on Sunday night," Quarles said absently. He was on his own knees now, peering under the body at a scrap of white that was showing. The scrap proved to be a piece of paper, clutched in Foldes' left hand.

Gently Quarles disengaged it from the gripping fingers. It had been torn from a larger sheet, and the fragment had only a few words on it. Quarles, who had a rough and ready knowledge of Foldes' native language, translated: "Memorandum on Leakage of Information. It is unquestionable that the leakage of information through which Paul and Andreas were captured came about…" Then there were a few more words and phrases: "one of us… although the governing régime… precautionary measure… suggest that action…"

"That's the old man's writing," Ronny Dobson said. "Do you suppose the murderer tore part of it away, thinking that he'd got the whole thing?"

Before Quarles could answer, the front door closed. Ronny Dobson went to the door of the living room and down the passage.

"Rita?" he called. "Rita, how are you?"

In a slightly surprised voice she said. "I'm all right."

"But your ankle? Is it better now?"

"Yes, quite better. Don't fuss, Ronny. Why are you looking like that? What has happened?"

"Rita, you must prepare for a shock. You must be brave."

"What do you mean?" she said, almost angrily. "Is it about Father? Or Jimmy? Let me go by."

Quarles thought it time to end a scene which could only become more painful. He went out into the passage where Ronny Dobson was trying to prevent Rita from passing him.

"Miss Foldes," he said, almost harshly. "It is nothing to do with your father or with Jimmy Clayton. Your brother Charles has been shot. I am sorry to say he is dead."

She stood perfectly still for a few moments, then said quietly, "I must see him, of course. Do not be foolish, Ronny. I am not a child."

She came into the room and stood looking down at the body on the floor. "Poor Charles," she said. "So angry and so foolish and so young."

This dry-eyed grief was more affecting than the hysteria Quarles had expected. He said to her, "Did you see him after he left Briffitt's office today?"

She shook her head. "I had lunch, then went to a masseuse this afternoon. She worked on my ankle—I had only turned it, as they say, not sprained it—she was able to put it right." While she spoke she continued to look at the body on the floor.

Now the door opened again, and Briffitt's clipped, cultured voice could be heard. "Hallo, Dobson. What's been going on?"

He came into the room without waiting for an answer, took one look at the body on the floor, and bent down to examine it. After a couple of minutes he straightened up.

"Shot from behind, distance of six or seven feet I should say, killer stood near the door, Foldes was on the telephone. Agree?" He glanced at Quarles.

The detective nodded. "This scrap of paper was in his hand."

Briffitt looked at it. "Killer presumably tore the rest away. Doctor Foldes' writing, isn't it? Doesn't help us much, as it stands."

"Mr. Briffitt," Rita said hesitantly, "what about Jimmy? He is—well, I mean, how is he mixed up in this? Did the man who killed my brother kidnap Jimmy from Wimbledon?"

Briffitt looked at her almost with pity. "Miss Foldes, this is a day of shocks. I may as well tell you now that nobody kidnapped Jimmy Clayton. He walked out of his own free will."

They sat in Briffitt's flat again, Quarles and Rita Foldes and Ronny Dobson, Victorian conversation pieces, English and Italian decadents looking down on them mockingly, while the dapper, rosy-faced little man smoked one of his black cigarettes and talked about Jimmy Clayton.

"Let me make this clear, first of all. Jimmy Clayton is a nice normal young man. He is in love with a beautiful girl, he likes playing tennis. But there are two other things about him that we must remember. The first is that he loves playing practical jokes. The second is that he worships his older brother Ralph."

They sat listening to him, Ronny Dobson with fingers plucking at his mauve waistcoat, Rita clasping and unclasping her black handbag, Francis Quarles with closed eyes, his bulk extended in an armchair.

"Here is the sequence of events. On Monday morning Jimmy Clayton receives a telephone call from Ralph. I think it's safe to assume that Ralph fixed a place of meeting, and told Jimmy that for obvious reasons he mustn't be followed.

"Easy enough, you may say. But not so easy, in fact. Supposing Ralph suggested a meeting at six o'clock, Jimmy had to play his match with Gladkov. Then he had to escape from autograph hunters and get rid of Bobo Williams. You've seen Bobo for yourself, you know what he's like. He was determined to have a talk with Jimmy after the match, and no amount of persuasion would have stopped him. Even outside the ground, Jimmy Clayton would have been recognised. After all, just at the moment, he is a pretty famous young man. So he decided to play one of those practical jokes which as everybody who knew him well told me, he enjoyed so much. He decided to disappear for the evening."

A little sharply, Briffitt said to the apparently sleeping detective, "Do you agree, Quarles?"

Francis Quarles opened one eye. "So far, yes," he said, and closed it again.

"Don't you think this was just the childish kind of practical joke that appealed to Jimmy?" Briffitt asked Rita.

"Yes. But I still don't see how he did it."

Briffitt stroked his moustache. "It was simple. He arrived with a zipper bag which contained a spare suit of clothes, a blond wig, and probably a false moustache. After the match he told Bobo Williams he was going to take a shower.

"He went into the bathroom, changed his clothes, put on the wig and moustache, deliberately made those misleading scratches on the window sill, dropped his zipper bag out of the window, came out of the bathroom, and walked out of the dressing room unnoticed. As Colonel Macaulay said, a watch is kept on people coming *into* the dressing room, but no similar watch is kept on those going *out*. Once outside, he simply picked up his bag and strolled off. Are we still in agreement, Quarles?"

"Yes," the detective answered lazily, from the depth of his chair. "Those hairs must somehow have come off the wig when he was putting it on—it's easy to distinguish real hair from false. The zipper bag Clayton brought with him had vanished. And it was much too great a coincidence that he should have picked just the one bathroom which had a window from which something could easily be dropped into a quiet passage outside. That wasn't accident but intention."

"Fascinating," Ronny Dobson said. "And what happened next?"

Briffitt looked at the tip of his cigarette. "We don't know. That is, we don't exactly know, yet it's not merely a matter of guess-work. Jimmy Clayton went to meet his brother. What happened when they met? Why did Ralph telephone at all? Remember Doctor Foldes had vanished on Sunday night, and the telephone call came on Monday morning.

"There's only one possible answer. Ralph was here as a secret emissary, to persuade Doctor Foldes to go home—or perhaps to take him home by force. Something went wrong with his plan. He was in need of help. Who should he turn to but the young brother who worshipped him? Are you still with me?"

"No," Quarles said from the depth of his armchair. Briffitt ignored him.

"When Ralph saw his brother he must have made an appeal for help. 'Help me and Foldes to get away. If you don't I'm done for. I shall have to stand trial.' Something on those lines.

"So Jimmy Clayton was faced with a terrible choice. On the one side was love for his brother, on the other the desire to play at Wimbledon. What arguments Ralph used to persuade him that this wasn't just a conspiracy to smuggle Doctor Foldes back into his own country I don't know. We only know that he stayed—he stayed to help. And when he did that he crossed the Rubicon." With a final, decisive gesture Briffitt stubbed out his cigarette.

"You mean he's not in England any more?" Dobson asked.

"I should say it's almost certain that Ralph and Jimmy Clayton are now behind the Iron Curtain, mission accomplished."

"And my father?" Rita Foldes asked.

"My dear Miss Foldes, I am sorry to say it, but in a couple of weeks we shall probably hear of him as another Doctor Otto John, attacking Western corruption, and back in his country's Communist-controlled but now slightly pseudo-Liberal government."

Quarles opened his eyes. "You seem to have omitted the murder of this young lady's brother."

"Charles Foldes?" Briffitt sighed. "Naturally there are still agents left in London, watching all of us—the note I received was sufficient proof of that. Charles Foldes discovered something, got in their way, and was removed."

"Poppycock." Now Francis Quarles, lethargy forgotten, was on his feet, striding up and down the room, talking with bitter, powerful emphasis. "Absolute rubbish, Briffitt, and if you weren't so blinded by your own conceit you'd know it."

Briffitt's rosy colour was a little heightened. "You agree with my explanation of Jimmy Clayton's disappearance—"

"Of course. It was obvious that he was playing some sort of practical joke. But the rest of it—I put this very question of yours to his mother, to Bobo Williams, and to Miss Foldes here, and they all agreed that nothing on earth would stop Jimmy from playing his men's singles semifinal." He whirled on Dobson. "What do you say?"

That elegant young man plucked at his mauve waistcoat a little uncertainly. "He's very fond of Ralph. But I know he was keen on tennis. I just don't know which he would do."

The telephone rang. Briffitt answered it. He said "Yes" three times, and then, "I'll come at once." He put back the receiver and stood looking at them, with the rosy colour entirely gone from his face.

"Well?" Quarles said.

"That was Inspector Leeds. They've found a body down in the docks. They think it may be Doctor Foldes."

They drove down to the docks under a darkening sky, with few words spoken. Quarles sat hunched in a corner of the car, his heavy face broodingly intent. Briffitt scraped at his nails with a nail file. Ronny Dobson whispered what were obviously comforting words to Rita Foldes who sat upright, paying no attention to any of them.

They passed the place where the taxi had dropped Doctor Foldes on Sunday night, and turned off into a side road. Warehouses reared their menacing bulk on either side, uninterrupted by houses. The street seemed utterly deserted, until a burly figure stepped out from the shadows and raised a hand.

It was Inspector Leeds. A sergeant was with him. They walked along the street in the dark evening, under thin rain, while the Inspector explained in a low voice what had happened.

"Street's all warehouses up this end, but there were houses at the other. Caught a packet in one of the raids on the docks, nothing much left now. Old air raid shelter there that you'll see in a minute. Stinking dirty place it is—been shut up for years.

"You know what kids are, though, they'll get in and play anywhere. This afternoon some kids playing cops and robbers down there came across this body. Might not have been found for months."

Quarles said, "Miss Foldes has very courageously offered to come down to look at the body."

They turned off the street onto waste ground. In a voice carefully devoid of feeling Rita Foldes said, "Are you sure it is my father?"

"Not sure, miss. We think so." The Inspector paused. "It's not very pretty."

"I did not expect so," she said, with the same artificial composure.

"Here we are." Another figure emerged in the light of the sergeant's torch. It was a policeman who said, "All correct, sir."

They went in, guided by two torches, past a wooden barrier and then down a sloping tunnel, which widened out at the bottom into a kind of central room from which four passages led off. Dust and dirt were everywhere, with odds and ends of clothing and scraps of old iron that had been left there at different times, broken saucepans and battered washbasins and bits of bicycles.

"Second left," the Inspector said. They made some turns in this passage and came upon the body of a man, stuffed into a small alcove that had once probably housed bunks for sleepers.

"Now just a minute, miss," the Inspector said, but Rita Foldes had already run forward to the body.

"Yes," she said. "Oh, yes, yes."

"You confirm that it's your father, miss?"

"It is my father," she said, and turned away.

Ronny Dobson put an arm round her and escorted her back along the dark tunnel. The sergeant stayed with them.

"Cause of death?" Briffitt said, in a weary voice.

"We shall have to wait for the doctor's final opinion," the Inspector said. "But I don't think there's any doubt. He was hit on the head with something heavy and it fractured his skull. Must have happened near here. Then the murderer brought him down here and dumped him in the shelter."

"How does this fit in with your theory that Foldes would reappear as a puppet Minister?" Quarles asked Briffitt.

The little counterespionage man made no reply.

They dropped Rita Foldes at the flat of a friend of Quarles, a woman doctor named Mary James, with whom she was to spend the night. Quarles went in with her and spoke to the doctor.

"Mary, Miss Foldes has had some terrible shocks today. She needs a sedative. But there's a question I want to ask her first. May I do that?"

Mary James was neat, bright, and birdlike. "Just one question."

Quarles put his hands on the girl's shoulders. "My dear girl, I know what you have been through. I wouldn't ask you things tonight unless it were vitally necessary. Jimmy's life may depend on it. Now, can you remember any place where Jimmy and Ralph used to go when they were children and on holiday, and you came over to see them?"

"Any house, do you mean?"

Quarles made an expansive gesture. "A house, a mill, a cottage—somewhere that was their own particular place."

She said despairingly, "I can't think, I just can't think." She put her head in her hands.

"You must leave it at that," Doctor James said.

Quarles nodded, concealing his disappointment. "If you think of anything, anything at all, telephone me at once." He said to Doctor James, "Take good care of her, Mary."

On the way home Quarles bought the latest editions of the evening papers. CLAYTON MYSTERY DEEPENS, he read in one, and in another, CLAYTON SCRATCHED FROM DOUBLES. STARS TELL OF DRESSING ROOM DISAPPEARANCE. There followed the story of how Joe Richards had helped Bobo Williams search the dressing room. Quarles read the story, and cursed Bobo Williams.

As he turned into the entrance of his flat, four figures suddenly advanced on him from both sides of the entrance. The happenings of the day had been such that his hand dropped to the hip pocket where he kept his gun. But these were no more dangerous characters than reporters in search of news. They fired a fusillade of questions.

"Is there any news on Clayton?"

"Can you say whether he'll play tomorrow?"

"Is it true Clayton's been involved in a car accident?"

"Been kidnapped by the Russians?"

"Lost his memory and wandered off somewhere on the South Coast?"

"Boys, boys," Quarles said placatingly. "I can tell you the answer to all those questions. I just don't know where Jimmy Clayton is. Happy?"

They were not happy. "Does that mean he's disappeared and you've been engaged to find him?"

"Ask Mrs. Clayton."

"She won't say. That's what Bobo Williams tells us."

"If you think you can rely on Bobo Williams—" Quarles said with a chuckle.

"Mr. Quarles, if you've not been engaged to find Clayton, why won't your secretary answer questions?"

"That's one of the things I pay her for, boys—not answering questions. Good night."

Quarles looked out of the window of his flat and saw that the reporters were talking together. Then two of them settled down in front of his flat, while the other two went off. Taking turns, Quarles thought, and chuckled again. Then he telephoned Mrs. Clayton, and asked her the same question he had put to Rita Foldes.

"I can't think of anything," she said. "At that time we had a large house called Roking Place in Kent, near Maidstone. The boys used to spend the summer there, and friends came over to see them. But we sold it years ago—it was an enormous, rambling old place—I don't think there's anything in that. Mr. Quarles, is there any news? Is Jimmy all right?"

Quarles chose his words carefully. "He is in danger, but I hope that somebody will show us the way to him."

"Will that be soon?"

"Perhaps tomorrow."

The telephone call that brought the case to a climax came sooner than Quarles had expected.

It was just after half-past nine in the morning, and the newspapermen had trailed him from flat to office, when he heard Rita Foldes' anxious voice.

"Mr. Quarles? I have news for you. It is perhaps of some use, I do not know. When I was a girl we used to come and stay sometimes with the Claytons at a house named Roking Place."

"But that was sold a long time ago. Mrs. Clayton told me about it."

"Yes. But it has been empty now for two years. Ronny came in this morning to see me, and we talked. He told me this."

"Miss Foldes, can you be ready in fifteen minutes to come with me to Roking Place? Are you equal to it? This is important."

Over the telephone she whispered, "Yes."

"Molly, listen to me," Quarles said to his secretary. "Ring Briffitt and tell him to get down to a house called Roking Place, near Maidstone, as quickly as he can. Tell him it's life or death. He must bring some men with him. I suppose he'll have to tell Leeds. But first of all, go and open the doors of that lift as if you were going down in it."

Molly did what she was told, watched with interest by the two reporters outside the office door. At the instant the lift doors opened Quarles came out of his office like a runner in a hundred-yard sprint. He had pressed the button taking him down to the basement before the reporters had begun to rush down the stairs.

From the basement he let himself out of the caretaker's door, and went to the garage where he kept the black and green Bentley which he hardly ever used for driving in London.

Rita Foldes was waiting for him, and with her was Mary James, a disapproving look on her face. "You've no right to be taking this girl out, after what she's been through," she said.

"Mary, if her presence wasn't vitally important to the case I shouldn't ask her to come."

Rita Foldes was in the car before all these words were spoken. Her face was pale, and she wore no lipstick.

It is a tedious journey from the north side of the river to the point at which the Sidcup bypass is reached, and Quarles generally reckoned that it took half an hour. On this occasion, by avoiding the Elephant and going down the back streets which skirt the Old Kent Road, he did it in twenty-two minutes.

Once on the main road to Maidstone the Bentley moved with effortless ease at a speed which made almost no allowance for other traffic on the road. Rita Foldes said once, "You are driving dangerously. Or it would be dangerous with most drivers. Is that necessary?"

Quarles shot the Bentley forward into the gap between an oncoming truck and a car just moving out to pass. They cleared the two by inches. "Yes."

"You expect to find—?"

"I expect to find Jimmy Clayton. Tell me where to turn off."

"Beyond Wrotham. There is a turning that takes you to Mereworth. Then Wateringbury. After that a narrow lane to the left. I will tell you."

They turned off down the Mereworth Road, and roared through the placid Kent countryside. "Here," Rita said when they were a mile out of Wateringbury, and Quarles turned sharp left up a narrow road.

"How far?"

"About a mile and you come to the drive. Then it's half a mile farther to the house."

Just inside the lion-topped entrance gates that said "Roking Place," Quarles stopped the car. "From here we go on foot. I hope we are in time. Can we approach the house without being seen?"

"Yes. It's a way we used when we were children. Along here." They pushed along an overgrown path tangled with briars and brushwood. "There is the house."

Through a tangle of bushes Quarles saw the front of the house. It was a Victorian Gothic monster, all spires and towers and arched doorways. In front of it stood a courtyard, and as they watched, two cars roared up into this courtyard and half a dozen men tumbled out of them.

Quarles saw Briffitt advance toward the house. Then a shot came from a first-floor window—a crack and a puff of smoke. Briffitt started back as if he had been stung by a wasp.

"He must be mad," Quarles said. "This is senseless. He can't possibly get away unless—did the eccentric Victorian who built this place put in any secret passages, that kind of thing?"

"I don't think so." She added slowly, "Of course, there is the passage that goes through the cellars and comes out by an old ruined chapel in the grounds, half a mile away. Would that be—?"

"Yes. Take me there now. Hurry! But we want to keep out of sight."

They moved round the side of the house and then, as it seemed, away from it. Their clothes were torn by brambles. A branch that whipped back struck Quarles across the face, and when he put up his hand he felt blood.

At last, after what seemed to him half an hour but was perhaps five minutes, they came to the chapel, a narrow building with only the walls still standing; it looked as though it had been put into a machine and squashed.

"It's along here, by the side of the chapel. There's a big stone with a ring in it. Here it is."

The surrounding wild grass had been cut away from the stone, which lifted easily when Quarles pulled at the ring. A flight of steps led downward into darkness.

"We go straight ahead and come out into the cellars," Rita said. "I know the way."

Quarles followed her along a narrow passage in which there was hardly room for him to stand upright. Cobwebs brushed their faces, but they encountered nothing worse until they opened the door that led into a cellar, full of empty wine bottles and old packing cases.

Above them was a thunderous knocking. That must be Briffitt and his men, Quarles thought, attacking the front door. But much nearer was the sound of feet coming down to the cellar, of something being dragged along.

Quarles moved behind a packing case and motioned Rita to do the same.

Now they heard a high voice speaking, a voice on the edge of hysteria. "You're wondering why I've taken the trouble to keep you alive all this time, my fine fellow. It was to provide the finishing touch. But not much longer—no, it won't be much longer. A bullet in the head, a quick and merciful end, you'll agree. Then the body discovered in the passage leading to the chapel. And by the time they find it, Ralph the wicked brother will be a long way off where they can't possibly catch him. Wicked, wicked Ralph."

The voice came nearer. Quarles called out loudly, "It's no use. Put up your hands."

From the end of the cellar there was a spurt of flame. Quarles fired as soon as he saw the flash, and was rewarded by a howl of rage and anger. He rushed forward and grappled with an assailant who was no more than a shape in darkness, bearing him to the ground at the same moment that the door above opened and the pencil beams of half a dozen torches pierced the darkness.

"Why, it's you, Quarles," Briffitt's voice said. "Have you got him? Have you got Ralph Clayton?"

Quarles straightened up, retaining his grip on the thing that now whimpered beneath him on the floor. "Ralph Clayton died in Korea, Briffitt, years ago. Here's your murderer."

The beams of light played now on the face of the man on the floor.

"Ronny Dobson," Briffitt said. "But why—"

"You call him Dobson, but don't forget that his name is really Dombos," Quarles said. "But there's someone else here who's much more interesting."

"Jimmy," Rita Foldes said. She bent down by the figure beside Dobson, bound hand and foot and a gag in his mouth; but the torchlight showed the bright unmistakable red hair.

Quarles cut the bonds with a knife, and Jimmy Clayton groaned and stretched.

"Take them upstairs," Briffitt said.

In the great empty drawing room upstairs, its windows looking out on the desolate courtyard and drive, Jimmy Clayton told them his story.

"I got the telephone call early on Monday morning," he said. "Chap said he was Ralph. I suppose I should have been suspicious—the voice wasn't much like Ralph's really—but at the time I fell for it hook, line, and sinker. Trouble was, I suppose, that I wanted to believe, and so I did. Anyway Ralph, as I thought it was, told me he was here on a mission, couldn't explain on the telephone, had run into trouble, and needed my help. I was to meet him here on Monday evening at seven, and he'd explain. Mustn't tell anyone, mustn't be seen coming here. I expect you think that should have made me suspicious too, but do you know it was all so very much like Ralph. He always loved a secret.

"I knew getting out of Wimbledon after playing the Russian wouldn't be easy, and I couldn't resist playing a little joke on Bobo, putting the wind up him a bit." He gave a sly, little-boy grin.

"We worked that out," Quarles said. "Then you came down here."

"That's right. I took a taxi from the station to a spot on the main road, and walked up. Opened the front door, something hit me, and I went out like a light. I always thought my head was hard, but this raised a bump on it that's still there. When I woke I was tied up in the room upstairs that we used as a playroom, wondering who'd hit me on the head and why. When Ronny came down and gave me food a couple of times I learned who, but I never did find out why."

"If you don't know now you never will," Dobson said. The expression on his face was one of intense, venomous hatred.

"I don't know about that," Quarles said. "We may be able to help you—"

He was interrupted by a shout from Jimmy Clayton. "What day is it? Wednesday? And it's half-past twelve. I must get to Wimbledon." He stood up and swayed on his feet.

"You're not fit to play tennis today," Quarles said. "And perhaps you won't need to. Look outside."

They looked. "Rain," said Jimmy Clayton ecstatically. "Beautiful, beautiful rain."

"If it goes on raining they'll postpone your match until tomorrow, isn't that right? And if the weather men are right, it *is* going on raining. But let's get to London."

They drove back in a rainstorm that was blended with thunder and lightning as they approached London. They telephoned Wimbledon and discovered that the rain had washed out play for the day. Then they deposited Jimmy Clayton in a Turkish bath, which he swore would be a cure for all his troubles.

"Just stiffness and cramp," he said. "I must say Ronny didn't beat me up, after that one blow on the head. Can't bear to miss that explanation, though."

"Miss Foldes will tell you tomorrow," Quarles said.

Later, in his office, he talked to an attentive audience composed of Rita Foldes, Mrs. Clayton, Inspector Leeds, and a subdued Mervyn Briffitt.

"I'll tell you first of all what happened, and then how I got on to it," Quarles said. "The whole thing was precipitated by Doctor Foldes' discovery that Dobson, or Dombos, was the traitor on the committee who had sent some of his friends to their deaths. Foldes must have told Dobson, and insisted that he leave England. Dobson agreed, and it was arranged that Foldes should come down to the docks to make sure that he had gone.

"But Dobson had no idea of leaving England. In another country he would be penniless, and it was certain that Doctor Foldes would spread the word that he was a traitor—though, incidentally, I doubt if Dobson regarded himself in that light, but simply as a sensible man who worked for the side that paid him best. Besides, Dobson was still in love with Rita Foldes, and didn't want to leave her. So he met Foldes down at the docks, killed him, dragged his body into that air raid shelter. He hoped that it might not be discovered for a long time but, as we know, he was unlucky.

"Then he had a brilliant idea. Dobson hated Jimmy Clayton. There was one genuine emotion in his life, and that was love of Rita Foldes. He had been engaged to marry her, and Jimmy had taken her away.

"Dobson's idea was this. Why not get rid of his hated rival and at the same time provide a convincing motive for Foldes' disappearance, simply by reviving the ghost of Ralph Clayton? He did it very cleverly at times, as when he drew my attention to Ralph at the beginning of the case, and clumsily at other times, as when he sent that note to Briffitt which was meant to be from Ralph Clayton. In fact, that was more than clumsy. It was the clue which led me to Dobson."

"I don't see why," Briffitt said.

"When you read the note you pointed out that it must have been written by somebody who had followed Miss Foldes, her brother, and me from my office. Now, outside my office, Miss Foldes tripped and hurt her ankle. By the time she saw Dobson after her brother's death it was all right—she showed no sign of a limp. Dobson said that he hadn't had a chance to see her or her brother that day. Yet he inquired tenderly about the injured ankle.

"How could he possibly have known about it—unless he was the man who followed us to your office that morning, and sent the note supposed to be from Ralph Clayton?"

"Very clever," Briffitt said, a shade grudgingly. "I missed that."

"You missed some other things too," Quarles said softly. "The significance of that torn memorandum in Charles' hand, for instance. That was the clearest possible indication that he had discovered the identity of the traitor, and had been killed because of it. Dobson realised that he had left a fragment of the memorandum in Charles' hand and came back for it, but I had already arrived on the scene. His last effort was to stage a good finale, in which we were meant to think that Ralph Clayton had killed his brother, and then vanished. Again, he wasn't quite successful. An ingenious, but a careless plotter."

Quarles strolled across to the window. "The clouds are clearing. I am happy to say that Jimmy Clayton has promised me a ringside seat for his match tomorrow."

Jimmy Clayton walked up the steps which, during the tournament, may only be used by those playing on the centre court. He entered the anteroom where Harry Parker was already sitting.

The young American smiled. "How are you, Jimmy? Fit?"

"As a fiddle," Jimmy Clayton answered.

The swing doors opened, and they stepped out onto the centre court. Once there, once he had bowed to Princess Margaret and the Duchess of Kent in the Royal box, and waved his racket to Rita and to Francis Quarles who sat together watching him expectantly, all nervousness dropped from him. He remembered only that he was the first English tennis player in the men's singles semifinal at Wimbledon for goodness knew how many years, and that this was the chance of his lifetime. He threw up the ball, pivoted round, swung his racket, and served.

THE DROP SHOT

Michael Gilbert

Michael Francis Gilbert (1912–2006) was, together with Julian Symons, the leading male British crime novelist of his generation. Like Symons, he received the CWA Diamond Dagger and was made a Grand Master of the Mystery Writers of America, but although the two men had a long friendship, they were very different in terms of personality and as regards their approach to writing crime fiction. Gilbert fought in the Second World War and his experiences as a prisoner of war in Italy provide background material for *Death in Captivity* (1952), one of the finest British "impossible crime" stories of the post-war era. By the time of its appearance, Gilbert was well-established as a partner in a prestigious law firm, and had also made a name for himself as an author of considerable talent. His urbanity is reflected in the smooth, readable prose of his whodunits, thrillers, spy stories, legal mysteries, and police stories. Although perhaps less ambitious as a novelist than Symons, he demonstrated that fiction written primarily to entertain can have enduring appeal, and was equally adept at writing novels, stage plays, radio plays, and television scripts.

Gilbert had a flair for the short crime story, as this example illustrates. It originally appeared in the *Evening Standard* on 27 November 1950, and was eventually collected in *Even Murderers Take Holidays* (2007) edited by John Cooper. He played squash and, in his twenties, rugby for Salisbury. After his marriage, he enjoyed playing cricket for Luddesdown Cricket Club, and in later life became their President. He also took up archery. At home, he is remembered by his children as highly competitive on the croquet lawn.

I SQUEEZED MY WAY INTO THE NARROW, CROWDED GALLERY and found a vacant place next to Bill Birley.

This squash match was likely to be the decider in the County Championship.

"Six-four in the first game," said Birley as I sat down beside him. "It's going to be damned good."

Birley is my solicitor—Horniman, Craine and Birley, of Lincoln's Inn—and, believe it or not, one of my closest friends as well.

"If Cavendish wins," I said, as I settled down to watch the game, "it'll be a triumph of experience over youth."

It was going to be a terrific fight.

Cavendish—you must have heard the name, he has been in the front rank of squash players for twenty years—was over forty to my knowledge; and he was playing a young pilot officer, who knew how to hit the ball very hard and who knew how to run.

He never let up on anything. But Cavendish was holding him—and doing it, chiefly by mixing good length shots with drop shots of amazing delicacy, a lot of them off the half-volley.

If you've never watched a squash match I'd better explain that a drop shot is one which is played very softly and as low as possible above the tell-tale. The real artist puts a bit of cut on it as well, so that it just falls to the floor and dies a natural death.

Time and again Cavendish dropped that ball dead, and time after time his opponent hurled himself across the length of the court and managed to get his racket under it.

Flesh and blood couldn't stand too much of it. And sure enough Cavendish was drawing away. He took the first game 9—5 and the second one 9—7. The match was best out of five games, so he only wanted one more to clinch it. And on that form he didn't look as if he was going to have much difficulty over it.

I said so to Birley.

"I'm not so sure," said Birley. "I'll back the airman."

"He's killing himself," I said.

"He'll survive," said Birley. "He's young. And he's learning. You can get an awful lot of education, even during one game. If he's learnt his lesson he'll win yet."

"It's that drop shot," I said.

"The way to beat a drop shot," said Birley, "is by anticipation."

As he said this he gave me a very odd smile I hadn't much time to wonder about it, because the third game was starting.

But Birley was right. Under the stress of total war the Air Force was learning the hard lesson of survival.

Cavendish still managed to deceive him occasionally, but his opponent was holding his own now, and he won the next two games with a little in hand.

"Right as usual," I said to Birley.

The players were taking the two-minute interval that the rules allow before the fifth game.

"It's not the first time I've watched him play," said Birley. "Not by a long chalk. And I've seen that drop shot in action before, too. In fact—look here. This fifth game is only going to be an anti-climax. The youngster's got his measure now. Come down to the bar and let's get a drink before the rest of the mob makes it impossible."

The bar was almost empty and we took our drinks and retired to the window seat with them.

"You've seen the end of a story up there on the court," said Birley.

He stopped for a minute, so I said: "What sort of a story?"

"That story you often hear about," said Birley. "The perfect murder. It happened years ago—before the war—when everyone had more money and a country house *was* a country house. You've heard of Sir Godfrey Heyward?"

"Biscuits," I said. "Millionaire. Used to have a big place just beyond Epping."

"That's the chap. He was one of my clients. Nice old boy, and game for most things. He wasn't exactly the hunting type, but he'd have a fling at anything else. Had his own squash court at Rowdens. Took to the game rather late in life.

"I shall never forget one weekend. I got down in time for tea on Saturday, and I found a lot of good-natured excitement going on, and even a few mild bets being laid over a match that was going to take place on the squash court that evening. I got most of it from Rufus Marks, the Harley Street man who was down for that weekend with his wife.

"'They had one game this morning,' said Rufus, 'which the old man just won. Then they had another this afternoon—very close thing indeed. Robert just managed to win that. So they're having a decider before dinner this evening.' 'Robert who?' I asked. 'Robert Cavendish,' said Rufus.

"It took a few seconds for this to sink in: then I said. 'Well, if you've got any loose money, put it on Cavendish.'

"'I don't know so much,' said Rufus. 'I saw this afternoon's game. It was a very close thing.'

"'But, good heavens,' I said. 'Don't you know that Cavendish is—' and then I stopped. It struck me that it was quite possible that no one down there except myself did know what sort of squash player Cavendish was.

"'Is he really good?' said Rufus.

"'Absolutely first class,' I said. 'Sir Godfrey would have no chance against him if he was really trying.'

"While I was in the middle of saying this the idea hit me, and I got quite a shock when I looked up and saw that Rufus had got it, too.

"'How's Sir Godfrey's heart these days?' I said.

"'It hasn't been terrific since he had pneumonia two years ago,' said Rufus.

"'Is there any chance of keeping him out of the court this evening?' I asked bluntly.

"'Have you ever found that he listened to his professional advisers?' said Rufus.

"'Only when it suited him,' I admitted.

"We both sat on the sofa and looked at each other like a couple of schoolboys who have gone treasure-hunting and turned up a skeleton.

"'Why?' said Rufus at last.

"'Just what you said. He'll never listen to his professional advisers. I don't know how many times I've told him to make a will. He always promises to do it next time he sees me.'

"'Who gets it all if he dies without a will?'

"'I don't suppose he's even troubled to work it out,' I said. 'He hasn't got any very close relatives. As a matter of fact it goes through his father's only sister—she died last year—to...'

"'I can guess that one,' said Rufus. 'To Robert Cavendish.'

"'Surely,' I said. 'If you told him—'

"'I've never known Sir Godfrey do anything I've told him,' said Rufus. 'Besides—this may sound unethical. But supposing we're right, and supposing it does happen—is it such a bad way to go?'

"'He won't last for ever. Some day soon that heart's going to catch up with him. It might be running up stairs or it might be just getting up from table. Why not go out in a blaze of glory, playing your favourite game—'

"'That's all very well from his point of view,' I said. 'I'm thinking of Cavendish.'

"I shan't forget that game as long as I live.

"It's the only time I've ever seen murder committed, under the blaze of electric lamps in front of a gallery full of spectators who cheered the murderer's every stroke.

"Cavendish, you understand, was not only playing the most perfectly judged drops and lobs, but he was playing them so that they were just *not quite good enough*. He always allowed his opponent a chance of getting to them. Not much chance, but enough to make a sporting old boy like Sir Godfrey go for them.

"The end came in the fourth game. A drop shot in a million. The old man started to jump. There was a clatter as he dropped his racket, and then he was in a heap on the floor.

"Rufus Marks was the finest heart man in England, and he was on the job inside five seconds, but he might just as well have been back in his consulting room in London.

"There wasn't a thing to be done."

★

I listened in silence. If I hadn't known Birley so well I should have thought he was making the whole thing up.

"I never heard that Cavendish came into money," I said at last. "He must have kept very quiet about it."

"Of course he didn't come into the money," said Birley. "I told you what the answer to the drop shot was. Anticipation, I persuaded Sir Godfrey to make his will before he went on to the court. Rufus and I witnessed it in the gunroom after tea. He left the bulk of his money to very sound charities—"

There was a burst of applause from upstairs and a clatter of feet, as the spectators left the gallery.

The first man down in the bar happened to be someone I knew.

"How did it go, Duggie?" I asked.

"Victory for the Air Force," said Duggie. "By that last game there was really only one man in it. Poor old Cavendish, he literally murdered him."

"Not literally, I hope," said Mr. Birley, mildly.

DANGEROUS SPORT

Celia Fremlin

Celia Margaret Fremlin (1914–2009) made a dazzling start to her career as a crime novelist. *The Hours Before Dawn* (1958), her first book, won an Edgar award from the Mystery Writers of America, and remains a classic of domestic suspense. For more than three decades she continued to produce gripping novels such as *Appointment with Yesterday* (1972) and *The Spider-Orchid* (1977). Fremlin's acute eye for characters must surely have benefited from the time she spent working on the Mass Observation project after leaving Somerville College, Oxford. Her understanding of human behaviour was complemented by a sharp sense of humour, evident in such novels as *Possession* (1969), while her presentation of quiet, sometimes desperate lives was accompanied by a touch of menace. Her own personal life was blighted by a series of tragic bereavements and she became a vocal advocate of assisted suicide and euthanasia.

Fremlin was an accomplished writer of short fiction and the virtues of her novels are equally on display in her elegantly crafted tales with a twist. This story first appeared in *Ellery Queen's Mystery Magazine* in September 1976, and was subsequently collected in *A Lovely Day to Die and other stories* (1984).

"DARLING, I'D JUST LOVE TO BE ABLE TO STAY. YOU KNOW I would. I'm just as disappointed as you are. But—"

But.

But, but, but. What would it be *this* time, Stella wondered bitterly. Whatever it was, she'd have heard it before, that was certain. After five years of going around with a married man, a girl knows his repertoire by heart.

But I have to help Wendy with the weekend shopping. *But* the man is coming to fix the hot-water boiler. *But* I have to fetch Carol from the Brownies. *But* Simon is away from school with a temperature. *But* I have to meet Aunt Esmé at the airport.

This last had been the funniest "but" of all; and though in fact it had happened quite near the beginning of her relationship with Gerald, it still made Stella laugh, and grind her teeth, when she thought about it. For it had come so soon after that golden September day when, lying in the long grass by the river outside Marlowe, Gerald had been confiding in her, as married men will, about his loneliness. Even as a child he'd been lonely, he told her.

"No brothers and sisters. Not even any uncles or aunts," he'd explained sadly. "I used to long sometimes for one of those big, close, quarrelsome families, all weddings and funerals and eating roast chicken and bread sauce at each other's tables, and running down each other's in-laws. I yearned for a group larger than just myself and my two parents—I wanted my own tribe, and that

wonderful feeling of *belonging*. Particularly at Christmas I used
to feel…"

Stella couldn't remember, at this distance of time, what it was
that Gerald used to feel at Christmas—something about tange-
rines, and somebody else's grandfather out in the snow sawing
apple logs—or something; it was of no importance, and that's
why she'd forgotten it. What *was* important was the discrepancy
she'd instantly spotted between these maudlin reminiscences and
the cock-and-bull story about meeting "Aunt Esmé" at the airport.

She'd given him every chance. Why couldn't *Wendy* be the one
to meet the woman, she'd asked, watching him intently while she
spoke. After all, she was Wendy's aunt, not his—"Oh, no, darling,
no, whatever gave you that idea? She's *my* aunt. She was awfully
good to me as a kid, and so I feel this is the least I can do. It's an
awful bore, but—you *do* understand, don't you, darling?"

Of course she'd understood. That's what mistresses are for.

"*Of course*, darling!" she'd said, not batting an eyelid; and afterward, how she'd laughed about it—when she'd finished crying!

She had to be so very careful, that was the thing: call Gerald's
bluff even once, and the whole relationship could have been
wrecked forever. He had made it quite, quite clear to her, very
early, that suspicion, jealousy, and possessiveness were the preroga-
tives of the wife, and of the wife alone. It was in the nature of
things (Gerald seemed to feel) that *Wendy* should cross-examine
him about his business trips, ring up the office to check that he
really was working late, go through his pockets for letters and
for incriminating theatre-ticket stubs; for *Stella* to do these things
struck him as an outrage, an insult to the natural order of things.

"Look, darling," he'd said (and the cold savagery of his tone
had seemed to Stella quite out of proportion to her very minor

misdemeanour—a single tentative little phone call to his secretary asking, just simply asking, what time he was expected back from Wolverhampton), "Look, darling, when a married man starts an affair, it's because he wants to get *away* from that sort of thing, not because he wants more of it! He has enough trouble getting a few hours' freedom as it is, without having his mistress waiting for him like a cat at a mousehole every time he steps outside his front door!"

A speech both cruel and uncalled-for, and Stella had been dreadfully upset. But being upset never got her anywhere with Gerald, it just made him avoid answering the telephone; and so after a while she'd stopped being upset, and had resolved to watch her step even more carefully in the future. And so that was why, when the Aunt Esmé "bit" cropped up, she'd let it pass without a flicker of protest. Dumber than the dumbest blonde she'd been, as she sleeked back her wings of black burnished hair and listened, her dark eyes wide and trusting, while he floundered deeper and deeper into a labyrinth of lies and evasions from which he would never (unless she, Stella, chose to assist him) be able to extricate himself.

For the lies hadn't ended with the meeting of "Aunt Esmé" at the airport; they had gone on for weeks. Because that hypothetical lady's visit had proved to be a long one, and packed with incident. She had to be taken to the theatre on just the night when Gerald usually went out with Stella; she caught the flu on the exact weekend when Gerald and Stella had planned a trip to the country; and when Stella herself caught the flu, she had to have it alone because it just so happened that Aunt Esmé had to be taken on a visit to an old school friend in Bournemouth at just that time.

And Stella had taken it all smiling. Smiling, smiling endlessly down the telephone, making understanding noises, and never questioning, never protesting. It had been over a year later (surely a *year* is long enough, surely no one could accuse her of checking up after a *year*?) before Stella had ventured, warily, and with lowered eyelashes, to ask after Aunt Esmé. Had they seen her lately, or had a card from her, she'd asked innocently, one late December day when Gerald, preoccupied, filled and brimming over with family life, had driven over hastily with Stella's present. Jewellery again, and expensive—Gerald was good at that sort of thing.

Stella thanked him prettily, even warmly; and then, still prettily, she tossed her bombshell into his face. "Have you heard from Aunt Esmé lately?" she asked, and enjoyed, as, she only rarely enjoyed his lovemaking, the look of blank uncomplicated bewilderment that spread over his pink, self-absorbed features. Not even any wariness, so completely had he forgotten the whole thing.

"Aunt Esmé? Who's Aunt Esmé?" he asked curiously, quite unsuspicious.

Stella had intended it to stop there, to brush it off with a light "Oh, well, I must be mixing it up with some other family"; to leave him unscathed, untouched by guilt, and to savour her triumph in secret. But the temptation to go on, to spring the trap, was irresistible.

"Aunt *Esmé*, darling! You know—the one you had staying with you for all that time last winter"—and as she spoke Stella watched, with terror and with glee, the dawning of guilt and alarm in his plump lazy features. Fear, calculation, and panic darted like fishes back and forth across his countenance; and then he recovered himself.

Of course! How stupid! Dear old *Esmé*, she must mean! Not an aunt at all, but the old family governess from Wendy's mother's old home—the children had been taught to call her "aunt" because, you know...

And of course Stella *did* know, smiling and lying and letting him off the hook. She, too, had had an "aunt" like that in her childhood. An Aunt Polly (she quickly improvised) who had made gingerbread animals. Smiling, inventing, chattering, breathlessly easing the embarrassment, Stella was nevertheless already making her plans. In a year's time—or maybe two years—"How's your mother-in-law's old governess getting on?" she'd ask, all innocence, watching his face while he blundered into the trap. "*Governess?* But Wendy's mother never had—" And while his words stuttered into silence, she would be watching his face, never taking her eyes off it as it disintegrated into terror, bewilderment, and guilt.

Guilt, that was the important thing. Guilt so richly deserved and so long outstanding, like an unpaid debt. Such a sense of power it gave her to be able to call him to account like this, just now and again—a sense of power which compensated, in some measure, for the awful weakness of her actual position, the terrible uncertainty of her hold on him. To be able to make him squirm like this every so often was a sort of redressing of some desperate balance—a long-merited turning of the tables without which Stella sometimes felt she could not have gone on.

Oh, but it was fun too! A sort of game of catch-me-if-you-can, a fun game. Not quite as much fun, though, as it used to be, because of late Gerald had been growing more wary, less easily trapped. He was more evasive now, less buoyantly ready to come out with giveaway remarks like "*What* trip to Manchester, darling?" or "But they've never *had* measles." Now, before he spoke, you could see him checking through the lies he had told recently, his grey-green eyes remote and sly.

And as Gerald grew more wary, so did Stella grow more cunning. The questions by which she trapped him were never direct ones now, but infinitely subtle and devious. It was a dangerous sport, and, like all dangerous sports, it demanded skill and judgement, a sure eye and perfect timing. Push Gerald too far, and she would have a terrible, terrifying row on her hands. "Possessive! Demanding!"—and all the other age-old accusations hurtling round her head.

Push him not far enough, however, and the opposite set of mishaps would be set in motion. He would start thinking he could get away with anything, leaving her for days on end without so much as a phone call, and then turning up all smiles, as if nothing had happened, and expecting her to cook him steak and collect his shoes from the repairers. Taking her for granted, just as if she was a wife—and what sensible woman is going to put up with all the disadvantages of being married *as well as* all the disadvantages of not being?

It was a cliff-hanger business, though, getting the push exactly right. Only a few months ago Gerald had actually threatened to leave her if she didn't stop spying on him—though surely "spying" was an unduly harsh term to apply to Stella's innocent little show of interest in the details of the business conference he'd pretended to attend the previous weekend?

"But darling, Lord Berners wasn't *at* the dinner!" she'd pointed out, with a placating little laugh, just to save Gerald the trouble of inventing any more humorous quotes from a non-existent speech. "I read in *The Times* the next morning that"—and at this, quite suddenly, he had gone berserk, and had turned on her like an animal at bay. His rage, his dreadful, unwarranted accusations, were like nothing she had ever heard before, and they threw her into such terror that she scarcely knew what she was doing or saying.

In the end he had flung himself out of the flat, slamming the door on her tears and screams, and vowing never to set foot in the place again. It had taken an undated suicide note, no less, to bring him back again. It was just about as generous a suicide note as any woman has ever penned to a recalcitrant lover, and Stella still remembered it with a certain measure of satisfaction, despite the misery pertaining to its composition.

"You mustn't blame yourself, darling," she'd written. "It is my decision, and mine alone. If I cannot face life without you, that is *my* problem, not yours. So don't, my love, feel that you have to come rushing round when you get this letter. The very last thing I want—or have ever wanted—is to inconvenience you in any way, or make you feel guilty. By the time you get this, darling, I shall be dead…"

The posts must have been slow that week, because it was nearly three days before she at last heard his feet pounding up the stairs, and had started taking the pills, stuffing them into her mouth in handfuls as he burst into the room.

It had been worth it, though. He'd been sweet to her for days afterward, visiting her often in the hospital; and even after she got home, he'd continued to shower her with presents, calling every day, and displaying in full measure all the remorse, the tenderness, the self-recrimination that such a situation demands of a man.

Until, of course, he got bored with it. First bored, then resentful, and finally beginning to throw the thing up to her in their arguments. "Blackmail," he called it now whenever Stella tried to get him to do anything he didn't want to do; and Stella began to realise, gradually, that she was right back at square one—having to be careful, careful, knowing all the time that the only way she could hold him now was by avoiding quarrels and by being infinitely tolerant and understanding—in short, by letting him get away with every bloody thing.

And this was why, this summer Saturday afternoon, Stella, her teeth set in a smile, was making herself listen without a murmur to what Gerald was saying. She had known, of course, the *kind* of thing it would be; married men always have such *righteous* reasons for letting you down. Sick wives, kids on holiday, family visits—all perfectly uncheckable, and all revealing what a kind, compassionate, virtuous, dutiful creature the lying, treacherous creature really is.

So what was it *this* time?

Simon's Sports Day. Gerald was potty about that son of his.

"You *do* understand, don't you, darling," he was pleading; and of course she understood very well, she understood that he preferred the prospect of watching a nine-year-old running across a field in gym shoes to the prospect of spending the whole long afternoon with his mistress, cool and mysterious in her darkened flat, the sunlight flickering across the bed through the slatted blinds.

"You see, darling, the thing is, he might *win*! Only nine and he might actually win the under-eleven two hundred and fifty yards! He's a marvellous little runner, Mr. Foulkes tells me—a real athlete's body!"

A real athlete's body. The light shining in Gerald's eyes was something Stella had never seen before. For a few seconds she tried to imagine what it would be like to be the mother of that athlete's body, to have produced it jointly with Gerald, to have a right, now, to a share in that idiotic pride. At the sight of those heavy, self-indulgent features thus irradiated, Stella felt a great darkness coming around her. It came like a black monstrous wave, engulfing her, leaving her bereft of speech.

"I wouldn't miss it for a million pounds!" she heard him saying, from somewhere outside the swirling blackness. "To hear his name called—Simon Graves—my own son! And then the clapping, the cheers! And him only nine! The others are all over ten, darling, *all* of them! He's the only nine-year-old who managed to…"

She preferred his lies, preferred them a thousand times. How could she have guessed that the truth, when she finally heard it from those evasive, prevaricating lips, would hurt as much as this?

The school gates were propped wide-open and welcoming, and through them, in the blazing sunshine, trooped the mothers and the fathers, the sisters and the girl friends, the aunts and the uncles. With their white sandals, their bright cotton dresses or pale freshly ironed slacks, women just like Stella, in their early thirties. Among so many, who was going to give her a second glance? Unless, of course, she gave herself away somehow—walking too fast, maybe, or letting her eyes flit too anxiously from side to side?

The fathers were less numerous than their womenfolk, which made Stella's task that much easier; they stuck out among the bright dresses like the dark stumps of trees. Stella's eyes darted from one to another of them ceaselessly, for he might be anywhere; and supposing—just supposing—he were to catch sight of her before she'd managed to locate him?

Not a big risk, really. For she had the advantage that the hunter always has over the prey—she knew what she was looking for, and what she meant to do when she found it; whereas Gerald not only wasn't on the watch for her, he hadn't the slightest suspicion she could possibly be here at all. On top of which she had, after a fashion, disguised herself with a pair of large round sunglasses, and a white silk bandanna wound tightly round her black shining hair.

Across the lawn, up under the avenue of limes, the slow procession wound, chattering, exclaiming, exchanging greetings; some were already fanning themselves against the heat. Slowly likewise, but with her heart hammering, Stella matched her pace with the rest; and it was not until she had settled herself on the grass at the far end of a long line of deck chairs facing the sports field that Stella began to breathe more easily. Hemmed-in by all these chairs, she could scarcely be seen from more than a yard or two away, and yet by craning her neck she could get a good view of the crowd still winding up from the school buildings. Here and there a dark head, taller than the rest, would make her catch her breath; but always, it was a false alarm.

And now, here was the junior master walking up and down with his loudspeaker, announcing the order of events. Already the crowd was falling into an expectant silence, the thousand voices dying away in wave after wave, fading away like the twitter of birds at twilight.

And still Gerald hadn't arrived.

Had he been lying to her after all? Had his afternoon's truancy nothing to do with Simon's Sports Day, in spite of all those passionate declarations of paternal pride? The swine! The double-crossing, treacherous swine! All that emotion wasted—not to mention having let herself in for a long hot afternoon of boredom, all for nothing!

I'll teach you, Gerald Graves! I'll teach you to lie to me, make a fool of me! Thought you'd got away with it, didn't you?—*I'll* show you!

Already she could feel a line of sweat gathering under the bandanna, along her hairline; she'd never worn such a thing before, and by the Lord, she thought, I never will again! *I'll* show him!

"Under sixteen hurdles…"

"Quarter mile, under fourteen…"

The sheer tedium of it was beginning to make Stella feel quite ill; her back ached, her eyes burned, and her brain felt half addled with heat and boredom.

Long jump. High jump… on and on the thing droned; whistles blew, shouts exploded into the shimmering air and died away again; the clapping and the cheering rose, and fell, and rose again. Cup for this, prize for that. The sun beat down, the voices swelled and receded, and then, just when Stella was on the verge of sleep, she heard it.

"Simon Graves! Winner of the under-eleven two hundred and fifty yards! Simon Graves!"

Stella was sitting bolt upright now, peering past the forest of chairs to get a glimpse of the sports field; but before she had time to locate the dark-haired little boy scuttling proudly toward the sidelines, she became aware of a little commotion going on in front of her and a few yards to the right.

"*Simon!* Our Simon! He's *done* it, Mummy! Daddy said he would! Oh, Simon—Si-i-i-mon!"

"Hush, darling, hush, Carol, you must sit down." A plumpish smiling woman was pulling at the sleeve of a wildly gesticulating little girl of about seven, urging her back into her seat. "Hush, Carol darling, not so loud. Simon'll be embarrassed. Oh, but won't Daddy be pleased!"

"Daddy will say," "Daddy will think"—and where the hell *was* Daddy, if one might inquire? "Wouldn't miss it for a million pounds," he'd said. Someone, somewhere, worth *more* than a million this bright afternoon?

Peering between the lines of chairs, Stella could see that the exultant mother and little sister were about to receive their hero. Pounding up the bank he came, wiry and brown and all lit up with triumph, hurling himself on his mother and sister amid a babel of congratulations.

Past the chairs, past the stirring smiling people, Stella watched, and kept very still. What *right* had the three of them to such joy, such total undiluted happiness? Didn't they know that the foundations of it were rotten, that their cosy little family life was based on a rotting, disintegrating substructure of lies and cheating? "Daddy" this and "Daddy" that—it made her feel quite sick to listen to the shrill little voices filled with such baseless adoration.

Quietly, unobtrusively, Stella got to her feet, and worked her way between the rows of chairs. She reached the little girl just when her mother and brother had turned away for a moment, receiving further congratulations. Quickly Stella dropped on her knees in front of the child, bringing their faces level.

"Do you know why your Daddy isn't here?" she said softly. "It's because he's spent the afternoon with me! In bed. Do you understand?"

The blank, almost stupid look on the child's face maddened her, and the blank look remained on the child's face. But Stella had the satisfaction, after she had squeezed back past row after row of chairs and had almost escaped from the enclosure, of hearing Carol, at last, burst into loud sobbing.

It was nearly ten o'clock when, at long last, she heard Gerald's step on the stairs; and even after all these hours she still could not have said if she had been expecting him to come, or to stay away.

He'd be angry, of course. But also, surely, relieved? Five years of secrecy was too much; it would be a relief to both of them to have it out in the open.

"Don't you agree, darling, that it is high time we had it out in the open?" she was asking, for the fourth or fifth time, of the silent slumped figure in the armchair. She'd been trying ever since his arrival to extract some sort of response from him. She'd tried everything, even congratulating him on his son's success.

"Pity you weren't there to see it," she'd been unable to resist adding; but even this had provoked from Gerald nothing more than the bald factual statement that he *had* seen it, thank you, from the Pavilion, where some of the fathers were helping to organise the boys.

Then more silence. She tried again.

"I'm sorry, Gerald darling, if Carol—if the little girl—was upset. I didn't mean to upset her, I just thought that the children should know about us. I don't believe in lies and deceit with children. I think they are entitled to the truth. Oh, darling, please don't look at me like that! It's been a shock, I know, but I'm sure that when you've had time to think about it, you'll see it's been for the best. The best for *us*—and for Wendy too. She can't have liked all this lying and deception all these years. I'm sure she'd rather know where she stands, and be able to start making sensible plans for the future.

"I mean, Wendy looks quite a nice sort of person. I don't think she'll make any trouble once she understands that we love each other. Oh, darling, what *is* it? Why don't you *say* something? Look, let's have a drink, and relax, and think what we're going to do when the unpleasantness is all over. This flat is a bit small for the two of us, but assuming that you'll be getting half of the value of your house, then between us we could—"

And now, at last, he *did* make a move. He rose stiffly, as if he suffered from rheumatism, and went to pour them each a large glass of whisky. He handed her a glass in silence, and then, swallowing his at a gulp, he walked over to the table in the window where Stella's typewriter stood, open. Laboriously, with one finger, he began to type.

Stella waited a minute, two minutes, then walked over to look.

GERALD B. GRAVES

27 FIRFIELD GARDENS

SYDENHAM WAY

The long Manila envelope stared up at her from the typewriter carriage; she watched, stupefied, while he finished the last few letters of the address. Then—

"Whatever are you doing, darling?" she asked, with an uneasy little laugh. "Are you writing a letter to *yourself?*"

And then she saw it, just by his right hand. Her own suicide note of last autumn—"*By the time you get this, darling, I shall be dead…*"

"The handwriting will be unquestionably yours," he observed conversationally, "and the address will have been typed on your typewriter. The post-mark will also be right, as I shall post it myself, on my way out. It should reach me at breakfast time the day after tomorrow, just in time to show to the police. And now, my dear, just one more little job, and we shall be finished."

And as he stood up and turned toward her, the light from the lamp fell full onto his face, and she saw the look in his eyes.

"No! No!" she gasped, took a step backward, and shrank, whimpering, against the wall.

"I intend it to look like suicide," he said, as if reassuring her; and as he moved across the carpet toward her, Stella's last coherent thought was: he will too! He'll get away with it, he'll lie his way out of it, just as he's always lied his way out of everything!

How accomplished a liar he was, she knew better than anyone, for it was she who had trained him—trained him, like a circus animal, over five long years.

EDITED BY
MARTIN EDWARDS

From picturesque canals and quiet lakes to the swirling currents of the ocean, a world of secrets lies beneath the surface of the water.

The stories in this collection will dredge up delight in crime fiction fans, as watery graves claim unsuspecting victims on the sands of an estuary and disembodied whispers penetrate the sleeping quarters of a ship's captain. How might a thief plot their escape from a floating crime scene? And what is to follow when murder victims, lost to the ocean floor, inevitably resurface?

This British Library anthology collects the best mysteries set on choppy seas, along snaking rivers and even in the supposed safety of a swimming pool, including stories by Arthur Conan Doyle, C. S. Forester, Phyllis Bentley and R. Austin Freeman.

EDITED BY
MARTIN EDWARDS

Forensic dentistry; precise examination of ballistics; an expertise in apiology to identify the exact bee which killed the victim?

The detective's role may be simple; solve the case and catch the culprit, but when the crime is fiendishly well-executed the application of the scientific method may be the only answer.

The detectives in this collection are masters of scientific deduction, employing principles of chemistry, the latest technological innovations and an irresistible logical brilliance in their pursuit of justice. With stories by early masters in the field such as Arthur Conan Doyle and L. T. Meade alongside fine-tuned mysteries from the likes of Edmund Crispin and Dorothy L. Sayers, *The Measure of Malice* collects tales of rational thinking to prove the power of the brain over villainous deeds.

EDITED BY
MARTIN EDWARDS

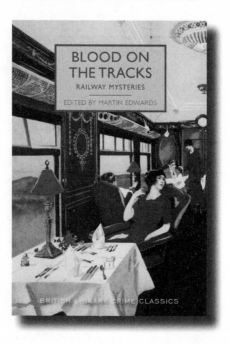

A signalman is found dead by a railway tunnel. A man identifies his wife as a victim of murder on the underground. Two passengers mysteriously disappear between stations, leaving behind a dead body.

Trains have been a favourite setting of many crime writers, providing the mobile equivalent of the "locked-room" scenario. Their enclosed carriages with a limited number of suspects lend themselves to seemingly impossible crimes. In an era of cancellations and delays, alibis reliant upon a timely train service no longer ring true, yet the railway detective has enjoyed a resurgence of popularity in the twenty-first century.

Both train buffs and crime fans will delight in this selection of fifteen railway-themed mysteries, featuring some of the most popular authors of their day alongside less familiar names. This is a collection to beguile even the most wearied commuter.

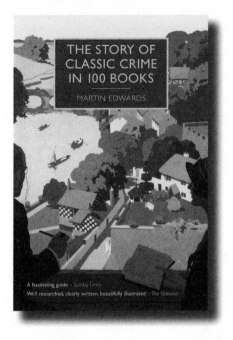

'A cabinet of criminal curiosities that novices and aficionados alike can happily search for titles to match their tastes.'   *Times Literary Supplement*

'No one could doubt the extent of Edwards's knowledge.'   *Mail on Sunday*

.   .   .

This book tells the story of crime fiction published during the first half of the twentieth century. The diversity of this much-loved genre is breath-taking, and so much greater than many critics have suggested. To illustrate this, the leading expert on classic crime discusses one hundred books ranging from *The Hound of the Baskervilles* to *Strangers on a Train* which highlight the entertaining plots, the literary achievements, and the social significance of vintage crime fiction.

BRITISH LIBRARY CRIME CLASSICS

ALSO AVAILABLE

Many of our titles are also available in eBook, large print and audio editions